THE BLOODY SEA

Anne Bonny incited the crew of *La Petite Mort* with loud shouts and curses. Then, amid loud explosions and with swords swinging, she and the pirates boarded the Dutch merchant ship.

"Once more into the breach!" shouted Alfred, dressed like a black-bearded Caliban. His resonant voice reverberated around the decks. "Cry havoc and let slip the dogs of war!"

"No quarter! We shall give no quarter!" announced Anne as she attacked the captain with her rapier. Roger tossed several Dutchmen overboard. Henri's knife pinned the boatswain to the mainmast. Nelson and Cuthbert, cutlasses in both hands, were ferociously slashing the air.

With her sword at the frantic captain's neck, Anne Bonny surveyed the scene with satisfaction. *The crew of the merchantman were on their knees pleading for their lives. The ship belonged to her pirates!*

THE CAPTAIN'S LADIES

Sandra Riley

For Gayle

Book Margins, Inc.

A BMI Edition

Published by special arrangement with Dorchester Publishing

Printed in the United States of America.

Acknowledgments

I extend hearty thanks to the energy essence of Fritz Ludington, who introduced me to Anne Bonny and Mary Read; to Sylvia Mull Heller, who insisted that I write a book about these pirates; and to my friends and family, both here and on San Salvador Island, who sustained me for six years while I researched and wrote this book. To Sue Herlihy for editing the final manuscript, and David Hankermeyer, friend, financial advisor, even lawyer when I needed one—*arigato!* Finally, to Bonnie Hance, whom I can never thank enough for struggling through my many drafts, and who was determined, in spite of my clumsy efforts, that this novel must be well written.

Sandra Riley
South Miami, Florida
January 1980

Plymouth, England: 1691

Molly twisted; ale splashed. "God's blood, if you pinch me arse once more, you bastard, I'll fetch me husband to slit your throat." Barely visible in the gloom of the smoky tavern, a man sprang up.

"Alfie!"

The knife glistened for an instant before burying itself in the abusive man's chest. He groaned heavily; then his flaccid torso slumped forward on the filthy table.

Alfred Read's anger flashed. "Hog-grubbin' thief! First me hard money, now it's me wife 'e's after." Alfred grabbed at the man's head. The candlelight created grotesque shadows on the victim's bloated face. "'E's the one, all right. Put that empty mug in his hand. This pack of drunken sots won't give 'em notice til mornin'."

"They'll hang you in the mornin' right enough," she said.

"They'll not find me to lay hands on, love. I'm off to sea this very night."

Swinging wildly, Molly's hand only glanced off Alfred's chin as she screamed bitterly, "The devil take ye, Alfred Read! How can you leave again, and me with child?"

"I must leave thee, Molly, girl. A man can get his fortune on the sea. Ye makes too much of it. Ah now, love. Go to me mother in Devonshire; she'll care for ye when your time is come. I want not to find thee here in Plymouth when I return. Stinkin' tavern, bloody fucking bastards," he

7

muttered as he inhaled the stale air and gazed soberly at the dead man. Then through a choking laugh he sputtered, "'Ere's one less prick to worry your arse, m' girl."

Not amused, she allowed the burning anger in her throat to abate before she uttered her deepest fears in a quiet, dead tone. "You won't return at all. You'll be spitted on a Spaniard's rapier and never see your child."

"Name 'im after me, will ye, love?" He kissed her hungrily. The gray smoke, heavy with the stench of sweat and ale, curled around them. Then he was gone.

Molly stared down at the dead man and watched his hand slide from the table. The mug dangling from a limp finger dripped its last vestiges of ale onto her small pink shoe.

A silhouette rippled through the uneven glass of the tavern window, but the figure disappeared just as Molly looked up and out onto the wet street. Feeling flushed by the stifling heat, Molly straightened her thin wrap around her shoulders and left the tavern.

A rainy breeze brought the smell of the sea to her nostrils and Molly, cold now from the evening's chill, drew her shawl up around her soft white neck. She was plump, pretty, lazy and deliciously appealing, with wisps of brown hair floating around her face. To look into her eyes was like being wrapped in the color of the sea.

The brawling taverns and bustling streets of Port Plymouth suited her mood and her paltry existence. Alfred Read was her man. She had had many like him, handsome, fearlessly independent, and all of them drawn to the sea. But, unlike the others, Alfred longed for the sea with almost frightening intensity. When a quiet peace supplanted passion, he would slip away from her and stand naked at the window staring across the harbor, and she felt utterly alone, with no touch of him anywhere.

This feeling invaded her soul now as she stood on the cobblestone street this cool May morning, searching through the mist for the only man who had made her feel this way.

Alfred had been at sea less than a month when his son

was born. Without money, Molly was not able to travel to Devonshire; and her mother-in-law, although well-to-do, refused her aid until she had seen, with her own feeble eyes, her son's namesake. Distraught over the woman's hard attitude, Molly had no choice but to return to the tavern and work until she had enough gold for the journey.

So it was that on a stormy night in August, with Buttons Read bundled in her arms, Molly arrived at the Green Lanterns. Battling a vulgar horde of thirsty mariners, Molly ducked into a cluttered storeroom. She laid the baby in his bed, which she had fashioned out of old cleaning rags cozily arranged in a crate placed on a shelf, and went reluctantly to her tasks.

Rain had slopped the tavern's worn and hilly hardwood floors, making them slick. Preoccupied by her own thoughts, Molly tumbled. As her feet slipped out from under her, a sailor deftly caught her loaded tray. "Got to save these, love."

The men laughed as they fell to their drinking again, leaving Molly sprawled in a puddle of muddy ale. A strong hand gripped her under the armpit, but it was the baby's scream that lifted Molly from the floor. She raced to the storeroom, barely a step ahead of the helpful gentleman. A rat perched on the edge of the box was ready to jump on the baby. The man pushed Molly aside and batted the animal with the flat of his sword while it was in midleap. It crashed against the wall and dropped into a pile of broken glass on the floor. The only sound remaining was the whimper of the child, safe now in his mother's arms. The man gathered Molly and her child under his cloak and they left the tavern.

Although the rain had stopped, except for occasional gusts, the slippery cobblestones made walking hazardous. Following Molly's subtle promptings, the man made his way through the narrow streets to her wharf-side lodgings on the harbor quay. Neither spoke. Once inside, Molly reclined on the sagging cot and began to feed her fretful baby.

She noticed that the stranger was much taller than most

men and that his body was well-proportioned and muscular. She allowed her thoughts to travel down his slim hips, reach between his firm thighs and dwell there momentarily. The graceful sway of his body cast shadows here and there about the room but Molly's attention now was drawn to his face.

The man watched with envy the child tugging ravenously at his mother's breast. Suddenly he came to her, snatched the swollen nipple from the baby's mouth, lifted the heavy breast and placed a gold doubloon under it. He stood staring into the blueness of her eyes, pulling her into the blackness of his own. After a moment he licked the milky mess from his fingers and smilled.

She was a comely wench, he thought. Such life in those eyes. I would give all my gold to feast one night on those succulent breasts. Aah, I have been womanless too long, I do forget myself. I am not a man to steal milk from babies.

The swing of his cape knocked over the chair; his sword clanked against the door jamb and he was gone.

Weeks passed. Molly's heartbeat accelerated every time she heard footsteps approaching her door, but the mysterious gentleman never returned. Keeping to her usual pattern, Molly had decided to return to the tavern only after the money was gone. Nan was to look after Buttons. Buxom and blowzy, Nan was a happy creature who served as Mother Midnight to these airy wharf wenches when they had the misfortune to conceive. Although she had brought hundreds of children into the world, she had had none of her own, nor wanted any.

Because Molly still hoped to meet the handsome stranger again, she wore a crimson velvet dress loosely laced in the bodice over a low-cut, freshly laundered white blouse. Faded in spots and mudspattered around the hemline, it was entirely unsuited to tavern work, but it was the best garment she possessed.

"Dressed in your finery tonight, eh, missy?" said Nan, eyeing her teasingly.

In a rapt voice Molly responded, "What is he, think you, Nan? He were dressed too fine to be any ordinary seaman.

A lord, per'aps?''

"What! Your gentleman with the Spanish coin, a lord? So's me arse! 'E's more likely some swaggerin' rogue who recently stole a fortune and has prob'ly spent it all by now, I warrant.''

Molly could not imagine how anyone wearing a hat with a white plume, a deep blue velvet greatcoat and a magnificent sword of Spanish steel could be anything but a lord; but rather than argue, she changed the subject. "I fed the baby. 'E'll sleep now.''

"Good.'' Nan bellowed, "I'll warrant some full-grown, sweating hulk of something will be feasting on those swollen melons this night. Ye are fine bait for a wencher. But remember m' girl, these be the middle days of the moon for thee an' I want not to haul another'n from ye.''

The port of Plymouth, England, in 1691 was no different in these days of the privateers than it had been in past eras. It had known the crews of Hawkins and Drake as well as the courageous *Mayflower* pilgrims. Richard Hakluyt had made his *Divers Voyages*, and Dampier his *New Voyage Round the World*. Captain Kidd was preparing to embark on his *Fateful Voyage*, which would conclude at the end of a rope at Wapping Dock. The taverns teemed with intrepid souls like Alfred Read, anxious to sign on a privateer bound for anywhere.

The Green Lanterns was packed with sailors belching, swilling, and swearing in the angry orange glow. Exhausted, Molly was resting in a corner of the tavern's largest room, intent only on her wriggling toes cooling in the damp Stptember breeze from the open window. Suddenly she was aware of a noise behind her—slap, slap, slap, like someone catching a ball. She turned just in time to see no more than a flash of steel cutting through a melon suspended in midair. Half of the fruit fell into her lap; the other half splashed to the floor. Her laughter filled the cheerless night.

"I'll have you to myself, wench; there's no babe at your breast tonight.''

Molly giggled and bit into the succulent meat of the

11

melon; the juices dripped down her chin onto her white bosom.

"Let me taste those melons."

She tossed the fruit his way. He juggled it awkwardly and laughed. "So it's games you want." He picked her up, threw her over his shoulder and carried her upstairs. No one paid any notice.

The images of the drinking men receded from Molly's distorted view. Her breasts popped out of her dress and her buttocks just cleared a cross beam. He dumped her onto the bed so hard that she bounced. Giggling, she threw her arms around his neck and pulled him down on top of her. As he buried his face in her bosom, he felt as though he were being drawn into the endless sea and the waves were folding over him. He lay there motionless for a long time. Her heaving chest subsided into the peaceful steady rhythm of her breathing. A feeling of death passed over him. How wonderful to die here this minute, drowned in a sea of flesh, he thought, as he held his breath. Cold fear swept over Molly. Somehow sensing a danger she could not explain, she struggled to push him off her. Grabbing two fists full of hair, she pulled him up. Gasping for air, he unleashed his codpiece, tore her clothes away and locked himself inside her, instantly flooding her fertile body with the warmth of his store.

Typhoid invaded practically every hovel on the wharf. Buttons had no strength to fight the insidious enemy which had violated his frail, undernourished body. Hard pains racked his intestines and he had been consumed with fever for days. Already in her ninth month of pregnancy, Molly prayed for Nan's speedy return from her visit in the country.

The handsome gentleman with the Spanish sword had gone away to London on matters of business. Their communication had been infrequent but effective, for it was his child Molly carried in her womb. Along with his sword, he had left an address where he might be reached in London, but Molly was too ashamed to admit to him that she could

12

not read the paper. She remembered his name—Miles Randall. What she did not know was that his real name was Miguel Rivera. Born in Spain of English mother and Spanish father, he was able to assume the character of an Englishman and gather information for the Spanish crown.

With the few coins remaining from the money Miles had given her, Molly sought to purchase medicines for Buttons. The barber advised no purgatives, while the apothecary urged her to use senna tea. Sensing it was harmful advice, Molly decided against the tea. So with no remedies and little comfort she returned to her room and wept.

Agonizing days and sleepless nights passed for both of them as the baby's fever mounted steadily. Tortured by her inability to east her baby's suffering, Molly went into early labor and, with the sick boy still in her arms, took to bed. Both of them screamed and writhed, seized by cramps and contorted in common agony. Struck by the desperate realization that she was utterly alone, Molly cried out to a helpless child and an empty room.

Her time had come. Fearing that the baby would fall from the bed when her pains became violent, Molly carefully laid him on the floor. She labored for hours, tearing at the bedclothes and clawing the mattress in futile attempts to grip a helping hand.

Sweat and pain blurred her vision, distorting the ceiling into a thousand hideous images. In her nightmare she witnessed a horrible cataclysm of nature. Standing on the edge of her nightmare, she felt the ground roll under her feet as she watched huge chunks of land break off and fall into the ocean. An entire city was being gobbled up by the earth and sea, before her eyes. Just as she was about to be pulled into the sea, she felt the child break from her womb.

Near noon on June 7 1692, Mary Read found her own way into the world. Molly did not know how long she had been unconscious, but she awakened to the healthy screams of her new baby. She severed the connection with her child and in a few moments all was silence. Too exhausted even to look at the infant, Molly followed the shadowy images on the ceiling and listened to the quiet—the first quiet in over a week. She was on the brink of sleep when a sudden realization jolted her back. Buttons! Molly pulled herself to the edge of the bed. Buttons was gone; he had crawled away. Molly dragged herself to her feet. Seeing him lying near the chest in the corner, she moved painfully toward him. He's dead, she thought. Dead! Dead! She looked down at his lifeless twisted form, then slumped to the floor.

Molly was still unconscious when Nan arrived. As she swung open the door her cheerful hello was choked off by the unexpected scene which greeted her. Molly was lying on the floor, naked except for her bedclothes which she had stuffed between her legs. Buttons lay beside her, drowned in his own vomit. Lying in the bloodstained bed, the screaming baby, remnants of afterbirth clinging to its tiny appendages, appeared almost inhuman.

Nan washed the baby first. Before reviving Molly, she wrapped Buttons in an old blanket and set him outside the door; then she put fresh linen on the bed and aroused Molly enough to get her back into it. Throughout Nan's gentle ministrations Molly did not say a word; nor did she look at the child when Nan placed her in her arms.

"Ye must needs feed this child, Molly." There was a look of cold indifference on Molly's face while she allowed the baby to nurse. "What will ye call her? The child must have a name." Molly refused to acknowledge the remark. "The child needs love, Molly, or it will die." Molly remained silent.

Taking the dead baby, Nan rowed out into the harbor. The water of the great sea swallowed him up as it had so many other nameless children delivered dead into its hands. Suddenly Nan was tired.

It was weeks before Molly said a word. Nan had been calling the baby Mary, and Molly had not objected. She wanted nothing to do with her. The child was allowed to nurse but was given no further regard by her mother. Nan supplied the love, attention and affection, and she was grateful that Mary was a healthy baby. Despite the ghastly circumstances of her birth, Mary was, at six weeks, already half the growth that sickly Buttons had been at twelve months.

Molly's nightmares persisted. She stood upon the earth and felt it moving, rolling, splitting, and then plunging into the sea. She saw an entire wharf town lying on the floor on the churning ocean. Bodies floated down, coming to rest on the tops of houses, in wagons, over cannons, across bar counters, even slumped in chairs sitting at table.

When the news of the earthquake in Jamaica reached Plymouth, the taverns burst with thankful sailors drinking healths to the good Lord Who had seen fit to spare them this time.

Nan brought the news to Molly.

"Molly, dreadful news has come just now on a packet from Jamaica. Port Royal is sunk! The town sits on the bottom of the ocean. Think o' that, Molly! It happened the very day little Mary was born, June 7th. There was a terrible rumbling sound, they say, and the earth moved. Then it broke off, carrying all the people and buildings into the sea. Only a few escaped to tell of it. Come to the tavern and hear their stories.''

Molly did not go, for she did not need to hear their gruesome tales. They could in no way compare with her nightmare or her vivid recollection of June 7th. She thought only of her dead boy and did not even wonder what fate held in store for her daughter, Mary Read, born at such an inauspicious time.

By the summer that Mary was two Molly had earned enough for the coach fare to Devonshire. Bigger than most children her age, Mary was a full year younger than her dead brother. Molly dressed Mary as a boy and called her Buttons. She was confident that Alfred's mother would give her enough money on a regular basis to provide the necessaries of life for her grandson.

Over-excited by the long coach ride, Mary could not sit on her grandmother's lap for long. She was anxious to play in the fields which had rolled past her view during their journey. The feeble old woman, her sight failing, fondled Mary in an attempt to memorize her grandson's features and build. Molly was grateful when Mary grew restless and bounded off the woman's lap to run outside into the wheat-field. If her plan should miscarry and the old woman discover her secret, the inheritance would be lost.

Mary did not want to leave her grandmother's. The old woman was kind to her. The beautiful fields of Devon, providing days of pleasure, had replaced the hardwood floors, wharf docks and cobblestone streets of Plymouth. Lost in the tall grass, Mary ran her tiny fingers up and down each blade. As the feathery wheat stalks stroked her face and arms, her little mind wandered into fields of fantasy where beautiful imaginings contented her energetic spirit.

Mistress Read went into her bedroom and came back, dropping gold coins into an already bulging sack. "This purse will keep ye til your next visit. Hide it well. These hills abound with murderin' thieves." Old Mistress Read held Mary tightly in her arms. "Take good care of our boy, Molly. 'E must grow up proud to be the son of Alfred Read."

"Yes, Mother Read," Molly said dutifully. "'E'll be proud."

Weeks and months passed, and Molly spent more and more of her now leisure time drinking. Something deep inside prevented her from establishing a physical closeness with Mary. The care of the child was left to Nan and the girl was fed well, due to Nan's thrifty housekeeping. But most of old Mother Read's money was wasted on rum.

At six Mary was a stocky child who was wont to venture out among the other wharf children. Looking like a brawny little man and displaying a mean temper, she terrified some of the others.

"Bet my roger be bigger 'in yours. Bet I can piss farther too. Let me see your roger, Buttons."

Mine is bigger, she thought, but how can I piss a distance?

I have never even tried to piss a distance.

"Show me yours first, boy," she demanded.

"No, you first," he said defiantly.

"You first!" she said, raising her fists.

Mary was amazed at the enormity of this strange-looking appendage. Running away, crying, holding her crotch in anguish, Mary went straight to Nan's lodgings.

"Where is my roger? 'Tis gone! How did I lose it?" Mary was so angry and crying so loudly and clutching her crotch so tightly that no amount of wrenching of her hands could make her release herself.

Nan struggled with the girl. "Stop this! Stop crying. There be nothing wrong with ye."

"Where be my roger, Nan? How did I lose it?"

"Quiet now, child. Listen to me. Ye has not lost anything. You are not a boy. You be a girl and girls do not have rogers. Your name be not Buttons but Mary."

Nan wept quietly to herself. She had not wanted to be the one to disillusion the child. Mary was so active, so free. No more, she thought. You be a fraud. You will be a fraud til your mother dies, perhaps long after that. From this day forth ye will think thy life pretense, when before this day ye were wont to be thyself.

The frequent trips to Hangmans Hill were prompted by Molly's incessant drinking. She was practically destitute. Mother Read never suspected the drinking, or that her "grandson" was not being properly cared for. For Mary these visits provided some of the most pleasurable days of her early childhood. She would always remember the beautiful fields, rolling hillsides and wooded valleys of Devonshire.

When Mary was eleven, Grandmother Read died peacefully in her sleep. As soon as Molly was in control of her drinking she made a journey to London. After days of interviews, she was able to impress old Mistress Read's solicitor that she was a responsible mother and fit charge for the boy on whom all the woman's money had been bestowed. The inheritance, although sizable, was not what Molly had expected; but in more provident hands it would have taken them far.

In Molly's case, in two years the funds were exhausted. Molly and Mary had no resources but the sword initialed M.R., a keepsake with which Molly refused to part. The inertness of this wharf town plunged Mary into the doldrums, but she was too vigorous a person to dwell within the calms. It was not long before the cyclone of her own turbulent spirit snatched her from lethargy. Having no constructive outlet for her frustrated energies, Mary plagued the fishermen on the wharf almost to the point of becoming a nuisance. Other young boys, seeing her humor and wishing to avoid her fists, left Mary alone. But Molly, weary of her presence, arranged employment for her as a footboy to Madame Beaulieu.

"What?" Nan said, surprised at this new development. "You would send the girl to work in a brothel?"

"Yes! What's more, she'll go, too! 'Tis time she went to work. I am sick to death of her!"

"When will you stop this pretense?" demanded Nan angrily. "Mary be a woman, more now than ever. 'Tis not right, Molly. 'Tis not decent."

"What if I refuse to go?" said Mary indignantly.

"You'll go!"

"But what if I be discovered?"

"See that ye be not discovered. Dost know what they will do to ye if they find ye out? You'll go to gaol and that's not all of it either. They'll stretch ye til your limbs break. You'll keep your secret, girl. If ye does not, they will hang ye up and cut off your teats and plunge jagged glass up your bite, and ye shall bleed yere life away. Ye will wish that day ye had never been born at all, let alone born a woman. So play your part well."

"God's death, ye be a vicious woman, Molly, to talk to the girl thus." Nan was unable to keep the bitterness from her voice.

"You stay out of our lives! She will live as it pleases me

18

she shall live. Dost understand me, then? Madame 'as promised to give thee schoolin'. Ye will learn to grace yourself . . . learn gentlemanly manners and such.'' Molly's voice softened.

"I must live there then, Mother? Day and night, in that place?"

"Yes, they will care for all thy needs. Your wages will be sent to me. I wish not to look on your face again.'' Tears welled up in Molly's eyes. It hurts me too much. I ache inside, she thought. 'Tis like a great choking. More and more this girl looks like her father. I can bear it no longer. I hate her for my boy's death. I do not wish to hate her father too.

Now in her thirteenth year, Mary Read went to work as a footboy to Madame Beaulieu. Always a free spirit, Mary found life there hard. It was not the nature of her work, for that was nothing, but the discipline of the routine. The morning spent with a tutor was her favorite part of the day; the afternoons and evenings were sheer boredom. Seldom out of Madame's sight, Mary performed perfunctory duties such as opening carriage doors, carrying parcels and forever standing, standing around in the elegant parlors and waiting—forever waiting. There was no patience that she could find for this. She took to bouncing up and down on the balls of her feet until she was summoned by her lady. Then she would leap across the room, bound off on an errand, and come back again to stand and bounce for several more hours. The customers complained to Madame about the rude boy who did not even have the courtesy to stand still. Madame Beaulieu, too fond of Mary to dismiss her, would lecture her on etiquette befitting a footboy in such an elegant establishment, and finally ordered two new suits of clothes for her, hoping to improve her manners as well as her appearance.

Mary fidgeted as the nearsighted, wizened tailor ran his pointed nose along the course of each stitch in her new frieze coat.

"Hold still, boy," said the tailor in a scratchy voice.

"What, will you ne'er cease moving, Buttons?" said Madame Beaulieu, as she swept into the room.

"Madame, I was just now rebuking this boy for his disgusting behavior."

"Buttons, how awful of you. How will we ever teach thee manners if we cannot get thee dressed properly?"

"'Tis tiresome, Madame," groaned Mary.

"Hush!" said the tailor. "You grow tiresome, lad. Madame, have you not some girl near his height and weight to fit this suit?"

"All right. I will send Lucy. Buttons, get thee dressed at once and come directly to my boudoir. We will begin your lessons today. And tailor, look to your hands. I will not have our Lucy ruined. She is a virgin, ripe for the Comte de Grasse, who comes here next month. Take care you stick to your trade. List me, tailor, thimble thy prick!"

Mary, admitted into Madame Beaulieu's boudoir, nearly swooned from the strong odor of perfume in the air. She had always been short of breath, especially at times when she was excited or nervous. Now she was coughing.

"Now what is the matter with thee, boy?" questioned the madame angrily.

"Nothing," sputtered Mary, gasping for a breath of air. "Oh Madame, I fear I shall swoon."

"Oh dear!" Madame Beaulieu rushed to Mary, helped her to lie down on the divan, and at once set her oriental fan into vigorous motion over Mary's face. Slowly Mary regained herself.

"Are you with us, Buttons? Dear me, but you gave me quite a fright."

Mary felt the color return to her cheeks. The woman's face was beautiful and made even more beautiful at this moment by the hint of concern slightly furrowing her brow. Mary had never seen the woman's face so close. She rubbed Mary's temples gently. Mary sighed and groaned a little, deliberately indulging herself, for she had never felt a gentle touch til now.

Nan is gentle, Mary thought, but not like this. Her fat hands are rough. But not this lady's—soft and delicate be her touch. Would this woman were my mother.

Distracted from the woman's face by the heaving motion of her breast, Mary thought she might smother in the woman's cleavage as Madame bent solicitously over her. As was the fashion, Madame Beaulieu's bosom, forced up by the corseted waist, was more out than in her scant bodice. Diverting her eyes, Mary noticed that she was half buried in the lady's skirts. For the first time in her life Mary was flounced and furbelowed in yards and yards of silk.

Mary survived that afternoon's lessons as well as the next and the next—weeks of lessons, months of lessons, dancing and reading, dancing and French, dancing and diction, as well as the etiquette of serving table.

At night Mary indulged in fantasies. In her dreams she rescued Madame Beaulieu from harrowing dangers—flood and fire, angry beasts and wicked djinns. Her youthful imagination devised perilous situations unequaled in any of the books she had read. She always rescued the lady at great risk to her own personal safety. Each time the lady was more and more beautiful in her suffering and more and more extravagant in her gratitude.

There was never a kinder lady; her very gentleness filled each day with such joy that Mary was carried through her chores as if on a cloud. Time spent away from her lady was anguish and nights were lonely, for the Madame's evenings were devoted to men, gentlemen not worthy of her company, Mary thought. She is too lovely a lady to waste time with fops such as these. I almost wish one of them would offer an insult; I would forget myself and buffet him.

One night at dinner, Mary could see that her lady was greatly annoyed with the long-expected Comte de Grasse. Rich as he was, she could no longer abide his bragging. In a moment of rashness Mary spilled into his lap the soup she was serving. While the comte was preoccupied with the hot broth in his crotch, Madame Beaulieu giggled triumphantly into her handkerchief. Recovering from his surprise, the comte slapped Mary hard across her face. Mary stood erect and proud even in the face of the dagger which the comte snatched from its jeweled sheath. Gladly will I suffer death for my lady, Mary thought bravely.

Ironically, Madame Beaulieu came to *her* rescue instead. "Oh, monsieur le comte, please." She laid her hand gently over his powerful fist which grasped the weapon. "He is but a boy. He means no insult. 'Twas an accident, I assure you."

"An accident? Why, Madame, look at him. He is almost proud of his action," snarled the comte.

The lady could not contain her smile. She knew what Buttons had been thinking and was more flattered by this gallant gesture than by all the expensive favors bestowed on her by other more mature admirers. She allowed her eyes to speak to Mary's long enough for the comte to notice.

"What is this?" he roared. "Marie, what is between you two?"

After a long silence the lady spoke. "He is my son."

Mary's heart, which had been beating wildly, suddenly stopped. For a moment there was no sound in the room, not even the whisper of breathing.

"Oh!" uttered the Comte de Grasse, slightly taken aback. Mary heard one of the candles dripping onto the tablecloth. She wanted to tend to it but the tension held her rigid. "I am sorry, Madame, that I struck the boy."

"Yes, I am sorry too." she said with a chill in her voice. "You have an engagement, monsieur le comte . . . if I remember myself."

"Yes, yes. I must take my leave. *Au 'voir*, Madame. A thousand pardons for my behavior. Forgive me, boy. Madame, good night." The comte bowed grandly and made a swift exit from the drawing room.

Madame Beaulieu took up her wine glass and stood by the window looking out into the night. Mary, afraid to move or speak, had resumed breathing and felt somewhat light-headed, enveloped in the warmth of the room and her own inner happiness. She looked at her lady. The soft candlelight illumined the loveliness of her face. The woman was young, only thirty-two, but her wealth and beauty commanded the respect of all within her empire here in Plymouth.

She is quiet now, Mary thought. I should leave her; yet I could stand here and look upon her face all night. She did call me son. 'Tis an honor I never hoped for. I wish I could tell her she has adopted a daughter and not a son, but I dare not. 'Tis a son she wants and a son I shall be to her.

"Shall I leave you, milady?"

"Yes, Buttons, leave me. I feel melancholy and would like to be by myself a while. Fill my glass before you go."

"Yes, milady." Mary carefully poured the last of the wine into the crystal glass. 'I give you good night, Madame."

"Good night, dear Buttons, and thank you for your gallantry." She kissed Mary softly on the cheek. The kiss was so soft, in fact, that Mary was not quite sure of it, for she dared not look up but rather stared at her own feet and waited for the wide skirt to leave her field of vision. Turning, Mary left silently.

As she disposed of the empty wine bottle, Mary thought of her mother. She had not thought of her in months and could not remember the last time she had seen her.

She is in her cups even now. I know it. Why do I think of her at all? I have a new mother now. Tears were running down her face and Mary was not sure for whom these tears were being shed, or why; was it from joy or sorrow or bitterness or hatred, or had all these feelings provoked her tears? It felt good to cry. It had been a long while since she had given way to tears.

Her tears spent, Mary closed her eyes. Nan appeared, surrounded by a blazing white light. Mary blinked the apparition away. What means this vision? Why does she beckon me to follow her? Where be thee, Nan? I cannot visit thee. I am forbid to leave this house. "No, don't leave me, Nan," screamed Mary at the vanishing illusion. "I need thee!"

June 7, 1706—Mary knew the date, but she did not know it was her fourteenth birthday. No one had ever regarded the event. She only knew that some time in the late spring, when the flowers were blooming, she was a year older.

Molly remembered well what day this was but for reasons other than Mary's birth. She spent the entire day in her room with a bottle of rum dreaming of her dead son. Going to the chest, she took out the faded crimson dress and unwrapped the magnificent sword. The blade was elaborately carved and the hilt inlaid with mother of pearl. She studied the intricate work. The initials M.R. were clearly marked within a triangle on the part of the blade nearest the hilt. More and more often these days Molly had removed the precious object from its hiding place to look at it. At times she had in mind to sell it, and in moments of extreme despair, she even thought to use it on herself. But no matter how great her state of intoxication, she could not do either of those things.

One afternoon in mid-July Mary was in the greenhouse, which was situated a short distance from the back of the main house. Perfectly at ease, almost lost in a daydream, Mary was watering the roses when two arms locked around her waist from behind. Her heart leaped to her throat. She pulled the arms away easily and turned around. It was fifteen year old Elinor, a pretty, green-eyed blonde. Backing away, Mary fell over a crate and Elinor jumped on top of her. They were rolling into the potted plants, crushing geramiums and pinks. Elinor's hands seemed to be everywhere at once.

"Get off me," Mary shouted, struggling to keep the girl's hands away from her private parts.

"Oh Buttons, I want you. I hate those old men. I love you. Kiss me. Hold me. Make love to me here. I've waited so long."

"Good God, get off me!" Mary was beside herself with desperation. "Get away before I have to hurt thee."

The girl kissed Mary hard on the lips, thrusting her tongue

deep into Mary's mouth. Mary had never been kissed before and was lost for a moment in this strangely terrifying sensation. Pushing Elinor away, Mary bounded to her feet. She felt a sudden dampness in her crotch which she did not understand.

"Don't come near me! I will have to strike you if you do." Her tone was so intense that Elinor stood staring in amazement. She had never been rejected before and didn't know quite what to say or do. "Stay where you are; I mean it." Mary held her fists in a fighting attitude.

"'You're a queer one, you are."

"Never mind," said Mary, lowering her hands somewhat. "Just don't you come near me." She bolted from the greenhouse, leaving the startled Elinor standing among the broken flowerpots; white, yellow, red and purple bits of crushed flowers were scattered around her feet.

Without bothering to inform anyone, Mary ran straight to Nan's hut and pounded on the door for a long time. There was no answer. Puzzled, Mary noticed that the flower boxes in the window were empty. Nan always planted in the spring. Straining to look through the cloudy window, Mary caught only glimpses of the few pieces of furniture. The place appeared deserted and a sick feeling gripped her stomach.

There was nothing else to do but go to her mother's. They rarely saw one another and their brief moments together had grown increasingly tense.

Mary exploded into the room. Molly slammed down the lid of a heavy chest and turned.

"What the 'ell be you doin' 'ere, burstin' in 'ere on me this way? Did they teach ye no manners at that place?"

"I'll not go back there," Mary said defensively. "I be almost discovered today. I'll not go. You cannot force me."

Molly, never in a mood for her daughter's wilfulness, retorted, "You'll go back, you stupid girl, and you will play your part well. What, will ye 'ave me starve in the streets?"

"I can't go back. What if I be found out? Sometimes

methinks my mistress can see into my soul.''

"'Tis not your soul she be interested in, I warrant ye.'' Molly removed Mary's coat and shirt. "Hold still!''

"What are ye doin'?''

Going to the sea chest, Molly pulled out an old shirt belonging to her husband and tore long strips of cloth from it. "We'll take no more chances. Ye 'ave no breasts now to speak of but we'll take no chances neither.'' She tied the strips around Mary's chest.

"Ah, I can't breathe, Mother.''

"You are goin' back to that house and this is to prevent your discovery. Don't take them off, not even to sleep. I'll not starve because of you. You are leavin' this house and are never to return again. I'll not look upon thee after this day.''

"I won't be used thus. I'll go to Nan.''

"You won't neither—Nan be dead.''

Mary pushed her mother away from her.

"How? When? Why did ye not tell me?'' she demanded.

"Why should I tell thee? Could ye stop her leavin'?''

"I could have seen her one last time, at least. Think you naught of my feelings, Mother? When did she die? Tell me that!''

"June, early June last.''

"God, I knew it, then,'' she said in sudden realization. Mary turned to her mother, attacking her through angry tears. "I loved Nan. I do not understand you! 'Tis more than the drink. Nan always said 'twas the rum, but 'tis more than that, I know. Why do you hate me so? What have I ever done to lose thy love?''

"Love! What would ye know o' love? Ye think love be the filthy buggerin' ye sees in your bawdy house. What do ye know o' my sufferin'?

Molly took a long gulp straight from the bottle and went into a violent coughing fit; tears streamed from her eyes. With sudden remorse, Mary rushed to put her arms around her mother. She felt the warmth of her breath, with its familiar odor of stale rum. Suddenly her arms ached to hold her close. When the coughing subsided, Molly pulled away and slapped her so hard she knocked her to the floor. "Don't ever touch me! I don't want you to touch me! I hate the sight of you! Your coming . . . killed my boy . . . my boy," she sobbed.

Mary sat in a daze, staring at this broken woman whom she so wanted to love. The burning of her face was nothing to equal the fire in the pit of her stomach just beneath her heart.

A sharp crash brought her back to reality. The floor around her was wet and there were heavy pieces of glass around her.

"Get up, you slut!" Molly screamed. "Get back to your whorehouse and make your ladies happy!"

The girl didn't move. Viciously Molly smashed another bottle, sending huge chunks of thick green glass bouncing up against Mary. A sharp piece glanced past her forehead; Mary felt the warm blood dripping down her temple.

Finally exhausted, Molly fell into another fit of coughing and dragged herself from the room. Mary couldn't stop her flood of silent tears. She remained on the floor until her tears were spent. Then, shaking off the bits of broken glass, she wearily picked herself up and without bothering to wash the blood from her face, dressed and went back to her mistress. There was nothing else to do, and nowhere else to go, for she had no spirit to start a new life on her own at this moment.

At sixteen litheness characterized Mary's physique. For a girl she was tall, almost five feet six—muscular and lean. The gawkiness which should have accompanied her height and shape did not appear; rather she showed a graceful bearing and a gentle manner. Her chestnut hair was cut short to accommodate a wig for Madame's formal occasions, and her dark eyes were the dominant feature of her boyish face.

During her four years at the brothel Mary had acquired the etiquette required in polite society. She had learned to read and write in both English and French and had been exposed to some good literature, but she had never been tutored in any such subjects as science, philosophy, Latin, mathematics or history. Knowing nothing of the world outisde the confines of Madame's house, she found the conversation of men boring, rarely having either the desire or the opportunity to listen to their political arguments.

Mary lived in a world of manners and sex. The former would be useless on the wharf or at sea, and the latter—well, she had seen enough to reject that kind of playful, promiscuous sexuality. It had nothing at all to do with love. If a time came when she was allowed to live the life of a woman, it would certainly not be in the manner of these women.

Her fantasies about Madame Beaulieu continued but they were never sexual. Now she was beginning to wonder about her lady's intentions and found that the looks she had been receiving lately showed more than motherly concern and parental love. If I am discovered, she thought, I could spend the rest of my life in this place, belly up—or, worse, on my knees and elbows with some Lord Flabby Arse beating his paunchy belly 'gainst my arse. Still worse would be to be brutally used by a ruffian such as the Comte de Grasse.

Genuinely afraid, Mary had given more and more thought to escape. Whenever she considered another kind of life, a vision of the sea would flash into her mind. But that didn't seem a very promising direction. Her mother had always hated the sea and had painted frightening pictures of dangerous ships and desperate men. Meanwhile, more and more often when they were alone together, Madame Beaulieu questioned Mary about which of the girls she found the prettiest. Her lady insisted that a boy's virginity was not a thing to keep forever.

"Come now, Buttons, there must be one of my girls you find attractive." Mary groaned and her face dropped into a sullen, angry expression. "What! You cannot remain celibate. You are sixteen. Come now, be reasonable. Think of where you are. You have the pick of the house's beauties.

28

Marie, or perhaps Elinor; Elinor is a pretty girl. Or Lucy; you're fond of Lucy, I know."

"No, Madame, I do not wish to bed any of these girls now . . . or ever."

"What did you say—now or what?"

"Not now, milady. I have no desire for girls."

"One of our boys, then?"

"No! Not that either," she said in a fierce tone. She prayed that might put an end to the conversation.

"Come here, lad, and sit beside me. Come on." When Mary sat down, the lady carefully removed Mary's wig and ran her fingers through her soft brown hair. Mary was uneasy but did not move away. "What's the matter, dear Buttons? You seem sullen and morose lately."

Mary felt little bubbles of perspiration on her forehead.

"We were wont to talk more in the old days. You would teach me then. You do not take the time to teach me now. We do not read in French or talk in English."

"Perhaps I have been waiting to teach you something more important than French or the drama. Perhaps we . . . ."

Sitting together on the sofa and looking straight into the woman's eyes, Mary could in no way mistake her lady's intentions now. Madame Beaulieu loosened her bodice, and as she talked her breasts became entirely exposed. Mary was so frightened she could not move. She sat staring at the floor.

"Look at these," the lady said, bringing Mary's head up to meet her breast. "On three continents men pay sacks of Spanish gold just to see them. You would not deny them your lips, now would you, Buttons? I offer them to you gladly. Think of us as mother and son. It is all one."

"'Tis not all one, Madame."

"But 'tis a beginning. 'Tis a woman you need, Buttons, not a girl."

With that, the lady pulled herself on top of Mary, smothering her with her breasts. "I love you, darling Buttons. My own dear boy. Don't you love me, your own Marie?"

29

Mary could not breathe. Her face was buried in the woman's breasts and she shifted her head to one side for air, all the while trying to move out of reach of the groping hands. The woman was not strong enough to hold her. Twisting and turning, Mary broke away. Once free, she ran from the house and headed straight for the wharf.

Just as she turned the corner, Mary saw Molly leaving their hut. Quickly she ducked behind some empty packing crates which littered the narrow alley.

Once inside the hut; Mary tried to quell her panting breast. Frustrated and angry, she breathed in halting gasps even after she had torn off her cravat and ripped away her red velvet vest. Looking for a knife and finding none, Mary went to her mother's sea chest. Opening it, she picked up the stained velvet dress and slowly unwrapped the sword. This was her first opportunity to look at it closely.

'Tis magnificent, she thought, turning the hilt and studying the detail. 'Tis even finer than the one the Comte de Grasse carries.

She slipped the blade from its tooled leather scabbard. The brightness of the metal sparkled in the last vestiges of sunlight which filtered through the grimy window. Mary ran her finger carefully along the edge. 'Tis very sharp. M. R. Who be that, I wonder? God, they be my initials! She slid the blade under one of the outer folds of her chest binding and cut through. The bands of cloth fell away. "Ah, I can breath again. I am free!" Brandishing the sword about her head, she danced barebreasted about the room, slaying foe after foe in wild excitement. "M. R. M. R. Mary Read, soldier! General Mary Read! Seaman Mary Read! Ha! Ha! Admiral Mary Read! Mary Read, the female filibuster! Ha! Ha! Take that and that, you scurvy dog! But soldiers do not fight in velvet, she said, having stopped long enough to notice her attire. Dropping the sword down the front of her breeches, she cut through the fabric as if it were paper. "I am free at last, of you Madame!" she proclaimed, swinging the sword high above her head.

Oh God, now what? she thought almost in the next breath.

What am I to do now? I cannot go back to the house. And I am forbidden to stay here. I cannot go into the street naked as I am. Jesus, what am I to do?

Scrambling through the trunk, she found a woolen shirt, then a worn blue coat and frayed tan breeches which had once belonged to Alfred Read. She dressed hurriedly. Oh, I forgot the binding, she thought. Ah, what of tha! I am small. I need it not. 'Tis a loose shirt, not like my tightfitting vest. Still, this new freedom will take some getting used to.

Where can I go, I wonder? Perhaps to the wharf to find a ship sailing anywhere in the world. It makes no difference. God, I have no money for passage. Once again Mary rifled through the belongings in the chest. She keeps it here, somewhere in here, I know. All her possessions in the whole world are in this sea chest. Mary found a purse and emptied the few shillings into her hand, then one by one put them all back. I cannot steal food from her mouth, thought Mary. I am no rogue. I'll walk. Mary closed the chest and, picking up the handsome sword, left her mother's hut forever.

It was dusk. A weathered old man, his face etched by the sun and wind, looked like the craggy rocks of the English coast. He sat on his haunches and scaled his fish. Glowing coals waited in a black iron pot nearby. A scrawny brown-black cat foraged ravenously through the meager scraps for a bite of fish. Rough fishermen hauled in their nets and sorted the day's catch. Amber lights from the newly trimmed lanterns jumped up and down, here and there. A tern bobbed gently near the rough wooden steps which led from the main dock, and disappeared into the water. Gulls squawked overhead, searching for their dinner.

Mary hid the sword under her coat and pulled her arms tightly across her chest to hold the weapon in place. Her chin securely pillowed in her collarbone, Mary was plodding along the harbor quay when someone jarred her shoulder. The sword dropped between the planks of the dock but the hilt arrested its fatal plunge.

"Sorry, lad. Let me help thee." The powerful man dressed in the uniform of the Royal Navy swung his bulging sack off his shoulder and plopped it onto the deck with a heavy thud. "There! Safe 'tis," he said handing the sword to Mary and watching her hide it under her coat again.

"Thank you," she said uneasily. She felt awkward in the presence of this man, who was looking at her with such intensity.

Sensing her uneasiness, he spoke again. "Where're ye off to with that fine weapon, m'lad?"

"West," she muttered. "West somewhere."

"Well, I hate to tell thee this, lad, but you're walkin' in the wrong direction. Besides, ye be needin' a ship to get to the far west from 'ere."

Mary turned and began to walk in the opposite direction.

"Would ye take a bite o' supper with me afore ye start your long journey?"

"I'm not hungry," was her firm reply.

"Suit yerself then. It be mess aboard me ship now, an' if ye won't join me, I must be along."

Mary turned and watched the sailor hoist the sack to his shoulder with remarkable ease.

"Your ship, ye say?"

"Aye, lad. I be Nicholas Brattle from the Isle of Wight, bo'sun aboard that man-o'-war ye sees in the harbour there. We be in need of a ship's boy just now."

Far out in the harbor a galleon stood at anchor. An unfamiliar longing stirred within her. Mary's future flashed before her eyes almost in an instant. Her present course was clear.

She ran after the boatswain. "Wait, sir! Wait for me, Mister Brattle. I'll go with you."

"Come along, then. Jump in," he instructed, pointing to the ship's boat tied to the dock.

"From here, sir?" she said, thinking it was a long way down.

"Aye. The tide be out but it be not such a great distance, five or six feet at most." He tossed his sack into the boat.

32

"What be your name, lad?"

"Buttons . . . Buttons Read."

"Well, let's be off, Buttons Read."

Mary pinched her nose between her thumb and forefinger, took a deep breath and jumped. Fortunately, she landed on the soft bundle. The boatswain jumped in after her. Mary clung to the edge of the pitching boat with a death grip.

"'Ave ye never been in a boat afore, Buttons Read?"

"No, sir."

"Well, come on then, leave hold of the side and I'll teach thee a thing or two. Take up this 'ere oar and I'll take t'other one."

They sat side by side on one of the benches in the boat. Mary gripped the fat oar with both hands.

"Now, lad, dip yer oar in the water behind ye, like this, and pull. That's it. Pull! Pull! Pull harder! That's it. Get the paddle deeper in the water or we'll 'ave to sleep ashore in a brothel tonight."

Provided with this strong incentive, Mary struggled with each stroke. The boatswain seemed to do it effortlessly. Once synchronized with the rhythm of his movement, Mary could relax. Looking out at the water, she could see the glint of moonlight shimmering on the edges of the easy waves. All was quiet except for the slap, slap of the oars and the swishing sounds they made as they lifted out of the water.

When they reached the galleon, the young boatswain caught Mary from behind as she dangled precariously from the hempen ladder, and, giving her a final shove, slipped her over the rail onto the deck. As she fell sprawled across the neatly stored circles of rope, laughter thundered in her ears and she looked up into the misshapen, elongated faces of the seamen.

"What a queer thing 'tis, eh mates? All legs an' no body."

"How old be ye, lad? Ten?"

"Get up from there and let's 'ave a look at ye."

"Where'd ye find this pasty-faced boy, Bo'sun?"

Mary scrambled to her feet, dancing on the thick ropes in an effort to find solid footing. Her small, firm breasts, bobbing gingerly under her tunic, went unobserved by the men intent on her fancy footwork. Mary was conscious of the movement of her breasts, but once her feet were firmly planted on the slanting deck, another kind of panic seized her. "My sword!" Rushing to the rail, she was prepared to leap back into the longboat.

"I 'ave it, lad," said the boatswain. "Come, get ye below with me. We'll see this safely stowed, and find some victuals."

The keeper of the ship's weapons unlocked a door, took Mary's sword and threw it onto a veritable heap of them. As the clanking of her sword reverberated in the arsenal, Mary felt a hollowness deep within the pit of her stomach.

"Yer sword be safe now, lad," said the boatswain as he led Mary to the officer's mess. "Safer than 'twill ever be again, I vow. The gunner's mate ties the key to the magazine to his private parts lest any man try to steal it from 'im whilst 'e sleeps. Damned clever bastard," he chuckled.

'Tis lost to me now, she thought. I cannot leave this ship without my sword, that's certain.

"Mister Brattle?"

"What lad?"

"What do you call this ship?"

"*Hawksnest*. This be the man-o'-war *Hawksnest*."

"Where bound, sir?"

"She ships to Flanders with the first light. We be transport for Her Majesty's soldiers in the Flanders wars. 'Ere we be. Let's feed! I be 'alf starvin'. What say thee, lad?"

"I am hungry enough, sir."

The boatswain took his heaping platter, scraped a third of it into an empty dish, and set the dish down in front of Mary. Crumbling a few dried biscuits on top of his food, he attacked his dinner with relish. Mary tentatively jabbed her spoon into a heap of what appeared to be bits of salt pork, turnips, and some form of potatoes.

Better scraps than these are set out in the alley of Madame's house for the dogs, she thought. Tastes of pure salt. I will starve aboard this vessel. 'Tis a comforting place, though.

"Per'aps the bill o' fare be not to yer likin', lad. Ye needs somethin' to fill yer innards and prevent sea sickness. 'Tis the best food ye will get til we return from Flanders."

"How soon will that be, sir?"

"Oh, a week to a week an' a 'alf, I'd say. Depends on the wind. 'Ere, drink this ale. Per'aps 'twill give thee some appetite."

Downing her ale too fast was a mistake. Soon boatswain, lantern, walls and table melted together in the soft amber glow. She felt warm, too warm.

"Will you walk with me, Buttons? 'Tis a fine starry night."

"Aye, sir."

The deck creaked beneath her step. She realized that the boatswain had stopped in his evening walk to look up at the stars. Intent on the sky, Mary had not noticed where she was walking until her foot struck flesh and a rasping voice came from the deck.

"Fuck you, you bleedin' bastard!" murmured the man at her feet into the dark night.

"There is a man lyin' just here, Mister Brattle. Do the sailors sleep upon the hard deck?"

"No, boy. This man is on the bildoes. 'E's chained to this grate beneath our feet. 'Tis common punishment in the navy for minor offenses. This man took a drop more o' rum than was 'is ration. 'E's been lyin' there a week now. Just stay upwind o' 'im an' leave the poor bastard to 'is mis'ry. 'Is breeches be as foul as 'is mouth. Yes, boy, ye must look to yerself if ye are to be a seaman in the Queen's Navy. The cat and the bildoes be common punishments. A man cannot avoid one or t'other. So tend to yer duties well."

"What be the other punishments?"

"In my day, lad, I 'ave seen men hanged from the yardarm, flogged through the entire fleet, and keelhauled."

"Keelhauled, sir?"

"Aye. The man is tied by ropes attached to the yardarms on each side o' the ship and thrown overboard; then he be dragged under the keel from bow to stern. If he escape drowin' he'll pro'bly die from the cuts and scrapes caused by the barnacles."

"God-a-mercy!"

"Once, lad, I saw a man marooned on a reef at low tide. The cap'n give 'im a pistol with a single shot in't so he could take 'is choice when the tide be risin'."

"Blast me! What happened to the man, Bo'sun?"

"I cannot be sure, but methinks I 'eard the pistol, tho' we be gone well out of earshot by the time the tide come in. But enough of these gruesome tales. Let's go below and find ye a hammock. Ye must take some rest afore the mornin'."

Huge cannons and piles of heavy rope occupied most of the space in the gun deck. Hammocks were strung up as close as fourteen inches apart.

"'Ere ye be, lad. Sleep well."

"Good night, sir."

After two or three tries, Mary was finally in her new bed. She pulled the thin, damp blanket over her. The hammock swung back and forth gently for only a short while before she was asleep. Seconds later, it seemed to her, the deck came up and hit her in the face.

"Out of it! This 'ere's my sack!" A man climbed into his hammock and grumbled and muttered himself to sleep.

Mary sat on the deck, stunned. She had been asleep, so she was not injured by the fall. Standing up, she bumped a man out of his hammock.

"By Christ, I'll break your bleedin' arse, whoever ye be," screamed the man so rudely awakened from his sleep. "Show yerself, you bloody bugger!"

Mary crawled away and hid behind one of the cannons. The sailor crashed about, waking his shipmates. Confusion and loud cursing forced Mary to find her way to a safer place in a pile of rope. Making herself as small as possible, she tried to insinuate her body comfortably into the coils of the rope.

The sour men were soon asleep again. Mary listened to the melody of their snores and farts, set to the background notes of the creaking ship, until a new strain was introduced to her right ear—the gnawing sound of a rat.

Oh God, I cannot be womanish and scream now, she thought fearfully. These men will kill me. I must think of something else.

Small feet walked across her back and disappeared into the folds of the rope. As another rat crawled over her, Mary tried to imagine that a fluffy kitten was walking on her body as she lay comfortable and warm in front of her grandmother's fireplace. Soon she was asleep again. There would be no further incident to disturb the damp sleep of the crew this night.

The next morning the deck was lively. The crew of the *Hawksnest* were busy with preparations for casting off. Some men inspected the shrouds and tackles; others secured the deck cargo or unfurled the mainsails. Mary looked toward the wharf and the town; the outline of its small buildings was barely visible in the early morning haze.

There is nothing that I leave behind, she thought. I wonder if Mother even knows of my escape. She will cry only because she will have to work again. My lady probably cried herself to sleep last night, but she will forget me by noon.

Mary stared in the direction of her mother's hut. I am off to sea, Mother, like your husband. Though I have not his blood, I share his destiny. I have only one question for thee. Why did ye never tell me who my own father was? If ever I return, 'twill be only to ask you that one question.

"Grab that line, boy, an' pull. That's it. Now tie it off like ye sees me do it. We'll make a seaman of thee yet," said a burly man, as he flashed a toothless grin at Mary.

"We must sling these ord'ances lest they roll about the deck. Will ye help me, pug?"

Mary worked with the sailor and together they made fast

the cannon on the main deck. Mister Brattle came to the quarterdeck with a tall, well-built man who possessed a military bearing that commanded respect. His sandy hair whipped about his face. As he straightened his square-cut coat, he allowed his sharp gray eyes to rest for a moment on the man in the bildoes.

He must be the captain, Mary thought. Will he release that man before we sail, I wonder?

Mary looked more closely at the man in the bildoes. Thick rods of iron were affixed to the deck and had sliding shackles which held the man's legs outstretched so that he could either sit up or lie flat on his back. No other choice was available to him.

A week for a minor offense, Mary thought. This navy has hard punishments.

"Is all in readiness to weigh anchor, Mister Brattle?"

"Aye, Cap'n, all is ready."

"Then instruct the men, Bo'sun."

"Aye, Cap'n. Prepare to weigh anchor!" The boatswain continued to shout his orders to the crew. The captain checked the wind's direction. "Weigh anchor! Briskly! Hoist all yards to their height. Put yere backs to't now, mates."

Leaping onto one of the heavy shrouds, Mary pulled with all her might. Laughing at her own strength, she fell into the rhythm set by her mates.

"Who is that?" asked the captain, somewhat astonished.

"New pug, sir. 'E'll be a fine seaman one day. That 'e will. No doubt of it, sir."

"Send 'im to me once this vessel is steady; and Bo'sun, release that man from the bildoes and put 'im to some useful work."

"Aye, Cap'n." Turning to the crew, the boatswain issued more orders. "Set taut the shrouds." Mary followed the toothless sailor and helped him to make fast the mizzen shrouds. She had forgotten her home and by the time she thought to look back, Plymouth Port had disappeared.

"Steady as she goes, helsman. We do but run down the coast til we reach the channel. Buttons, a word."

38

"Aye, sir." Mary flew up the stairs to the quarterdeck. "What is it, sir?"

"Cap'n wants thee below. Take 'im some hot tea."

"Aye, sir. Oh, how do I address him, sir?"

"Why, call 'im Cap'n; 'tis the proper way. Or Cap'n Glynn. Ambrose Glynn be 'is name. Now run, boy! The cap'n likes to take 'is mornin' tea afore noon."

"Aye, sir. Right away, Mister Brattle."

In the excitement of the morning's activities, Mary had forgotten to eat. As she waited for the cook to fix the captain's tray, she ate a dry biscuit dipped in fat and gulped hot tea from a mug.

Mary tapped lightly on the captain's door.

"Come!"

"Your tea, Cap'n."

"Yes, yes." He made no move and gave no further instructions. Mary stood quietly holding the tray. The captain was leaning over a polished mahogany table, poring over his charts, intent on one fixed point. The September sun broke through the windows of the stern, flooding the tiny cabin.

Mary regarded the handsome blondhaired man standing at the table. His white lace cuffs flopped about with the movements of his hands. He wore a beautifully embroidered frogged waistcoat and his boots were polished to the brilliance of a looking glass. In all, he was a fine figure of a man.

His sword slung over the chair was almost as magnificent as her own. Mary stared at it, trying to visualize the blade. She was so intent she did not realize that Captain Glynn had even noticed her presence in the room, until a hand pulled the sword from its scabbard and she saw the point of the sword practically at the tip of her nose. The tray began to shake and the tea made little waves in the mug. Mary was so frightened in the face of the naked blade that she could not take her eyes from the blackness within the pewter mug. She wanted to dive into it and disappear forever.

"My father's," said the captain.

39

Mary tried to regain her poise but was still much too frightened to look up from the try.

"This sword . . . 'twas my father's. It is so sharp . . . "

Mary saw the point of the blade approach her chest and she clamped her eyes shut and stood rigid. She heard the click of her jacket button striking the glass pane. Opening her eyes, she saw the sword resting across the tray.

"Your tea, sir." Mary's words came out in a highpitched tone and her throat felt as though she would strangle.

"Yes, set it on the sideboard."

She stumbled over to the sideboard and set the tray beside a crystal decanter.

"You be the new lad? Report to cook. Mister Warren, the first mate, be sick. Have cook fix some broth an' ye take't to 'is cabin."

"Aye, sir."

"On your way, now."

"Aye, Cap'n."

Oscar Warren, first mate of the *Hawksnest*, tossed in his feverish bed. The rank smell of his cabin threatened to make Mary sick. Just as she was preparing to feed him, Mister Warren turned over onto his back and opened his eyes. One red eye stared in bleary delirium. There was a gaping hole where his other eye should have been. Mary stood up and backed away in fear.

'Tis a mean man, she thought. I know it. 'Tis not the one eye or his foul sickness, but he be mean throughout.

One day when Oscar Warren had been but thirteen, his father, in a monstrous fit of rage, had plucked out the boy's eye. Young Oscar had killed him on the spot. Then he had run away to sea, to wait. Year after year of bitterness seethed within him, until one day he had become an officer—first mate of the *Hawksnest*. Now he could take out his vengeance on his fellow man in the name of military discipline. All men would suffer under his hand. It was he who had put the man in the bildoes.

The eye closed. The other eyelid sagged into the hollow

of the man's face. Mary put the broth aside within his reach and picked up the wooden bucket. As she carried the bucket to the deck, the putrid liquid sloshed out, fouling her jacket. As a footboy she had always been relatively clean, at least; now she would have to live in stained and sweaty garments. She tossed the contents of the bucket over the side, casting up her stomach after it. Then for a long while she hung over the railing, dizzy and nauseated.

At high noon Mary was sent to scour the below decks with salt water and vinegar. As she worked she noticed the movement within the walls of the ship as the bedbugs wriggled their way out of the newly painted boards. Already the unpleasant odor of the bilge had begun to turn into the rancid stench of rotting carcasses of rats and other vermin.

When she emerged from the foul tomb, Mary gulped quantities of fresh air. Perspiration beaded her forehead and ran down her cheeks. The troops were sitting about on the quarterdeck cleaning their pieces, sharpening their swords and knives. Two men were fencing. Fascinated by the speed and agility of their movement, Mary came nearer. The blades of their swords were so thin that Mary could hardly see them flashing through the air.

"Like to 'ave a go, boy?" asked one of the soldiers.

"Oh no, sir, I have duties." Mary snatched up her bucket and quickly tossed the filthy water overboard.

"What be yer name, lad?"

"Buttons Read, sir."

"Well now, Read . . . . " The soldier leaned in very close to her face and his voice dropped to a harsh whisper. "Why don't ye come with us? This navy life be not healthy for a boy such as yerself."

"How can fighting a war be healthy, sir? I might get myself killed in a battle."

"But look 'ere, lad, ye'll be dyin' in the service of yer Queen, not hangin' over the bleedin' rail with the seasickness or burnin' up from the bloody flux. Think on't, lad. We 'ave some days yet afloat. For myself, I'd gladly walk

41

fifty miles a day rather than rock me arse on the deck of this bloody ship. Oh, Will's me name. Will Dever, one of the Duke of Marlborough's soldiers of foot, and damn proud of that too, boy. Find me if ye wants to get off this stinkin' scow. I'll show ye how to do it.''

Will Dever had a kindly face and seemed to have her best interests at heart, but to leave the navy to enlist in the army made little sense.

That evening the crew lay about the deck with their ration of rum and sang songs of the sea, of sailors and of the women they had left at home. Lying flat on her back, Mary looked up at the stars, half listening to the music and their conversation.

"Ye know, lads," a sailor said softly, "a man what goes to sea for pleasure would pro'bly go to hell for a pastime."

The boatswain interrupted their laughter. "All right, men, get about your duties. Some to the watch, some to sleep. Buttons, dost thee bunk on the hard deck?"

"Huh? Oh, Mister Brattle, it's you." She yawned.

"Get thee below and sleep. Ye must watch the glass in the early mornin'. 'Tis orders of the first mate."

"Is he well again, sir?"

"Well enough, I fear," groaned the boatswain.

Mary crawled into a warm hammock recently vacated by a sleepy sailor gone to the watch. At least she was sure of four hours of uninterrupted rest. Before she had hauled her legs up into the hammock she was asleep, one long leg dangling out.

"Out of it! Get about yer duties. Think ye can lie in the sack all the day?"

Mary's hammock was flipped over and she crashed to the deck. As the first mate grabbed her shirt and pulled her to her feet, the dancing stars began to clear from in front of her eyes. A giant of a man, his one eye gleaming like the blackest devil, Warren now wore a black patch over the empty socket. His dark wet hair hung like strings down the sides of his face. The tiny red hairs of his short beard moved about and sometimes stood straight out from his face as he shouted at her. Mary's arms were clamped to her body as she felt her feet leave the ground. Warren's powerful arms lifted her up to his height as he shouted directly into her face. His teeth, although stained and rotting, were sharp and pointed. Suddenly she was tossed through the air, a hammock catching her in flight before she hit the hard deck again.

"Take advantage of me illness, will ye! Ye and that pasty-face bo'sun. I'll show ye!" He hit her hard across the face. "Now, mind yerself, boy, or the next time ye'll feel the cat instead of the back of me hand. This 'ere's a bloody military vessel and ye'll obey orders or I'll beat thee to a bleedin' pulp."

"Hard to starboard," shouted the boatswain. The helmsman pulled the wheel with his powerful arms.

The *Hawksnest* surged through the misty morning. Standing on the upper deck, Mary was lost in a fantasy of high adventure. Gramercy! The upper bell of the glass was empty. How long has it been, I wonder? I hope I'm the only one to notice this. Just as she took up the glass to turn it, she felt a powerful presence behind her.

"Turn that glass!" boomed the voice of the first mate. "Ring the bell! So, pug, ye cannot tend the glass without dreamin', eh!" Mister Warren gripped her neck so hard that she almost swooned from the pressure; then he threw her down the stairs to the deck. "Tie this boy to the mainmast. Knave's grease for a bloody woreson knave. Bo'sun, assemble the men and fetch the cat!"

The men stood, startled. Surely he would not beat a boy. They waited, hoping to hear a lighter sentence given.

"Don't stand there like bleedin' pricks. Tie this filthy wretch to the mast and fetch the cat!"

Pure fear gripped Mary. What is this cat? she asked herself, as her face was pushed into the mast. Blood flowed from her nose and mouth. The toothless sailor tied a heavy rope around her wrists.

"The mate is a heartless bastard. 'E loves to see blood. Be a brave lad, now."

"What be the cat?"

43

"Call the ship's company to parade!" shouted Mister Warren. "Mister Brattle, get thee to yer position." He began to address the entire crew. "This insolent wretch hath been negligent in his work. Bo'sun, do yer duty!"

Tense silence prevailed. Mister Brattle ripped Mary's shirt, exposing the soft white skin of her back.

"God-a-mercy, I am to be whipped. How shall I bear it?" Mary pulled at the ropes in an effort to free her hands, but had the presence of mind to press her chest against the wood of the mast to conceal her breasts.

"I command that six stripes be put upon this wretch," shouted the first mate. "Bo'sun, tarry not!"

"Six?" pleaded the boatswain. "He be but a boy, sir!"

"Dost thou dare to contradict me order? Per'aps a dozen suits thee better."

Hot fear rose in her throat and Mary felt she might choke. The splintered wood of the mainmast had scraped her cheek, blood was dripping down her neck. She was suspended in a moment of time when she knew not what might be the worst that could happen to her.

Suddenly there was a whistling sound, followed by a pain so acute that a scream of anguish escaped her. Her whole back was on fire. She felt her flesh tear in what seemed a dozen different places.

"Put some muscle into it, man," shouted the first mate to the boatswain.

First the whistling sound, then came the pain worse than before, gouging her flesh. She felt the lacerations as if her very bones were exposed to the raw salt air. Again the nine tails clawed her body. Only deep groans issued now. Her shoulders were afire and excruciating pain gripped her torso. The many knotted straps reached around and tore at her breasts. The sky flashed red, then blackness came over her. The whip lashed out again, leaving her back a red mass of flesh.

"Wake him."

A bucket of water was splashed in her face and Mary saw the blurred image of the boatswain. "I'm sorry, lad," he whispered.

"No talking there!"

Another sailor was ordered to douse her back with a bucket of sea water. She fainted again, but not before she felt her body explode into a million fragments of raw hot flesh. The boatswain began to cut the ropes.

"Leave 'im til high noon. It seems we need an example. With each bell, douse 'im with a bucket of sea water. Per'aps then this boy will learn to tell the time correctly."

A half hour passed in what seemed only seconds to Mary. She bit down hard on her lower lip but could not keep a deep groan from swelling up from her heaving chest as the stinging water hit her back again. A sadistic smile passed over Mister Warren's face, then he quickly went below. The boatswain came to her and, under the pretext of checking her ropes, shoved into her mouth a rag saturated with fresh water. Mary sucked on the water gratefully while the boatswain adjusted the ropes away from the raw spots on her thin delicate wrists. She allowed her body to mold itself to the mast, giving herself up to this humiliating exhibition.

Silently Mary called out to her dear Nan. As a young child she had been wont to wrap herself around Nan's full round body and bury her face in her ample breast. Hugging the mast, she dreamed of Nan's warm comfortable body and the magic of her healing salves. There was no hurt which Nan could not ease. Lost in this dream, Mary thought she could feel Nan smooth the balm over her back and sides, slowly extinguishing the fire of the burning flesh with her healing touch.

A sudden splash of water hit her, but this time she felt nothing. Her back was numb, sensitive only to Nan's easing strokes. She slept till noon.

The boatswain waited until after Mister Warren had left the deck before he cut Mary's bindings.

"Thank the Lord ye are alive, lad!" said the boatswain. "I would not 'ave thy death on me conscience."

Her pain returned as he picked her up and carried her to his cabin.

"I 'ave some ointment for yer wounds." He put her down on his cot and inspected her back. "These wounds be not so bad as they could be. I cannot understand it. Per'aps the salt water hath prevented 'em from goin' rotten. Now be brave, lad; 'twill smart a bit.'' He gently applied the paste over her cuts and the vibrant red welts which had risen up from her milk-white skin. "A travesty, by God, to lay six upon a mere boy, cruel bastard that 'e is. But ye know, lad, six dozen be common punishment for a navy seaman.'' She groaned periodically. Slowly the burning flame of her torso quieted into a warm glow. "Can't understand, these cuts 'ave sealed themselves already. In all me days I've never seen the like o' it. That be youth for ye. Ye'll be fit by mornin'.''

Mary slept until the next morning and was awakened by the urgent need to relieve herself. Swinging her feet to the floor, she sat on the edge of the cot. There was a clean white shirt on the bench next to the bed; she put it on. When her eyes began to focus, Mary looked for the bucket and, spotting it, slowly made her way to it. When she heard heavy footsteps outside, she quickly drew up her breeches. Just as the boatswain entered the cabin, she swooned.

"Gramercy! What are ye doin' out of bed?'' As the boatswain helped Mary to her feet, she clutched at her breeches, fearing they would fall open and reveal her.

"What ye are in need of now is a walk about the deck. A breath of fresh air will do thee good.''

Mary tucked her new shirt loosely into her breeches and, with his help, she made it up the stairs to the deck. The sun was warm, it seemed to burn her back through her coarse shirt. The boatswain left her clinging to the rail and went about instructing the men in their duties.

Will Dever stopped alongside her. "Be ye ready to come with me now? A day hence we be in Flanders. We must make some preparation if ye be comin' with us.''

The soldier stiffened and Mary sensed his fear. Turning toward the quarterdeck, she saw the first mate looking through his glass out to sea.

"Watch 'im close, boy,'' warned Dever. "'E 'as had thee whipped soundly. 'E's got thee by the tail now. Next 'e'll want in yer bung hole. Mark me words.''

Mary fixed upon the eye of Mister Warren and she could not conceal the enmity in her own eyes.

"If ye be alive, be about some useful work or I'll fling ye to the sharks," he barked.

Mary hurried below, quickly poured down a cup of watery broth and went to work cleaning the below deck. The scraping motion pulling at her wounds only inflamed her already burning anger.

That night Mary was alert to every movement of the sand in the glass, practically counting each grain as it dropped. Toward the end of her time at the glass she heard the first mate speaking to the helmsman below. His words were slurred beyond the point of intelligibility.

I hope he comes not up here she prayed. She heard Mister Warren speak an oath, and felt the ship lurch to one side, then right itself again.

"Check yer compass. 'Tis there for a purpose," slurred the first mate. "Damn yer eyes, man," he mumbled, as he climbed the stairs to the poop deck. His ascent was retarded. Mary heard him slide down several stairs at different intervals. Her body went rigid with fear. Striking the bell with the feeling of sounding an alarm, she turned the glass and waited.

That be seven, she thought. Would it were eight. I would leap o'er this rail and drop to the quarterdeck and run off like the scared cat that I am. He be drunk. I can smell him from here. If I kill him, the captain will hang me from the yardarm. God, what am I to do?

As she felt his hot breath on her neck, Mary gripped her belly in panic. Mister Warren thrust his loins against Mary's backside. She took hold of the railing. His penis hardened as he continued to drive it against her. All the while he laughed and murmured filthy words. When he backed away to thrust again, Mary, with a well-timed corkscrew motion, spun away. He toppled over the railing and crashed onto the quarterdeck.

Christ! The glass! Eight bells! Where be my relief? If he wakes, he'll come up here and kill me, surely. What if he does not wake? What if he be dead? I did not touch him. Who will believe that? No one!

"To the sack, mate." Frightened out of her wits by the relief, Mary nearly leaped overboard. "Watch ye doesn't trip over the first mate. 'E's lyin' on the quarterdeck, passed out from his cups." The man chuckled to himself as he checked the glass.

Fetching a lantern, Mary went to the below deck where the soldiers were quartered. The men were sleeping on the hard deck, pillowed on their knapsacks. Mary stepped over a few bodies and peered into several snoring faces before she found her friend.

"Mister Dever! Mister Dever!" Mary whispered harshly, and shook the man.

"What the devil!" he exclaimed, reaching for his weapon.

"Mister Dever, it's me, Buttons."

"Buttons! What be the matter with thee? Dost know the hour?"

"I think I have killed the first mate."

"Gramercy!"

"I did not touch him!"

"How can ye kill a man without ye touch 'im? Make sense, lad. Did ye kill 'im or no?"

"I was standin' at the rail an' he come behind me, beatin' his loins 'gainst my backside."

"I told thee! I warned thee, did I not?"

"When he reared back to 'ave at me again, I spun away and he fell over the railing to the deck below."

"God's Eyes! Thou hast killed 'im, right enough!"

"What am I to do?"

"You must desert this ship, that's what ye must do. Else ye will hang."

"What if Mister Warren be not dead?"

"Then 'e will kill ye for tryin' to kill 'im. So, lad, ye has no choice in the matter. 'Tis death either way."

"But I had not figured to go to war, Mister Dever. I be no soldier."

"Ye will be one tomorrow. 'Ere, take these things."

Mary climbed over the sleeping men, doused her lantern, then made her way to the magazine. She found the gunner's mate stretched out on his back in front of the door. A sack of meal served as his pillow. How am I to rescue my sword? she wondered. I have never touched a man's privates before. Yet I need that sword, and I'll not get it without I filch it.

Looking at the paunchy sailor, she saw that he was wearing loose-fitting pantaloons, tied low under his mountainous belly. Long snores issuing from his lips were followed by blasting snorting sounds. Mary watched him intently and checked the corridors to see if anyone was stirring about. The rolling motion of the galleon lulled him deeper and deeper into sleep. An empty jug of sack hooked to his forefinger scraped almost soundlessly across the wooden floor. There were no other noises except the incessant creaking of the timber.

He's well in his cups, she thought. Would almost take a cannon to wake him. Be bold, Mary. Untie but a few strings and 'tis done.

After carefully undoing the ties of his pantaloons, Mary foraged in the hair at the base of his belly in search of his organ. Surrounded protectively by his testicles, it seemed to be locked between his thighs. What! Hath he got it up his arse? Be bold, Mary, be bold. Gathering all her courage, Mary touched the base of his penis and felt along it in quest of the key. The large limp member began to stiffen and rise up slowly from its furry hiding place. Sensing what was happening, Mary looked to see if the man had awakened. He hadn't, but a smile had appeared on his face. She continued the stroking motion until his appendage was standing straight up. She was relieved to find that the string had been tied in a neat little bow. One tug and it was off; she had the key.

Silently she unlocked the door, but she had to pick up several swords before finding her own. The movement of the weapons on the pile made a soft clanking sound, but the keeper did not stir.

After she secured the door, Mary felt confident enough to return the key to its hiding place. The penis, which had maintained its erection during her absence, looked ridiculous standing up at the base of his gigantic belly.

'Twould be an amusing picture, she thought, if 'twere not such a dangerous proposition. 'Tis beyond my understanding why women lust after this so much. It must do something besides stand up like a bishop or, as it did before I put my hand to it, hang like the neck of a dead chicken. Whatever it can do, it cannot be much. But 'tis a handy pisser. Would I had it.

After tying the key to his penis, she fastened his pantaloons, picked up her sword and other equipment and hurried away.

Mary spent the night wedged between two cannons on one of the gun decks. Using her shirt tail, she polished the blade of her sword. I will wear this sword for convenience now, she thought. Perhaps someday when I learn to use it, I will wear it proudly. I wonder if I will ever know what it is to live as a woman, like other women?

Through the gunport, Mary watched the sun rise. The sea was calm, reflecting the pinkish cast of the sun's morning rays. In the distance she could see the coastline of Flanders.

Mary remained hidden waiting for Will Dever to find her. In an hour she heard Mister Brattle issuing orders for their putting in to shore.

"Lower the sails! Lively now. Get into the chains port side, mate, and toss out the sounding lead. Stand by to let go the starboard anchor."

Will Dever found her and strapped all manner of equipment onto her body: jacket, canteen, munitions pack, bedroom, and a rifle.

"Any word of the first mate?"

"'E's alive, lad. Bastard broke 'is bloodly leg, 'tis all. Down in 'is hole now 'e be, screamin' 'is fuckin' 'ead off. There now! Pull this hat over yer ears. Come with me. We be the first to go ashore."

"What is this place?"

"Ostend. The French 'ave Dunkirk. Come now, we best leave this vessel afore the first mate sends for thee!"

The soldiers spaced themselves evenly on both sides of the longboat and pulled oar to the chant of the tiller's, "Heave to, heave to. Pull, you lazy land rats. Ye're slappin' at the water like a bleedin' whore. Work as slovenly in these wars an' they'll bury yer arse 'ere in Flanders. Jesus God, pull!"

Intent on her own thoughts, Mary struggled with her oar until she felt a hard drag and realized the boat had beached. The soldiers hopped into the water and hauled the longboat onto the shore.

Fallen soldiers littered the beach; their wounds dripped blood onto the creamy white sand as they groaned in misery. A hand touched her leg.

"God-a-mercy, soldier, a drop of water for a dyin' man."

Mary lifted the man up slightly and gave him a drink from her canteen. Tearing a piece off her shirt, she saturated it with water and wiped the man's bruised and blackened forehead.

"Thank ye. You're a fine lad. Bless thee, boy."

She stopped over another man lying face down in the sand. Fearing that he would smother, she had intended to turn him over when Will Dever took her arm.

"'E's dead, lad, can't ye see that? Come along now, and leave 'im."

Will marched away; then Mary turned the man over onto his back and knelt there, staring down at his face.

He be but a boy, no older than me, she thought. A hairless boy like me. Grains of sand, looking like gleaming quartz beads, stuck in his long black lashes and on his lips. One side of his face had been completely blown away. Flesh mixed with blood and sand gave it a grotesque appearance. The other side of his face was smooth; grains of sand clung to his pale cheek. Mary brushed the sand from this cheek and covered his face with the remnant of her shirt before hurrying after the soldiers.

It was a long way up to the wooded area and the sand

was so soft that it seemed to draw her into it. Once or twice she fell to her knees and had to struggle up under her heavy load. For every step forward she felt she was sliding one step backward. Once on harder ground, she regained her land legs and ran down the path until she saw the men up ahead. Only then did she slow down to catch her breath.

At Ostend Mary was hastily inducted as a soldier of foot and outfitted to take part in the Flanders wars. She was handsome in her uniform of gray breeches, tricornered hat, and red coat lined with the brilliant blue of her regiment. With the addition of her sword, which now hung smartly at her side, her equipment totaled almost fifty pounds of dead weight.

Mary had arrived in the very thick of a war which had been waged for five years and would not conclude for yet another five. She was one foot soldier in one battalion of the hundreds actively engaged in Brabant and Flanders.

Laying her equipment under a sprawling tree, Mary sank into her own feelings. A bitter stab of desolation churned the emptiness in the pit of her stomach. Will Dever, her only friend, had been separated from her with no word of goodby.

Unfamiliar men milled about the area where she sat. Hugging her knees, her chin resting on her folded arms, Mary stared straight ahead. Gray and white breeches floated by, patches of red, a pair of black boots, bright swords flickering in the sunlight. She heard a clank, a whish, a footfall. Colors, sounds and bodies, now disconnected and separate, would soon mass into a great fighting force to engage in the destruction of the enemy.

Mary buried her face in her arms. The enemy? Who is this enemy? Her hand fell from her knee onto the flintlock musket. Tracing with her finger the cold, smooth metal of the loop and trigger, she then opened her eyes and regarded the oddly shaped spring hammer of her weapon. The paper cartridges were new, the sergeant had said, but she had no earthly idea how the weapon was to be used.

She approached a short, thick-set man with black hair, sharp features and penetrating black eyes. The flesh of his protruding stomach was hard. He wore nothing except breeches, stockings and shoes. Tufts of black hair covered his shoulders and grew halfway down his back. The man was shaving. Logically this sergeant should be the one to assist her, since it was he who had issued this mystifying weapon to her in the first place.

"Sir?"

"Eh?" He stopped and peered up at her. His thick hands fell from his face and he rinsed the razor by sloshing it in the soapy water of his cooking pot.

"What is it, lad? Can't ye see I be busy 'ere?"

"I see that, sir, but I needs must learn this weapon afore the fighting and I know not who to ask. You seem a patient man, sir . . . . "

"'Enry Jaspers, sergeant-at-arms."

"Yes, sir, sergeant-at-arms. How am I to learn this weapon?" Mary lifted the musket waist high, the barrel pointing at the sergeant's chest.

"First I would suggest ye point it at the ground, for if an accident should occur, who would teach thee then, eh?"

"Sorry, sir sergeant."

"Sorry, sergeant, no sir sergeant, ye foolish boy."

"Yes, si . . . sergeant."

"What be yer name, boy?"

"Buttons Read."

"Come along then, Cadet Read; let's be off into the woods." He dried his face with his shirt before stuffing both hairy arms into it. Swooping up his hat, he settled it on his head, took up the musket, and walked briskly to a clearing at the edge of camp. Mary followed.

"Now . . . um . . . we be ready to load and shoot. Watch me." The sergeant prepared the musket for firing and repeated the process several times. "Now, you try it."

Mary slipped the cartridge into the barrel, primed the lock, pulled back the hammer and squeezed the trigger. The recoil knocked her back against a tree and bruised her shoulder. She was more startled than hurt. When the ringing in her ears ceased, she heard laughter coming from all about. The heartiest laughter was that of the sergeant. When the smoke cleared she saw faces in the woods. Three women, hands on hips and heads flung back in laughter, were pointing toward Mary, who was slumped against the tree. The young women were wearing low-cut chemises and red petticoats with black velvet ribbon running through. The white cheeks of their pretty faces were highly rouged.

"He be down, girls. Let's jump on 'im," said the heftiest one.

Mary leaped to her feet, quickly loaded the musket and pointed it in the direction of the taunting women.

"Oh, look now, girls, *all* his guns be loaded." The women broke into peals of derisive laughter.

"Get thee hence, we have serious work 'ere, ye miserable hedge whores," blasted the sergeant, shaking his fists at the women. "Lazy bitches, hangin' 'bout 'ere all the day. Strumpets, off with ye!"

"We'll see thee later, handsome boy."

"What be women doin' at the wars, sergeant?"

"Don't ye know, lad? They follow the campaign to ease the soldiers. For a tuppence these bangtails will be thy mattress. For meself I 'ave no need of them. Too old now to wrestle one of those busy wenches after the day's hard battle. Ye may indulge yerself as ye wish, lad. Yet, by the look of ye, I dare say ye 'ave never had a woman. Am I right on that score?"

"Yes, Sergeant Jaspers, I've never had a woman."

"Well, take up with one of these and they'll teach ye how to use yer equipment!" He broke into a great burst of laughter. "But, me boy," he said, shaking his head and growing serious again, "ye must not indulge thyself grossly on the eve of battle. 'Twill drain thy energies. Now enough of this talk. Back to work. Here now, brace yerself 'gainst that tree and try it again. Hit that dead branch stickin' out from that tree over there."

Mary missed breaking the branch off but she did hit a

piece of it. "Ye got a twig, boy! Ye'll improve with practice, if ye lives."

They worked and worked until dusk made target shooting impossible. Once back at the camp, the sergeant spoke of his favorite weapon. "I be an old soldier, lad. I prefers the pike to these fancy guns. Me pike thrust be deadly. 'Ere 'tis, lad . . . sixteen feet in length. I keeps the point sharp, see." Mary could hardly lift the pike, and handling it with any degree of accuracy was impossible.

"Try to hit me."

Mary swung the unwieldy weapon in the direction of the sergeant, who jumped out of the way with time to spare. She swung again. This time the force of her movement carried her around full circle. The sergeant took the pike from her and demonstrated. "I can batter a whole line of musket men with just one stroke. They topple like dominoes. She is my war prize, an' me only bedmate. I depends on her for me very life and that of me friends."

That night, wound in her great cloak, her head propped against her knapsack, Mary ritualistically played her fingers over the parts of the musket. She fell asleep, repeating the load, fire, reload procedure in her head.

On September 27, 1708, the convoy left Ostend for Menin. The next day, expecting to be intercepted by the French, Major-General Webb placed most of his six thousand troops in a triple line at a small clearing in the forest of Wynendael. In an effort to disguise his number, the Major-General dispatched some men, including Mary and the sergeant-at-arms, to hide in the thick woods.

Fluttering streaks of light filtered through the trees as they walked on a quiet path of moss. 'Tis now, she whispered to herself. I sense a danger behind a fallen tree trunk. The convoy moved steadily behind them.

"Be ye ready, lad? I smell the French. They be nigh," whispered the sergeant, lying beside her.

Mary's throat was too dry to respond. She loaded, then primed her musket. Sweat dripped from every pore as her fear mounted. Dear God, she prayed, did I live all these miserable years to die this day?

Parts of the Flemish line dispersed and the French, thinking they had an easy time of it, entered the forest, marching toward the convoy. Then the soldiers jumped up like rabbits from their holes, throwing the French into confusion. A man came into Mary's sights; her finger froze on the trigger.

"Shoot, lad!" screamed the sergeant. Mary stood paralyzed. A ball nicked one corner of her hat. The sergeant dispatched several Frenchmen around them with his pike. Then, coming to Mary, he grabbed the musket from her frozen hand, causing it to fire into the empty air.

"What be the matter with thee?" he cried. "Take this and use it, for God's sake. Be ye coward?!"

Fear gave way to anger and Mary drew her sword. The sergeant, believing himself threatened, instinctively thrust the bayonet of her rifle at her, failing the notice the Frenchman who was sneaking up behind him. Mary quickly ran the enemy through. The sharp steel slipped easily into the man's gut. When she drew out her sword there was blood on it. Leaving the soldier groaning and writhing on the ground, Mary stepped behind a tree and rested her back against it.

I have killed a man, she thought, her panic subsiding. But I have saved my friend. What now? I can either hide or fight. The choice be mine. I be no giant, I must use my wits in battle.

Hearing a sound from the other side of the tree, she swung out and was face to face with the enemy. His bayonet was no match for her sword and he was down. For two hours Mary flashed in and out of trees, dispatching any man wearing a white rosette. She was not yet skillful with her sword; success for her was in the element of surprise. It was fortunate that she had been placed in the woods, for she would have been killed had she stayed in the line.

At the end of the battle the sergeant found Mary lying on the blood-spattered ground, passed out from exhaustion. He cleaned and sheathed her sword, picked her up and carried her over his shoulder until the convoy made camp for the night. She never woke. The sergeant placed her under a tree and tried to rouse her to take some nourishment. Mary opened her eyes and stared, unmoving, up through the branches fluttering in the evening breeze.

"Thou didst well in today's action, Cadet. I thank thee for me life."

Mary nodded, for she could move no part of her body, and her jaws ached from grinding her teeth during the battle. Once again that night she was awakened, this time by the heavy moans and gasps of women and the grunting noises of the men. For a moment she thought they had been besieged in the night. Besieged they were, but by women, not soldiers.

Mary turned over on her stomach. Moments later a woman straddled her body, sitting on her buttocks. Gentle hands rubbed her aching shoulders and arms, which still trembled from the activity of the day. If it were not for her fear of the situation Mary would have indulged herself awhile longer, for she felt her torn, tired muscles repairing under the woman's touch.

"Leave me, I be weary," Mary said sternly.

"Please, do not send me away, brave soldier. Let me soothe thee. I'll not encourage thee to further action this night."

The woman lay prone, covering Mary's body with her own. Mary felt the softness of the flesh against her own, the downy legs, ample breasts, thick waist and fleshy arms. The woman whispered softly in Mary's ear snatches of old poems, and presently she slept.

The next day they arrived at Menin. Marlborough's tension abated and his dispatches heaped extravagant praise upon Webb and his troops for their behavior in the celebrated battle of Wynendael. The campaign continued.

The winter of 1708/09 was to be the worst ever experienced in this part of the world. It was a sixty-mile march from Ghent to the town of Breda in the Netherlands, where

Mary's garrison was to be quartered for the winter. The soldiers, fatigued from the overlong campaign, walked over rough roads, broke through ice-covered ditches, and marched across rolling fields of snow.

When the leather of Mary's shoes had worn completely through, she had to tear pieces from her cloak and tie the strips around her feet. The night fires never warmed her. She would unwrap and rewrap her hands and feet a dozen times. Almost afraid to go to sleep lest she not wake up again, Mary fantasized for hours, dreaming of the warm waters and hot sun of the Caribbean, which the sailors on the man-of-war had spoken of.

During the day she marched on. Men dropped in the snow. No one stopped. The ground was too hard even to bury anyone. Mary talked to herself, babbling nonsense all day. Discarding most of her gear except for her drinking cup and sword, she was able to walk faster. It had been more than a day since Mary had been able to feel any sensation other than numbness in her feet. Once or twice she faltered and fell but somehow raised herself up onto her feet once more. She saw a horse and rider frozen, standing upright in the snow.

Stumbling along, she tripped over what seemed to be a pole, but uncovering it she discoverd a pike. Henry Jaspers' pike! Where be he, I wonder? Several yards ahead she saw the sergeant lying face down, dead in the snow. Mary tried to drag him to a place nearby, under the shelter of some trees, but she could not. Cutting a few pine branches, she laid them over him.

The cold penetrated her spirit. She wanted to lie down beside the sergeant and die. It be not painful to freeze to death, thought Mary. I heard talk that ye just goes to sleep. No, it be only a few miles more. I can make it. Farewell, Henry Jaspers. Mary turned and started off again. Think of one step at a time. 'Tis all that matters now.

In a few hours, as twilight was descending to darkness, Mary saw a castle loom up in the distance.

"What be that, soldier?" she slurred through icy lips.

"Breda Castle," he shouted back. "Our camp be nearby now, thank the Lord!"

For the infantrymen, winter quarters consisted of a few miserable huts where they survived huddled together. The wind whipped through the gaping boards, and the small wood stoves provided little warmth. Mary began to think she would never be comfortable again.

Men who had not died of frostbite or exposure along the way were now dying from rotten wounds caused by amputated fingers and toes. Fever raged through the camp like blasts from the enemy firing line. The stench of the rat-infested huts drove Mary into the cold outdoors.

I would rather freeze to death in the open air than thrash about on that mat of straw hung all over with horse dung. I almost wish I had died in battle. 'Twould have been a brave thing, at least. Have I survived these battles to die of a rat bite?

The burial details were busy. Because the ground was frozen, dead men were simply laid in ditches with rocks placed over them. It was backbreaking work. Mary's physical state was weakened even more from the lack of food. There was barely enough to sustain the numbers in the camp. She had lost weight but, despite her constant hunger, she thought she had grown an inch or maybe two, judging from where her breeches hit her.

By the end of February Mary's duties had fallen into the boring routine of cleaning her sword and gathering kindling for the fires. She had the afternoons to herself and began to wander into other areas of the encampment. One afternoon she came upon the field where the cavalrymen were practicing maneuvers. The men sat handsomely upon their fine steeds, practicing the various gaits and charges, as well as mounted sword fighting.

Now that be a way to keep shoe leather, she thought. I wonder if I could sit a horse. 'Twould be fun to try. Mary made some inquiries and discovered that, upon certain easily obtainable recommendations, she could secure a place in the Dragoons. It was soon done and Mary was issued a long red coat, a white crossbelt and heavy thigh boots. The Dragoons was not the elite part of the cavalry; a trooper was essentially a mounted infantryman. But they were being used more and more in cavalry positions in battle.

When she learned to sit on the horse rather than fall off it, Mary would be instructed in the use of her sword. She worked day and night for weeks before she could handle the simplest maneuver of her horse and feel confident that she could fight from the saddle. It was many weeks more before she could keep her horse from turning in circles, and days after that before she could strike her opponent's sword with any degree of accuracy.

During one such exercise, Mary had so exhausted herself that she cried quarter. She hung her head down upon the horse's neck, panting heavily. A strong arm gripped her rein. Mary saw the blond hairs of the man's muscular forearm glisten in the sunlight and, raising her head, she was drawn into the bluest eyes she had ever seen. The man's face broke into a broad smile but Mary, still lost in the sea of his eyes, did not see it.

"My name is Maximilian Studevant." His voice was soaked in the melody of a heavy Flemish accent, rich and deep, yet gentle. Mary almost forgot herself.

"Mar . . . Read. Read."

Maximilian Studevant was a Corporal of Horse and a Fleming by birth. Young and vibrant, he was slight of build but muscular, with fair skin and bright blond hair. The features of his face were clearly chiseled into handsome lines. His eyebrows, somewhat darker than the hair of his head, gave his eyes a striking intensity.

"I have been watching thee, Read. Thy horsemanship improves. Come down and give thy horse a rest."

Mary dismounted and her knees gave way. Max caught her under the rib cage before she hit the ground. Mary's small breasts heaved with excitement at his touch and her sudden weakness mystified her.

"There now, on thy feet. Thee has been spinning round

up there too long. Thee must learn to keep thy horse steady.''

Steady, she thought, as she weaved down the path to the stable. First I must get rein over myself. Her knees were weak, her body limp, her arms useless and trembling so much that she could hardly put her sword into its scabbard.

"A fine sword thee has, worthy of an officer.''

"I be no officer, sir.''

"I know that. Perhaps thee should be.''

"I have no money to buy a commission. Be ye an officer, sir?''

"Yes, a corporal. But thee need not call me sir. My name is Max.''

Max did not know why he was so attracted to this young man. As a rule Englishmen bored him, but there was something about the lad, something warm and genuine, exciting.

I must know him better, he thought. This lad is sensitive and fresh, not like my coarse comrades.

After Mary's horse was groomed and fed, they left the makeshift stable and had a meager lunch by a blazing fire. Since the last light snow a few weeks ago, supplies had come through.

"This is the first good soup since the hard winter,'' he said, relishing every spoonful.

"Aye, 'tis hearty,'' she replied. Every time Mary looked at Max she felt a queasy sensation in her stomach and could not eat; a tingling glow of urgency flooded her privates and her breasts ached. Can this be love, she wondered? Oh, God, methinks it might be. But here in this place? Whoa! If it be, I needs must govern myself closely. I almost blurted out my rightful name today. Go slow, Mary.

"Let's shoot,'' he said.

"Shoot? Shoot what?'' asked Mary, bewildered.

"Our pistols, of course.''

"Aye, of course.''

Pistols in hand, they went into the Mastbos Wood within sight of the castle. Max talked about his military experiences and Mary listened intently to his stories of battle and his humorous camp tales. She wanted to learn everything about this man to whom she was so very much attracted.

How handsome he be, she thought. I do love the sound of his laughter. I would so wish to tell him a story or two of my own. I could keep him laughin' and cryin' til the morn. Instead, Mary listened and kept silent.

They practiced until their munitions ran out, then walked the rest of the afternoon. The world around seemed brighter to Mary. The sky was cloudless and bluer than she had remembered it to be in past weeks. Tufts of grass had sprung up through patches of bright snow. Touching tree after tree, she sensed their life and energy. It was easy to be natural and free with this man. For the first time in her life Mary wanted desperately to pour out the strange experiences of her childhood, but dared not.

In the weeks that followed she was constantly in the company of the young Fleming. Rising early, she would tend to her regular camp duties, wash, clean her equipment, polish her boots, and be off to join her friend. Most afternoons were spent drilling with him to perfect her horsemanship and pistol shooting. Mary was exhilarated during every precious moment of fencing practice. Neither she nor Max had any doubt that she could fight with a sword better than she could shoot or ride.

After supper they talked for long hours by the outside fire. Struggling to stay awake, Mary willed herself to converse so that he would not become bored and leave her company. Veiling the circumstances of her background, Mary was able to tell enough about herself to make him feel that he knew her well. Their conversations had turned to serious matters, far beyond the familiar banter of messmates. In their moments of silence Max caught himself looking at Mary with somewhat of a lover's eye.

He be a handsome lad, thought Max, lean of leg and tall. Yet there be a softness that I long to touch. Good God, what am I thinking?

"Read, we must to bed." Jesus fuck, what have I said! "I mean, I must be abed. Me to mine and thee to thine. Oh, I will see thee tomorrow."

"Good night then, Max. Sleep well."

Mary could not bear to be separated from this man. As she returned to her quarters a longing gripped her. It was a hunger which she could not satisfy, although she walked for hours in an attempt to quiet the ache of her desire. She felt herself drawn to his barracks as if by a powerful magnet. Sheltered from view by the tall trees, Mary would sit and stare at his window. On a few occasions she saw him mount and ride off in the direction of the town. Almost by reflex, she started to call out his name, but checked herself in time.

One afternoon they walked out by the wide stream near the castle and sat watching the lordly swans. The trees hung barren branches over the glassy water and waited for spring.

"Max, dost thou know aught of women?"

"Well," he said, somewhat taken aback by the boldness of her question, "what can I say? Women are wonderful, lovely, wild creatures, brimming with love and tenderness. Most of all they be soft to the touch, not hard like ourselves, and they be eager and willing to make love."

"How does a man know when he be in love?"

"When a man be properly aroused, he will know how to handle himself. Do not worry, thee will know. Once in the embrace of a lusty wench, thee will draw up and be a man. It will just happen."

I do not want to draw up like a man, she thought. I want to love as a woman loves. I cannot bear to go on this way but I know not what to do. I must leave it to him.

Word came in early April that the duke himself was coming to inspect the Breda Garrison. A week of preparations was hastily outlined to get camp, men and especially "The Horse" in readiness. Max and Mary worked together as much as possible until his duties of administration took him to another part of the camp. Mary usually managed to attach herself to any detail that was under his supervision. She watched in admiration as he walked about inspecting their activities.

There were times of separation which grieved Mary. As an officer, Max spent a large portion of his day in special battle training. The duke depended on the expertise of his officers in these wars. His officers were reputed to be the finest. Since she had no money to buy a commission, Mary was determined to be the best trooper in the Duke of Marlborough's regiment of horse.

If fate has landed me here in Flanders, into these very wars, then I will distinguish myself in some way. Life must be more than the daily problem of hiding my sex. If I am to be a woman in a man's world, I will be the best. I will be the finest trooper in the Dragoons. The duke himself will hear of me, perhaps Queen Anne as well.

Mary practiced every day, perfecting her all but passable skills of riding and shooting. In her fencing matches she had become the master, although Max was not totally aware of her skill. She allowed him touches she could easily have avoided. It was enough to know that she was the better swordsman. There could be no greater happiness in her life now except to possess him utterly, but she would have to discover a way to do that when the time was right.

As for Max, these preparations had removed him from his friend, giving him an opportunity to think on their past conversations. Mixed with his feeling of comradeship and brotherly concern was something he could not explain. He had deferred examining this impression for too long now. More than once he had found Mary staring at him with a look of more than friendly feeling. It was a loving, adoring gaze which embarrassed him. Obviously Mary was unaware that he had taken notice of it. Even though she had worked at repressing these visible expressions of her emotion, it was in her nature for her feelings to show in her face automatically.

Am I a sodomite? he pondered. I had never thought of it til now. Do I love him? I can see that he loves me. Is he a sodomite? I cannot deny there be more than friendly feeling here. What am I to do? Surely the other men observe his looks.

These thoughts played on his mind and disturbed him enough to bring about a sudden, almost violent change in his behavior. Max found himself boasting about his increasingly frequent excursions to the town, when talking to the other men in Mary's presence. On the pretext that their preparations took his activities in another direction, he drifted away from her. They were no longer seen in each other's company.

I cannot understand this. What power does this boy Read have over me that I ache when parted from his company? Yet I am tortured in his presence. I have hurt him, I know. It is in his face, in the black anger of his eyes. Why does he not leave my society? He is like a devil possessing me. Dear God, what am I to do? Women! I will seek solace in women! They will cleanse my body and mind. I will rain my bitterness into them until my guilt be purged and all thoughts of sodomy washed away.

Each night Max held himself firmly clasped inside a village wench. Her looks mattered not to him; it was her regenerating chamber he needed. When he finally pulled away, it was as if he had never been inside her at all. He carried nothing with him except his own weariness as he rode into camp the next morning empty, spent and tortured. Deep circles began to appear under his lusterless eyes, and his drawn face had a yellowish cast.

Since I can neither forswear his society nor bed him, he thought, I will let this next campaign end my life.

Mary was deeply saddened by the changes that each day brought to him. Their infrequent conversations became brief and he was always wont to turn away from her. The stink of whoring was all about him.

If only the campaign would begin, she thought. We would leave this place and these women who have such a hold on him.

Mary did not fully understand Max's actions, and therefore could not help him, any more than she could bring herself to any decisive action. It had not yet entered her mind to reveal her sex to him. In recent weeks her womanly feelings had been so strong she had quite forgotten that Max saw her as a man, and that might be the cause of his suffering.

She fought for understanding. Why this sudden rejection?

There be only coldness betwixt us now. I should leave him to himself, but I cannot. We were so close. What altered that? I cannot remember. Oh, I am miserable! Had I only the courage to reveal myself! But if he hates me now as he seems to, he will have me put out of the army. Perhaps he is in love with one of the women in the town and is rejected by her. That's it! He doth pine for some lady. Max's rejection of her preyed on her mind. It was, for Mary, the culmination of a childhood of rejection. Her thoughts drove her to distraction, and with each passing day she slipped deeper and deeper into depression.

One spring afternoon, when the sun was especially bright and warm, Mary left the camp. Pistol in hand, she entered the Mastbos Wood. Her pace was aimless, yet persistent and steady. Moving too close to a tree, she scraped her shoulder on the bark, breaking her stride. When she reached a clearing, Mary stopped and looked around a last time at this, their favorite resting place. Snatches of past conversations invaded her dismal thoughts. Mary lay on the soft new grass and stared up at the sky. She was transported back in time and saw herself as a young girl playing in the tall summer wheat. Images flashed into her mind: purple heather blanketing a rolling hill, wisps of lamb's wool like patches of snow on a Devonshire sedge.

A wispy cloud went floating by her eyes. Mary did not move. Then she seemed to be staring into a small black hole. Her entire concentration entered into this gloomy tunnel, this circle of blackness. She felt her consciousness shrinking to the size of a tiny dot and preparing to disappear forever into this murky aperture. She was not frightened; it seemed as though she were outside of herself looking down at herself and her little-girl self who lay stretched beside her on the grass. She saw that her own body was flat and straight, except that both arms were raised, holding a pistol, its black barrel pointing at her brow. Then both thumbs squeezed the trigger. The circle of lurid darkness detonated into a fantail of purple rays sparking out in every direction.

Moments later, Mary was awakened by sharp pains in

her hands, produced by the feathery breeze fanning her now skinless palms. The little girl was gone. The woman rose and looked at the inconstant weapon dangling from a raw forefinger. Blast! Blast it all to hell! Why did ye misfire now? Betrayed by my very own weapon. I'll use my sword. 'Twill not fail me. But just touching the hilt caused her to scream out in pain. Resigned to failure, she began her long painful walk back to the camp. Even when tucked protectively under her shirt, Mary's hands burned from air that seemed to float up under her blouse. She trudged into camp, noticing no one, though many looked in amazement at her face blackened by the impotent flashfire.

Two weeks passed before Mary had the use of her hands again. One the day of the duke's arrival they were still tender in spots. Manipulating the reins was difficult at best, without the added strain of executing a perfect maneuver for the duke. Her grip tightened and her hands stiffened. The platoon performed well under the direction of her corporal. As they stood at attention, she was so situated in the column that she could study the imposing figure of the Duke of Marlborough.

The man was handsome despite his sixty years. His manner was graceful and he displayed litheness of form, hands with long tapering fingers, and a broad face with a high forehead, full lips and large, slightly bulging, almond-shaped eyes. His deteriorating health made him irritable at times but today there was no evidence of this. He sat his horse well, patiently inspecting each platoon of horse and infantry. Then the parade ended and Marlborough remained a few moments to speak to individual members of the rank and file. Mary was among those chosen to be addressed by him personally. The duke expressed concern for her bandaged hands. Trying to hide the fresh bloodstains on her right palm, Mary told him her pistol had misfired during a practice. She did not remember all that he said to her but she recalled ever after the gentleness of his manner and the sincere regard he had for the welfare of his men.

That night, meetings were held and the officers were duly

instructed for the forthcoming march. Afterward Mary and Max had a few moments alone. Excitedly he talked of strategy and tactics. Then suddenly, his energy spent, he examined her hands. Since the day of her accident his indifferent attitude had changed to one of gentle concern.

"Thee did well today, Read. Remember the day we meet? Thy horse did spin thee around like a top." His laughter lifted her spirits. This was the first time in weeks that he had spoken of friendly matters. At the end of the week they would begin their march to Malplaquet, over one hundred miles outh of Breda. This battle was supposed to provide a decisive solution to these lingering wars.

During the sweltering summer march, the cavalry rode in columns and in pairs; Mary rode at Max's side. Usually they talked, but this particular day Max remained silent. He was greatly troubled. Last night a campaign lady had come to him and, although he had tried, he could not take her. Mary had been lying next to him. I have taken women in the presence of other men afore, he thought. 'Tis the necessity of war. Either that or go without. 'Twas not the reason. I was too aware of his eyes upon me; they were like burning coals on my back. That's not the whole of it, either. 'Tis plain I love him. But I will die afore I touch him in a loving way. His resolve newly strengthened, Max vowed to make this campaign his last. He would die in a blaze of glory.

Mary was more than weary. Throughout the campaign she had ridden gallantly at the side of her beloved. What she could not understand was why Max had thrust himself into dangers he could easily have avoided. He had made foolhardy drives into the bulk of the enemy's cavalry, time and again galloping into a swarm of men and horse, shooting and slashing his way through entire platoons, with Mary beside him.

Her comrades wondered at her bravado, thinking her at the very brink of madness to pursue a friend this way.

I know what I am doing. I'll ride through the very fires

of hell to be near him. If he needs must fight this way, I will also. If he dies, then will I, and gladly.

"Get out of here!" she could hear Max shout above the clamor. There were many anxious moments of separation, but most times Mary could feel his vibrant presence next to her. Sometimes there would be only the two of them left to battle as many as ten of the enemy horse.

For just one moment on this bloody day at Malplaquet, Mary lost him; she could neither hear his resounding oaths nor feel his presence. Oh God, where is he? Not dead! He cannot be dead! Pausing for a dangerous moment, she tried to spot Max amid the dense smoke. It was then that a sword penetrated her left shoulder. Instinctively Mary brought her blade down across the man's sword arm, then ran him through. She rode out of the engagement carrying the enemy sword in her shoulder. Once removed from the thick of the battle, Mary was unable to stand her horse any longer, and she fell to the ground face down, driving the sword through her shoulder up to the hilt.

The sun fell off the west end of the world. Dusk spread over the bloody field of battle. Mary's groans mingled with the sounds of the dying around her. A wagon train of scavengers, headed by the notorious Mother Ross, was nearby. They were collecting anything saleable from the dead bodies: weapons, clothing—especially boots—and other personal items, to resell to the troops when the army reached the next encampment. Mother Ross also provided medical aid on occasion. Since the army's service was entirely inadequate, consisting mostly of surgical removal of damaged extremities, the appreciation of Mother Ross's aid far outweighed the resentment resulting from her foraging activities.

A wooden wheel ground past Mary's head and the next wheel stopped. She felt her sword being pulled from her right hand. Mary summoned all her remaining strength into her right arm, gripping the hilt so hard that only death itself could wrench it from her. The tugging stopped and she felt herself being jerked onto her right side.

"Easy with the lad, ye bird-witted arse worm. Aah, get out of it! Let me see 'im. Dimwitted bastards, the lot of ye! Alive are ye, laddie?"

"Don't."

"Don't what, lad?"

"Don't take sword. Bury with me . . . ."

"Ye won't be needin' the box yet, and ye can keep yer bird spit since ye have the strength to hold on to it. Besides, it be the sword in ye that I covet. So hang on tight to yer own whilst I remove this one. 'Ere, bite this rag."

Mary bit the sweaty cloth and felt an excruciating grinding in her chest, just before consciousness left her.

Hours later, she woke from a restless sleep to find herself lying on her side with her shirt completely off. Panic set her heart pounding at a tremendous rate. She tried to move but the pain in her shoulder prevented her. Mary sank back down, wondering what new fate lay in store, now that her sex had been discovered. The moon threw bright beams over the pitch darkness of the forest. Lifting her head back slightly, she could see a burly figure bending over a black pot on the fire. I be lost now, she thought. She felt utterly defeated by the one enemy she could not fight. Discovery meant discharge from the army—no questions, just dismissal. It mattered not how much she had distinguished herself. Her record for bravery stood for naught under this kind of attack. I be a better soldier than any of them, she thought. 'Tis because I be a woman that I have had to be better. Now what good is it? I am undone.

The burly figure was striding toward her. What if my mother be right? Perhaps he'll rape me or, worse, cut off my breasts. Mary could see his knife shimmering in the moonlight as he approached. She waited and watched his every move. Boiling hot rags, placed across her shoulder, started her scream of anguish.

"Now, lass, be still."

Heavy hands pressed the fire deeper into her chest and back. Tears welled up in Mary's eyes and dropped over the bridge of her nose.

"Ye be a fine, strong girl. Ye'll be fit soon enough."
A hand brushed Mary's breast as one cloth was removed
and another replaced it. This time Mary ground her teeth
into her jaws and waited for the searing pain to abate. Not
a sound escaped her. The man had a strong thick body,
muscular arms and large but gentle hands. Mary caught a
glimpse of his face as it turned from time to time into the
moonlight: middleaged, with handsome features, high
cheekbones and keen eyes. His long dark hair, streaked
with gray, was tied back. Mary looked away from the face
and concentrated her gaze on the man's hands. There was
a wide gold band on the third finger of the left hand. Fine
strong hands, she thought, but somehow not at all like a
man's.

"Ah, lovely, small, but round, firm, white and soft to
the touch," said the man, stroking Mary's breasts.

The voice was deep and smooth and the touch aroused
Mary, yet she jerked away from the hands, suddenly causing
the pain to renew itself.

"Now lie still, lass, yer secret be safe with me. I be
Mother Ross. No one will 'ear of yer pretense from me."

"You be a woman, then?" Mary asked in astonishment.

"Why yes, does that surprise ye?" She proceeded to
bring Mary's hand to her own breast. "Feel these jugs of
mine. Ample, eh! Sometimes I hide my sex as thee does.
Some know, some do not. It does not matter. I get by on
me physical strength. 'Ere now, let me see thee once more
afore I must wrap up these beauties."

Mary could see the woman's face now. Her smile spread
small graceful lines about her dark eyes. The face was
beautiful in a strikingly handsome way. Her bigboned frame
gave her a manly aspect. The smooth fingers caressed
Mary's breasts and she felt a tingling sensation that thrilled
through her body.

"Ah beautiful! Ye be fortunate to be alive, do ye know
that, lass? It be some time afore I could stop the bleedin'."

"Thank ye." I be alive, but what of him? Ah, Max! Be
ye alive or dead? Ye cannot die now. I have not told thee

71

of my love for thee!

Long bands of cotton cloth covered Mary's breasts and were wound up over her left shoulder.

"Ye see, yer secret be buried. Now lie beside me and lean yer back up against my bosom. The hard damp ground be not good for yer wound." Mother Ross wrapped her arm around Mary and held her so that she would not turn in the night and open her wound.

An amber ray of sunlight filtered through the ancient oak under which they lay. The first glow of morning light fell upon Mother Ross's hand, which firmly clasped Mary's right shoulder. Awakening, Mary studied every wrinkle and line of the hand, including the deep blue veins and the worn gold ring.

Mother Ross awoke and carefully extricated herself from under Mary's thin body and laid her on a cushion of rags. Mary's entire torso ached from lying on the hard ground. She tried not to move, but rather stared through the branches of the large tree spreading its limbs overhead.

Mother Ross awoke and carefully extricated herself from under Mary's thin body and laid her on a cushion of rags. Mary's entire torso ached from lying on the hard ground. She tried not to move, but rather stared through the branches of the large tree spreading its limbs overhead.

Mother Ross returned with a bit of bread and some warm broth. The soup was good and Mary could feel strength easing into her body, but she could not drink much. "I needs must take relief, Mother Ross."

"Let's to yer feet then, lass, an' remove ourselves apace. We must soon be on our way to find your regiment." Mother Ross lifted Mary to her feet. The ground swirled for a moment, then Mary swung her good arm around the woman's broad shoulders. Her knees were weak but she was able to put one foot in front of the other and shuffle her way into the woods.

"Thee be tall for a lass. How tall be ye?" asked Mother Ross.

"Five feet and six last I be measured, but that were over a year ago."

"Ye be taller now, that be certain. How old be ye?"

"Seventeen."

"Thee could grow yet. 'Ere, let me help thee with thy breeches."

"No, thank ye, I can manage."

With one hand, it was some time before Mary could untie and let down her breeches. Mother Ross watched the entire proceedings with amusement. Then she opened the front of her breeches and gingerly extruded what appeared to be a penis and urinated through it. Mary was so amazed that she halted her awkward operation at half mast to watch.

"What be that?" asked Mary, astonished.

"This 'ere? This be a grand pissing device. It be fashioned of silver and painted over in the color of flesh. It be strapped to me body, see." Mother Ross pulled the ingenious invention out of her breeches for Mary's inspection. All she could do was to marvel at it.

"Fore God, a handy pisser!"

Feeling considerably more comfortable, Mary laced her breeches and walked, unaided, back to the camp. Mother Ross issued a few sharp orders and camp was broken, wagons were loaded, and the ragged convoy headed north to meet the army.

Mary rode with Mother Ross for the first few hours of the journey, talking in order to occupy her mind and ease the discomfort caused by the jolting ride.

"Why be ye here in Brabant, Mother Ross?"

"Oh, it be a place to survive. My husband was a soldier, ye see, and I 'ad no mind to stay back while 'e went to the wars. So I followed 'im as a campaign lady at first. Thee must have met that sort by now."

"Where be your husband, Mother Ross?"

"He be gone now, lass. With the saints he be. One day long ago I found 'im lyin' in the field as I found thee yesterday. Only 'is 'ead was what I met first, 'is body was somewhat removed from it. I took the clothes off 'is body

73

afore I buried 'im. After I had washed out the blood, I dressed meself in 'is uniform and followed the wars disguised as ye be now. But I had no head for killin'. I deserted the army an', findin' this abandoned wagon, set out to salvage what I could in the aftermath of battle. Now ye be up to date with me present occupation." Mary was silent. "A woman does what she must to survive. We be great survivors. I 'ad to live, girl, since I were not ready to die."

"Did ye ever think to live as a woman?"

"I thought on't, but I be too old to change me ways now. 'Twould not suit me to sit in a warm house and bake bread and sew, rockin' by the fire. I needs a more active life. The field is home enough for me. This tattered bunch of vagabonds be me family and I do what I can to relieve the sufferin' humanity 'ere. I cannot leave a wounded soldier to die on the battlefield without I do all I can to ease 'im."

"I for one be in thy debt, Mother Ross."

"No, no debt. We all be in each other's care. Thee were there because I needed to help thee. It be my gain, too. As for thee, lass, how long does ye think ye will follow these wars?"

"I be in love." The words came out unconsciously; it was the first time she had said them out loud to anyone.

"Ah, that do make a difference. A fellow trooper, eh?" Mary nodded. "Does he know it?"

"No, he believes me to be a man."

"When do ye plan to reveal yerself to 'im?"

"I am not sure he loves me. If I were sure, I would tell him of my love. It would be a danger for me otherwise, and a disgrace for him. He be an officer. But this silence be misery for me."

"And what of 'im? Dost thou not think the man has stirrings too? Ye say it may be worse for thee. But thee knows ye be a woman. Think of 'im, feeling thy love and 'e be wonderin' about 'is very manhood, thinkin' 'imself in love with a boy."

"I never thought of that."

"Well, thee should 'ave. Ye must reveal thyself to 'im for both yer sakes."

"Dost thee think so?"

"Aye, lass, I know so. What will happen, will happ⟨
Thee must take a chance if ye truly love 'im."

Mary considered the woman's words and thought over all the events which had passed between herself and Max during the past months. When they stopped to water the horses, Mother Ross checked Mary's bandages. The wound had started to bleed again. She put a wad of clean linen rag under the wrapping next to the wound.

"Girl, ye must ride in the back now. Lie upon this straw. We should meet thy troopers at dusk encamped on the river Trouille. Try to sleep, thee will need all thy strength."

When next Mary opened her eyes, she saw streaks of red across the sky. Balancing was difficult in the moving wagon, but she managed to pull herself up and hold onto the back of the driver's bench. She could see the river in the distance.

"See there, lass, yer encampment be ahead. I dare go no closer." Mother Ross reined in the horses and lifted Mary from the back of the wagon. "'Ere ye be, lass, safe 'monst thy friends."

"Thanks to thee."

"I would hug thee but I would hurt thy wound. I did not nurse thee all last night to injure thee yet again."

Mary flung her right arm around Mother Ross's neck and kissed her cheek. The woman blinked back a sudden tear and turned away, cursing at her retinue to make camp. Mary watched for a moment, then walked toward her encampment.

"Luck to thee, lass!" shouted Mother Ross after she had collected herself.

Mary turned. "And to thee, Mother Ross."

"What is thy name, girl? Ye never told me thy name."

Mary hesitated, then boomed out in a loud clear voice as if making an announcement to the whole world, *"Mary Read!"*

"Good fortune to thee then, Mary Read."

Mary turned and walked on into the encampment, past the artillery guard, through the infantry officers' tents and on to the horse camped on the right flank. It was there that she saw Max standing next to her horse, a brush in one hand, the reins in the other, his forehead buried in the horse's mane. His posture seemed mournful and despairing. Mary approached silently and, taking up another brush, began to stroke the animal's flank. Mary's horse stamped a welcome, bringing Max out of his reverie.

"Read! By God, Read, thee be alive!" He grabbed both of Mary's shoulders and pulled her to his chest, holding her tightly. The pain was almost unbearable but Mary would not be the one to break this passionate moment. Max held her close, resting his cheek next to hers and rocking back and forth. At the same moment that he realized he had held her longer than propriety warranted, he also noticed the bandages at her collar. "Read, be ye wounded? Why did ye not tell me?"

"'Tis nothing. I caught steel in my shoulder, that be all."

Max pulled open her shirt and saw the wrappings and the bloodstains on her chest and back. "It went clean through thee and ye acts like it were but a scratch. Ye be mad as a buck."

"I be fine. I had luck to meet a woman named Mother Ross. It were she who bandaged my wound and brought me here."

"Mother Ross? I have heard tell of her. Oh, Read, I thought thee dead."

"And I feared ye dead too! I lost ye for an instant in the fray and looked for ye. 'Tis then I caught the steel."

"I was knocked from my saddle and dragged off some distance by my horse before I was able to right myself. After the action I found thy horse but despaired of ever finding thee mongst the many dead." He squeezed her hand to convince himself that she was really alive. "Come, ye must be starved. There be stew on the fire, and hot coffee."

Max put his long cloak around Mary's shoulders as they sat by the dwindling cooking fire. The September breeze bestirred the tall fir trees. Each had stories to tell the other of their time spent apart. Mary's story was largely lacking in detail, falling short as her narratives generally did. She so wanted to tell Max about Mother Ross's grand pissing device but knew not how to do it.

"The duke all but has these wars," was Max's final assessment of the campaign. "There be a slacking off now. Methinks a few more years an' we'll see an end to the fighting in Flanders."

Mary was disheartened. Secretly she had hoped to continue this joint occupational effort. Perhaps Mother Ross be right, she thought. I should seize the moment for love, for 'tis indeed fleeting. Death or the end of the war could bring about separation. A sudden chill coursed through her body, bringing with it a stab of pain to her chest.

"Come, let's go in. The damp night air does thee no good. I have a tent to myself now. Our losses at Malplaquet were considerable. Share it with me, since ye have no bed. I would welcome your company."

Mary followed him, catching her breath. What happens now is up to me, she thought. Be skillful, Mary; discover yourself to him gently lest ye turn him away in fear. Straw scattered in the corner, with a coarse woolen blanket tossed carelessly upon it, was to serve as a bed. Mary sat down on a wooden keg near the entrance, her knees unable to carry her any farther. Her face was flushed from a slight fever and her heart pounded up against her throat, choking her. Clutching the cloak around herself, she shivered with apprehension.

Max stood at the opening of the tent, peering out into the night. Moonlight began to flood their little space. Whither this night may lead me, I am quite prepared to follow, he thought! My feelings be too strong now to reject them. Other men indulge quite happily in the practice. Why not see for myself what delights be here? Max turned and looked at the lean, graceful figure now slumped on the keg. Why does this boy excite me so? 'Tis beyond my reasoning.

Lifting Mary to her feet, he gazed upon her handsome face: her sharp nose, the smoothly cut lines of her jaw, the sensuous lips and those eyes, eyes so piercing that no one could fix upon them for more than an instant. Yet there was no end to their depths.

The intensity of his feeling pervaded her whole being and Mary was powerless against its keen assault. Accidentally his fingertips touched her wound; her breath was caught in a sharp pain.

"Your wound, I quite forgot it. We should tend to it. I'll fetch clean linen."

Mary removed her shirt and loosened the bandage only enough to expose the wound, no further. Max lighted the lantern and Mary again situated herself on the keg. She watched his face while he tended her wound. He was quick and expert, having tended many soldiers in the field.

"Your bandage is too large. I can make a smaller." He wrapped a thin strip of cloth high under Mary's armpits, crossing twice over her shoulder to hold the wads of linen in place over the wound, front and back. Pausing in his work to stare into her eyes, he said softly, "You won't be needing this old linen."

Rising, she moved to the tent opening. He doused the lantern and drew near, admiring the graceful sloping curve of her back. Placing his arm gently on her shoulders, he kissed her softly on the cheek and neck. His lips brushed over her yielding mouth. Mary dropped the hand that was holding the bandage over her breasts and it fell about her waist in easy folds.

Max kissed her left ear, then her neck, and ever so gently pressed his lips against her wound. Bending low, his lips settled into the pliant flesh of her breast. His tongue swept over the protruding nipple. Only when his face pushed under her bosom to allow his lips access to her slender rib cage did he realize the deviation. Straightening up, he saw the loveliest breasts he had ever beheld. They stood high like delicately chiseled Carrara marble, glimmering very white in the moonlight.

He stood fixed for a long while, staring at the two firm fleshy mounds lifting up and down with Mary's rapid breathing. Then he took them in his hands, still disbelieving, and ran his thumbs across her swelling nipples.

"Read, be ye a woman or am I dreaming?"

"No, Max, you do not dream. I be a woman and have been all this while. My name be Mary."

"Of course! Of course!" He looked at her, inspecting every inch of her womanly form. Mary brought his face to her lips and kissed him tenderly. Max's lips moved over every part of her face and neck in a flurry of soft kisses until they met her anxious lips. Their kisses deepened into a passionate embrace. Max lifted Mary off her feet and carried her to the straw bedding, laying her down gently. He drank deep kisses from the roots of her throat and fell upon those welcoming breasts. His hand reached down and deftly untied her breeches, seeking her private place, moist and hot. He slipped his fingers in and out, holding her tightly and drawing his own legs together in sensual agony.

"Be God, ye are a woman!" he whispered to her. As his fingers slipped in and out and around her vagina, Mary opened herself in a flood of warmth. Moving her hands over his body, she accidentally touched his privates. He was hard as iron. Their breathing quickened. Ripping open his breeches, Max brought himself flesh to flesh upon her, rubbing himself harder and harder against her pelvis. The weight of his body bore down upon her but Max was careful not to hold or lean upon her wound. For Mary there was no thought of pain. She wanted to feel every inch of his body touching her own, to carry the impression of his form with her forever.

Anxious to gain access to her, Max lifted up.

"No," whispered Mary. "Don't leave! I want to hold thee close, so very close."

Max, reaching down, found his penis and bid entrance. In his eagerness he missed, nudging instead the crevice of the outer fold. Again he lifted up. "No, no, come back!" Mary tried to draw him down upon her once again but her strength gave way to his superior force. At last his member penetrated harshly. She gasped.

"Oh, I have hurt thee. Forgive me."

In his excitement Max had not thought to ask if Mary were a virgin. He regretted his rude advance, drew out and lay still upon her, his penis throbbing on the threshold. With his full weight upon her once again, Mary felt sheer bliss. She ran her fingers through the soft hairs of his neck and felt the taut muscles of his back ripple under her stroking fingers.

She would prevent him for now; she knew that. It was not the pain. Mary knew full well what was to come. He was large but she knew she could contain all of him. But it was not the time. I love this man, she thought. I want him. I also want him as my husband. I will not be his whore; I'll not be any man's strumpet. Consummation must and will be delayed til our wedding night. This be the right way. Mary still longed to draw him inside of her this instant, and Max, sensing this, prodded and pushed against her passage but could not gain entrance.

"What be the matter, Mary, does thee not want me?" he whispered.

"Yes, I want thee."

"Be thee afraid? Be thee virgin, then?"

"Yes, I be virgin."

"'Tis enough, then, for now. These matters take time." Pulling off her, unfulfilled, his penis felt as if it might explode. "Ye must excuse me." Max sprang to his feet and left the tent.

Mary could hear his efforts to stifle groans and finally she heard the soft stream hitting the leaves like rain. His seed is wasted upon the earth when I should receive it. And where be my relief? She lay there holding her own privates, feeling the heat soak into her hand.

Max returned and lay quietly beside her anguished body. "We will try again. The time be our own now. Besides, ye need time to heal. We must sleep now. We have but a week here for rest and care of the wounded."

"Where do we go hence, Max?" asked Mary, her thoughts still concentrated on the future of their relationship.

"To join the siege at Mons. It should be the last of the campaign. Pray God ye be fit soon. 'Twill be a long siege."

"A long siege," she murmured. "Pray God I can endure it."

The week went by quickly. Max and Mary spent leisurely hours on the river bank talking. It was good for Mary to tell the strange story of her life to someone. Some of the bitterness was loosed with the telling of it. Each day love flowed subtly into their souls and flourished there. Each night Mary slept in his arms, yielding to all but the final act of love.

Will he never ask me to marry? she wondered. Has he even thought on't? I will not follow these wars as a campaign woman like Mother Ross. 'Twould be humiliating. He needs must leave the service. But 'tis his life. Can he do that? Does he love me that much? I will not submit to sexual communication without I be married. I have lived a man in this world of men. I have lived by their rules. Now I be a woman and I will live as my heart directs me, seeing that I have had no proper woman to teach me.

On October 1st the month-long siege of Mons began. Heavy mortar fire battered the gate. Cadogan himself was wounded in the neck. Max's advances became more fervent each night but he was always stopped short at the brink of entrance. Angered, he would turn away and think to himself, what is wrong? Why does she deny my access, no matter how gentle my approach? How long must this go on? Does she think to remain a virgin forever? Women! There be no understanding them.

The movement of her horse relieved the burning anguish of Mary's desire, for this abstinence was painful to her as well. Mary was acutely aware of Max's unrest and, sensing the growing anxiety between them, she anticipated an argument, for an explosion was inevitable.

One night as they lay together, Max burst out vehemently, "Be ye cold and heartless, woman? Can ye not feel my despair? Have ye no feeling heart? Do you not want me? What is wrong with thee? Answer me, don't lie there like stone. Speak thy mind, woman, or foreswear my bed entirely.''

Pricked by anger, Mary spoke at last. ''I'll not be your convenient, private tent whore!''

Anger seized him. He gripped her jaw, vicelike, between his fingers. ''What did ye say? Did ye say whore? How can ye believe it? By God, woman, what must I do to make thee trust me? I love ye. I loved ye even when I thought thee a boy! What must I do? How much longer must I wait? When we reach Breda we'll not have this privacy.''

Mary made no answer. He thrust her rudely aside and turned his back on her. Women! All alike. Even when they be men, they think like women still. Camp whore, indeed! Be that what she thinks? What be in this woman's mind? Surely she cannot be thinking of marriage.

''Mary . . . be ye thinking of marriage?'' She did not answer. He turned over, confronting her. ''Ye are! Ye be thinking of marriage. Ye has some damned notion to remain a virgin til your wedding night. Answer me, damn ye!''

''Ask me a proper question and I'll answer thee.'' she shouted back.

''Will ye marry me?!''

''Yes, I'll marry thee!''

There was a moment of stunned silence between them.

''Ye know what this means, don't ye? We'll have to leave the army,'' he said soberly.

''Yes, I know. I be willing. What be your mind in the matter?''

''I do not know. This is the first such thought to enter my head. Have ye thought about this long and hard?''

''Since that very first night. I knew I would be your wife, Max, and meant to keep myself virgin til then.''

''I knew it. I sensed it be some such nonsense as that.''

''Nonsense? 'Tis proper and fittin'. Furthermore, I'll not have it otherwise.''

''Ye will persist in this even now that I have asked ye to marry?''

''Yes, I will persist. 'Tis my way.''

"Ye are a strange and wonderful woman, Mary Read. Any woman who be so loyal to her own beliefs needs must be loyal to her husband."

"Always, Max, ye must believe it."

They kissed sensuously and lay a long time in each other's arms. He thoughts kept him awake for a time. "I never did think to quit the army alive. What will I do, think you?"

"Well, ye be a carpenter, and a good one. Some position will show itself. There must be honest trade at Breda." His chuckling grew into roaring laughter. "What be so funny?" she asked.

"Oh, God," he said through his laughter, "can ye not see old Cadogan's face when we tell him our intention to marry? He'll piss in his pants. I bet he'll fart and fume for days." Suddenly he said soberly, "Ye will be famous, Mary Read. Are ye prepared for that?"

"As long as I be your wife, nothing can go ill with me."

"We have a few days' time before we reach Breda. Ye may change your thinking. I'll not think harshly of thee if thee changes thy mind. It cannot be an easy thing to become a woman after having been a man for so long."

Mary was certain that her mind would not bend. She had not considered, however, that this situation might cause a stir. But he was right. For herself she would be content to desert the army and be quietly wed somewhere in England, but she could never ask that of him. Max was too much a military man to consider desertion. Besides, they would be shot on the spot if caught. No, they would have to announce themselves to the Quartermaster General. There was no way around it.

The Breda garrison was home at last. Winter quarters were established once again and provisions were laid in for the long hard months ahead. Firewood was gathered, fodder stored, bread baked and barracks readied for long-term oc-cupants. The camp was as busy as the woodland squirrels, bustling about storing nuts against the winter's harshness.

One afternoon Mary emerged from the woods, logs piled

on her chest up to her chin. As she made her way to the main cooking circle, Max crept up behind her, grabbed her wrist and swung her around to him.

"Oops! Great God, man, what are ye about?" she said, as the wood dropped and scattered in all directions. She brushed the bark from her tunic.

"Mount up, girl; we be headed for the Quartermaster General's tent. Smooth your hair and tie it back neatly, for we be seeking permission to wed."

A shriek of delight pierced the calm afternoon. This was the moment she had been waiting for. Hand in hand they ran to the stables and leapt upon their horses, riding off in the direction of Breda Castle. The brisk autumn afternoon sun brightened the trail. Loud whoops rent the air as they flew along, bent low under the leafless branches.

At length they stopped by a small rivulet to let their horses water. In the distance Breda Castle was imposing, austere. The dying leaves dropped their colors into the water. The air was fresh. A gust twirled a pile of leaves, sending their vibrant hues scrambling across the road. Listening to the sounds of the quiet afternoon, Mary felt suspended in time, lost in an ecstasy of her own making. This stillness was broken by the restless stamping of the horses, snorting their impatience. "Why must we see the Quartermaster General?" Mary asked apprehensively.

"'Tis fitting. We seek honorable discharges. Cadogan be the only man to see. Ye are not afraid, are ye, Mary?"

"Somewhat."

"Thee has not changed thy mind, has thee?"

"No, it's just the thought of it. After this day I can no longer live as a man. I be somewhat used to that, you understand. Thou dost love me, do ye not, Max?"

"With all my heart."

"Well, the sooner we see old Cadogan, the quicker 'twill be over."

They remounted and charged off in the direction of the Duke of Marlborough's headquarters. General Cadogan's aide-de-camp greeted them. Two hours passed before they were admitted to his tent. The burly general was standing behind a campaign table studying a paper, stroking his sagging jaw all the while. Max coughed. Mary punched his side with her elbow, causing him to hack louder. General Cadogan interrupted his work and peered out over his spectacles at the two handsome troopers standing at attention before him. His long curly white wig fell over his massive shoulders. His complexion was swarthy, his eyes puffy and red. "Well, what is it ye be wantin'?"

"Sir, we would like permission to marry," said Max, his voice cracking slightly.

"Thee does not need my permission to marry, Corporal. But thee has my blessings all the same."

"General Cadogan, we must ask to be discharged as well."

"Why so? 'Tis not necessary to leave the army. Ye both can take wives betimes and return to the campaign in the spring. Now leave me, I have work to do." The general went back to his papers, but they did not leave.

"Sir," said Max clearing his throat, "we wish to wed each other."

General Cadogan looked up, removed his spectacles and rubbed his burning eyes. It had been an exhausting campaign. He still had not recovered completely from the wound in his neck. Sinking his hefty body into the chair, he said, "What do you say? I don't believe I heard thee accurately."

"We desire to wed each other."

The general replied testily, "And ye does not think that is highly irregular?"

"No, sir," Mary said assertively. "You see, sir, I be a woman."

"No, I do not see!" he said, slamming his fist on the table. "Nor have I time for foolish banter." Rising to a half-standing position, leaning over the table, he looked Mary full in the eyes. "What be your name, soldier?"

"Mary Read."

"God's Death! Persist in this foolishness and I'll slap thee in the gaol!"

Oh, I feared that above all, thought Mary. My mother did warn me 'twould be so.

General Cadogan shuffled among the papers on his desk. "Read . . . Read . . . Ah, Read. Buttons Read. I have a citation for one Buttons Read for meritorious bravery in the face of the enemy during this recent campaign. Be this you, mister?"

"Yes sir."

"And you, Corporal Studevant, we had in mind a promotion for thee, to captain. What say you to that, mister?"

"Captain! Why, sir, 'tis . . . 'tis an honor I dreamed not of."

Captain, thought Mary. Oh dear God, I hope he does not foreswear me. Oh, I fear I am undone.

There was an awkward moment; then Cadogan spoke again. "So, dost thee both persist still in this preposterous marriage?"

"Oh, yes, sir," said Max. "I be honored at the promotion, sir, but I love Mary and wish to wed her."

"What is this? Be it buggery? What are you, soldier? These actions you propose be perverse and shameful."

"No, sir, I am a woman."

"A woman, you say . . . a physical woman?"

"Aye, sir, do ye wish to see?" Mary reached up to undo her shirt.

"No, no, no, no, that won't be necessary," he said hastily. "You be a disappointment to me, Read. Time and again you have distinguished yourself in battle after battle, never faltering, always in the forefront of danger. And now thee tells me thee be a woman! 'Tis beyond belief! 'Tis disgraceful! You will be examined, you know that?"

"I had expected it, sir."

"'Twill be looked into! We will get to the bottom of this deceit, I assure thee."

"Aye, sir!" said Max impulsively.

"And you, Corporal, how long has thee had intelligence of this soldier's true identify?"

"Only since Malplaquet, sir."

"And how hast thou used her since? Tell me that?"

"Sir, she be a virgin still. My life on't."

"Let us hope so for thy sake, Corporal. For if thou didst press thy suit too far, it will go hard with ye. If it be as you say, I shall be the first to wish thee luck."

Max and Mary took each other's hand.

"None of that here. You be in uniform. Remember yourselves! She needs be proven yet."

"Yes, sir," said Max, dropping Mary's hand and standing at attention.

"Dear God, how am I to explain this to the duke—two of his most distinguished fighting men, and one of them a woman. He'll have my arse thrown to the hogs. Come, both of you. We'll ride to town in my carriage and fetch a doctor there."

Mary's apprehension grew. It was uncomfortable riding in this carriage with such austere company. She longed to take her lover's hand but dared not. Old doubts entered her mind, along with new fears.

What have I got myself into? I am to be publicly acknowledged a woman. The entire army will know of it, if not all of Flanders. And how will I ever be used to dressing and acting like a woman after so many years a man? They'll put me in skirts first thing, I'll warrant. Bloody skirts! Nor do I like the prospect of this examination. No one has seen my privities, not even Max. And now a stranger. 'Tis unbearable. I could leap from this carriage at the next turn and run into the woods. Then she felt Max's knee against her own and all was well once more. I will suffer anything for his sake, she reaffirmed in her mind.

Once inside the doctor's office, Mary was instructed to remove her breeches.

"Lie back, soldier—beg pardon, mistress. Put your feet flat on the table and spread your legs wide. Come on now, let's 'ave a look at thee."

Mary was embarrassed and angry at being placed in such a degrading posture.

"Come now, the general awaits news of thy virginity. Open your legs!"

The general was waiting in the adjoining room. Max had gone straight to the tavern.

Just like a man to leave you when you need him most, she thought. Here I am alone, bare arse before God and the world.

"Spread your legs! How am I to look into thee?"

Reluctantly Mary unfolded herself. "Ah, I see . . . hum," he said, as if about to make a startling discovery. He pushed his thumbs inside her and wrenched her apart.

"Blast ye, man, does thou mean to tear me apart?"

"Easy now, girl. I needs must have a better look at thee. "Hym . . . ah . . . " He moved his finger inside her and pressed her stomach with his other hand to make certain she was a full woman. After a few pokes at her taut hymen he instructed Mary to dress.

Mary angrily jerked up her breeches, and laced them hastily. The doctor was washing his hands in a basin; his back was to her when Mary strapped on her sword. When he turned around he met her black eyes and was instantly afraid. Quietly, so not to alarm the men in the next room, Mary slipped her sword out of its scabbard. The doctor screamed. General Cadogan entered, sword drawn.

"Fret not, General, I'll not kill the old pisspot, though 'twould please me greatly. Old . . . twat-scourer!" Mary shouted, as she slammed her sword into its scabbard. Pushing past the general, she bounded out onto the street. Max was waiting by the carriage. Mary flew past him and stormed into the tavern. She slammed her hand on the bar and demanded a pint. Puzzled, Max pursued her.

"Ye cannot stay here now!" Max whispered harshly. "Women are not allowed in here!"

"I'll do as I please."

"Come out. The general is on the street looking for thee and a crowd is gathering."

"Leave me be!" Mary downed the ale in one long gulp,

then bounced the tankard off Max's head. She tore out of the tavern and marched past general, carriage and townspeople. As she approached the group the doctor moved judiciously behind the general. Max was scrambling to catch up with her but her pace was determined.

General Cadogan burst into laughter. "After her, soldier. She be a fine wench but a salty one. She'll brighten your days and liven your nights, I warrant ye."

Every time Max caught hold of her arm, Mary jerked free and took off down the road, kicking up dust and setting a terrific pace. After a quarter mile of this chase, Max wearied, and throwing his hat down on the road, crossed his arms doggedly. The carriage pulled up alongside him and the general leaned out. "Get in, soldier. She be too hot for thee now. She will cool by the time she reaches the camp. Leave her to herself. Ride with me." Max picked up his hat and watched Mary's figure growing smaller, arms swinging, head down, until she almost disappeared around the bend in the road. Thumping hs tricornered hat on his head, he snorted. "You be right, General. There be no reasoning with the woman now." Climbing into the carriage, he sank into himself, to ponder the fate he had wrought.

"Don't worry, lad," urged the general. "She will fall into your arms when she returns. But she needs to be with herself awhile now. We'll make every arrangement for thee. The good Reverend Hare will perform the service, a military wedding as befits your station as an officer. And I will inform the duke and make preparation for your discharges. 'Twill take time but everything will be taken care of. You will have all ye can do to get your lusty wench into attire befitting the ceremony before spring be upon us."

Max was waiting outside the general's tent holding their horses when Mary arrived. Gathered around him already was a group of soldiers, who, having heard the news, waiting to set eyes on the female soldier. All turned and looked at Mary as she walked into the camp. The silence was portentous and she sensed their ribald curiosity.

When she reached her horse she spat on the ground,

snatched up the reins, swung gracefully into the saddle and rode off with lightning speed. Mary was gone almost before Max had realized it. Excusing himself, he clumsily mounted and turned in circles several times before he could point his steed in the right direction. The band of troopers burst into laughter. "Look at 'im! Can't even rein in his 'orse!"

"'E'll never catch that wench. Ye'll have to get that girl belly up to slow 'er down."

"Arse upward, Corp'rl. Arse upward!"

The news of this extraordinary union spread about the countryside, reaching the principal cities of Rotterdam, Antwerp, Paris and even London. The couple were interviewed by the countless chroniclers, among them a journalist from the *London Gazette* who was curious about the comely seventeen-year-old woman who had concealed her sex from an entire army. They asked about her family background and her childhood years, and even rudely inquired how she had managed to hide certain necessary bodily functions from the crude eyes of her fellow troopers. Never once did any of them ask how she had learned to ride, fence or shoot, or how she had managed to keep herself alive, let alone distinguish herself in battle.

In the face of all the publicity, the army was reluctant to honor Mary in public. But the Duke of Marlborough, who had come for the ceremony, presented her with a ribbon in his private quarters. Mary understood and was deeply moved. With these honors came certain awards of money. Collections were also taken up among the troopers, and even the duke, who was famous for his thrift, made a donation.

During the interim prior to the April wedding Max had negotiated for an inn near Breda Castle. Secretly he had been repairing and painting the old tavern in order to surprise Mary on their wedding day. The Three Horseshoes, as it was called, was well situated near the garrison and, once restored, would attract the soldiers from the camp.

The day approached. At the bride's request, a little altar had been erected outside under the tall birches flanked by hedgerows. Reverend Hare stood proudly in his vestments. The entire garrison was present. Officers were smartly dressed, the rank and file spruced up with brass shining for the occasion. Mary was lovely in her wedding gown of Brabant lace. Her proudest moment was when Cadogan escorted her to the altar. Max had never been so handsome as on that day. As he lifted her veil, Mary's hair fell softly about her radiant face, and the twilight ceremony ended. The couple walked arm in arm under the crossed swords of their regiment of horse, leaving the garrison and towns-people to a night of revelry. Buttons Read was no more. At last Mary was free, free to be a woman and to love the man she so adored.

Once at the Three Horseshoes, Mary went about excitedly inspecting everything: tables, chairs, glasses, kitchen, even the storage rooms. Max finally was able to lead her up the stairs, but she had to open every door and investigate every closet, bed and washstand of each room before they reached their own. Opening the door, she saw the bed strewn with flowers. Mary leaped upon it, rolling over in sheer delight. "A real bed. My very own, lovely, wonderful, real bed."

"Our very own wonderful bed, if you please!"

Mary placed a flower seductively in her bosom and tossed a handful of roses at Max. A bright smile spreaad over his face. He came down upon her, sinking into mounds of lace.

"All right, wife, this is what you have wanted from the beginning. Is everything all right now, Mary?"

"Yes, yes, I will have all of you now, every inch."

Bath Town, North Carolina: 1711

Their ponies raced the wind. As they went flying down the hillside and rushing across the plain, the tall grasses bent beneath the ponies' hooves. Anne's mind was no longer in the classroom.

"Thomas Braddock, when was Bath Town first founded?"

"I don't know, teacher."

"Mister Henderson, if you please, Thomas."

"I know not, Mister Henderson."

"Thomas, what *do* you know? Do you know at least where we are now?"

"This be the Carolinas, Mister Henderson. Everybody knows that."

Her pony pounded after the frightened rabbit. The Indian hunter urged the young girl on. "Keep your eye on him, Annie, or you'll lose him. Keep close or he'll take a turn on thee. Think on what you do. He be your dinner and you must go hungry if you lose him."

With tremendous concentration she focused on the head of the small rabbit racing before her. Tightening her legs around the pony's belly, she leaned in and pressed him onward.

"Anne O'Brannon, tell me about the English city of Bath after which our little town is named. Annie, are you paying attention? When you brought me this apple this morning, you said you had completed your assignment. Do you hear me? Answer me this minute or I'll fetch the rod!" He was hunched over, his arms spread wide, his hands clutching the sides of his desk. "Anne O'Brannon, answer me!"

Straddling her desk, Anne stood, her face contorted with excitement and rage. Her keen eyes pierced the back of the animal's head. I have ye now, she whispered to herself. "HAIIEE!" Her hatchet sang through the air, splitting the apple into neat halves and burying itself in the desk just inches from the teacher's nose. The Reverend Mister Henderson stared at the hatchet; then he fainted.

After a moment of shocked silence, the chaotic outcries of the other children routed Anne from her daydream; she bolted from the room and ran down the dusty road leading to her father's plantation. She ran and ran, never looking back. Turning into a dense wood, she clawed her way along an almost imperceptible path. Dried branches lashed her face, moss caught her flailing arms and strong vines tangled her feet. "I'll kill him! Next time I'll kill him dead. I'll . . . tear him apart! I'll . . . I'll cut out his heart and eat it!

Suddenly she was seized by powerful arms which seemed to squeeze the very life out of her. Still she thrashed and kicked and bit.

"Devil! A thousand devils take ye! Stop, wildcat, stop, I say!"

Recognizing a friend's voice, she went limp and buried her face in his chest, sobbing uncontrollably. The pungent odor of rawhide, mixed with sweat and earth, assailed her nostrils. His body was hard but his deep voice was soothing.

"Tell Joe who you want kill."

"Joe, Joe, swear you will be my friend no matter what happens! I need thy kind of understanding."

"Till death take me and after. Joe Buck be Annie's friend. I swear upon your hatchet, Annie. Give it me."

"I lost it . . . at school."

"Lost! Your father forbid you take hatchet to school."

"I do not care. I needed it. I should have split his head instead of that apple. It matters not that I lost it. I'll not go back there again. I be finished with school! I wish to live

93

free with you, ~~in the~~ woods, and hunt and swim in the river and do as I please. I be twelve years today and I will be free!''

It was April 18, 1711, and the Carolina spring was late. The O'Brannon plantation was located on the Pamlico River, Near Bath Town, North Carolina. William O'Brannon was a gentleman planter and a thriving merchant. Although he was a barrister by education, he had left the practice upon coming to the colonies from his native Cork, Ireland. He had also left behind a wife and a twin boy and girl. Scorned by his countrymen, he was forced to leave Ireland with his mistress, Mary Flanagan, and their daughter Anne. Almost destitute, Will had received certain grants of land from the Lords Proprietors and had come to Bath Town with its first settlers in 1706. Diligent and enterprising, he was soon in a position to acquire several valuable parcels of land, which acquisitions made him a highly respectable member of the community.

Mary Flanagan passed these days as Mistress O'Brannon. Having been Will's servant girl in Ireland, she had found this new life as a merchant's ''wife'' strange at first. But in a very short time she had become acclimated to the opulent yet rather crude society which surrounded her.

Anne's parents gave her everything any young girl could desire. She had servants purchased at the slave markets in Charleston, magnificent horses carefully bred on the plantation, the best tutors, including a fencing master, imported from England and France. But lately Anne had kept too much in the company of Joe Buck, an Indian hunter who, for less than twenty shillings a year, had agreed to supply the O'Brannon household with as much venison and as many fowl as they could eat. Joe had taught Anne to ride and to hunt with knife and ax.

Will watched his strongwilled daughter grow and, strive as he might to better the conditions surrounding her, he was secretly afraid that his own temperament, as well as the chaotic circumstances of her birth and early years, had contributed to her wild behavior. He was no saint but rather a full-blooded, hotheaded Irish tosspot, as he was the first to admit. He knew full well he could not legitimatize her, but he was determined to give her every other advantage in life.

Whether it was fate or a series of happy accidents, Anne O'Brannon had the benefit of an unparalleled education. With maturity she would learn to combine the knowledge derived from her learned tutors with Will's enthusiastic love of literature, Joe's practical and natural philosophies and sciences, and her mother's genuineness and sensitivity for humanity, to become a cultivated, sympathetic and dynamic woman.

Anne had always been interested in the circumstances of her birth. To quiet her questions, Will, in a besotted state, had promised that on her twelfth birthday he would tell her about her origin. He had often heard it said that "bastards had the best luck" and he certainly hoped this would prove true in Anne's life. When she came to him this night demanding to hear the entire story of her birth, he at first refused. She did not know that she was illegitimate and Will had no idea how the girl would react to this news. Taking his courage and a decanter of claret in hand, Will began his curious story.

"Your mother was a maid in me house in Cork, Ireland. Ah, Annie, she were a plump, comely wench with fine green eyes, bright red hair and skin the color of milk. I see her youth in thee now. Well, having taken a fancy to her, I would make some advance from time to time and a tinge of pink would come to her cheeks and she would stifle a tiny giggle in her wet dishrag. 'Oh, Mister O'Brannon, the mistress will see.' Then I would give her a resoundin' slap on her fine round arse, and that would set into a fit of laughter. Now, me wife Kathleen were a big buxom woman. . . ."

"What! Your wife, ye say?" Anne interrupted. "Does ye mean to say me mother be not your wife?"

"Aye, daughter, I fear 'tis true."

95

"That doth make me bastard, doth it not?"

"Aye, lass, 'tis even so."

"Zounds! I did never think I be bastard."

"Now, daughter, don't upset youself. There be worse things in the world than bein' born bastard."

"I'm not upset!" she shouted. "And tell me not there be worse things, when I have yet to digest this shockin' piece of news."

Will waited until Anne had composed herself, then continued. "Well now, as I were sayin', me wife were about ten years me senior and possessed of an ugly, shrewish disposition. She had taken ill at her last unsuccessful lyin' in and gone to recover her health at me mother's house a few miles distant. There were no issue betwixt us and I began to despair the fact that there would ever be any. In fact," he said, "I had had no communication with the woman for four months because of her illness. So when she goes to me mother's, I takes advantage of her absence and beds with my lovely lass, Mary, your mother. Uh . . . humph . . . dost cry, girl? Be ye tired?" he asked, somewhat embarrassed.

"No," said Anne, firmly. "I will hear this story from first to last."

"All right, then, list." Will was on his fifth glass of wine and his ears had begun to turn red and his freckles stood out on his round, heavily jowled face. His large hands touched Anne's knee often as he emphasized a strong emotion, and he gestured wildly with his long clay pipe. Soon he was so liquored and entirely engrossed in the telling os his story that he might well have been recounting these events to his alehouse friends rather than to his own daughter.

"Well, then, durin' me wife's absence, your mother and me consorted on a regular nightly basis. But while I be in the town about some work at the bar, she has another suitor, a tanner. Mary had taken such pity on him as to give him supper from time to time as she oft fed stray dogs and cats. She have a good heart, your mother, as ye well know. But she give him no other favor, mind you."

"Be ye sure of that?"

"On me life!"

"Be ye sure I be not the tanner's bantling?"

"Fore God and all the saints, thou canst not think it, girl!"

"All right, if thee be certain, but know I will ask Mother."

"God strike me dead if she say otherwise."

"Go on with thy story."

"Well, this cub, not havin' the fear of God afore his eyes, takes his opportunity to steal three silver spoons while your mother was about some household business. Mary soon misses the spoons and threatens to go to the constable. The tanner is frighted and tells her to look about some drawers, and while she does this he slips into her room and puts the spoons betwixt her sheets, thinkin' she must find them when she retires.

"Well, you see, Annie, your mother had been sleepin' in my room durin' Kathleen's absence. She did not once get into her own bed. This foolish tanner finds out the next day that the constable have been lookin' for him and he thinks that Mary had filched the spoons and be tryin' to put the blame on him.

"In the meantime me wife Kathleen returns home perfectly recovered from her indisposition. The knavish tanner goes to her and tells her the whole story, sayin' he did it for a jest. Kathleen finds the spoons in your mother's bed and, as jealous women will, concludes that the maid had not been to her own bed but had supplied Kathleen's place in my bed. Well, bein' of a jealous nature, she devises a plan to take her revenge against your poor mother. Women seldom forgive injuires of this kind, believe it, Annie.

"So, upon the excuse of my snorin', Kathleen orders Mary to make up her own bed, so that she, Kathleen, might lie in't, and tells Mary that she must sleep in another part of the house. Mary makes up the bed and, much to her surprise, finds the spoons. She quickly puts them in her trunk till she can find an opportunity to put them back where they belong.

"That night Kathleen lies in the maid's room. And I, poor fuckin' bastard, knowin' nought of this change, come to your mother's door and call out, "Mary, be ye awake!' Kathleen makes no answer. She thinks, ye see, to expose me for the very rogue I be, which she did. I think Mary dost tease me by not answerin', so I approach the bed without invitation. I did not know I were walkin' into the hangman's noose. Well, I drilled her proper, thinkin' all the time I were enjoyin' your dear mother. I pumped so violently that the bed did rise up from the floor and bang down again hard. I would not find out till later just how thoroughly I had fucked her. However, it were a fine fuckin', and she, bein' passive, bore it like a Christian."

"Now wait," Anne interrupted. "Where be the spoons?"

"In your mother's trunk."

"Why did she not put them back?"

"She had not the opportunity that night, with Kathleen sleepin' in her room. And the next day it did slip her mind, she bein' so busy about the household chores."

"How could you bed your own true wife, Kathleen, and not know it were she?"

"Well, I was a mite in me cups, she havin' nagged me all through our dinner. That's the truth of it."

"And it were the tanner what stole the spoons and later put them in Mother's bed?"

"Yes, bastard that he was to cause all this trouble and confusion betwixt us."

"Go on, then. What happened in the morning?"

"Well, early, before daybreak, me wife Kathleen steals out of bed, leavin' me asleep, and goes straight to me mother's to tell her all. I get up and go into the town and loiter about till noon. Me wife returns and fetches the constable, who searches Mary's room, and, findin' the spoons in her trunk, has the poor woman committed to the gaol. God's Death! Whereupon I hear this news in the tavern and go at once, after several pints, to confront Kathleen with her vile deed.

"I bursts through the door, ravin' and shoutin', 'Where

be ye, you miserable bitch!' I storm around all the rooms, slammin' doors, knockin' over furniture, till I come to the maid's room. And there be Kathleen, lyin' naked on your mother's bed, revelin' in her triumph. "Woman! What have ye done?' says I. And she, the hobbyhorse, what does she do but opens her arms to me and spread her legs in an invitin' manner? 'What in the name of the Holy Saints be ye up to?' says I. 'Have ye no shame!' Now she begins to play her hands in her twat rug. 'Ye be a shameless woman! Look at ye! And that poor girl . . . that fine girl . . . to toss her in the gaol like that. For what? Tell me, why did ye send Mary to the basket? What did that sweet thing ever do to thee? Answer me!' I yanks her out of the bed, her kettledrums a-bouncin'. Now, aware of her nakedness, she grabs up the counterpane and winds it around her fat body. 'Ye better give me answer, gipsy.'

" 'Mary took me spoons,' she says, a-blubberin'.

" 'Spoons?' says I. 'What's this? Did ye say spoons? I cannot understand ye through all your squallin'.'

" 'Yes, spoons,' she says. 'A thief she be; Mary filched three of me best silver spoons!'

" 'I don't believe this!' says I. 'Ye mean to tell me that ye went and locked up a servant girl what has been faithful to thee these past seven year, all on account of three bloody spoons?'

" 'They were me best! I'll show thee.' She stumbles out of the room, trippin' over her wrap, and goes to the sideboard in the dinin' room. 'Here, see for yourself. It were these very ones! She has stolen from me, more than ye see here, too!' she cried.

"She be holdin' the evidence out before her nose like a Chinese fan. I says to her, 'Ye be a ravin' madwoman. Six months that girl must rot in a stinkin' gaol with the rats, and for what?' I snatched each spoon and hurled them behind me, resultin' in two chinks in the plaster wall and a smashed teacup. 'Ye be a rantin' bitch,' says I. 'Six months!'

" 'I'll not change me mind. She can rot there, for all I

be carin'.' Now she dragged up a portion of the counterpane to cover her dairy, like a proper whore.''

Anne's laughter encouraged Will to add even more expressiveness to his delivery.

'' 'Oh, so that's the way 'tis.' I be ravin' now, Annie. I takes up the silver chest and dumps it on the floor at her feet and flattens each piece o' silver under me boot.

''I'm leavin' you!' Oh, she be wailin' good and proper now.

''Good,' says I. 'Be on with ye, the sooner the better, you stupid slut, you bangtail, fishmonger's bawd, tweak! Ye have no feelin' heart, you bloody cunt.' I bellowed and cursed and smashed every fine piece of porcelain in the house. Then I calmly puts on me hat, takes up me walkin' stick and leaves her standin' in the debris.

''Then I goes to your mother at the gaol. She tells me she have been pregnant some five months already and that she fears the prospect of bringin' a child into the world in that festerin' rathole of a gaol.''

''God's Blood!'' exclaimed Anne, as an icy chill passed through her veins.

''I cried, bein' powerless to prevent it. Oh, Annie, how I cried to see her lyin' on her little bit of straw. Ye see, Annie, the dampness have got to her lungs. 'Tis why she coughs so much. I fear she will die soon. Well, Kathleen had gone back to me mother's, and I was refused entrance. Dost believe it? Me own mother would not help me. Oh, how I despaired. Kathleen remained hardened and your mother stayed in the gaol, where she birthed ye. I had found a good woman, one Anne Fulworth, in the town. She were a midwife. This eased my mind. And poor Mary, thank the Lord, did not labor long afore she were delivered of ye.''

''What! I were born in the gaol, after all. Born in a stinkin' gaol! Poor Mother.''

''Oh, I cried to hear her sufferin'. I were standin' outside the gaol. When I heard your cries, me heart burst with joy to think I had a child, and that me Mary's pain be over. 'Twere around eight o'clock in the evenin', April 18, 1699.''

Anne climbed into Will's lap and hugged him tightly. Both of them sobbed for some time before Anne asked, "I did not stay in the gaol with my mother until her relase? Ye will not say so. Tell me, Father."

"No, child. 'Twere arranged that Anne Fulworth would give out that the baby had died. I had a little coffin brought in and we carried you out of the gaol down the street, past the watchin' eyes in all the taverns, to the potter's field. I dug the hole and put in the empty box, and Mistress Fulworth carried you to her home in her market basket. Ye be named after that fine woman who brought thee into the world and cared for thee in thy early years."

"Father," asked Anne, not wanting him to fall asleep, "how long did I live with Mistress Fulworth?"

"Oh, three or four years. When your mother was set free from the gaol, she stayed with ye at Mistress Fulworth's cozy hut on the outskirts of the town."

"Did Kathleen stay at your mother's?"

"Well now, that be another story." Will poured off the last of the claret and opened a bottle of brandy, stomping about the room to revive himself. "Three months after your mother were released from the gaol I heard the news, through a very reliable source, that me wife Kathleen were delivered of twins, a boy and a girl."

"Who fathered them?"

"Well, I learned later that I were the father."

"You mean I have a brother and sister?"

"Yes, child. It were all the result of that one night of love when I thought I were in bed with thy mother. But ye see, I did not know it were Kathleen in your mother's bed and I be thinkin' the bitch be whoring all this while. So methinks to confront her with this and goes to me mother's house. I had long since sold me horse and carriage to buy food for your poor ailin' mother during her long imprisonment. So I walked twenty miles, me fury growin' into a whirlwind by the time I reached me mother's house. And I burst in on them like all the furies of hell and said, 'God damn thee and thy brood to the everlastin' fires of hell!' Well, me mother were sittin' by the flickerin' fire, and she crosses herself a dozen times and beats her breast and runs her fingers over the pearl beads of her rosary, movin' her lips in silent prayer, only little whistlin' sounds escapin'. And there sits Kathleen, one babe at the breast, the other lyin' across her lap a-waitin' his turn. There were many exclamations of 'Oh dear Lord, save us!' from the both of them but I continued to rave on in spite of their prayers.

" 'Be it not true, Madam, that I have had no communication with thee since they last unfortunate lyin' in? How came you by those bastards? You woreson bitch, you bawdy wench, you magpie's nest you! Paradin' your gear like a gipsy in front of any besotted hard cock strollin' in the streets. Who be he? Where be the bastard? I'll beat his arse to a bloody pulp. Let me at him. I'll teach 'im to use another man's wife.' '

"Thou did rail against thyself," laughed Anne.

"Aye, lass, but I did not know it. Then me mother pipes up and suggests that Kathleen return home with the children, and at that I exploded.

" 'Not on your life! I'll not have those bantlings in me house. Nor you neither, woman. I be disgraced in the town. A man cannot be cuckolded in this manner and retain the respect of his friends.'

" 'And what about a wife ill used by her husband? Hath she no recourse? Hath she no pride?'

" 'She be only a woman. It does not matter. It be expected.'

"Oh, expected, is it? A man can slapdash his cock into any wench in the village and his wife must sit back and watch and say nothin'. No justice for the woman, that be the way of it. All right then, go home and keep your tarty slattern Mary and her bastard.'

" 'Her bastard be dead. Another disaster I have to thank thee for, ye heartless bitch!' '

"Did ye leave then?" asked Anne.

"Aye, lass. I left, cursin' their graves, and a year later me own mother died. Yes, and what's more she leaves all her money in trust to Kathleen for those bastard twins.''

"How did ye find out they be your own?"

"From the barrister who proved me mother's will. He practically drowned in sack one afternoon and babbled everything to me. Whereupon I discreetly questioned your mother and found out that at Mistress Kathleen's request she had not slept in her room that night. Now, with that information and my drunken remembrance of Kathleen's great breasts, tight gear, and her usual passive acceptance, I put all events together and admitted to meself that the twins must be mine own."

"Father, what manner of child was I?"

"Oh, wonderful, the joy of our lives, warm and lovin' ye was to us. I would visit each night and we would kiss and hug as if we had not seen each other in a week. And Mistress Fulworth was good to thee. She would make thee clothes, yet for the life of her she could not keep thee in 'em. All the day ye was wont to raom in the fields and walk in the woods and streams, quite naked. Ye does that still, does thee not?"

"Yes, I do, I feel free then. Oft I ride my pony naked as the day I be born."

"Dost do so in the presence of that Indian, Joe Buck? I forbid it! I'll not have it! I'll lock thee up, chain thee in the cellar!"

"Ye will not either. This be a ruse to put off thy story. Tell the rest!"

Will was well into his brandy now; he tried to gather his recollections. Skipping over several years, he came to the end of his story.

"When thee were six I dressed thee as a boy, brought thee to me house, and gave out that ye be a nephew from England, apprenticed to the bar. At six ye looked more like a strappin' lad of ten. This be how I saw to your early education. Thee was quick of mind and loved your books. We had but a few then which did bore thee—*Livy's Roman History*, *Pilgrim's Progress* and some plays of Master Shakespeare. We would act the plays at night. Thee did love *Macbeth*, I remember. Thee did delight to say the word 'anon.' Ye would go about all day saying 'anon' to the birds, to the ants, to the flowers.

"Now Kathleen, knowin' I have no nephew in England,

suspected deceit and sent her agent, a foppish gentlemen, to spy on us. He came one day when I was in the town and tricked thee into revealin' that ye were a girl.

"Well, one night soon after came a dreadful knockin' at the door. This did fright us, because I was in the midst of a stirrin' rendition of the porter's scene in *Macbeth*, and I says to thee, 'There's a knockin', indeed,' and I shouts out, "Anon, anon!' I can hear thy laughter yet. Well, I goes to the door and there be Kathleen and her fancy bespectacled agent. And Kathleen starts right in a-shoutin'. 'So here's your brat. To think ye tried to pass that slut's whelp off as your nephew. Does ye think me stupid? And as for thee, miss, someone ought to tan your little hide.''

"And ye responds roughly, 'Ye lay one hand on me, ye fat bitch, and I'll carve yer arse and serve it to the dogs.' ''

"I remember her now! She be a woman with uncommon breats; they did stick out like a shelf.''

"That be Kathleen, all right. Now she says in response to thee, 'Oh! She hath a tongue like her father's. I be not suprised, that is all I can say.'

" 'Good,' says I, 'because I like not to listen to thy tongue wag, nor do I like to look on thee. Yes, she be mine and I be proud o' her!'

"All this while thee has been starin' daggers at the agent, and suddenly ye picks up a carvin' knife and challenges him, sayin', 'Why, ye traitor!' and ye slices a candle cleanly down the middle.

" 'Oh, my goodness,' he says and you slide another knife across the table to him, and he says again, 'Oh, my goodness!' 'Tis all he can say: oh, my goodness. Now he be about to faint, and thee says, 'The devil damn thee black, thou cream-faced loon. Prepare to fight like a man, for I am goin' to slice ye from the nave to the chaps.' He tries to get away but ye jumps on him and holds the knife to his throat. Again he says, 'Oh, my goodness!' and thee says, 'You barnacled sot, you wormy fellow. I cannot kill thee if thee dost not fight me.' Now Kathleen swoons, distractin' you, and the foppish agent slips away.

"We pack up quickly and leave the house afore Kathleen wakes up; then we fetch thy mother. Oh, how ye did cry to leave Mistress Fulworth, and she cried too. We dresses you once again in girl's clothes."

"I did not like that, I warrant."

"No, you did not like it then and ye still don't, I notice. Oh, Annie, it would so please thy mother to see thee in a dress again. Think on it, love, for Sunday supper maybe."

"I'll think on't. Well, is that it? Be that the whole of it? Did we come to the Carolinas straight from Ireland?"

"Aye, lass. Oh, thou didst enjoy that passage. Ye spent the entire voyage on the deck watchin' the sea and sky."

"I do love the sea, I know that. 'Tis another world to me." Lost in a sea dream, Anne was awakened hours later by the fierceness of her father's snoring. That be some story, she thought, as she went out into the damp morning. I wonder if it be fiction. Whether it be true or not I be a bastard all the same. She walked into the fields and repeated the more humorous parts of the tale to one of the spotted ponies grazing there. With its retelling all the story's details became solidly planted in her memory.

The treaty of Ulrich in 1713 ended the Wars of the Spanish Succession. Thousands of Marlborough's troops returned to their homeland from Flanders and found unemployment their only welcome. Because England was no longer at war with France and Spain, privateering was made illegal; nonetheless pirates stormed the West Indies to menace trade, French, Dutch, Spanish or Enligsh, indiscriminately. In just one year New Providence would be taken over by these sea brigands. The golden age of piracy had begun.

Anne was now fourteen, wild and headstrong, a strapping, vivacious, energetic girl. She maintained a close relationship with her father. They would ride and hunt together, sometimes spending the entire day in the woods. She was a deadly shot with a pistol or musket.

Her schooling finished, Anne spent whole days with the

Indian, Joe Buck. He was more than a friend to her; he was her trusted mentor. From him she learned the use of the spear, the bow, the tomahawk and the knife, as well as hand-to-hand fighting and wrestling.

During the long summer afternoons spent among the moss-hung oaks, he would talk to her about the delicate balance in nature, and about principles of honesty, loyalty, fair play and honor.

On the days they would hunt, however, Anne was most excited. For many months much of Joe's game had been lost, due to Anne's impatience. Planning and waiting were the hardest lessons for her to learn.

In August of that year a young gentleman came with his father to visit the O'Brannon plantation. Baldwin Sommerwood came down to dinner dressed as befitted a prosperous planter's son; Anne wore her soiled riding clothes. The Sommerwood plantation was at St. Thomas-in-the-East, in Port Morant, Jamaica. Anne's first impression was that this Baldwin was too dandified for her taste. His face was ordinary. In fact, there was nothing at all distinguished about his person. Anne was totally uninterested.

Although her father had asked her to include Baldwin in her activities the next day, Anne fully intended to ride off without him. The next morning she got up earlier than usual for that express purpose. Grabbing a few biscuits and stuffing them in the pocket of her breeches, Anne went out. But Baldwin was mounted and holding her pony, waiting for her. Stripped to the waist and barefoot, he wore only faded breeches which were cut off at midthigh, exposing his cocoa-brown skin. The wiry muscles of his arms, shoulders and legs had been hidden beneath last night's formal attire.

Anne mounted and, whooping and hollering, they took off into the open fields. Baldwin had sparked her interest; now she felt he might have potential.

They met Joe Buck by the river. He had promised Anne that he would take her on a wildcat hunt. The prospect was stirring.

Restless with apprehension Anne and her young companion followed Joe. The Indian stopped to say, "Ye must calm yerselves. Yer breathing be too loud and ye disturb the air with violent movement. Take a deep breath and continue behind me."

Joe is leading the way, thought Anne, but I must be the first to spot this animal. It must be my kill. Anne was all eyes and ears; all her senses were sharp.

The Indian was concentrating so intensely, anticipating the event and predicting the results, that he did not hear the cat above him. But Anne heard it and looked up to see the animal about to leap from a high ledge onto Baldwin, who was only a few paces to the rear of her. Raising her musket, Anne took deadly aim and fired, hitting the cat squarely between the eyes. Joe tackled Baldwin and moved him out of the way of the animal's fall. The cat was dead the instant it landed. They tied the cat to a pole and carried it to Joe's cave, where he skinned it experly.

"Oh, 'tis a fine skin!" said Anne.

"Magnificent!" shouted Baldwin.

" 'Tis yours, Annie; you earned it," said Joe, offering it to her. "Young lad, now you owe Anne a life. Perhaps some day ye might snatch her from some danger. And you, Anne, once you save a man's life you be responsible for him always."

"Yes, I know. Is it a thing needs swearin' to?"

"Yes, I think so." Anne and Baldwin placed their hands on top of their hatchets, which Joe held crossed before them. They stared into each other's eyes and silently communicated a mutual promise.

"Yes, yes, 'tis done," said Joe, breaking the spell.

"I have a plan for further adventure," whispered Anne, once she and Baldwin were out of Joe's hearing. "By the time we reach home I will have the complete plan worked out in me mind." Taking up her prized skin, Anne mounted and was off, with Baldwin riding after her.

Today the parlor of the O'Brannon house was buzzing with the conversation of the society ladies of the Bath district. The room was stifling. Slaves stood about fanning the air with large palms. An old white-haired Negro man leaned over, holding a heavy silver tray filled with wonderful cakes and rich pastries. The squat woman talking to Mistress O'Brannon took no notice of him for a long while. She was engaged in vivid conversation with Mary concerning the dreadful abuse of slaves on vessels newly arrived from the Guinea coast. The old man's back ached under the weight of the tray. Huge beads of perspiration ran down his face and dripped into his painfully tight collar. Still she took no heed of his tormented efforts to serve her.

"Ye know, Mary, me husband, Mister Knight, did not want me to see his ship when I was last in Charles Town, but I insisted. He made me wait a full week till his crew could air the hold of its foul odor. Last Tuesday I was finally admitted. Oh, I can't begin to tell you. . . ."

Mary was beside herself. She looked at the old man and felt his agony, but could find no graceful way to interrupt Mistress Knight's dissertation on the injustices of slavery. "Mary, I just don't know how people can treat others in such a dreadful manner."

"Cake, Mistress Knight?" Mary finally said. The insensitive woman leisurely selected six different pastries and put them on her plate, settling them into her fat lap. "Thank you, Samuel. Simply disgusting, I tell you, Mary. . . ." The old man lifted his tortured shoulders into an upright position and went on to the next guest.

Suddenly, with an enormous catlike growl, Anne, wearing the bloody wildcat skin, leaped off Baldwin's horse into the middle of the room. Loud whoops rent the air as Baldwin, painted from head to toe, rode about the parlor, swinging his tomahawk over the heads of the ladies. Cakes, spoons and teacups flipped into the air and bounced off the terrified guests. Baldwin's horse circled the room and ground the cakes into the Persian carpet. Anne bounded from chair to chair, hissing at the ladies. Mistress Knight, fainting dead away, slumped into her high wingbacked chair. Servants ran from the room screaming. The shrieking guests huddled together, pleading for their very lives. Anne filled a corn sack with as many edibles as she could gather, then swung up behind Baldwin and sped away, leaving the parlor in a state of total upheaval and disarray. The two fearless warriors took lunch by the river, laughing a long while about the capture of the tea cakes.

That night in Mary's room after their guests had retired there was a heated conversation concerning Anne's latest escapade. Will was livid at first, Anne sullen, and Mary, weakened by the excitement of the afternoon, soon gave way to tears.

"Be ye possessed of a devil?" said Will in a harsh voice. "I will dismiss the Indian, ye know that."

" 'Tis not his fault. He teaches me only good things. If I am devious, 'tis by me own will."

"Thou dost drive us to extremities!" said Mary, blubbering through her tears. "How can I teach thee? I cannot whip thee; 'twould do no good. Why can yet not understand that ye must not behave in polite society like a wild thing?"

"Listen to your dear mother here!" said Will, in a quiet but threatening voice. He did not wish to rouse the entire household. "Have ye no care for her delicate health?"

Anne said penitently, "But Father, 'twould have done thy heart good to see Mother laughin' at those fat hens runnin' out of the house and waddlin' down the road like the devil himself were on their tails."

" 'Tis true, Will," said Mary, somewhat ashamed. "I did laugh. 'Twere not proper but I could not help meself."

"Did thee now?" Will started to chuckle.

"Oh, Annie," said Will, taking her into his arms, "I do love thee, girl. Ye be the true darlin' of me heart. Without thee, life would have no excitment, no delight or humor." Anne threw her arms around him and kissed him on his whiskered cheek. "Ah, that's the girl I know. Now tomorrow, Mister Sommerwood and I must go to Charles Town on some business. Dost think ye and young Baldwin can find some peaceful entertainment for the next few days?"

"I think so, Father."

"Aye, that's me good girl. Now sit awhile with your mother." Will wiped away a tear as he left the room. He would drink half a bottle of brandy before he retired for the night.

Anne went over to her mother's bed and kissed her softly on her cheek. Mary took the girl into her arms and hugged her tightly. "Me darlin' Annie, dost know how dear thee be to me? Dost know what a special girl ye be?"

"I am bastard, Mother. There is nothin' special in that."

"Ye be wrong there, girl. 'Tis not a high birth that makes a person great. Whatever be in thee to do, thee will accomplish; believe it."

"Ye may be right, Mother."

" 'Tis true, girl, and ye be a human bein' besides and needs must respect thyself. Let no man use thee."

"No man shall, Mother. Never fear it."

"And if thee dost respect thyself then thou must needs respect thy fellow man. I be reminded of this just this afternoon. We did talk of slavery. I have oft spoken with thy father of this business. A human bein', be he black or white, straight or lame, rich or poor, be not a thing to be bought and sold. Ye must see that, Annie. Ye be bastard, 'tis a fact, but the name is all it be. Some men be black, 'tis a fact too. But ye all be human and equal in the sight of God. I hope to convince thy father of't afore I die."

"I believe thee, Mother. Joe hath told me something of this afore."

"Treat every person the way thee wishes them to treat thee and ye will never have reason for regret. Ye be bastard and have no name. I be sorry for't. But I love thee dearly, better even for that."

"Do not fear, Mother. I will make my own name."

"I believe it, darlin' Annie." Mary closed her eyes and was soon asleep.

The next day Will and John Sommerwood left for Charleston. Standing by the coach, Anne and Baldwin listened to their fathers' instructions. Will issued a heavy warning to his daugher.

Anne was true to her promise. After searching Will's library for some interesting reading, they took a picnic lunch and rode down to a pond which was one of Anne's favorite places on the plantation grounds. She and Baldwin stretched out on the soft grass and each picked up a book. Anne had chosen to scan the *History of the Low Country Wars*, and Baldwin had selected a work Will had recently acquired called *The Buccaneers of America* by John Esquelmeling. Anne was somewhat content with her choice until Baldwin's intermittent "Good God's" piqued her interest.

"What is it you read?" she asked.

" 'Tis a work concerning the bloody buccaneers. Says here that Henry Morgan was a buccaneer. I never did know that. He were the governor of Jamaica once."

"What is a buccaneer?"

"They ride upon the seas, capturing ships and stealing precious cargo."

"Let's swim," said Anne, smiling. "I am weary of reading."

Before he knew it, Anne had stripped naked and was in the water."

"Well, don't stand there; take off your clothes and jump in."

God's Death, she is beautiful, he thought as he removed his shirt and boots; but he left on his breeches and jumped into the pond. They swam and splashed and wrestled one another in the water. Finally they tired and swam to the shore, pulling themselves up onto the grass to dry off in the sun. Beads of water glistened in Anne's reddish hair. Baldwin leaned on his elbow and watched her eyes change color.

"What is this?" she asked, pointing to his penis, its outline revealed by his wet garment. He turned over on his stomach. "No, remove your breeches; I want to see you. I am curious."

Somewhat self-conscious, he pulled off his wet garment. Anne stared at his penis a long time. He giggled in embarrassment. Mary had given Anne no instruction in this

111

matter of sex and Joe had only preached at her, saying the young maidens of his tribe never think to give themselves to a man until the day of their marriage. These thoughts now incited her curiosity even more.

"Methinks I have been too busy all this summer hunting, fishing and riding. Now I wish to examine this male apparatus and observe its function. Show me what it can do."

"Well, for one, it can piss." He demonstrated.

"I see that. What else?"

"I know not, Annie, for I never have touched myself except to wash and piss."

"What, are ye afraid of thyself?"

"I am not!"

"I am not afraid to touch it." She grabbed him quickly as though she were catching a bird. He gave out a startled gasp. "I'll not hurt thee." Anne fondled his testicles. He groaned a little. She watched the limp penis harden and rise up slowly. "Put it inside me," she demanded.

"What? I cannot. I know not how to do it."

"I want to know what it feels like inside me. Do it now, or pay the price," she said, with a threatening squeeze. He was awkward and Anne had to help him. Once he was inside her, she waited. "Now what?" she asked. "Well, do something! I think it be up to you now." He pushed in further and she winced.

"God's Blood, I did hurt thee," and he slipped out immediately.

Anne began to laugh and pushed him off. "Oh, I tire of this foolishness. 'Tis more fun to wrestle." They rolled about on the grass, pinning each other in various holds and laughing. Anne thought it might be interesting to see if his organ was a debilitating factor. She clutched it firmly in one hand and found that he was completely and utterly powerless to break the hold. "Quarter, quarter!" he shouted. " 'Tis not a fair fight." He was at her mercy now. She gave a few hard jerks and he screamed. "Not so hard, please, Annie. You'll pull it off." He tried to get at her hands, but she only pulled harder. "Ahhhh, stop." But

Anne kept on, softening her tugging motion until she established a steady rhythm. His screams of pain turned to moans of pleasure. She was determined not to stop until she found out what this interesting appendage was capable of. And she did not cease her motion until a warm stream shot up and sprayed her breasts. "So that's what it does."

"What?" he said, not fully understanding himself what had happened.

"Ye will have to learn to do that into a woman, I warrant. 'Tis certain that man is not meant to squander his seed in the open air. As for me, I'll wait till thee has had more practice."

The next day they went sailing on the Pamlico River. It was Baldwin's turn to teach Anne something. He could sail as well as she could rid.e With his instruction, Anne was maneuvering the small sloop handily by the time they decided to anchor and take lunch.

"I hear the Caribbean waters be the most beautiful in the world. Is that true, Baldwin?"

"Oh, yes, 'tis true, but seas can be rough sometimes."

"You leave for Jamaica tomorrow?"

"Yes, and I am sad to go."

"What will you do there?"

"Oh, I will go to school in England next year. Till then I will help my father on the plantation."

"I will miss thee."

"Do you see what I did here?"

"Now, what is it?"

He showed her where he had scratched the initials A and B inside a heart on the tomahawk Joe Buck had given him.

"Now, that is bloody foolish," she said.

"I do not think it foolish. We may meet again some day, Annie O'Brannon, and what's more ye may wish to make love to me again—after I practice."

They laughed. Anne kissed him affectionately on the cheek, then he kissed her tenderly on her lips. He hauled in the anchor while she hoisted the mainsail and Baldwin, taking the tiller, guided their vessel home.

Will had returned from Charleston with a young Englishwoman whom he had purchased from a prison ship recently arrived from Newgate. The prisoners had been so tortured during the passage that Will was hard pressed to find one who could survive the coach ride back to Bath. Although weak from lack of food, and sullen of temperament, this girl seemed hearty and young enough to prove a useful addition to his household.

Clara Hawkins had accidentally stabbed a gentleman of the nobility during a moment of intense love play. Since he was a member of the aristocracy, the law of the realm dealt harshly with her. Her bitter resentment of what she termed the falseness of the upper classes made her a vengeful antagonist to people of wealth and position.

Mary O'Brannon be no better than meself, she thought. This story of how Mistress High-and-Mighty got to be the lady of the house be common gossip among the servants. Will O'Brannon be easy to bed. I be not the only girl to know that either, I warrant. Silly bitch!

Sparks flew between Clara and Anne the very moment they laid eyes on one another. Anne did not know why she hated the woman, but she was certain there was no way she could trust her.

One day at the noon meal, Clara burst into the kitchen in a rage, slamming the silver tray on the table and cursing the fate that brought her to this desolate country and pompous household. Her dark hair flew about and the few fine strands sticking to her sweaty face caused her further annoyance.

"That little slut, I'd like to kill her. What gives that fuckin' bitch the right to treat me like dirt under her feet? 'Fetch this, fetch that.' 'This be too cold, that too hot.' Called me a clumsy wanton gypsy, she did! Here!" she said, throwing a beaker of soup at the cook. " 'Tis too cold for Mistress Hot Twat. 'Fetch me a hotter or I'll brain ye,' she says to me. I'll brain her, that's what! I'd like to pour these victuals down her bleedin' neck." Clara was quite beside herself with emotion. She left the kitchen and made her way into the dining room. A wisp of hair tumbled down over her eyes, blinding her momentarily, and she tripped, pouring the hot soup into Anne's lap.

"Bloody, fuckin' bitch!" cried a startled Anne, as she rendered a stinging blow to Clara's cheek.

"Who be ye callin' bitch, slut?" Without thinking, Clara pickèd up a carving knife and held it high over her head. Instinctively and with lightning speed, Anne took up her case knife and plunged it into Clara's stomach.

Will jumped up from his chair, as the woman slumped to the floor, quite dead.

As a criminal, Clara had no legal rights. The inquest was routine and speedy. Damaging evidence was spoken by some of the servants against Clara's character and it was stated that she had threatened to kill Anne several times before that last attempt. With Will's eyewitness account, the judge finally ruled that Anne be acquitted on the grounds of self-defense. She was released into her father's custody and Will was warned to keep a good eye on her.

One tragic event seemed to follow another. Soon Mary's consumption worsened and in a matter of weeks she was dead. Will was despondent and wept continually, and Anne slipped into a melancholy mood and did not set foot out of doors for two weeks. The incident with Clara Hawkins had left her with a stunned, empty feeling. Her father could not help her; she needed the comfort that only a woman could give.

I am thankful thee was not at the table that sad day, Mother. 'Twould surely have hastened thy death. I cannot bear the thought of't even now. Joe was right. Anne went over his biting words in her mind.

"A woman with a knife. Fogh! And thee, Annie O'Brannon, could do naught but kill her! What threat were she to thee, tell me that? None! Ye could disarm her in a minute. Do not tell me thee needs must kill her. I'll not believe it!"

"It were reaction. I did not think."

"What! Think ye be a bear or some other wild beast in

115

the forest? Man does not act on instinct alone. You be human. Methought thee knew to respect life, for it be a precious thing. I be disappointed in thee and myself too. I thought I had taught thee better.''

''You did. I know better. 'Twas just that in the anger of the moment I did not think.''

'' 'Tis no excuse, I tell thee! Ye must learn to control thy temper. 'Tis something I cannot teach thee. 'Tis a bitter lesson thee must learn for thyself. When next you be in serious trouble, look to yourself and see if it be not impulsiveness that got thee there.''

Anne was crying now, just as she had at other times when Joe had spoken harshly to her. I feel like a child now, not like a woman at all. Oh Mother, why are you not here to comfort me and give me thy womanly strength?

Will pulled himself out of his bereaved state and made plans to expand his ever-growing business. Anne must learn to manage the household, he resolved. And now that she was of an age to marry, he would set about finding a profitable match from among the wealthy planters of the neighborhood, and thereby expand his Carolina Estate.

Anne was fifteen and was as aware of her beauty as the young gentlemen of the district who were seeking to court her. There was a constant stream of suitors to the house but Will encouraged only the wealthiest. Anne was by no means free with her favors. She had the highest regard for her person and would allow a lad to kiss her only if she liked him. And a kiss was the full extent of her favor. In this manner she drove the young bucks of the neighborhood to extremes.

One lad, Philip Daniels, wealthy and impetuous, so bragged to his fellows about Anne's one kiss, that he overshot his latitude and had to make good the rest of the story. Heaping one lie upon another, he boasted how he had had his way with Anne under the bushes, behind the barn and in every other place imaginable on her father's plantation. Daniels was so deep in his story and the lie had spread so in the district that he had to bring this matter to the attention of Mister O'Brannon if he was to save himself at all.

This foolhardy boy boldly repeated to Anne's father in her presence how often, where and when he had had certain private communication with his daughter. Profuse in his repentance, he stated that now he was willing to do the honorable thing, at which point he brazenly asked for Anne's hand in marriage.

Will was surprised and outraged at Philip's tale. He raved on while Anne, angered enough to kill, somehow managed to control her wrath.

"What, have I sired a whore! Tell me, girl, be ye naught but a harlot? Have ye no shame? The saints be blessed that your mother be not alive to see this."

Will, sure that his daughter would burst into a tirade at any moment, was amazed at her control. He felt daggers from her eyes shoot past him at the boy and marveled that the lad had not run off then and there.

"I should like to have one or two words with Mister Daniels in private, if you would please excuse us, Father?"

Oh, he be in for it now, thought Will. But if they are to be wed, the lad must learn to handle his wife's temper. God help him!

"Very well. I'll inquire after our supper."

Will had no sooner left the room when the lad realized his fatal mistake. He was certain that Anne's eyes flashed red before she began to hurl china ornaments at his head. While he remained stunned by the barrage of porcelain missiles, Anne cudgeled him with a chair until it broke into pieces too small to strike him with.

"You bloody fucker! I'll teach you to make up lies about me. Miserable bastard that ye are, I should kill you."

Wrestling him to the floor, Anne bit him severely in several unseemly places.

"God help me, Mister O'Brannon!" he whimpered.

"Shit! Scab! Cowardly wretch! You were brave enough a moment ago. Fight back, you bloody prick!"

Will entered the room to find Anne sitting on the lad's

stomach, holding him by the ears and banging his head on the floor. He ran for help. It took a half dozen of his strongest servants and himself to pull Anne off the boy, Philip had to be carried to his home. Many days passed before anyone knew whether the boy would live or die, he languished so under his hurts.

The news of Anne's assault upon the Daniels lad spread through Bath Town and the surrounding district. It did not matter to Anne if any of her erstwhile suitors knew that the boy had lied. She had convinced her father, and she felt sure that none of the boys in the neighborhood would ever speak a word against her again, whether it were true or not.

At sixteen Anne had matured into a captivating woman. Standing five feet six inches, she had developed a most curvaceous form. Her hair was rich gold with hints of red, and her face, with its alluring green eyes and sensuous lips, was beautiful to look upon. Since Will had been entertaining lavishly in recent months, he had spared no cost on Anne's wardrobe. The bodices of her exquisite dresses displayed her voluptuously full breasts and her tiny waist.

Anne received guests at the plantation with the ease of a highborn lady trained in the social arts since birth. Will watched his daughter tantalize prospective customers from all parts of the world.

One new and unwelcome resident of the Pamlico River area was Edward Teach, soon to become notorious as the infamous Blackbeard. It had recently been his practice to anchor his pirate vessel, the *Queen Anne's Revenge,* at Ocracoke Inlet and watch shipping in the Pamlico River and on the open ocean. The inhabitants of North Carolina were in absolute terror of his presence, for he roamed about the province as freely as he rode the seas.

It was the night of December 31, 1715; Will had invited Charles Eden, Governor of North Carolina, to join in a New Year's Eve dinner. Will's old friend John Sommerwood had arrived the evening before with a planter from Barbados, one Stede Bonnet—Major Bonnet, as he was called—who had been retired for some time from the king's forces. The major, a handsome man in his midforties, was excessively well dressed in a wide-skirted gray velvet coat, a brilliant blue satin brocade waistcoat, voluminous lace falls at the wrist and throat, red-heeled shoes and a full wig. He kept himself well scented, but Anne was grateful that he did not paint his face as well. She found his conversation most engaging, for he was a cultured, learned gentleman with a most agreeable voice.

Two men, Charles Bellamy and his associate of dubious character, James Bonny, had just arrived from Charleston. Captain Bellamy had come to propose that Will finance an expedition to the Bahamas. Governor Eden arrived without his wife, who was ill; and Anne was the only woman in this gathering, as she often was when entertaining her father's guests. She went in to dinner on the arm of John Sommerwood.

"My son Baldwin asked me to inquire after your health, Mistress Anne."

"Oh, my old friend—how nice. How is he? Where is he now?"

"In England, at his law studies. In these two years he has grown into a tall, fine-lookin' young man. You would scarcely recognize him, or he you for that matter."

I dare say, thought Anne to herself. If my very life depended on't I could not remember his face, it were so ordinary. "Give him my fond regards when next you write him."

Will beamed, as always delighted to see his daughter so amiable and gracious. He knew that someday she would make a fine match, and secretly he hoped it would be with Baldwin Sommerwood. The lad had promise; he was bright and enterprising, and their marriage would join two expanding plantations, one in America and the other in the West Indies. But Will knew his daughter—headstrong, determined to have her way, much like himself; her husband, whoever he was, would ultimately be Anne's own choice.

Once at the table, the group was startled by a short burst

of gunfire issuing from an early reveler outside. Will sent a husky servant to look into the matter.

"I be not usually alarmed," said Will, "but lately rumors of this villain Teach menacing our countryside have put me on me guard."

"You have good cause to be alarmed, Mister O'Brannon," remarked Governor Eden. "I have heard harrowing reports from the citizenry regarding this man's outrageous exploits. I hear 'tis his practice to invade a planter's home, abuse his hospitality by eating at his table uninvited and consuming great quantities of liquor, then to take the man's wife and daughters, bulling them, beg pardon, Mistress Anne, right before the man's eyes, he being powerless to restrain him."

"Let him but try it with me and I'll cut off his balls and feed them to the swine."

"Annie!" exclaimed Will, "remember yerself!" He added, "What does this wretch look like, Gov'nor?"

"Oh, he is a great hairy fellow, most frightful to look upon, they say. He dresses all in black and is most noisome, a wild-mannered character. I am responsible for the government in this district and am at a loss to know how to handle this dread visitor. The town looks to me for protection."

"Have you no force at your disposal, Governor?" asked Major Bonnet. "A small contingency of militiamen, properly armed, could easily blow this man and his vessel straight to hell's door!"

"Guns will not stop him," said Bellamy, "for he be the very devil himself. I have never seen him, but I lately shipped with a Captain Hornigold who knows him well. He says Teach be capable of any deed and be most unpredictable in his behavior. But old Hornigold do say he be a man of great personal courage and uncommon boldness."

"Boldness! God's Death! His boldness may like to cause the ruin of our prosperity here. Fuck the saints! Has he no fear of God afore his eyes?" expostulated Will.

"That he has not, I warrant thee." Bellamy was a short stocky man with very close-cropped white hair, intelligent and interested in the affairs of the world. He indulged in piracy on occasion and believed that he understood Edward Teach. "Governor Eden, Mister O'Brannon, I put it to thee this way. Piracy be a thing to live with, for 'twill not go away overnight, in a year's time, or maybe never. It be right here on the Pamlico River, in Charles Town, and in the West Indies as well. I know this for fact. Now, if ye cooperates with Ned Teach in matters of economy, perhaps providin' him a fair market for his plundered goods, he may protect thee."

"What! Compromise with the devil! Never!" roared Will.

"Wait, Father, let the man have his say," cautioned Anne. "Continue, Captain Bellamy."

"Now he, bein' your neighbor, will not allow you to suffer at the hands of other villains. What think you, Governor?"

"Well, 'tis worthy of consideration, since we have no force here."

"You see, I came by coach from Charles Town," said Bellamy, "to avoid sailin' past old Teach. 'Tis best to keep clear of the man, when thou canst, or to cooperate with him, for ye cannot brave him. 'Tis certain death."

"Are you a pirate, Mister Bellamy?" asked Anne.

"Anne, 'tis not a proper question for our guest," said Will.

"Let him answer, Father."

"Not at the moment, Mistress Anne. James Bonny here be a pirate, if. . . ."

"God's Death! Cap'n Bellamy, what are ye sayin', and in this company. He doth jest . . . he be always jestin' with me. Cap'n, tell 'em ye be jestin'."

"I jest. But he be a damned clever bastard all the same."

I warrant ye be too, thought Will. Ye be presentable enough in yer person, but there be somethin' about thee I do not like. Besides, thee be gazin' with a lewd eye upon my Annie. Another damned rascal lookin' for some opportunity, I warrant.

Anne had as yet no opinion of James Bonny. She was

121

most interested in pursuing further conversation with the colorful Charles Bellamy. "What is your business, then, Captain, if you are no pirate?"

"I be an old sailor, Mistress Anne, an' have used the sea all me life in one fashion after another. But lately I have been fishin' the wrecks in the Gulf of Florida."

"What do you mean by 'fishin' wrecks'?"

"I dive seeking the treasure which lies about wrecked galleons on the ocean's floor."

"Have you ever gone diving in the ocean, Major Bonnet?"

"No, I have not, Mistress Anne." Then he lowered his voice so that she alone could hear. " 'Twould be a most tempting prospect if you were in the water. I would be jealous of the fish and would petition Neptune himself to come to my aid and endow me with the skill to swim after thee."

A most charming gentleman, she thought, refined and handsome. They continued their discourse in low voices well out of range of James Bonny, who was straining to hear. During the main course of the dinner, Governor Eden questioned John Sommerwood about his Jamaican background. Charles Bellamy solicited Will regarding investing in his wreck-fishing operation. Being thus excluded from all conversations, James Bonny retreated within himself.

Get thy wits together, James Bonny, he thought. Look around ye. In your whole miserable life ye has not been surrounded by such wealth. Ye have not a groat, yet here ye be. Sharpen thy wits and turn this association to thy own advantage.

He looked about him. Besides wealth, he recognized other qualities which he did not possess: the political position of the governor, the gentility of John Sommerwood, the education and social grace of Major Bonnet, the energy and drive of Will O'Brannon, and above all the honesty of Charles Bellamy.

I like not to work as these men do. They love to toil, for without work they would not feel alive. I need money, and what's more I'll devise a means to get it without workin' me arse off. I'll have more pieces of eight than old Bellamy can dream about, a mansion bigger than the governor's and a plantation twice the size of Sommerwood's and O'Brannon's put together. I can see myself dressed finer than this dandy Bonnet, and I'll have this beauty to boot. If I have naught else, I'll have her, and her money as well.

The noise of gunfire shattered the evening's quiet.

"Must be midnight," said Will, looking at his watch.

"Yes, by God, on the very stroke. What the devil!"

Edward Teach burst into the room, a pistol in each hand, and fired at the crystal chandelier above the table, sending a shower of fine glass all over the guests.

"Happy New Year and many fuckin' more of the same!" he shouted. His long black beard was braided and tied with colored ribbons in the manner of the Ramillies wig. Gunner's matches stuck under his hat fizzled and sparked. His eyes had a fierce expression, created by the fact that his beard grew high on his cheeks under his eyes and great bushy black eyebrows grew down to meet the beard. He was frightful to look upon. Anne was so amazed at the appearance of this man she did not notice that James Bonny had slipped under the table and remained there.

"A fuckin' Happy New Year to ye!" Teach shouted again, waiting for someone to offer him a drink. Major Bonnet stood up and drew his rapier.

"Damn your eyes, man, dost draw on me when I wishes ye Happy New Year? Best return that bird spit. Be that the way to treat a guest? Zounds! Be there no brandy? Who be the lord of this fuckin' manor house?"

"I be, ye whoreson wretch!" Anne cried out, seeing her father's hesitation. She stood up and continued in a threatening voice, "If ye steps one foot nearer without invitation, I'll carve thee and serve thee for dessert."

"Aye now, a saucy, spicy wench. I like thee well!"

"Too good for thee, villain. Thee be all bull beef and very little wit. Thou hast not the courage to brave me, I'll warrant."

"Oh, be that so! Dost know my name, girl?"

"Aye, thee be Edward Teach. Thy vile reputation precedes thee."

"Aye, it do! And ye be not afraid of me?"

"I am afraid of thee no more than of an actor in a play. I hear tell ye be a man of uncommon courage. Are ye brave enough to stand afore me whilst I plant these carvin' knives in the door around thee, or dost thou piss more than ye drinks?"

He stood and looked into her eyes. Braved by a woman, by God, and afore these gentlemen here. This never has happened afore. I cannot even bully this hellcat. I must be brave, for all of these cowardly whelps are not. They be not brave enough to still this girl's tongue.

"Well, I have had little entertainment of late, so I will see what thee can do with thy knives, lass. I hope ye be skillful at throwin', for old Ned's sake."

"Dost want to tie this napkin around thy eyes?"

"What! God's Balls!" he bellowed. "Think Ned Teach fears a flyin' blade! I am afraid of nothin' any man can do . . . nor woman either."

"All right, then." Anne took up half a dozen carving knives and, from twenty feet, and without pause, threw one after another to outline Teach's head and torso.

"Fuck thee, wench. . . ."

"Best not try that either." Anne stared straight into his eyes, making sure he received the full import of her last message.

"Now, Mister Teach, won't you take a brandy with us?" Anne smiled graciously.

A pause followed. Everyone trembled, wondering what this man would do now. He could as easily kill them all as drink with them. Teach roared a laugh which shook the remaining bits of the chandelier.

"Don't mind if I do, Mistress ah. . . ."

"Anne."

"Mistress Anne," he said, bowing low before her. " 'Tis a bonny name. It be the name of me galleon.

Queen Anne's Revenge. To Queen Anne,'' he said, raising his glass before her. ''May she never need revengin'. If she do need it, 'twill be done by Ned Teach fuckin' proper.''

''Allow me to introduce my father, William O'Brannon.''

''How do, sir.''

''Yes, ah. . . .''

''And Governor Eden.''

''Aye, Gov'nor, to your fuckin' good health, sir!''

''. . . ah . . . yours.'' Eden lifted his glass.

''Why, thank thee, sir; 'tis been a long time since a man willingly drank me health, aside from me crew; they always be drinkin', me health or no.'' Teach laughed.

''These gentlemen were speaking about you earlier, Mister Teach. Methinks it be in the way of business; be that so, Governor?''

''Ah . . . well. . . .''

''Perhaps the gov'nor be thinkin' to give me leave to auction me goods in the town?''

''Well, Mister Teach, I. . . .''

''There be profit for thee.''

''Oh, I could not. . . .''

''I mean for some private charity, of course.''

''Well, now, I think. . . .''

''Good, 'tis concluded. And perhaps Mister O'Brannon has it in mind to purchase the whole of what be left?''

''Ah . . . I might consider. . . .''

''For a very respectable price, that is.''

''Well, perhaps. . . .''

''Good! Now, Gov'nor, since our business be concluded, I would move to other matters. Methinks I shall wife.''

''Dost not have a dozen wives already, Mister Teach? asked Captain Bellamy.

''A dozen? Nay—thirteen, to be exact. I look to take me fourteenth from your fine city here.''

Anne laughed, Mister Sommerwood was choking on his brandy and the governor was beside himself.

''Thou'rt a lusty wencher, Mister Teach,'' said Anne.

''Aye, lass, I be a healthy man. Well, what say you,

Gov'nor? She be a sportin' lass of sixteen, and 'twould please her if ye was to perform the ceremony.''

"Oh, God help me!''

"I care not a bleedin' fart if God be there, just you, man!''

"Well. . . .''

"Good, bedad, good! Sunday next then on the village green.''

"Methinks we can all rejoice now to have gotten this New Year off to such a rousin' beginning," said Anne, lifting her glass. "Happy New Year!" Everyone drank.

Teach sat on the table. Wine sloshed out of the glasses onto the lacy linen tablecloth. Tearing off a turkey leg, he began to gnaw on it. After a great belch he said, "Ah, Mister O'Brannon, excellent victuals. Thank thee for thy generous hospitality. I know I did break your chandelier, but I did not like it; I'll get thee a bigger. Think no ill of't." Teach smiled at Will, then at John Sommerwood.

"Mister Teach, this is John Sommerwood, a planter from Jamaica.''

"Jamaica! Fore God!" He offered a greasy hand to Mister Sommerwood, too quickly for him to refuse it. "Jamaica, 'tis me old home. Drummond was me name in those days. Hast heard of me?''

"No, sir, I have not.''

"Beautiful country, Jamaica. I do long for the mountains. But 'tis not a healthy place for a pirate these days. And who be the gentleman with the pissin' bird spit?''

Major Bonnet stood and introduced himself boldly. "Stede Bonnet, Esquire, late major in the king's army, retired, now a planter in Barbados.''

"Ah, the Windwards." Teach filled a wine glass with brandy. "I know those islands well, and often cruise there—Dominica, St. Vincent, Barbados. That is the site of Carlisle Bay, is it not?''

"Yes, there's a Carlisle Bay at the south end of Barbados.''

"There be a place near there where Barbadians come to perform their voudou. Have ye heard of that, Bird Spit?"

"Aye, I have heard stories of their secret rites but I think they cannot be true."

"They be true, Mister, believe it. 'Twas at Carlisle Bay, in the dense palms there, that I saw them do their witchery. One evenin' meself and a small crew pulls up our piragua onto the beach. The dead of night it was. And we finds this band of eight or nine Negro men and women far in on the beach chantin' and dancin' in the trees. We steals closer. 'Twere a fine moonshinin' night an' everyone of them were naked, naked as the day they was born. Then they chants louder and commences to dance in a circle around a woman who were standin' in the middle of them. They danced themselves into a frenzy and soon cut her throat."

"Gracious!" exlaimed the governor.

"Oh, there be more, Gov'nor. They take up their knives and commences to drain out all her blood and then they pours it all over themselves and dances once more into a frenzy till they all falls to the sand in a trance. We takes them all up, including the dead girl, and carries them down to our piragua, and lays them all over the side. Now we removes our breeches, which were all smeared with blood, and lays them aside; then, linin' up behind these bare-arsed creatures, we begins to bull the woman and bugger all the men, one after one, each man takin' his turn. They never woke, dost believe it? So we goes another round and another. Now some of me men have dropped to the beach. So settin' up me pipes I holler, 'A keg of rum to the man what can fuck the longest!' I had company awhile longer. I buggered me last man as the day broke and had not one drop of fuck left in me, but I still has the strength to toss each man of me crew into the sea to wake 'em up. Now tell me, Bird Spit, that there be no such thing as voudou!"

"Ah, I do not know what to say, sir," said Bonnet.

"Well, I know naught of voudou, but I am somewhat exhausted at thy lusty tales, Mister Teach," said Anne.

"I pray ye excuse me."

"Aye, Mistress Anne, and thank thee for thy hospitality."

"Oh, look at thee, Mister Teach, your hair is afire!" said Anne, laughing.

He pulled the gunner's matches out of his hat and doused them in a water glass, then poured a pitcher of water over his head.

"Will you impart a secret to me, Mister Teach?"

"Perhaps, Mistress."

"Canst tell the formula for those fuses you wear? I am curious, is all."

"These be but ordinary gunner's matches, Mistress Anne, hemp cord dipped in saltpeter and lime water."

"How slowly do they burn?"

"Twelve inches in an hour, I'd say."

"By God, it be one o'clock now!" said Will. " 'Tis time we all retired. Good night, sir." Anne left on Stede's arm.

"Weren't there one more at your table, Mister O'Brannon, at the evening's start?" asked Teach, looking at the company remaining.

"Fore God, where be Mister Bonny?" shouted Will.

Charles Bellamy seemed to know where to look for James Bonny and, dragging him out from under the table, he threw him into Teach's arms. "I'd like you to make the acquaintance of the famous Mister Teach, James, my lad. Shake his hand, that's a gentleman. James Bonny at your service, Mister Teach."

"I am not surprised that he should hide," said Will to Mister Sommerwood and the Governor as they left the room. " 'Tis a snivelin' coward and a sneakin' puppy to boot."

"The night be young, Mister Bonny. Come, wash the milk off thy liver and let's to me vessel and drink in the New Year proper. Why do you shake, sirrah? Be ye cold? Here, let me warm thee." Putting one powerful arm around Bonny's waist, he lifted him off his feet and carried him out of the room under his arm. "We will revel this night and all day tomorrow. Come, friends, let's away!"

128

During the weeks remaining in the brisk month of January, Anne was properly romanced by the gentleman planter Stede Bonnet. Their conversations were intellectual, stimulating, and often witty.

Will had taken an extended buying trip to Charleston and Mister Sommerwood had returned to Jamaica. Anne and Stede spent the winter afternoons by the fire in the parlor, where he recited poetry to her by the hour. She studied every line of his handsome face as he read aloud.

How gentle is his voice, she thought. 'Tis not difficult to admire such a man. I wonder what sort of lover he would prove. In four months I will be seventeen and I am a virgin still. Is my maidenhood such an important thing to keep till marriage? I wonder. Seems an unnecessary luxury meant for the man's benefit.

He stopped reading and took her hand in his.

"Anne, you know I am married."

"Why do you tell me this?"

"Because I think I am in love with you."

"Oh?"

"Dost surprise thee?"

"No, Mister Bonnet, many men are in love with my beauty."

"Oh, 'tis not thy beauty. Ah . . . I mean, 'tis not *only* thy beauty. I love thy beauty well. It is more than that."

"Explain, if you will."

"Well, you are a woman I can talk to."

"Your wife does not talk to you, Mister Bonnet?"

"Only with a most rude tongue, Mistress Anne. I will not speak against her, for 'tis not a courteous thing to do. But I love her not, and of late I have devised many ways to be out of her company. I cannot marry you, nor would your father permit it, I being over twice your age, yet I would. . . ."

"You would what, Mister Bonnet?"

"I would . . . I humbly ask permission to make love to you."

"Dost know I am a virgin, Mister Bonnet?" She spoke louder and in a harsher tone than she had intended.

"No, I. . . . Forgive me, Mistress Anne. I do most humbly beg your pardon for my boldness."

Anne got up and went to the parlor door. Bonnet stood and bowed, thinking she meant to exit the room. Anne stood facing the door for a long while. His body slumped in despair to have so bungled the affair.

Anne thought, I dare say I could not lose my maidenhead in a gentler or easier manner than to this gentleman. 'Tis time the thing were done. Her hand was on the knob but instead of leaving she locked and bolted the door. Then she turned and faced him.

Major Bonnet proved that afternoon a most considerate lover, bring Anne to several orgasms before inserting himself within her. She was in such ecstasy that she did not even feel her hymen break. Before he brought himself to climax he asked if she was in her fertile cycle.

As the days progressed Anne learned the meaning of sexual gratification. She would never forget this man, her first lover, nor did she regret having kept herself a virgin till now. All lovemaking did not contain such fulfillment, she was sure, but she was enjoying completely this time with this man.

If he could have made love every minute of the day, she would have been ready. She was as insatiable in love as in all her appetites. Stede Bonnet was thankful that he was a strong, healthy man.

Soon it was time for Stede to leave Carolina and return home to Barbados. His goods were being loaded on January 21st and he was to sail the next evening.

"I must go now, Annie; the vessel leaves Charles Town tomorrow night."

"Let me ride as far as Charles Town with you. I cannot bear to part from you so soon."

"You cannot. 'Twould be difficult for both of us. And you know a lady cannot travel without a female companion."

"I'll take one of the servants. Besides, Father is there. I can return with him. It would give us a few more hours together. Please say yes!"

"All right, but we must go *now*, Annie!"

Anne had the entire household in a state of pandemonium, but she was packed and in the coach, the reluctant duenna perched atop with the driver, within an hour. They spent the entire journey in each other's arms. At their infrequent stops for food, Anne would stare across her plate at him, feeling no hunger. He could not eat either.

Why did I let this go so far? he thought. 'Tis torture for both of us. But I treasure every precious moment we had together. Perhaps I will see this beautiful creature again someday. But these things are never the same after a space of time, I know that. We have had our season and I needs must be happy with that.

The coach thundered onto the wharf just as the crew was letting go the lines. Stede jumped aboard in time. Anne stood on the dock and watched until the vessel was no longer in view. How can he leave? she thought. Barbados might just as well be at the other end of the world; I fear I shall never see him again.

Will was overjoyed to see her. Anne lied and told him Stede Bonnet had left the plantation weeks ago, and, being bored, she had decided to come here, make some necessary purchases and hobnob with Charles Town society. Not fooled by her smile, Will took his daughter into his arms. Anne wept softly.

"What is it, daughter? What sorrows thee?"

" 'Tis a private grief, Father. I would prefer not to talk about it."

"As ye wish. These lively Charles Town parties will cheer thee up, I warrant. Did'st bring thy prettiest frocks?"

"A few."

"Well, thou must needs buy more. Here's money. To-morrow you must visit the best shops and have a new wardrobe made up. Annie, I know the fabrics will dazzle thy eyes, cloth from all over the world, India, Japan. 'Tis like London here at Charles Town. Spend the money in this purse. There be more when that be out."

Anne's room overlooked the harbor, crowded with vessels. Small portholes beamed in the dusky night. In the distance the lofty sterns of the great galleons were aglow. She thought about her lover, Stede Bonnet, riding on the vast ocean, and pictured him in his cozy cabin sipping madeira. Her musings now did not ameliorate her situation but only served to make her more miserable. Even tears did not relieve the hollowness of her feelings. She cried the entire night.

Eyes puffed and red, Anne went down to breakfast. Will studied his daughter. 'Tis a deep hurt, he thought. Some man, I warrant. Thank God, the creature be resilient. Many women would have taken to their beds long before this.

"Annie, tonight be a grand ball at the house of Nicholas Trott, judge and councilman of this province. We are to attend. Buy something befittin' the occasion, will ye, girl? And stay away from the docks, and the taverns too, mind ye. Judge Trott be a fartin' tyrant, and has hung up many a pirate in the bay, but still some despicable brigands roam this port, and I would protect thee from such rogues. Take thy woman along."

"Yes, Father."

"Well, I be off about some business now. And remember this, girl, the more ye cry the less you'll piss."

Anne burst into laughter. Will's smile beamed at her. In all the world he wanted nothing more than to see her happy. However, he had his own idea of what would make Anne happy.

Anne made several quick purchases in a few of the shops in the fashionable district of town. After lunch, she told her woman that she meant to nap the entire afternoon and would no longer require her.

But trying to sleep only made her more restless. Bored with her own melancholy, she got up, put on her dark blue breeches and woolen camel frieze coat. After tucking her hair up under her plumed hat and concealing a dagger in the sheath in her boot, she went out.

Anne walked out to the bay, then along the wharves

running down to the water. The odd-shaped buildings intrigued her, as did the motley assortment of humanity who paraded in and out of them. The cast of characters was astounding: fancy gamblers, slick thieves, tattered cutthroats and bloated merchants. A loud voice, sounding like that of a street barker, brought Anne to a part of the wharf where African slaves were being auctioned. Black men, their genitals barely covered, their wounds seared closed, were led roughly by chains anchored to heavy iron collars, and urged forward with a whip.

Flesh for sale, and not even much of that; I can see every bone in their bodies. Disgusting. She looked around for her father and, seeing him at the rear of the crowd, moved away from the group.

She stepped into a tavern, ordered a pint and watched with curiosity and delight the big bosomed, tawdry whores. Loosely laced bodices allowed easy access to the hands of sailors, who caroused with no inhibitions. A lusty seaman was working enthusiastically with one hand under the skirts of a comely wench while his other hand fondled her delicious bosom.

Anne did not at first see James Bonny, who was sitting alone at a table in the corner of the room. A full-bodied doxy descended the stairs, came over to him and sat on his lap, dropping several coins into his hand. He held his hand extended for a moment after she had finished and, with a disgusted sigh, she rummaged in her bodice, hauling out one breast, then the other, until she found yet another coin.

Fired by liquor, men arguing over women, over dice or the price of sugar, all ultimately came to the same folly—fighting. Bawdy language accompanied a myriad of blows, knocks, thwacks, licks and wallops.

Just the thing to cure my melancholy, she thought. Anne downed her pint and leaped into the center of the fray. Smashing chairs and onion bottles, she issued stinging blows to several patrons, driven on by the energy of the vilest phrases she could think of.

Anne managed to exhaust herself in ten minutes. Fighting

her way out of the thickest part of the struggle, she stood on the fringes of the battle and watched. James Bonny was being severely pummeled by nearly a dozen wenches who, obviously caught up in the spirit of the fight, had decided to seek revenge. Anne took two deep breaths and resolved to rescue the unfortunate man, who was now at the bottom of the heap of women.

"Off it now, get out of it, you bloody fens, whoreson bitches!" she shouted as one by one she propelled the women into tables and chairs. One undaunted wench returned and jumped on her back. "Mount some other bull, ye fuckin' cunt." And again that one went flying. Anne bit, scratched, punched and tore her way into a veritable heap of bodies. Finally she pulled away the last and looked down at the man who was curled up with his arms protectively over his head. When he felt no more blows he unfolded himself and looked up at his rescuer, his face sweaty and beet red.

"Why, Mister Bonny," said Anne, startled. "I did never think we would meet again, and certainly not in such a perilous circumstance."

"Mistress O'Brannon," he whimpered, "be that you?"

"Aye," she said, pulling him to his feet. "Methinks you could use an ale."

James Bonny chuckled nervously. "I almost did not recognize thee, Mistress Anne, in men's clothing."

" 'Tis convenient sometimes, Mister Bonny."

"Aye, most. 'Tis fortunate for me thee was about today."

"Why were those women angry at thee?"

"Ah, they be jealous, is all."

"All o' them? Ye are a bold rascal indeed to have so many."

"The lot be not half your worth, Mistress Anne."

"Now, no need for flattery. I did only save thy life, no more."

" 'Tis the truth, no flattery intended. I would have spoken sooner but I was shifted away from your party by that fulsome blackbearded fellow, and I had no opportunity to return. If I had, I would have stood outside your window all night."

"Sir, surely you overstep yourself."

"Nay, Mistress. I mean no offense."

He ordered rum punch and continued talking without pause. "There be so many wonderful places I would love to show you. We have been received in the best houses here. Tonight we are to Judge Trott's."

"And I also."

"Oh, wonderful! May I escort you?"

"My father takes me tonight, but. . . ."

Captain Bellamy approached the table, swatted James on the shoulder and said, "Come on, move your arse, man, we have work!"

"Oh, Cap'n, remember Mistress O'Brannon?"

"Well, damn me eyes! 'Tis she." He pulled up a chair and ordered punch. "Why Mistress Anne, what brings thee to Charles Town?"

"The shops and other pastimes."

" 'Tis good to see thee. We be off soon, in two days I think. My sloop is bein' careened even now."

"Where are ye off to, Captain Bellamy?"

"The Bahamas. New Providence."

"Is it pleasant there?"

"Overrun with pirates, like Bonny here."

"Nay, cut that, man. It be not funny any more."

"Really, Captain, are there pirates there?"

"Yes, hundreds of 'em. 'Tis an excitin' place, I tell thee. Nary a dull moment in Nassau Town, I warrant ye that. No place for a lady, though."

"Why is that?"

" 'Tis a rough bunch there, swearin' and fightin' all the day sometimes."

"Worse than this place a few minutes ago, Mister Bonny?"

"Oh, about the same."

"Well, that be not much."

"Were there a fight here?" asked the captain.

"Aye, a grand fight," said James. "I would have been killed if Mistress Anne had not stepped in."

"You mean ye were rescued by this woman here?"

"Aye."

"And ye be not ashamed of that?"

"Why? It were a dozen against one."

"A dozen what, rats? Ants?"

"Women."

"God's Death, man, ye be nothin' but a bleedin' cock-bawd. Ye should have let them eat him up, Mistress Anne. It be no honest employment for any man of salt."

The winter ball given by Nicholas Trott, Esquire, was the event of the season. It was a grand affair; any person of consequence within reach of the Port of Charleston was sure to be there. As judge of the Vice-Admiralty and Chief Justice of the Province of South Carolina, Trott was looking for political support among the colonists. The merchants depended on the Admiralty to keep trade safe from piracy and Trott's political life depended on the prosperity of the province. In this way a practical code was established, one hand washing the other.

Tonight the judge was maneuvering his way through his guest list, working under the premise that whatever God in His infinite wisdom did not provide, he, Nicholas Trott, Esquire, would buy.

Anne arrived with her father. She had never looked more beautiful. Dressed in a dove-colored damask gown patterned with large emerald trees, Anne brought every eye in the room to herself. Almost popping all the buttons on his best waistcoat, Will paraded her past scores of gaping eyes and introduced her to their host. As the judge, a good-looking man in his fifties, took her hand, Anne noticed that his skin was as soft as a baby's.

Leaving them to converse, Will retreated to the punch table and began to fortify himself against the evening.

Anne was trapped. How rude, she thought, to dump me on this old fart, this pulpit thumper, with not even a glass of punch to see me through it. This man will talk all night,

I fear, and naught but platitudes. He has not looked into my eyes once, only stares at my cleavage. He is a man the same as all the others, no matter how much religion he spouts.

"Yes, we all be ambassadors of Christ, Mistress O'Brannon, whether we wear the cloth or no," was the judge's pious remark.

"Really, Judge Trott, women, too?"

"Oh, women most of all, since they be responsible for the moral upbringing of the children. A child cannot be saved if he hath an unholy mother."

"Even so."

"Aye, Mistress Anne. Who else will teach him?"

"Education be an important thing all around, think you, Judge?"

"Aye, Mistress. Yet I fear the principles of religion instilled by education be defaced by the infidelity and skepticism of these wicked times."

"If this be true, I be possessed of much wasted knowledge."

"You, my dear? Hast had the benefit of much learning?"

"Aye, sir, a most thorough education."

" 'Tis unusual for a woman, and most unnecessary."

"Unnecessary! How unnecessary? Thee didst say a moment ago the child's education be the responsibility of the mother. How can she teach if she is ignorant?"

"Only religious training be the mother's duty."

"Oh, she need know naught but her Bible; is that the way of it?"

"Yes. Only that, no further education be needed for the woman to perform her function."

"And to thy mind, Judge, what is a woman's function? I am most anxious to heart it."

"Why . . . to provide a good home, be an obedient wife, bear and raise up many children in the sight of the Lord."

"That is all? Hath the woman no mind which she must use to her advantage and to the well-being of her family?"

"No, not a mind like a man's mind. 'Tis not the same."

"What is the difference?"

"Well . . . I cannot rightly say. All I know is that it be sinful for a woman to have any thought contrary to that of her husband."

God's Death, this man is impossible. Mother has said all creatures be equal, but if this narrowminded, ignorant son of a bitch is my equal, I am a toad.

"Woman is the root of Adam's sin and sin be the debasing of human nature."

Sin now, I was wondering when the old pisser would get to that subject. "Dost mean, sir, that woman is sinful by her very nature and can do naught to help herself?"

"Yes." Jesus God! "I have heard, Judge Trott," Anne ventured, trying to introduce a new topic of conversation, "that you are the scourge of all those who steal from the sea."

"Aye, my dear, I be that, for they are thieves and murderers. What's more, Mistress Anne, as if it be not sin enough for these rogues to steal and kill, they be also perverse."

"How perverse?"

"I cannot say, lady, in thy presence, for it be related to matters of intimacy. 'Tis unseemly."

"I am no prude, Judge Trott." How dare he! This man has raped me with his eyes this half hour as we stand here and now he has the gall to call other men's actions perverse. God's Death, the thing in all the world I can least abide is a hypocrite. "Wilt say, please, what you mean by perverse?"

"Well, 'tis common knowledge, and I have it from their own vile lips, that they be . . . sodomites. It doth befoul my soul to say the word e'en now."

"If they are willing, and they harm no one, where is the sin in that?"

"Why, Mistress, those actions be most perverse and unnatural. 'Tis against the law of God."

"Where in the Bible does it say that?"

"I . . . cannot recall, but 'tis there, I know it. 'Tis a most unnatural, sinful, wicked action."

"I do well believe thou wouldst hang a man for it."

" 'Tis even so. I would pray for his repentance, for no sin is unforgivable, but I'd see him dangle surely."

"Oh, Mistress Anne, how good to see you," gushed James Bonny. "Evenin', Judge Trott, wonderful party. It doth befit your greatness. I thought you might take a cool drink with me, Mistress Anne. With your permission, Judge."

"Why, yes, of course."

Walking away eased Anne's tension. She tightened her grip on Bonny's arm. The entire evening so far had been a strain. Bonny misunderstood and took her touch to mean affection.

"Now we are even, Mister Bonny; you have saved me."

"How so, Mistress Anne?"

"From that vinegar-pissing old judge."

"Oh, there be no uncommon courage in that."

"It takes courage for a pirate like you to come so near that tyrant. He could send thee to the gallows and sun dryin', dost know that?"

"I know it, but I am no pirate, Mistress Anne."

"I do but tease, Mister Bonny. Wouldst fetch me a glass of punch, sir? I am about to perish from thirst."

"At once, milady." He bowed and hurried off.

Anne looked around, observing the other ladies somewhat critically. God, what a life, she thought. Doth make me shudder to think I must spend the rest of my days in this fashion. It took these biddies an entire day to dress—and for what, just to get their husbands some advancement. Or, worse, to bandy words with self-righteous hypocrites like the judge there. 'Tis not for me, that's certain.

I need to free myself from this inane society afore I am swallowed up by boredom. 'Tis like quicksand. I must marry, there is no other course for a woman. Listen to me, I sound like the psalm-spouting, old holier-than-thou-hot-Trott, but 'tis true nonetheless. This society provides no other choices. I could marry James Bonny and go to sea. I have always loved the sea. 'Twould be for convenience only, for 'tis certain I do not love him. Oh, he knows the value of flattery and would woo the world if he could. I can play the opportunist too and turn the tables on him. He doth woo my money, not me, for I am in for a handsome sum the day I marry. The whole world knows it.

Bonny was at her side again. She said, "Oh, you have returned. I perish here from lack of company."

"Ye are truly radiant tonight. Such a lovely gown, picturesque yet subtle in color, but 'tis no match for thy beauty."

"You are too kind, Mister Bonny."

"And this gown does blend so well with the brilliance of thy hair, and the warm glow of thy complexion. Your beauty dost rival the goddess Venus, Mistress Anne."

"When do you sail for New Providence?" queried Anne, eager to change the subject. That she was beautiful was scarcely news to her.

"Tomorrow," he said with a sigh.

"So soon?"

"Yes, there be high adventure for us in the Bahama Islands, excitin' times and good fortune."

"Indeed! By high adventure, dost thou mean pirating?"

"Oh, Mistress Anne, ye are too clever for me," he said with a glint in his eye. "Dost know I have a house in New Providence, the largest on the whole island. And I have many acquaintances there. We do lead the high life."

"Gracious! High adventure, high life, 'tis most tempting."

"Oh, if I could tempt ye, Mistress Anne. Just think, a sea of jewels awaits the finding, galleons laden with gold just for the taking."

"A lady cannot travel without a husband, Mister Bonny. 'Tis not proper."

"Oh, that be easily managed."

"Indeed!" Too easily, I fear, for him. "Dost have any money, Mister Bonny?"

"Not yet, but I will."

'Tis my money he thinks of, I warrant. This marriage will be to my advantage or I'll none of't. He is easy to manipulate and used to being cuckolded by both his wenches and his "buisness parnters," I'd wager.

Turning around, she saw another acquaintance. "Ah, Mister Bellamy. I hear you leave us tomorrow."

"Aye, Mistress Anne, my sloop be ready and the sea awaits, fresh and beautiful. Would that you could go with us."

"What think you of marriage, Mister Bellamy?"

"Ah . . . well. Mistress Anne, I do not know what to say."

"I mean in general, Captain Bellamy. I but seek your opinion; 'tis not a proposal."

"Oh, my opinion. Well now, methinks marriage be a grand thing for them that wants it, but it be worthless as a social institution. 'Tis only another means of revenue whereby the clergy robs poor people."

"Mister Bonny here has asked me to marry him. What think you of that, Captain Bellamy?"

"Why, Bonny, you old rascal. I never thought ye had it in you to bed one woman for more'n a fortnight."

"I know you be the cap'n, Charles Bellamy, but ye go too far. Kindly step outside with me."

"Oh, come now, James, I do but tease. 'Tis a fine idea. What says the lady's father?"

"Ah. . . ."

"Well, old man, that be a thing must be done first, ye know. Well, there he is, be about it." Bellamy walked away.

"Ah . . . Mistress Anne, didst meant that . . . you would marry me?" Bonny stammered, suddenly realizing that Anne was in dead earnest.

"Yes, and go with thee to New Providence. But I know my father. We will wed and ask him later."

God, thought Bonny, I never did think it would be so easy to get her. I was almost prepared to stay ashore and become a gentleman planter like Major Bonnet. I could do that yet if her father demands it. It matters not to me if money comes withal.

At dawn they were married. Anne put all her belongings aboard Bellamy's sloop in secret. She had no idea how her father would react but she feared his reaction would not be kindly. James Bonny was not a man of means and there was always the possibility that Will would disinherit her. She must prepare for the worst.

Will looked at the young couple standing hand in hand before him and was momentarily struck dumb. All his dreams were shattered. He could not believe that Anne had betrayed him so.

" 'Tis true, Father. I have married him."

"How could thee marry such a worthless fellow with not one penny to his name?"

"He has other qualitites."

"Name one." James waited, but heard no response from Anne. "God's Death, woman, how could ye cheapen yourself so? You be both rich and beautiful. Ye could take your pick of the province. And what does thee do, choose a man of the sea, a shiftless fellow with not enough wit to wipe his own arse."

"I be honest in my proposal, sir."

"Don't birdmouth with me. Thou hast stolen my daughter and now ye want her money too. Well, y'll not have it, hear me! Never! You fishfaced milksop! An arse worm for a son-in-law, God's Blood! Girl, I cannot understand thee! What is he, a good fucker? Be that it?"

Anne controlled her response to this last comment. Their marriage had not as yet been consummated and very likely it never would be, but Anne did not want her father to know that. He would have dragged her away to annulment forthwith.

"At least we be lawfully wed. If I have issue they will be legitimate." Anne wished she could retract her words but it was too late. "Oh, Father, I did not mean to hurt thee."

"Thank the Lord your dear mother be not here to see this. Thou dost decry her too, ye know. Ungrateful bastard! I have given thee every opportunity, and ye chooses to roam the seas with this pirate! Yes, and smuggler too. Dost think I know naught of your activities, puppy? Ye are a coward and a thief and a pimp besides. Pray God ye have not issue of him, girl, for ye will regret it. 'Twould be good, however, to see thee fry in thy own grease. Don't come to me! No, never! I disown thee! Think not to collect your dowry! I disinherit thee this minute!''

"You will give me nothing, then, in parting?"

"Only me everlastin' hatred!"

"Goodby." After a moment she said, "Willst bid me farewell, then? If only for what we have been to each other?"

Will wanted to take Anne in his arms but he could not do it, especially in front of James Bonny. Tears fell down his cheeks and splashed onto his satin waistcoat. They were tears of frustration and loneliness, for he knew he could not stop her and he would miss her. God, how he would miss her.

"All right, then," she said, as she turned to leave.

"List me, one more word," he said portentously through his tears. "Rashness will be thy undoin', remember that, Anne, Mistress Anne . . . *Bonny!*"

The variant blue greens of the Bahama Bank were awesome. The water, as clear as crystal, reflected the milky white sands of the shallows. Anne watched the gentle action of the waves and calmly reflected upon this, her daring new venture in life. She was as rootless now as any sailor who must claim the great ocean as his home. The active February breeze enlivened her and the warm sun embraced her like a reassuring mother. Although she saw her life stretched before her like an imperceptible ocean void, Anne was not afraid. She felt at home here in this warm part of the world, and free with nature, not confined in the restrictive bricks and walls of society's conventions.

That night, still at the rail, Anne watched the caps of white water fold into the blackness of the sky and ocean. She was fascinated by the green sparks of phosphorus dancing in the wake of the vessel. Dense black clouds floated across the sky, mantling the lights of a thousand stars.

By morning the sloop was nearing its destination. The anticipation of her arrival in New Providence increased with every dip of the bow. James Bonny was lying on the deck, shirtless, basking in the bright sunshine. They had not spoken since their departure from Charles Town, he being acutely disappointed at the loss of her dowry and the denial of her bed, and she too upset at having left her father in his lonely condition.

The man is empty inside, she thought, staring at Bonny's inert body. No amount of money could fill up the void within him. No amount of sunshine can bring even a blush of honesty to his character, for his soul is ashy.

"Look, a man-o-war bird!" Anne's eyes shot up to view the large black bird sailing by; then she spoke to the boy who had alerted her.

"Is this your first voyage, lad?"

"No, Mistress. I 'ave been bred up to the sea an' 'ave sailed all over the Caribbean."

"How old are you, boy?"

"Fourteen, Mistress, but I will be fifteen next month."

"Where were ye born?"

"Barbados. Me name be John Burn."

"Dost know a man, a planter there, named Major Bonnet?"

"No, Mistress."

Bellamy came up to the deck.

"Excuse me, but I must be about my work."

Captain Bellamy ruffled the boy's hair affectionately as he walked by him. He inhaled the fresh sea air and scanned the sky for birds. Thick deposits of rich brown sargassum, looking like floating carpets, drifted by.

"Cap'n," shouted the helmsman, "we should be within sight of New Providence very soon now."

"Thank thee, mate. Keep her steady."

"Aye, sir."

"Who be your helmsman, Captain?"

"That be Dennis McKarthy. He's a bold fellow and a good pilot, not shiftless like some men I know. I mean no offense, Mistress Anne, I just speak God's truth." He went over to Bonny and kicked his boot. "Wake up, man, get thee indoors afore the sun fries thee."

"It be winter," Bonny said listlessly. "How can the sun be so hot?"

"Well, look at yourself, man. Worthless sot," Bellamy muttered, as he stared out to sea; he had better things to think about than James Bonny. Greater issues were always on his mind: the wretched state of the human condition all over the world and the unpredictable shifting sands on the ocean floor. One day a wreck might be in one place and a month later it might be buried in sand or moved away by the strong currents. He was obsessed by Spanish plate. The sunlight glistened on the water like billions of pieces of eight, and New Providence stretched low and flat before him.

Lying at twenty degrees north latitude, the island of New Providence was almost inaccessible in every direction due to the unbroken violence of the sea. Dennis McKarthy skillfully maneuvered the sloop into Nassau Harbour, formed by Hog Island, which ran parallel to Nassau Town for five miles from east to west.

"That cay belongs to Judge Trott," said Bellamy. " 'Tis called Hog Island."

" 'Tis aptly named," said Anne.

"He were the government here till 1698."

"Is there any government now?"

"One Cap'n Thomas Walker, so called judge of the Vice-Admiralty, but no one pays him any mind. The place is slowly bein' overrun with pirates. In a few months' time this island will be headquarters for all the Caribbean. The harbour here guarantees safety. No ship of war can pass over this bar and, the harbour bein' open at both ends, 'twould take two men-o-war to close her up."

"Be that the town?"

"Aye. Nassau, 'tis called."

From a distance the tiny thatched huts improvised from driftwood looked quaint and comfortable nestled among the giant palms which were flexing gracefully in the breeze. But once inside the harbour the atmosphere took on a more vulgar character. Assorted buoyant garbage, including a bloated dead body, floated past the sloop. James Bonny clung to the rail, adding to the refuse problem by casting up his accounts into the harbour. His pallor turned from bright red to greenish yellow before he collapsed on the deck.

The arrival of any vessel was an event of import, so a representative group from Nassau society greeted them. The welcoming committee included a cross section of Nassau's elite. Sprinkled amid gaudily dressed pirates were thieves, slaves, Conchs, mulattoes, escaped criminals, doxies, derelicts, gypsies and peddlers.

A few of the colorful pirates sported equally colorful appendages: a wooden leg painted with yellow flowers, a hooked hand of etched silver, an eyepatch of batik print. Tattered shirts were stuck into soiled pantaloons or breeches which terminated in shreds at the knees. Waists were wound thick with striped sashes large and long enough to be used as blankets. Most pirates wore their wealth rather than lose it to thieves. Great jeweled crosses hung irreverently from swarthy necks amid numerous twisted chains of gold. Arms were braceleted from wrist to elbow and fingers ringed with precious gem stones. Hoops of gold dangled from pierced ears.

Anne was amazed at the amount of artillery worn. Pistols hung in braces across hairy chests, cutlasses hung from gem-studded baldrics, knives were stuck in massive leather belts slung low under Falstaffian bellies. One man even had his wooden leg stuck round with pistols.

Pregnant women restrained barefoot children, whose little arms strained almost to the point of popping out of their shoulder sockets with their efforts to free themselves from their mothers' grasp. Shyer children hung tentatively to the dresses of old grandmothers whose bosoms drooped to their waists. Dogs barked, babies cried, cats hissed and parrots shieked gross obscenities.

Captain Bellamy took Anne's arm and helped her onto the dock. As they walked through the crowd the black women reached out to touch Anne's golden hair, beautiful face, high round breasts and curvaceous hips. Her hand tightened on Bellamy's arm.

"Nothing to fear, Mistress Anne, they do but admire your beauty. These people must touch; 'tis their way. They be like children—no offense intended, only admiration. Come, we will go to the King's Head Inn for refreshment. 'Tis always the first stop of any seaman what loves his grog. My friend Cap'n Jennings be the proprietor. We will receive splendid attention, fine victuals and excellent liquor."

"Where is James? I had quite forgotten him."

"There he be, laggin' astern."

Bonny, head down, was dragging himself along the narrow road some distance behind them. A tall, massively built Welshman bolted from the tavern and stamped down the road past Bellamy and Anne.

"Hey, Bart," shouted Bellamy. "Can't ye speak, man?"

The man stopped and, turning toward them, said, "I be in no humor for conversation, Charles. I be too angry now to be civil to anyone, even you, old friend."

Anne was struck by the richness of his appearance. It was not so much the crimson damask breeches and waistcoat he wore, but the diamond cross which hung from what seemed to her a dozen gold chains about his neck. The magnificent jewels flashed and sparkled in the sunlight. He turned, and, blustering down the road, flattened James Bonny, who was bent double with stomach cramps and did not see him coming.

"What, further delays?" shouted Roberts, picking Bonny up by the scruff of his neck. "Your name, sirrah?" His voice was so loud that everyone stopped on the road to witness the scene. Bonny stuttered for a half minute, unable at first to spit out his name.

"Who is he?" Anne asked, almost amused at Bonny's plight.

"That be one Cap'n Bartholomew Roberts—Black Bart he be called by them that know and fear him."

"Where do ye come from, James Bonny?" boomed the captain as he took a pair of pistols out of a silk sling.

"SSSSSSouth CaCaCaCaCaCarolina, ssssssir."

"Pity, 'twould be a kindness to kill thee. Ye needs killin' to mend thy speech. Step aside." One sweep of his hand and Bonny was in the gutter. Once again the man barreled down the road to the harbor.

Before he was completely out of sight Roberts stopped to have a few words with young John Burn, who had just come swaggering up the road, carrying his knapsack over his shoulder.

"Wait," said Bellamy, "that be me ship's boy Roberts be talkin' with now. God help him, I hope he does the lad no mischief." They watched John Burn drop his bundle and extend his hand, just as Roberts raised both pistols to the boy's head and fired.

"God's fuck!" Anne could not believe what she had seen. Bonny had fainted. Charles Bellamy turned away with his head hanging, and beat his fist against his thigh. Roberts walked away, swinging the smoking pistols at his side, leaving the boy lying dead in the road.

"Jesus God, a boy's life, his dreams afore him, snuffed out like that! Why?" demanded Anne. "Dost seek no revenge, Charles Bellamy? What kind of friend is he to kill thy ship's boy?"

"He did not know he were my boy. The man be dangerous. The devil himself dares not tangle with Bartholomew Roberts when he be in one of his dark moods."

"But why kill the boy, just a boy he met on the road offerin' a friendly hand?"

"Roberts were thwarted but two times in his life, once at Barbados and once at Martencia. They applied their cannons from the battlements and would not let him stop and take on water. His crew were near dead from thirst. This angered him. Since that time he takes his revenge by executin', in the very manner you saw there, any man he meets who comes from either of those two islands."

"God's Mercy, the lad was from Barbados," cried Anne in astonishment. "Poor lad, he never knew why he died.

He was so hopeful at this new venture. Only this morning. . . ."

"Dost no good to ruminate; the boy be dead. I be sorry too, he were a good lad. But," philosophized Bellamy, "as hypocrisy is essential to politics, so killin' be a necessary part of piracy. I have seen men killed for less reason."

The King's Head Inn was at the end of a long line of thatched huts facing the bay. The yard was decorated with bowsprit figures of several wrecked galleons, a few rotted iron anchors, and fishing floats of colored glass encased in net. Conch shells, their coral-pink fans turning chalk white in the sun, bordered the path to the door.

Hinged to the tops of the two small windows on either side of the door were flat boards covered with palm fronds. They were both propped open, allowing only some slight breeze into the tavern and very little light. A cutlass and an ax were crossed and nailed up on the flimsy door made from bamboo strips.

Captain Jennings was waiting to greet them at the path. "Bellamy, how be ye? Hast been some time, has it not?"

"Aye, Commodore. This be Anne Bonny."

"Cap'n Jennings, at your service, Madame," he said, taking her hand and kissing it graciously. "It have been some time since such beauty have graced our little island. Be that James Bonny coming behind? What, James, hast married this beauty?"

"Aye," he said wanly.

"Why, James, what ails thee? Come inside, man."

"Sun and fear ail him, Captain Jennings," said Anne. "He hath met with Captain Roberts just now."

"Ah yes, I heard some noise. Thee be lucky to be alive, James. Some country hath lost a citizen. Bart doth not expend shot lest he aims to kill someone. Which be it this time, a Barbadian or Martenican?"

"A Barbadian, and me ship's boy, worse luck," grumbled Bellamy.

" 'Tis a pity," said Jennings. "I do believe the man intends to depopulate those islands singlehanded. Well, on to happier business, I trust. Welcome to my humble establishment, Mistress Anne.'' Jennings swung open the door, flooding the smoke-filled room with light.

"Shut the fuckin' door! Dost mean to blind us, Cap'n?"

Once out of the bright afternoon sunlight Anne could see nothing. But she could smell out the patrons who were sweating in the closed room and she noticed a strange odor to the pipes they were smoking. As her eyes adjusted to the darkness she began to recognize some of the men who had been standing at the dock less than half an hour ago. Jennings introduced her around and familiar aspects took on names. The Falstaffian figure with the massive leather belt was Benjamin Hornigold. Wearing more gold crosses than the Archbishop of Canterbury was Thomas Burgess. The hairy chest, hung all over with half a dozen pistol braces, was that of Captain Edward England; the wooden leg outfitted for battle belonged to George Allen, and the print eyepatch to Captain Benjamin Edwards. All extended their greetings in the form of grunts, clanking tankards or how do's.

One gentleman, however, rose to his feet and, bowing, said, " 'Oh, she doth teach the torches to burn bright! Did my heart love till now? Foreswear it, sight! For I ne'er saw true beauty till this night.' "

"Sit down, you arse hole. The lady would like to eat, not listen to thee spout Billy."

Romeo and Juliet, Act I, scene V," said Anne.

"Correct, milady. Now 'ere's a lass after me own heart. Alfred Butler at your service, Madame. Whatever your pleasure. . . ."

"Sit down afore I toss yer arse out of 'ere!" shouted Captain Edwards. "Yer spoilin' me dinner drivelin' all over it."

"Beg pardon, Madame, for the crassness of me mates 'ere. . . ."

"Ah, bugger off!"

One man belched, another farted loudly, several of the others were smacking their lips so loudly that one could hear nothing else. More food was spattered about the surface of the wooden table than was in the plates, and eating utensils consisted primarily of knives and fingers.

"Here's our supper at last," said Bellamy, rubbing his hands together.

A fat lively middleaged woman with peppery hair brought in a portion of roast pig and set it before them.

"Anne," said Jennings, "this be me woman. Emma, meet Anne Bonny."

"How do, Mistress Anne," said Emma with a curtsy. "And what brings thee to New Providence?"

"I wanted adventure, so I married that lout over there," Anne said, looking at James, who was sitting at a table in the corner playing in the bosom of one of the doxies. One by one women were coming into the tavern. As the door opened Anne caught glimpses of the beautiful lingering colors of the Bahamian twilight.

"A beauty like yerself can find a better man than 'im, surely," said Emma, sipping her ale and wiping her mouth with the back of her hand. "I warrant ye'll find adventure without 'im. There be fine strappin' men in and out o' Nassau; ye'll not want for entertainment, either." Anne laughed. Emma reached up and lighted the oil lamp which was hanging over the table. Then she got up, took their cups and went to the bar to fetch more ale.

With the eating over, the captain's patrons began to do some serious drinking. Each man had his favorite doxy perched on one knee. The lanterns allowed more illumination and Anne looked around at the room and its occupants.

The ceiling was decorated with black flags and pennants, many of which displayed the skull and crossbones. Gaudy trophies, silver cups, jeweled chalices lined the shelf behind the serving bar. Rich tapestry and mats of plaited straw hung on the walls. The furniture was an odd assortment of driftwood tables, barrel kegs and stools, and hand-carved velvet chairs, obviously unwilling contributions from the Spanish and French governments. Carved on the beams were the names of a few of the pirate captains who had terrorized the Spanish Main: Benjamin Hornigold, Henry Jennings, Edward Teach, Charles Vane, Edward England and Bartholomew Roberts.

Emma returned and sat down. "Whew, 'tis crowded tonight. Many vessels be in. 'Tis like to get even more raucous as the evenin' wears on, if I know these boys. I hear from Cap'n Bellamy that you be capable of protectin' yerself if there be trouble 'ere. I did fear thee would not be safe amongst this crowd. Methinks ye be the only woman 'ere what come on 'er own account. We all be rescued either from slaver or hell ship, even the men waitin' table. They be a scurvy lot, all thieves and murderers, like these women. Jennings be the only man on the island to give 'em work. Now ye know why 'e calls this tavern the King's 'Ead Inn."

"No, I don't see the significance. I thought at first it was misguided loyalty for an outlaw of the king's justice to be so bold."

"Well, King's 'Ead Inn be but another name for Newgate prison. 'Tis a grand joke, ain't it?" Emma said, laughing. "Wilt excuse me, Anne? I must get back to me tasks and watch awhile lest these boys steal too much of me rum."

"Aye. I think I'll step outside for a breath of air."

The night was warm and the growing number of bodies crowding into the tiny inn made the air close. Anne went outside and looked out to sea. The sky was filled with stars and the cool ocean breeze was refreshing.

This is my first night on a Caribbean island; I want to remember it. She listened to the rustling sounds of the palms and watched their graceful leaves sway in the light of the waning moon. The fresh smells of orange blossoms, jasmine and pine cleared her head. She watched the surging whiteness of the ocean waves striking the outlying reefs and saw the stillness of the shadows of the small vessels in the harbor. Locking all these sensations in her memory, Anne went back inside, drawn by the music of the hornpipes.

She jigged until she was too tired to lift her feet any more, then plopped herself down in a green velvet armchair and surveyed the scene like a grand dame at a play. Chairs and tables had been overturned; a few drunken pirates were passed out on the floor. In the corner, one burly corsair was molesting his equally brawny messmate. One sailor was drilling his doxy on top of the banquet table, while another was issuing like treatment to his woman against the wall. When too many bodies cluttered the floor, some were thrown outside by the waiters. These interruptions seemed in no way to disturb the rising pitch of their merriment. The music, singing and dancing mingled with the sounds of sexual activity until the whole room reached one hideously colossal climax.

At the very flootide of the action the door swung open and a tall blond man swept into the room. He was dressed entirely in brilliant blue satin, and was hatless. Running his fingers through his white-blond hair, his Lydian figure slumped into an attitude of despondency.

"Oh, *merde!* I have missed zis grand orgy once again. Oh, *c'est la vie. Ah, M'sieu James, mon cher. Comment ca va?*" Crossing the room, he lifted James Bonny out of his chair and whisked him to the dance floor, Bonny being powerless to break away. The graceful gentleman was swinging and dipping Bonny about the dance floor, completely oblivious to his protestations. When he was finished, he escorted Bonny back to his chair, kissed his hand, bowed and sat him down.

"Henri, you shit!" shouted James Bonny, too frustrated and angry to say anything else.

"Zis man lacks all sense of courtesy. Ungrateful bastard! *Au 'voir,* James." Hitching up his testicles, the man turned and walked away. Seeing Emma, he flew into her arms. "Emma! *Ma cherie!* I have missed you. Where have you been all zis day?" Hugging her tightly, he puckered his lips and kissed her on the mouth.

"Onree, wait here. I want you to meet someone," said Emma. "Fix Onree a rum punch."

"Oh, *merci,* zis dancing, she make me so hot." Stepping up to the bar and slamming down his fists, he said in a loud deep voice, "Rum and water, leave out zat fruit juice, she gives me loose bowels. I cannot afford to be tender zere!" He laughed and slapped the buttocks of the seaman standing next to him. Emma took Anne's hand and brought her up to the bar.

"Onree, I would like you to meet Anne Bonny." He swung around. "*Mon Dieu!* She is gorgeous. *Cherie,* you are as tall and as beautiful as a man. Look at zose eyes, like fire, and zat hair. What I could do wiz zat hair! And zis body! I am tempted to make love wiz you. *Sacre bleu,* for ze first time in Henri's whole life, he desires to make love wiz a woman, God forgive him."

"I am pleased to meet you, Henri."

"Ah, such music, listen to ze music of zat voice. Henri Duplaissez, *a votre service,* Madame," he said, taking Anne's hand and kissing it tenderly. "Oh, Emma, I am hopelessly in love."

"Oh, Onree, you be always hopelessly in love."

"Emma," said Anne, "I am very tired. I think I will return to Captain Bellamy's sloop and retire for the night."

"What! I will not hear of zis. Sleep on a filthy scow? Never! Not when Henri have an entire house. Come wiz me, you beauteous creature. Good night, Emma. Perhaps tomorrow we shall see you."

"Take good care of the lass, Onree," said Emma warningly.

"What! *Mon Dieu!* She is safer wiz me than wiz most of zese men, is she not?"

"That be true," said Emma. "Goodnight, Anne. You will be comfortable with Onree. He has the best house in all of Nassau."

"Zis is true. Sorry, gentlemen," he said, addressing the entire tavern. "I shall attend you some ozzer night. Zis lady is weary. Goodnight."

He glided out of the room with Anne on his arm. The patrons watched in silence as if a king and queen were exiting a throne room.

154

Anne awakened early but lingered in the wide brass bed, luxuriating in the fragrances carried on the fresh sea air and listening to the music of the morning birds. When she had saturated those senses, she bounded out of bed, went out on the veranda and stood naked, allowing the sea breeze to caress her body. The cloudless sky, gleaming white sands, clusters of coconut palms, lush green vegetation and azure sea looked like a painting at first. A gull swooped low over the calm, bright blue water and the painting came instantly to life. Anne inhaled the Caribbean morning.

Will I feel this renewed vigor with each sunrise? she wondered. Is it possible to tire of such beauty?

Henri was standing by the well, staring up at her. *"Exquise, ravissante.* Anne, you are ze most ravishing beauty in all ze Caribbean. You are even more beautiful zan him." He pointed to the sinewy black man who was loading his fishing boat at the edge of the bay. But the man was too far away for Anne to see. "Come down. I have a surprise for you. Have you ever tried zis drink zey call coffee?"

"Oh, is that the strange odor I smelled earlier?"

"Yes. It is wonderful, much better zan tea in ze morning. It is from South America. Come down. We shall have some *petit dejeuner.*"

Anne dressed quickly, thankful that Henri had made no comment on her lack of apparel, and came downstairs. Henri's house had three stories, each one with a wide veranda which ran east and west, the north side of the building faced the sea. The first floor served as a mercantile shop. Henri sold fabrics, cosmetics, clothing and all manner of personal accessories for men and women. As *maestro sastre* for the Pirate Republic, he set the fashion for the corsair captains and repaired the damages that time and ill fortune had wreaked upon the ladies of the community. The second floor was Henri's general living and entertainment quarters. His rooms were tastefully appointed. Anne now occupied the third floor. While Henri was in the cookhouse preparing breakfast, Anne wandered through the house. It was spotless, and neat almost to a fault.

155

"Ah, Anne, you are about to have a Bahamian breakfast, boiled fish and biscuits. Come sit on ze veranda. Let us enjoy ze view."

"You have a beautiful home, Henri."

"My house is yours. Be free to come and go as you please."

"I hope I do not intrude."

"Ah, no, stay as long as you like. I sew all ze morning long. But zen we can take lunch by ze sea, and you can swim, ride, whatever pleases you. I like to play in ze bed in ze late afternoon." He laughed. "I be no good at night. I am getting older and work too hard all ze day. You have no idea ze effort it takes to beautify zose ugly women and prepare zem for ze evening. I am quite worn out myself. I take a late supper here wiz a few friends. I cook for myself. Ze food at ze tavern is absolutely inedible, fit for pigs only. You must take supper here wiz Henri. I insist. Zen, if I have energy left, I go to ze King's Head for a nightcap. So you see I lead a very quiet life here."

What a pleasant, generous fellow, Anne thought. I think I have found myself a home here.

That afternoon the women arrived and Henri busied himself altering new dresses for some and styling hair and apllying makeup to others. Anne was exhausted just watching him.

"Emma, fix a punch, will you, *cherie?* I am parched," he shouted through the pins in his large white teeth. He worked on for over an hour on what looked to Anne a hopeless enterprise. She went down to the bay for a swim. After the ladies had punch and cakes, they began to be restless with Henri's fussing.

"Oh, 'tis too hot for all this, Onree," said Agnes Bassett. "Come on girls, let's go for a swim."

"*Impossible;* you'll ruin all ze work I've done," screamed Henri.

But they were gone. Removing only their bodices and blouses, the women waded into the water. Henri fluttered all about the beach, cursing loudly in French at the bare-breasted women splashing and playing the water. Anne, who had been swimming a distance away from the group, could not help laughing at the scene. Henri ran into the bay and pulled at the women to come out, fussing at them to watch their coiffures and not to smudge their cosmetics. He carried on in this frantic manner until his sharp eye fell upon the muscular African who was pulling his boat into the shore. Wading out of the water clad only in his skintight breeches, throwing his tape measure around his neck like a scarf, Henri paraded up to the man, who was whacking at a conch.

"You fish every day?" Henri asked.

"Yes."

"Bring your conch to ze house later. I would like to buy from you." Henri smiled provocatively.

The black man smiled back but made no reply.

"You have green turtle?"

"Not today."

"Bring me some pieces of succulent turtle meat sometime. I will pay well for zat." Henri pushed at his member and sighed amorously at the half-naked man. "Would like?" asked Henri, indicting the bulge under his codpiece.

The African shook his head from side to side.

"Chacun à son gout; c'est la vie."

"Henri! Henri!" The husky voice caught his attention. A well-built seaman was running down the beach toward him.

"Cheri!" screamed Henri, and ran to meet him. Both the African on the beach and Anne in the water watched in utter amazement as the two men hurried toward one another, arms outstretched. They met and embraced passionately, then, arm in arm, walked up to the house. Anne's eyes met those of the black fisherman, but only for an instant. He took his cutlass and chopped a gash in the side of the conch, releasing the muscle, then pulled the slimy meat out of the shell. Anne's attention went to the ladies, who were dragging themselves out of the water, their long

skirts clinging comically to their odd shapes. Anne remained in the water until they were gone and the African had left the beach. She had been swimming naked and did not want to astonish all the citizens of the island, at least not on her first day.

Anne installed herself at Henri's. She had forgotten about James Bonny. Most of her days were spent shocking the citizenry by riding stark naked along the beach, on Captain Jennings' horses.

Evenings were spent hostessing Henri's elegant dinner parties. Afterward she would remove her gown and dress in masculine attire to carouse until early morning with the patrons at the King's Head Inn. Soon bored with her daily routine and the same company every night, Anne became as restless as the other islanders. She too began to pray for a vessel to put into the harbor, any vessel, it mattered not, as long as there were people and not cattle on it.

One idle afternoon Anne sat on Henri's veranda with her legs stretched before her and her feet propped on the railing, staring at the sea. Her elysian existence had degenerated into utter boredom. She sat, elbows propped on her stomach, chin resting on the the thumbs of her folded hands, and contemplated the meaning of life.

Henri was perched on a stool beside her, his knees pressed together, sewing on a cocoa brocade for a new pair of breeches for Anne. *"Café?"*

"No, thank you," Anne replied listlessly.

"Are you ill? Do you have ze fever?"

"No, just bored."

"Ah, ze island *maladie.*"

"Henri, who is Charles Vane?"

"One of ze pirate captains, very *sinistre*, you know what I mean? I do not like him."

"Is he handsome?"

"I would not say so. He is a wiry man; not Henri's type at all. Why do you wish to know about him?"

"Just curious. Of all the names carved at the King's

Head, he is the only one I do not know. Does he have a lover?''

"*Mon Dieu!* If you need a lover, why did you not tell Henri sooner? I will bring a dozen men to ze door.''

"I don't need a dozen, just one, but he must be a man of substance.''

"I know many men wiz substance in their codpiece but very little between ze ears.''

"Yes, that is what I wish to avoid.''

"Well, Charles Vane is clever, perhaps too clever. But do not trust him. I hear he enjoys to hurt people, prisoners he captures and also his partners in bed. Besides he has a lover, a devil, I should say.''

"Is she here in New Providence?''

"Yes, but she will not come out till he comes, thank God! She is *diabolique!* She is black Haitian, obeah woman, voudou, you know ze practice?''

"Hum.''

"Eyes like ze devil. No woman go near Charles Vane when he is in Nassau. She will kill her wiz her cutlass or her voudou. Both are deadly. Henri locks himself in his house when she comes into town. Charles Vane, believe me, he is not worth ze trouble. Now his quartermaster, he is somesing else. A very handsome fellow, dark hair, fine eyes and ze smile make you melt away.''

"What is he called?''

"Calico Jack Rackam, ze man after my own heart. I have fabric here now to make him new breeches. He love ze large pattern prints. Now zere is a man for Anne Bonny.''

"Perhaps.''

"Oh, piss,'' he said, tearing the cloth. "How can I create wiz rags?'' Throwing down the garment and putting the back of his hand to his forehead, he got up and stepped languidly from the veranda. Then, closing his eyes, he held his face up to the hot sun, stretched his long arms to the sky and shouted, "Piss! Piss on all ze rags in ze world!'' Suddenly he did a pirouette and screamed. "I have it! Anne, we shall go pirating.''

"What?"

"Pirating, you and me on ze small venture. What say you?"

"You must be joking. You are no more a pirate than I am."

"You underestimate ze both of us, *cherie*. Oh, I am desperate! At night I dream of rich silks, fancy brocades and plush velvets. We could do it, *petite amie*. We get outserlves a little sloop and a crew, a few handsome men, one for you, two or three for Henri, and we sail off on high adventure! What say you, Anne?"

"We will do it! Jennings has a small sloop in need of repair. I am sure we can borrow that. Henri, we can do it! But we will need the talents of Alfred Butler."

"Why him? This is piracy, fighting. We do not need zis actor."

"*Au contraire, mon ami,* an actor be the very person we need. Hast never meet Edward Teach?"

"Ze man zey call Blackbeard? I don't know. He has been here in New Providence?"

"Yes." Anne was on her feet, performing. She wanted to give Henri the full effect of Blackbeard's style. "If you met him you'd remember it, for he is a huge grizzly man, over six feet tall, with a terrifying physique. He has a long blue-black beard all braided and tied with ribbons. I swear by the saints, Henri, that water has never touched the man. He is encrusted over with black powder mixed with sweat and sea spray—a giant devil, soot under his eyes, his teeth tarred, his fat lips curled in a sinister smile." Anne demonstrated. Henri laughed. "You see, 'tis all an act. Even his laughter sounds like ten thousand demons. No one dare come near him. We can do the same, and put on a better show to boot. I'm off to the harbour to find someone who will make our vessel seaworthy and find us a crew."

"Pick only beautiful men, *cherie!*"

Anne leaped on her horse and galloped down the beach in the direction of the town. Captain Jennings had been gone over a month now and his sloop was half submerged at the edge of the harbor. Stopping at the King's Head Inn, Anne discussed her idea with Emma, who quickly gave her permission for the use of Jennings' sloop.

"Dost know a shipwright, Emma?"

"There be one lives near the wharf, methinks. Toby!" shouted Emma. "Come hither, lad." A Negro boy came out from the back of the tavern. "Take Mistress Bonny to Ned Hornshby's hut. I think 'e'll serve thee well, Anne. 'E's a Bristol man. An' McKarthy be 'angin' around 'ere scratchin' 'is arse ever since Bellamy smiled. Perhaps he'll go with ye. These waters be more dangerous than they look. Ye'll need a good pilot."

"I'll ask him tonight. Thanks, Emma. Come on, Toby."

They found Ned Hornsby standing at a workbench outside of his hut. As they approached he squinted up from his work. Anne gave Toby a coin and he ran off. Ned wore a short, square-cut blond beard. A red kerchief anchored his blond curls to his head, except for the few ringlets which had escaped his headband just behind his ears. Anne noticed his heavy rolling walk as he stepped out from behind his workbench and came toward her. His left calf was much thinner than his right and the leg was shorter. Up close, Anne saw that his mustache had been bleached almost white from the sun and tiny hard lines splayed out from the corners of his eyes. Curls of yellow pine clung and mingled in the twirls of his blond chest hair.

"Good day, Mistress."

"Good day. Are ye Ned Hornsby, master shipwright from Bristol?"

"Aye."

"I have need of ye, Ned Hornsby."

"Whatever your pleasure, Mistress, shelves for your cookhouse? Ladies is always needin' more shelves and cupboards."

"No, I need ye to repair Captain Jennings' sloop; I am going on a privateering expedition."

A smile ignited Hornsby's dancing eyes. Seeing her earnest expression, he flushed suddenly under her scrutiny. The man looked down; his blond lashes were thick and full.

Coughing slightly, he said, "Take me to your vessel, Mistress."

"Anne Bonny's me name."

"Aye, Mistress Anne Bonny. Let me fetch me tools and we'll 'ave a look at your sloop." Adjusting his tool sack on his shoulder, he lumbered after Anne, whose long strides put her far ahead of him.

Once at the harbor, they hauled the sloop up onto the beach and bailed out the water. Hornsby then made a quick appraisal, arranged a fair price and immediately set about his work. The damage to the sloop was minimal. Only a few days' work was needed to make the vessel seaworthy.

That night, after six rum punches, Anne convinced Dennis McKarthy to pilot their sloop. Alfred Butler went to his hut immediately after supper to select the costume most befitting the occasion, rehearse his lines, and collect his makeup. Henri signed on the rest of the crew.

The next morning Ned was startled to see Henri and three other men holding hands and skipping down the beach toward him. Anne rode up in a horse-drawn cart bringing lumber, paint and other supplies.

All day Hornsby wore a smile as he watched this crew busy themselves about the vessel. Henri flitted here and there getting his boys situated at some job. Then he diligently set about the difficult task of mending the sails. The crew flapped about the deck, scraping, painting and polishing. They were all dressed in wide striped pantaloons and billowing shirts, and each wore a handsome collection of jewelry.

Each time Nelson Chillingsworth lifted his paintbrush his bracelets clanked to his elbow, causing his hand to shake and spatter paint all over his face. He was spitting and sputtering all day. Cuthbert Goss carried a parasol in one hand while scraping the deck with the other. Roger Gillmore, a great burly fellow, was destined to perform all the heavy tasks. Each time he carried a barrel or crate aboard the sloop, he paused to give Henri a big wet kiss.

Anne studied the charts with Dennis McKarthy. It would

be a short run. A merchantman was expected through the Gulf of Florida any day. Since their sloop was of shallow draft, McKarthy could take the vessel between the Berry Islands and Andros, then stretch over to the Bimini Islands where they planned to wait, hoping to intercept the merchant vessel.

Hornsby came up from the below deck, drying his sweat-soaked body with his blouse and surveying the endeavors of this "pirate crew." He said, smiling, "Well, your sloop is seaworthy, Mistress Bonny. I hope your crew be likewise fit." Shaking his head, he stretched down and lifted his heavy tool sack to his shoulder. He thought to himself, what a group o' worthless seamen. This sloop will never sail out of the harbour, I'll wager that.

Henri emerged from below dressed in a flamboyant outfit of bright yellow pantaloons, green-and-yellow print blouse, and a wide-brimmed hat with a large ostrich feather. He wore a rapier and a heavy leather belt with several knives stuck in it.

"Dear God, unbelievable!" said Hornsby, as he watched Henri sharpen half a dozen knives on a grinding stone.

"Perhaps we are more than we seem at first glance, Ned," said Anne. "Best not scoff and anger us, we be dangerous when roused." Ned could not contain his laughter.

Henri stood up and flicked six knives in rapid succession at the deck, perfectly outlining Ned's withered left foot. Ned was too astonished to move. He stared dumbly at his foot, then looked up at Henri, who was standing, feet spread wide, his hands on his hips and laughing loudly. Anne offered Ned a small bag of coin which was dangling on the point of her rapier. As Hornsby reached for it, she deftly flipped the sack into the air and sliced it open with the rapier, letting the coins spill everywhere on the deck.

"God's teeth!" cried Ned, staring at her in amazement.

"What were you saying, Mister Hornsby, about our unseaworthy crew? Would you like to see what big Roger here can do?"

"No, Mistress Bonny, I believe you. Please forgive me. I did mistake meself. Ye 'ave one dangerous crew 'ere for pirating. Yes indeed, very dangerous."

"Will ye join us then, Ned?"

"Oh, I would like to, Mistress Bonny, but I be afraid I'd be too slow for ye," he said, patting his left leg. "I be crippled, ye know."

The crew gathered up the coins for him. Henri tied the money in his own lace handkerchief and handed it to Ned.

"Well, even if you are crippled, Ned Hornsby, you are the most agile crippled man I've yet to meet," Anne said goodnaturedly.

Ned sniffed his perfumed money pouch. "Perhaps another time. I have some work to finish on Cap'n Hornigold's vessel this week."

"I'll see thee tonight then, Ned. I fear thee has not received proper payment for your labors here." There was a pause; then their eyes met, and both smiled. Ned flung his tool bag onto the dock and jumped from the boat. Swinging his bag onto his shoulder, he limped off down the beach. His step was heavy, the weight of his body planting his right foot deeply into the sand. Anne watched him for a long time.

"You like that boy, *cherie?*"

"I like him well, Henri."

"You will make fine love tonight?"

"Perhaps."

Anne replaced her rapier and went over the charts once again. "Don't drink too much tonight, Dennis. The pilot must have his head about him."

"I'll be as sober as Bartholomew Roberts. He drinks nothin' but tea."

"That, I dare say, is his only virtue. Henri, get your fill of lovin' tonight. I'll not have you tiring my crew once we're at sea."

"Do not worry, *ma cherie*, I have half a dozen handsome devils waiting for me now. Zis will be one beautiful night of love for ze two of us."

The crew giggled and Henri chased them about the deck, swatting at their behinds with the flat edge of his cutlass.

"Find zat amusing, do you? Well, we'll see who's laughing when I stick zis cutlass up your bunghole."

Leaving her crew screeching on deck like squealing pigs, Anne went with Dennis to the tavern.

They departed the next morning but had great difficulty getting the vessel underway. Due to the totally debilitated condition of the crew, the anchor, mainsail and halyard were not properly weighed, raised or manned.

But, in spite of everything, *La Petite Mort* was finally underway and gliding smoothly through the blue-green waters of the Bahama Bank. Henri, Alfred Butler and Anne were planning the strategy for their encounter with the merchantman. One idea inspired another and soon *La Petite Mort* looked like the stage setting for the last act of *Hamlet*.

As for the crew, no gruesome detail was missed: fantastic tattoos, hideous scars, blackened teeth, frightful hair, fierce eyes and ghastly mouths were applied with great skill by Alfred.

Anne wore a Roman centurion's helmet, a souvenir of one of Butler's great roles. Looking a little like Cleopatra in armor, she was making a kind of bomb by filling rum bottles with black powder, small shot, bits of iron and lead; all of which was packed around Blackbeard's gunner's matches.

Cuthbert and Nelson had so many weapons strapped, hung and stuck into their garments that they could hardly walk. Finally they were ready for the encounter.

By late afternoon *La Petite Mort* had reached the Bimini Islands, where they would wait. They waited all night and were provisioned to stay for a week if necessary.

The merchantman was spotted early the next morning and *La Petite Mort* gave chase. The heavy-bottomed Dutch merchantman could not outrun the fast sloop. Hoisting several black flags, Henri shouted, "Anne, smear your beautiful face wiz blood while I load zis perrier." He primed the ancient weapon with powder and loaded a ball.

"Dennis, you must be ready to rush against the side," shouted Anne. "Alfred, remember what I told you, loud and monstrous noises when we board her."

"Fear not, I have prepared some few dastardly lines which, when I recite them in a booming voice, will frighten the crew into the hold, I warrant."

They could see the hands of the merchantman preparing for close fighting. Henri fired the cannon, but it blew up in his face, throwing him several feet across the deck. Anne left her post and rushed to her friend, forgetting everything. An intense feeling of hopeless fear swept over her. When the smoke had cleared she saw that he was alive. Henri was shaken and covered with black powder, which added an awesome touch to his already startling appearance.

"Oh, my lovely shirt, she is ruined!" he said, coming out of an almost unconscious state.

"Is that all you can think about, you prick—your shirt? I thought you were dead. Are you all right? Can you get up?"

"Am I dead? Oh, I hope not." He clasped his genitals firmly. "Oh, thank God! I am alive, *Mon Dieu!* Come, prepare to fight! We must board zis vessel at once!"

The crew was positioned in various attitudes of fierce attack poses. Dennis pulled the sloop too close and rammed her. The bowsprit snapped and everyone tumbled to the deck, momentarily stunned. Anne scrambled up and, inciting the crew with loud shouts and curses, hurled the bottles onto the deck of the merchantman. Amid loud explosions, and with swords swinging and pistols blasting, they boarded.

Henri was cursing loudly in French. Anne was using Will's best Charles Town dock language and the others were whooping like Indians, just as she had rehearsed them to do.

"Once more into the breach!" shouted Alfred, dressed like a blackbearded Caliban. His resonant voice reverberated around the decks. "Cry havoc! and let slip the dogs of war!"

"To horse," cried Anne. "My kingdom for a horse"

"Ring the alarum bell!" raved Alfred. "Blow wind! Come wrack! At least we'll die with harness on our back." The Dutch crew offered no defense in the face of this grotesquely frightening assault. The fact that they did not understand what was being shouted at them terrified them even more.

"No quarter! We shall give no quarter!" Anne shouted. She held the captain's chin at the tip of her rapier. Roger tossed several Dutchmen overboard with ease. Henri's knife pinned the boatswain to the mainmast. Nelson and Cuthbert, cutlasses in both hands but opponentless, were ferociously slashing the air. The crew of the merchantman were on their knees pleading for their very lives.

The pirates of *La Petite Mort* had raised such a hue and cry that the Dutch were quite subdued. Henri went immediately to the ship's hold and emerged moments later with bolts of silks and taffeta wrapped around his lithe figure. Prancing about the deck, the material billowing behind him, Henri issued orders to his dangerous crew to unload the merchantman.

Cuthbert and Nelson, eyes closed now, were still engaged in battle. Cursing and swinging their cutlasses in a most violent manner, they cut down riggings, hacked at railings, and stabbed the water barrels, thinking all the while they were engaged in murderous battle. Roger loaded the cargo onto the sloop and Anne plundered the captain's chest, taking all the coins she could find and all the jewelry she could wear. Eyes shut still, Cuthbert and Nelson, each believing himself to have encountered an aggressively barbarous opponent, fought hard.

"Nelson! Cuthbert!" shouted Henri. "What are you doing?"

"We are fighting, can't ye see that?" shouted Nelson, over his partner's din.

"Shits! You crazy bastards! You fight each ozzer."

They stopped. Dropping their swords to their sides, and opening their eyes, they looked at each other, bewildered. "What am I to do wiz you? Come here and help me wiz zese sings!" ordered Henri. Very embarrassed, they put away their weapons and relieved Henri of the fabrics. Cuthbert tripped on one of his dangling swords and fell to the deck.

"Don't soil ze lace, idiot, crazy bastard!"

La Petite Mort reached Nassau Harbour at sunset. Henri was posed in the bow, wrapped in silk and reciting love poetry in French to Anne, who lounged barebreasted at his feet. The crew was cheering and singing drunkenly. An African standing on the beach blew into a conch shell and people poured out of the taverns onto the dock. Anne observed the man who had alerted the town. His breeches were bloodstained from cleaning fish, and he was shirtless. His black skin was streaked with salt from the day's laboring. The strange sound his shell made aroused something within her. Her eyes studied every part of his muscular body.

Lines were thrown out and the sloop was moored. Ned Hornsby helped Anne out of the sloop. "I see ye 'ad a little accident," he said, noticing the absence of the bowsprit.

"Yes, 'twas a wild time we had."

"Looks like ye got what ye went after," he added, looking at the multitude of golden and jeweled chains adorning her bare breasts and watching Henri unload his silks.

"Indeed we did." Anne showed him her purse, bulging with coins. "I can pay thee properly now when you repair our bowsprit."

"I liked it better when ye was poor." Ned's face creased into a broad beaming smile which Anne could not resist. Taking his hand, she ran down the beach toward his hut, dragging him behind her. She dashed into the sea and pulled him in with her and they stood together in the waist-high water.

"Here, let me clean this ghastly blood off your face. Ye are a sight, ye know that? Am I to believe from this that ye have been engaged in dangerous battle?"

"Believe what ye will," she said tauntingly.

Splashing up water and rubbing the side of her face, Ned

suddenly stopped his efforts and, taking her into his arms, kissed her. Just at that moment the sun slipped out of sight beneath the horizon.

The next morning Anne walked from Ned's hut to Henri's house. She had not bothered to dress. The beach was usually deserted in the early hours of the morning, except for the shore birds skimming over the wet sand, pecking at morsels, then running away from the advancing waves.

The African who kept his boat in front of Henri's house was busy repairing his nets and fishing lines. He was Anne's height, muscular yet lean of form, and wore nothing but a bleached muslin cloth which barely covered his loins. The folds of the cloth served only to amplify his genitals and heighten Anne's imagination. His skin was blue-black and she knew it would be as smooth as ivory to the touch. His face was not particularly handsome, yet his features were striking.

She stopped. His penetrating eyes met hers and she smiled. The African smiled inwardly; his countenance remained immobile. He stared at her large, firm breasts.

"What is your name?" she asked boldly.

"Tombay," he replied.

"Are you a free man, Tombay?"

"Yes, I be free," he said proudly.

As she turned and walked up to the house, he studied her nude form; her trim legs and the rise and fall of her round buttocks were like a ship lolling in a calm sea. She was bronze from the sun, unlike the other white women who kept themselves covered. Her small waist fanned into a broad back and her golden hair hung just past her shoulderblades.

The African went back to work, thinking of the dark tips of her distended nipples, and stuck himself with a fish hook. Sucking his thumb hard, he turned and looked again. She was gone. He spat and stained the white sand red.

Breda, Flanders: 1716

Mary stared down at the dirty plate for a moment before setting it on the floor for the dog. He licked the dish listlessly, barely rearranging the scraps; then, with a grunting sigh, he flopped under the table. In the corner of the almost empty dining room an old farmer drowsily contemplated the void at the bottom of his tankard. A soldier in a worn uniform sat with his legs stretched straight out in front of him, his chin buried in his chest.

It was quiet. Too quiet.

The late afternoon sun shone through the tinted panes of the western window, spilling colors on the swirls of dust filming the tables.

Mary wiped her greasy hands on her soiled apron and sank onto the bench of a booth, resting her head back against the wooden partition. On the other side of an open window a leafy branch danced in the spring breeze.

Her mind drifted back to happier times, six years ago, when this dining hall was bustling with activity and merriment. Vaguely, through her dream, Mary heard a wagon roll to a stop; but she did not return from her memory until the door burst open and robust laughter shattered the quiet Sunday afternoon.

"Where be she, where be me girl Mary?"

"Mother Ross? Be that you?"

Mary sprang to her feet and rushed into Mother Ross's

open arms. Burying her face in the woman's ample bosom, she began to sob bitterly.

"Now, now, girl. Surely ye cannot be grieved to see old Mother Ross again. Enough of this womanish blubbering. Because ye puts on a dress does not mean ye must go soft in the head. Let me look at thee. How pretty ye looks in country clothes. And where be the handsome Fleming who captured the love of his young comrade?"

"Dead." The sobs ceased momentarily as the thought crystalized in her mind; then tears came again with renewed vigor. Max had been dead these three months and she had not shed one tear until this moment.

"There, there, now, let Mother Ross hold thee quietly. Hush, girl, hush!"

Mother Ross hugged Mary, stroking her soft brown hair as she tried to absorb this new tragedy which had befallen her young friend.

"What am I to do now, Mother Ross? I am only four and twenty years old and have nowhere to go. Me life be spent." Utter loneliness swept over her, initiating new sobs. Mother Ross continued to rock Mary gently in her arms.

"Your life be far from spent, me girl. Hast thee children?"

"No children."

"Perhaps 'tis best. What happened to thee here in this place? What caused thy young husband to die?"

"When the peace came and the business went bad, Max took to drink. I do not know if that be the cause or not. Oh, I hate this place. God, what am I to do?"

"Ye can go back to the army. Have ye not thought of that? 'Tis where thee belongs. Ye be a soldier, not a serving maid."

"But these wars be done."

"There be something useful yet for thee to do. 'Tis a better life than this. Go now, put on thy uniform. There be a regiment of foot near Bergen-op-Zoom. I will take thee there. Come, I'll help thee. Tell me, where do ye keep that precious sword?" Mother Ross looked at Mary apprehensively. "Ye have not sold it? God's Death!"

"No, I have it still. Why can I not just travel with thee?"

"Ye have said it. These wars be done. Mother Ross be goin' to work her farm in the low country. 'Tis no life for thee. 'Twould be a worse boredom than ye suffer now. My life be over and yours be just beginning. There be high deeds in store for thee, Mary Read, and they will not be accomplished sittin' by the fireside with old Mother Ross."

Enlisting under the name of James Morris, Mary soon found life in the regiment of foot in peacetime to be dull, almost as wearisome as keeping a failing tavern. The monotony of camp life tired her very soul.

And so, Mary deserted her company.

At Rotterdam she booked passage on a small merchant-man, crossed the Channel to England, then made her way to Liverpool, where she hoped to fulfill a secret dream and crew aboard a vessel bound for the West Indies to follow a life of the sea.

The streets of Liverpool were crowded. Mary drifted in and out of the merchants' stalls through a confusion of scents: sweet candies, ambergris, tobacco, braziletto and other woods, all manner of island spices, and the pungent odor of rawhide. Her fingers ran over the white and blue linen fabrics, calicoes, chequered Guinea stuffs, taffetas and velvets. Her eyes were captured by the brilliance of the amethysts, blue coral, amber, pearls and purple beads. She tasted a variety of exotic fruits, which was all the purchase her slim purse would allow. Snatches of conversation between merchants and their customers faded in and out as she walked. All had one theme—the Islands: Sugar Islands, Spice Islands; groups of islands called the Windwards, Leewards, Virgins and Bahamas. Their names were like music: Antigua, Martinique, Barbados, Trinidad, Nevis, Anguilla, Dominica, Saba and Jamaica.

After days of steady wandering in a trancelike state through the same shops, seeing everything but inspecting no particular item, she stopped. Of all the beautiful merchandise gathered from every part of the known world, the object that had captured her eye was a branding iron, used to mark slaves. What be these things, she wondered. They were for purchase, along with padlocked handcuffs and other iron instruments of this cruel traffic. She studied a small object that had two circular holes at the top.

"What be this?" Mary asked the merchant.

"A thumbscrew," he replied curtly.

"What be its use?"

He looked into her questioning eyes, then turned and walked silently away. Receiving no satisfaction, Mary moved out onto the street.

The strong odor of bitter ale and sweet rum disclosed a small tavern wedged between two shops on the narrow street. Entering, Mary inquired of the bartender how she might sign aboard a vessel bound for the West Indies. He pointed out several captains sitting together at a table in the center of the room.

Tankard in hand, Mary moved close enough to overhear. Because their vocabulary consisted almost exclusively of seafaring terminology, and because they spoke of nothing but trade, their conversation made no sense to her. Mary's life had been the bordello and the battlefield; she knew nothing of trade goods or trade winds, let alone the geographical triangle of trade so important to these men. Mary listened carefully, trying to grasp the significance of this triangle. England was one point, the islands of the West Indies and the Carolina Coast in America were another, and the third the coast of Guinea. From their dialogue Mary gleaned that their crews were full and they would set sail tomorrow for Africa.

That night Mary visited the taverns searching for news of a ship in need of a seaman. She downed many tankards of ale just for the opportunity of a few moments of conversation with a boatswain or gunner's mate. The little money she had left was kept in a leathern pouch, safely stowed in her wide belt. Stepping into another tavern, she made her way through the noisome crowd to the bar and ordered ale.

Over the years Mary's voice had acquired a rich, resonant

quality. The accent of the British, mingled with hints of Dutch intonation, rendered her speech more husky than musical. At five feet eight inches, Mary stood taller than most men of her day. Her lithe figure had lost its girlish softness, and her sinewy thighs showed handsomely in the fitted camel breeches tapering just below the knee. The chocolate brown coat had been her husband's and was slightly large, perfect for concealing her swelling breasts. An open graceful collar of a white linen shirt revealed her lovely neck, long and sleek. Across her chest she wore a crimson damask baldric, from which hung her fine sword. The baldric had been her husband's, a badge of his military rank. In all, her clothes were comfortable, and necessary for her deception.

But nothing could hide her face. It was more than handsome with its high cheekbones, fair complexion, strong jaw and penetrating black eyes. Other than a thin scar above her left eye, there was not a mark on it. Rather, it had retained a boyish quality, as yet unmarred by the brutal sun. Tied in back, her rich brown hair lay in one soft twirl between her shoulderblades.

Her natural walk was too graceful and Mary had to affect a kind of swagger. A still graver problem was hiding her beautiful hands, with their long tapering fingers. Often she stood with her left hand grasped firmly around her sword hilt and the right tucked into her belt in back. At sea my hands will roughen and my face weather to suit a sailor's aspect, mused Mary.

She looked around at the beaten wrecks of humanity in the tavern, searching for that one face which would be instrumental in pointing out her destiny. These were men worn by the sea, tired, hard, wrinkled and misshapen, anxious to seize life in their few fleeting nights asore, and eager to spend on women, spirits, a bed to sleep in or a new pair of boots the money they had not lost at gambling aboard ship.

Everywhere in the squalid room, men silently whispered their dreams. At the table across from Mary's, a young sailor signed away his service on a slaver to pay a gambling debt. The quill dug defiantly into the parchment; then the pen fell from his trembling hand, leaving an inky blot where his soul had gone. His face darkening, he sank down into the chair, put his face in his hands and wept. Two stocky sailors lifted him up and carried him from the room. As they passed her Mary glanced his way, but thought nothing more than that the boy was drunk. She pushed her tankard away and stared absently at the table top, making swirls in a spill of ale. A hefty doxy plopped herself in Mary's lap.

"Say, mate, how's about a wee drinky for Old Sal?"

Mary stood up, dumping the Irishwoman to the floor, and walked over to the bar.

"Well, I never," the woman shouted. "I been fucked by better'n the likes of you." Picking herself up, she joined several other drabs at a table well situated in the midst of the turmoil. She talked in loud tones, pointing Mary out to the others. Mary ordered another ale and was about to take a sip when a resounding slap on her back made her lurch forward, sloshing her beer over the bar.

"Hey there, mate. Mind if I join ye? Very few pleasant-lookin' fellows to talk to in this place."

Without bothering to wait for Mary's response, he ordered a tankard of ale and continued speaking. After a few moments Mary discovered that the old sailor was a Hollander, and they continued their discourse in Dutch.

A sinister pair at a nearby table were listening to their conversation.

"The lad speaks Dutch, Cap'n."

"I 'ave ears, don't I?"

"Shall we take 'im? 'E's big enough. It would take the two of us, though. Fancy that, the lad speaks Dutch!"

Still listening, the younger man looked around to see if anyone had taken notice of them. "What I mean, Cap'n," continued the ship's master in a lower voice, "is that most of our crew speaks only Dutch. I could give the orders to this 'ere Englander and he could repeat 'em in Dutch to the crew. Save me grief, Cap'n Thomas. 'Tis a stubborn crew ye has when it come to heedin' commands. Let's take this one. What say you?"

"Suit yourself, but ye'll have no help from me. I be goin' outside to piss. We sail at midnight with or without yer Dutch-speakin' Englander."

After a long belch, the burly captain raised himself from his chair and shouldered his way out of the room. The master watched Mary intently.

Giles Deegan was an ugly little man. Vileness seeped from the grease-filled crevices of his piglike face. When he was scheming, which was his common practice, his pig's eyes would dart anxiously in their sockets, as they were doing now.

Finally the old sailor fell asleep and Master Deegan sidled up to the bar. "Would ye take an ale with me, lad?"

"No, thank ye. Me head swims now. I'm off. Goodnight to ye, sir." She moved as quickly as possible through the crowded tavern.

Once outside, she took a long breath of much-needed fresh air. As she did, something heavy struck the back of her head with a solid thud. Blackness enveloped her. Deegan rushed onto the street and found Mary sprawled in the mud and his captain standing over her, urinating on her face.

"I told ye I had to take a piss. A good long one." Laughing heartily, and without bothering to put his parts back in his breeches, Captain Thomas hoisted Mary over one shoulder and with long strides made way to his ship.

"'Tis time we cast off."

"Aye, Cap'n."

When they reached the wharf, Captain Thomas dumped Mary into the longboat. "Unchain the Guinea man. If he be not drowned, we'll take him back to his chief and demand me money back. I've lost enough on his account already."

"Can't we sell 'im here? He be a jinx; I fear 'im, Cap'n."

"Do as I say!"

"Aye, sir." The master forced his black captive to row. Once aboard, all made ready to depart. The captain instructed the master and the galiot slipped silently through Liverpool Harbor out into the open sea.

Mary lay unconscious on the deck.

Master Deegan struggled with the black man. Finally the captain assisted him, and together they tied the man to the mainmast.

"God's fuck, you're a useless milksop. If ye were not such a loyal bugger I'd throw ye to the sharks. We'll put in at the Canaries to take on water and brandy. Set the course and stand by."

"Aye, sir."

It did no good to hate Captain Thomas. Where else could Deegan get such a position? On any other ship he would be cleaning the holds or swabbing decks. Nonetheless, he knew his captain to be a mean bastard. But they were compatible in that Giles Deegan also liked abusing people, and a slaver was a fit place to practice the cruelties and perversions they both enjoyed.

However, the last middle passage had been too much even for Master Deegan. What slaves had not been carried off by fever and the flux had been killed in a mutiny led by this lone survivor, now helplessly tied to the mast and staring longingly at the heavens.

It was still dark. Giles removed Mary's sword from its scabbard.

" 'Tis a pretty piece. Well-balanced. Methinks I'll trade it for me own."

He slipped Mary's sword into his scabbard and went below to secure his own weapon.

On deck the rolling motion of the ship lulled Mary from fitful unconsciousness into a deep and tranquil sleep, unaware of the dangers that lay in store for her aboard this ill-fated vessel.

A splash of water followed by a sharp kick brought Mary back from sleep. She immediately went for her sword.

"I 'ave it. 'Tis safe by me side."

The morning sunlight flashed off the hilt, blinding her

eyes. Mary fell back to the deck and held her throbbing head.

"Where am I?"

"Aboard the *St. Job,* a Dutch tradin' vessel bound for Curaçao. 'Tis what ye wished for, isn't it? I 'eard ye say last night you was lookin' for a ship bound for the West Indies. And a fine one 'tis, too, a galiot, ninety tons, and swift of sail. Oh, you'll be paid when we reach Curaçao, if ye be alive. I be ship's master; Giles Deegan's me name. Master Deegan to you. I am in charge of all discipline aboard this 'ere vessel. Take care not to overstep yerself or I'll see to it that ye 'ave more than an ache in your 'ead, Mister. What are ye called?"

"Read. Mar . . . Matt Read," she answered faintly.

"Read, eh. Well, Seaman Read, get to swabbin' this 'ere deck and see that I can eat off it if I've a mind to. And don't go near that nigger or I'll tear the skin off your back."

Her pilfered sword clipped her jaw as he turned and walked away. Mary looked at the black man tied to the mainmast.

There were only a few men scattered about the deck, fifteen or sixteen dirty, shirtless ones with their ribs showing through sagging skin, pantaloons falling under bloated bellies, soiled checkered scarves tied around scrawny necks. They were hatless, hairless, toothless men. Be there no able-bodied sailors to man this vessel? A foul odor wafted up from the hold. What be the cargo? Cattle? But this be not the smell of cattle. What manner of ship be this? Dizzy from the blow, Mary closed her eyes for a moment. When she opened them again she saw that the black man was staring at her despairingly. Giving way to its own weight, his head fell forward onto his chest. Mary wondered if he were dead but, hearing footsteps, she busied herself in scraping the deck.

"Bring that black bastard to me, Master Deegan."

The black man's head sprang up and a hate-filled glare shot from his eyes to the captain.

"Chain 'im well first."

The man had scarcely enough strength to walk under the

178

weight of his chains. Captain Thomas stood with feet wide apart, a long whip stretched between his hands. The man dragged himself across the deck. His knees buckled, but the captain's whip raised him to his feet again. Stopping, the black man brought himself to his full height, towering over the stocky captain. He had been tortured unmercifully all the way to the West Indies and back again and he would not suffer his body to be mutilated further.

Poking the handle of his whip into the man's genitals, the captain said, "Cut off his balls, Master Deegan. You should enjoy that. Have cook prepare them for me breakfast."

A broad grin of sheer delight spread across Deegan's face. The black man spat in the captain's eye. Thomas punched his whip handle with such force into the man's genitals as to double him over in pain. "Do it now, Deegan, in me sight."

Where the black man's strength came from, Mary did not know; but, summoning an inner power, he raised his arm and struck the captain square on the jaw with his wrist iron. A cracking sound was heard. Before Deegan could raise the whip against him, the black man made for the railing. Deegan's whip lashed out, halting the man for an instant. Then he grasped the whip in flight and, with tremendous force, flung Deegan against the railing where he landed with the wind knocked out of him. Dropping the whip, the man struggled on toward the rail. A shot caught his shoulder, another his leg, but, with his last bit of energy, he flung himself over the railing and crashed into the sea. Mary rushed to the rail to see his huge black fists sink defiantly beneath the waves and watch the bubbles dissipate over the surface of the water.

The master's groans startled her and, dropping to her knees, Mary picked up a brush and went back to work. Deegan's first thought on regaining consciousness was of the captain who was lying on the deck, his face bloodied, his arms stretched before him, a discharged pistol in each hand.

"Read! Give a 'and 'ere. Come 'ere, some of you men!"

As much scrambling about as these tired men could accomplish, they did, and after a good deal of awkward maneuvering Captain Thomas was taken to his cabin and placed on his cot.

"I fear his jaw be broken. Read, minister to 'im."

"But what shall I do? I know naught of medicines."

"How should I know?" replied Master Deegan. "But whatever ye do, take care it be all for his good or the cat will learn ye."

The cat. Mary knew well what that was. Captain Thomas turned over on his cot and raised himself up, choking and spitting. Mary slapped him firmly on the back. Up came bits of broken teeth, followed by large clots of blood. She turned away. Secretly she wished he would drown like the black man. Moaning fitfully, his lips formed unutterable curses and unintelligible sounds.

'Tis no great loss that the man cannot talk, she thought. A bulbous nose was a feature of his pockmarked face. Bushy black eyebrows hung like fringe over his angry dark eyes. There was a huge mole at the corner of his left eye and a long red gash across his right cheek. Now the left side of his jaw was crushed. Thomas was an Englishman, a criminal, a murderer, a rapist, a cannibal and a thief. He had been hanged once at Tyburn but had survived; the hangman's rope accounted for the thick reddish weal encircling his neck. When the hell ship from Newgate which carried him to the West Indies had been captured by Dutch pirates, Thomas had joined them and, for his valor in many engagements, was awarded a prize ship which he had later traded at Amsterdam for the *St. Job*. Slaving was more profitable than pirating, or so he had thought. Now he was not so sure, since his last crossing had ended in total disaster. This time his commission was to purchase three hundred slaves and deliver them to Curaçao.

On deck, Mary listened to Deegan's instructions to the helmsman. They were heading south to a place called the Gold Coast, but where that was located Mary could not find out to any satisfaction. The crew would not answer her.

Either they did not know or were not saying.

The voyage became even more mysterious when she was ordered below to make ready the hold. The stench was asphyxiating. Her eyes burned so badly that she could not see at first. Her head barely cleared the low ceiling. As her eyes stopped watering and became accustomed to the darkness, she studied the layout of the hold. Chains and wrist irons hung from iron posts placed at two-foot intervals along the narrow passage, with three tiers of wooden racks on either side. The only air in the place came from a large hatch amidships and a smaller one in the stern. A terrible feeling came over her, a sickness not so much from the foul stench but from something more, a sense of inexplicable suffering akin to that of hell.

Mary and a few other sailors began to scrape the slimy mess from the slats of the first tier, which had been washed in the scummy waters of the bilge. Along the front edge of each rack was a series of leg irons with little more than a foot of clearance between tiers. *Human cargo!* Mary's head came up suddenly and banged against the second tier. God! This cannot be what methinks it is! Her mind could not fully grasp the idea, even though she had heard some talk of it in Liverpool. *Black ivory.* How was she to know that that term meant trade, trade in people? *The Gold Coast.* Now it was coming to her. The merchant who would not talk—wrist irons, branding irons, thumbscrews. Pieces of conversations began to fit into a horrifying picture: Niger, Ivory Coast, Gold Coast, Angola, Cape de Verd, Sierra Leone were names she had heard over and over again in the taverns of Liverpool. The *St. Job* was sailing to Africa to pick up slaves and transport them to the plantations in Dutch Guiana, West Indies. *The traingle of trade.*

Mary accelerated her tasks. Tears fell as she thought about the black man who had killed himself in defiance. She felt despair and loneliness for all those who had suffered and died in the hold of this ship. Soon her herculean task was completed. The hold is ready for its occupants, she thought bitterly. A heavy hand gently grasped her shoulder but when she turned she found no one. Immediately the image of the black man flooded her mind. Does his angry spirit linger here? She wondered. Will it remain until vengeance been acted against this vile captain? She was uneasy. This vessel be ill fated, surely, and I be a part of its crew.

On deck, she rigged a sail to catch the wind and force it into the hold. Deegan was pacing nervously on the quarterdeck. I be his prisoner, his slave, but this man will not kill me. I will kill him first. 'Tis more than a promise; 'tis a fact. Mary spat indelicately over the leeward rail. She was a man again. She had to be.

The captain, his broken jaw preventing speech, was on deck to supervise the landing at Elmina, the Dutch slaving fortress on the African Gold Coast. He pointed to leech lines, halyards, shrouds, while cuffing Deegan on the ears if he issued the wrong order. Deegan in turn sent his whip singing in the direction of the offending sailor. Mary repeated the orders in Dutch and received a clout from the whip handle on her back for thanks. Once the *St. Job* was anchored in the Bay of Gambia, Mary was selected to be part of the landing party.

Captain Thomas looked drawn and haggard; Deegan appeared sullen and nervous. The June sun beat down mercilessly. Mary looked toward the shore, noting that the Dutch fortress commanded a strip of sand stretching for miles in both directions.

"Row; don't gawk. Ye'll get an eyeful soon enough," barked Master Deegan.

After pulling the longboat onto the beach, Mary was ordered to instruct the crew to stand close by in case it should slip its anchor. The captain and Master Deegan pushed through the deep sand in the diredtion of the castle. A litter carrying a richly dressed African king appeared through the trees. An enormous carpet was spread on the sand and the black king was placed upon it, litter and all. Very old and withered, he seemed almost to disappear into the pillows on which he sat. Two colossal black men held umbrellas of palm fronds to shade him from the scorching sun. Several women stood behind him fanning him with large feathers. One woman knelt beside him holding a silver tureen and carefully watching the movement of the old man's head in order to catch the saliva dripping from his mouth. Master Deegan and Captain Thomas stood in the sand directly in front of the king, shifting uncomfortably from foot to foot. Their boot leather was no better than the thin soles of Mary's shoes. She stepped back into the bay, wriggling her toes in the cool water that was seeping into her shoes.

Off to one side a group of men, part of the king's entourage, lounged in a cluster of trees, resting against canoes. Slightly removed from this altogether spectacular tableau were the captives, several groups of naked black people penned by spears driven into the ground in a circular fashion. No one moved. The various physical attiudes of the forms within displayed a haunting picture of the ultimate in human despair.

The fate of all these people is in the hands of this dastardly pair, she thought hopelessly. Mary sensed by their despairing silence that these prisoners knew it.

A young boy was carried in, his legs and wrists tied to a pole stretched between two bearlike white men. They rested the pole on their shoulders, removed their kerchiefs and wiped the sweat from their eyes. Four or five other young men were pulled down the path from the fortress, chained in a row, an iron bar extended between each collar iron. Mary wondered how they walked without choking one another. Tall, naked men were brought and tied to stakes in the sand, their well-oiled muscular bodies shining like those of bronze gods. But their eyes were closed and their teeth clamped shut in fear. There were the cries of children, the high-pitched wailing of women, the babbling of old men, and the intermittent staccato of the cracking whip.

Negoitations seemed to be reaching a climax. Captain Thomas rudely inspected the men chained to the stakes in the sand, brutally unclamping stubborn jaws with his knife to check their teeth and gingerly fingering their testicles.

The pens were opened and men, women and children herded out.

The men who had been lying around under the leafy trees began to move swiftly now, dragging their canoes into the water. Whips snapped. Master Deegan supervised the loading of each canoe.

Captain Thomas pulled a one-armed man from the line. The white merchant argued frantically, protesting the man's strength. On his own account the black man lifted the bow of the longboat up and out of the water, but Captain Thomas continued to shake his head. The merchant reluctantly removed his pistol from its brace, took aim and, seconds later, the one-armed man was floating face down in the surf.

Mary was flipped into the boat by the captain, who then pointed to the money chest, which she handed to him. It crashed open as he flung it to the sand, spilling bright coins onto a patch of rotting seaweed.

The rest of the cargo was loaded into the captain's longboat, among them a beautiful young girl whose skin was bright creamy brown. She was naked except for a covering wrapped loosely about her loins. Her small breasts bounced as she was lifted into the boat. She shrank among some of the other children. The girl could not have been more than fourteen. A small boy of two or three crawled into her arms and she rocked him protectively. The captain was hoisted aboard and immediately uncorked a flagon of brandy that he had stashed under a bench.

The beach was nearly deserted. The doomed souls were corraled into one of the empty pens while the back merchants swept their coins into the cask. A woman started screaming; one arm was nearly wrenched out of its socket by a burly Dutchman, the other stretched imploringly toward the captain. She was crying and pleading unintelligible words.Captain Thomas stood up in the boat. The crew cried out to him vehemently.

"No . . . no, Cap'n . . . witch, no, witch!"

Captain Thomas steadied himself and, taking a long swig

of the brandy, watched the woman on the beach. He kicked a sailor who was pulling at his trouser leg. Handing Mary the flagon, his sign language instructed her to offer it in exchange for the woman. Mary sprang out of the boat and pushed against the water as fast as she could. When she saw the merchant draw out his saber, she ran even faster and began shouting. "The captain wants to buy this woman!" The woman had understood, but in her excitement Mary was speaking English. Just before she could reach the merchant his sword swung out and decapitated the smiling woman. Her head rolled away in the sand. The woman's torso jerked spasmodically, then fell to the beach and, after several fitful motions, became still in the sand. Mary slowly sank to her knees and stayed there until a shot from the longboat roused her from her stupor. She dragged herself to her feet and stumbled down to the water's edge, clutching the flagon of brandy to her bosom. The captain snatched the bottle and Mary had to get herself aboard as the boat slipped into deeper water.

All was quiet as Mary took up her oar.

These things did not happen, she mused. This day could not have been. She slipped into a state of semiconsciousness and faintly heard a child's frightened scream. Through blurring vision, she thought she saw the captain struggle with the young girl and, wrenching some object from her, fling int into the ocean. Mary's arms moved the oar—over and pull, over and pull, over and pull.

The longboat struck the hull of the ship with a thud, bringing Mary back to consciousness. As Mary secured her oar, it accidentally struck the girl's foot and Mary looked into her tearstained face. The child was no longer in her arms and, looking around, Mary could not find him anywhere in the boat.

After much delicate negotiation, the captain was aboard his vessel and his precious cargo driven into the hull. The strongest men were chained standing, three to a post in the aisle. The women and children sat crammed on the shelf in the stern. The rest were packed spoon fashion on the tiers. The count was 414, almost twice the allotment for a ship of this tonnage. Mainsails unfurled and the anchor was weighed. The long middle passage had begun.

The night dropped over them. The ship rolled quietly through the waters of the Atlantic. The crew slept on the deck, hard and damp in the cool night air. Calmed by the gentle rocking of the vessel, Mary pursued the stars as they rearranged themselves in her vision. Her gaze shifted back and forth across the nameless constellations until the dolorous symphony of the chains from below initiated tears which blurred the stars and muddied the clear night.

Below, another woman was sobbing. She was Letla, princess of her tribe, young and beautiful, who had stood proudly on the rim of life before this unhappy accident had cut her off from all hope and desires. Her whim alone had coaxed a warrior to escort her and her little brother away from the camp. It had been curiosity, nothing more. One flower was like any other in the rain forest of that region near her home. All three had been captured in an instant, surrounded by what seemed an army of sweaty men with dirty white faces. And now the warrior stood chained only a few yards away and her brother lay dead at the bottom of the bay.

The vessel rode on through endless days of scorching heat and work and pain and hunger. At the outset of the voyage the crew had been allotted three thin slices of dried beef per day and one cup of water. Now, thirty-three days had passed and the crew's water ration was cut in half.

Thirty-three bitter agonizing days. Feeding the slave cargo only made Mary bitterly aware of her own hunger. Any of the crew would have gladly eaten anything left over of the gruel-like mixture of Indian corn and split beans. But what was left was always mixed into the next day's rations and any sailor caught stealing as much as a mouthful would be severely punished. One man received twenty lashes of the cat and was chained to the mast with a sack of bullets tied to his neck for taking a sip of water while watering the cargo. Slaves were worth good money in the Caribbean, and reasonable care was taken not to lose one to starvation, illness or ill treatment.

Once a week the passengers were brought up on deck to exercise. The sailors were armed on those days, ready for a mutiny should one occur. The bow chaser was loaded and manned by the gunner's mate. The crew lived in fear. If any slave escaped during the exercise period, the hand responsible would be sentenced to death. Mary was in charge of the women and children. She felt lucky to have drawn this usually uneventful duty.

This day was to be different. No sooner on deck, the princess dashed to the side of the ship and was almost overboard when Mary intercepted her. If she had struggled any longer, Mary, in her weakened condition, would not have been able to restrain her.

Deegan ripped the girl out of Mary's arms and, coming face to face with her unexpected beauty, was somewhat taken aback. Although he had had several of the women during the course of the voyage, he had not bothered even to look at this girl before now. His intentions were revealed clearly to the girl's frightened eyes. Mary turned away in disgust and helped hustle the prisoners back to the hold before there was another mishap. Mary had heard stories from the crew of wholesale suicides among the slave cargoes, and panic gripped her. It was one thing to die in a fight, another to be whipped to death. She was angry with the girl. Whips sang through the air. Bewildered children began to cry and Deegan threw the girl back into Mary's arms.

"Chain her to the wall of the hull. I'll attend to her later."

I wager ye will! Mary placed a firm hand on the girl's wrist and dragged her toward the hold. "Can't take any chances with ye. Almost had me killed up there. What do you care? End your miserable life. That's all ye care about. Maybe I be not as ready as I thought to end me life. I almost wish ye were successful, for you've bought it now, me girl.

Master Deegan will rip ye open like an orange. I've watched 'im with the others here. But they be women somewhat used to it." One delicately thin wrist was placed in an iron, then the other. Mary took the girl by the shoulders and shook her angrily. "Why did ye have to draw attention to yourself that way?" The girl did not understand one word Mary had spoken but her rough treatment puzzled her. Mary looked into her large round eyes, astounded by her beauty. Taking her own sleeve, Mary gently wiped away the girl's tears. Letla's eyes flashed to Mary's, trying to find the cause of such contrasting behavior. Mary averted her eyes, afraid of the intimate nature of this contact; she had her own survival to think of, after all.

As she made her way through the hold, hands reached out to her, hands responding to the mind's knowledge that someone of a sympathetic nature was among them. Squares of afternoon sunlight patterned the hold, but eyes blurring on the verge of blindness could not distinguish the hands held in front of them.

That night Mary kept a close eye on Master Deegan. Fighting against drowsiness, she stationed herself at the entrance of the hold. The night was especially clear. A bright full moon was blazing in the cloudless sky.

The next week the slaves were brought on deck ten at a time. Sailors gathered their buckets and scrapers and left their clothes scattered on the deck as they went naked into the hold. Luckily Mary had been assigned above to assist in the cleansing of the prisoners.

Mary was busy sweeping the filth through the scruppers when she heard Captain Thomas in a fit of rage. Waving his arms before one African, he had discovered that the man was blind. "God's Death! Blind! Blind as bats, Master Deegan! Test the rest! Fetch the blind men aside. I 'ave 'eard of this disease. He must not infect the others. We be not immune either. No man be safe while they be aboard."

Deegan went to work. Several men were dragged from the group and fell against the port railing. One man lost his balance and flipped over the side into the ocean, carrying his chained partner with him. His frightened screams heightened the terror of the other blind men, who knew they had been singled out but were as yet unaware of their fate. Racked with fear, they crouched down and clung to one another, jabbering unintelligibly.

The sighted prisoners were driven back into the hold. Deegan took the long whip and struck numerous times to hasten the departure of those to be spared. He then turned his whip into the group of bewildered men who, anguished at the loss of their sight, were now panicked in the face of these new circumstances which they could not understand. All the violence the captain and Master Deegan had held within these many days was unleased now as they laid stroke after bloody stroke upon these pitiful men. They were doomed.

Mary had never heard such cries and screams of agony. A man's genitals, snatched by the whip, were ripped from his body and flew into the sea. Bloody gashes followed the cat. White bones shone through dark skin, streaked with blood. Lashes struck ulcerated sores, bringing the tortured bodies to their knees. Men were sliding on the deck in their own blood and pieces of flesh. When the captain slipped and his own body came crashing to the deck, then, and only then, did he stop. Master Deegan had already given way to exhaustion. The screams died but moans deepened in intensity as shock wore off and men became aware of their pain. Mary's fists were locked tight in anger, her eyes shut against the horror.

The captain picked himself up and surveyed the massacre. Many were dead and the rest barely alive. The scene on deck resembled a field with mounds of earth scarred by the plow. Each heap of black flesh now writhed in anguish.

By this time Mary was heaving her guts into a bucket of slime. Nothing was being cast up, yet she could not stop the retching. The lash caught her squarely between her shoulderblades, straightening her body up sharply. The captain snapped his whip at the deck and those who could stand, did. "Read! Tie ballast to their feet and throw these fucking blind men to the sharks." He turned to go below. Mary did not move. "Did ye not 'ear what I said? Move yer arse!"

"I'll not do it!"

The words flew out of her mouth. She had not had it in mind to say them. She wished she could take them back into her mouth again, but even if it were as easy to do as breathing, Mary knew she could not. For the moment she felt totally free, as if the boulder sitting on her stomach had finally been cast up with those words.

"What!" shouted the captain. "Fuck me eyes! Ye dares to disobey a direct order!"

Now she would die. It was that simple. Mary could feel her heart beating rapidly but could feel nothing else.

"Master Deegan, see to it that these blind bastards are heaved over the side. Then use the cat on Read there. And do not let me see yer ugly face until it be to tell me that they be all dead." Captain Thomas made one last tour of the condemned men, devouring their suffering bodies with his hungry eyes. Then he shifted his attention to Mary. " 'Tis a pity to waste the only able-bodied seaman aboard this vessel. How many blind niggers are here, Deegan?"

"Thirty-nine, sir. Some already dead."

"I will put it to thee another way, Master Deegan. Listen well. If Read should survive thirty-nine lashes, he has me leave to live. Perhaps, 'earin' your punishment, yet wish to reconsider. What say you to that, Mister? I cannot 'ear thee."

Mary's tightly clenched teeth prevented her tongue from bursting senselessly from her.

"So be it. Do yer duty, Master Deegan. It would be a pleasure to watch ye, but I rather choose to be inspired by Seaman Read's screams while I skewer one of our passengers bumwise." He laughed and coughed as he went into the hold. Deegan, helped by a few emaciated seamen, tied ballast to the feet of the blind men and began tossing both the dead and the living bodies into the sea.

His selection made, the captain dragged a woman from

the hold. Her resigned silence contrasted with the screams of the still living blind men as they sank into the ocean. Mary was glad it was not the young girl. She had lately become accustomed to choosing between lesser evils. But not this day; she just could not obey one more inhumane order. It was not in her to do it.

Mary stood and waited, her thoughts muddled, her eyes and ears closed against the cries of the extermination. Some were alive enough to know that they were being sent overboard. All were chained together and heavily ballasted. Bodies struggling against the weight of the irons, choking one another with chains, danced in a ghastly, deathly ballet in the ocean depths. Then all was quiet.

The brightness of the midday sun struck Mary's burning, now-open eyes. The only sounds were those of the gasping sailors lying about the deck, contorted by cramps and exhaustion. Master Deegan was among them.

He cannot kill me. I will not allow it. He be too weary even to hurt me much. I will live to kill him yet.

At length Deegan drew his aching body to his feet. His sadistic smile broke Mary's guard and she was suddenly frozen in cold fear. Throwing her down roughly, Deegan lashed her arms and legs tightly to the stern grating. He did not bother to tear her shirt. It would be a wasted effort, and he needed all this strength. A second before the first lash reached her, Mary caught a glimpse of the young African girl. Then the cat struck, searing her skin. Mary refused to scream. She would not give the captain any satisfaction. Let him fuck his way to hell and be damned. Not a sound escaped her, but her body responded to the unbearable pain. She could feel the blood running down over her breasts. She drove her face into the metal grating and blacked out. Deegan took two or three more ineffectual strokes and collapsed. He had delivered twelve in all and could do no more.

Mary did not realize how long she had lain unconscious. Nor did she know whether she was alive or dead. She tried to move her body and at first it did not respond. Surely I'm dead. Then, with great effort, she pulled her back up and the searing pain told her that she was very much alive. The stench of the hold rose and filled her nostrils. Her eyes, crusted over in a salty rheum, broke open and and vague, darkened images appeared. Something wet touched her lips and, looking down, she saw the young princess. She was wetting her fingers in a small cup of water which she had saved back from her own ration and was forcing a few drops into Mary's mouth. Mary struggled to keep the precious liquid in her mouth, savoring it, rolling it around her parched tongue. She murmured grateful sounds weakly before she blacked out again.

The sun fell.

The moon rose.

The sun lifted out of the ocean. In half sleep, Mary heard footsteps approaching. A bucket of sea water assaulted her back before she could brace herself. Her agonized scream pierced the quiet of the morning.

The sun moved higher.

Sweat dripped from Mary's face into the hold. Her back burned and dried and itched unbearably. She squirmed and arched but could not relieve the steady torture. Tears came. She could not stop them. A hand reached up and wiped the tears and sweat from her face. The gentle stroking eased her mind and brought pleasant thoughts.

That evening Mary felt a mushy substance being forced into her mouth. She gobbled the horrible mixture greedily.

Days later, when she was finally cut away from the grating and was strong enough to think the matter out, Mary realized that the girl had been feeding her from her own meager ration. She felt a mingling of remorse and gratitude. She owed this girl her life, but she had no idea whether she would ever get the chance to repay this debt.

Days and nights passed and Mary healed.

One night, while sleeping near the grating of the stern, Mary heard a rapping sound. She awoke and saw the girl stuffing a wad of cloth through the grating. Mary took it up and discovered that it was a crude garment. Armholes had been carefully chewed out of the solid piece of material to make a vest. Mary put it on over her torn shirt and was thankful that she no longer had to spend time covering her exposed breasts. She reached down and took the girl's hand in gratitude. The drift of the moon's light revealed the girl's nakedness. Mary turned away.

Why does this wretched girl help me? 'Tis past my comprehension. I grow deeper in her debt. She sits in the stench of the hold and gives me comfort. Why? I am her captor, her tormentor. Lost in her thoughts, Mary almost did not notice Deegan enter the hold. Looking below now, Mary saw him cover the girl's mouth and carry her out of Mary's sight. So he finally wants her. Too late, Master Deegan. You will not enjoy this girl now or any other time.

Master Deegan emerged from the hold holding the struggling girl. Pushing the princess aside, Mary snatched her own sword from Deegan's scabbard and ran him through neatly. Being skewered on Mary's sword was hardly punishment enough and scarce vindication for the hundreds who had died by his hand, so Mary jerked the sword viciously in every direction until his guts spilled through the opening. Then she toppled his twisting body into the sea.

It was good to feel her sword in her hand again. There was more life in her tortured body at this moment that there had been at any other time during this foul voyage. "The devil take ye, Master Deegan," she muttered bitterly. "And remember who you deal with in the future. Mary Read be ever faithful to her promise."

After cleaning her sword, Mary slipped it under a pile of torn sailcoth. Only then did she think of the frightened girl. Searching for her, Mary found her crouched deep in the stern, hidden among boxes and barrels. The girl started when Mary touched her shoulder but her panic eased when she realized who it was. She had run away and had not seen the fierceness of the master's murder.

The next morning Mary watched the men move aimlessly

on deck, bewildered, yet relieved, that the drunken whip-snapping Master Deegan had not bestirred himself as yet.

The helmsman shouted some orders, pointing at the flapping sail with his free hand. A few sailors responded and trimmed up the sails in question and the *St. Job* went smartly on its course again. To what destination?

Later the men began to murmur among themselves concerning the strange disappearance of Master Deegan. Finally Mary relieved the helmsman, who went below to inform the captain. It was assumed that Deegan had fallen overboard in the night. He had often been seen by the helmsman retching his insides out over the rail. This seemed a reasonable explanation and the captain did not question the incident further. The helmsman was awarded the promotion.

Locks were installed on all the water barrels and the new master held the key. Mary watched him swagger about the deck like a child playing king of the mountain. Power had twisted his mind in a minute.

What good be your power? she thought. 'Tis a doomed ship. Lord and master ye be over a few bedraggled scraps of humanity. King of what? King of nothing. Going nowhere. All yer power could not put decent food into yer belly, for there be none.

The new master, Ferguson, ordered a bucket to be hoisted to the topsails. The ladle was placed at the bottom of the mast. Any sailor requiring a drink would have to climb the mainmast for it, the ladle in his teeth. In a few days hardly a sailor in this crew would have the strength for such a feat. Some few would try and fail. One afternoon a sailor who lost his grip halfway up the mast would come crashing to his death.

Mary maintained herself by sheer stubbornness of will. She would not die an ignominious death just to please a sadistic captain and a power-grubbing master. Remaining alive was an act of defiance.

The slave cargo was watered and fed only occasionally now. Nothing more was done. The hold was never cleaned;

even the dead bodies were left there to rot. The hatch cover was left open and those with energy enough to crawl out were allowed to spend the day on deck.

The *St. Job* was about to enter the Caribbean Sea; the hellish voyage was nearing its end.

At night, Mary fought off sleep for as long as she could. She did not want to die in her sleep: she wished to meet death bravely, sword in hand.

The tattered sails of the *St. Job* flapped almost uselessly in the breeze. Mary listened for a long time, lulled by their sound. Suddenly aware of a presence, she stood up. Moving to her, Letla offered Mary a cup containing a few drops of water. Mary accepted and, while savoring the mouthful, she felt compelled to stare into the girl's large, round eyes. They stood face to face for a long while.

Even in the dim light of the wasting moon, Mary could not help but notice the girl's nakedness. Letla touched Mary's face gently and kissed her hand, caressing it and holding it against her own face. Their eyes met and Mary was quickly brought back to reality. Her eyes revealed her confusion, which Letla misunderstood as rejection. A look of sadness came over the girl and she turned to go.

"No," said Mary, as she reached for the girl's hand. "You cannot go away thinking I do not love you. It be just that I be not what I seem. I be a woman . . . like you. Name . . . Mary . . . Mary."

Tilting her head to one side, Letla repeated in a puzzled voice, "Mary."

Taking the girl's hand, Mary placed it inside her blouse. When Letla felt the fullness and softness of Mary's breasts, she drew her hand out. Now she understood. Their tense stillness was broken when Mary took the princess in her arms and held her close. Their bodies melted together tenderly. There was no reason to deny themselves this time of comfort.

Alone among the barrel kegs, Mary and Letla slept in each other's arms through the night. Mary had not enjoyed a moment of any kind of physical intimacy since her husband's death; in fact, this was the first time she had thought of him in months. Months—it seemed like years, so much had happened. Before long she was dreaming. Max had taken her hand and together they were walking in golden fields, stopping by cool, refreshing streams, willows dipping into the water, and wandering along winding roads bordered by tall trees. Piercing light stabbed down through the dense forest of her dream and Mary awoke to find herself wedged between two crates. She felt feverish and dizzy. Had she been delirious? What had happened last night? Like a dream, images of subtle actions were fast fading—a kiss, a touch, a soft curl against her chin, a small head resting on her bosom.

When Mary stood up, consciousness seemed to leave her. For a moment even her senses failed. Lightheaded and dizzy, she could neither see nor hear. Feebly she stumbled across the deck and down into the galley, where she consumed her entire day's ration of salted beef. Going on deck to relieve the helmsman, she began to strain every muscle against the powerful ocean. Having eaten, she felt somewhat better; at least the painful inner gnawing had subsided.

Another sailor joined her and together they battled the mighty ocean. Will I live through this day? I wonder. Or be this the last? Will any of us survive? This was a constant thought. Scanning the deck before her, Mary saw the beaten faces of the surviving seamen as they hunched their shoulders over torn bits of sail or spliced rope, any work a man could do sitting. They toiled at these simple tasks as if their last vestige of sanity rested in that piece of worn sailcloth or length of frayed rope.

A vile stench came up from the hold, and there was no more music. The singing had stopped long ago, but the maoning of intermittent prayers went on in halting phrases.

Where be their gods? Have they deserted these people? Where be my God, for that matter? God does not keep me alive. The sea breeze is my god. The sea breeze keeps me alive. But they—they have nothing.

A few slaves crawled up out of the hold, gagging. One was dragging the dead partner chained to him. Master Ferguson unlocked the irons and the slave was left to maneuver the badly decomposed body over the side.

The men sat on gray haunches, staring blankly at the boards of the deck. The women seemed stronger, trying to walk straight with their heads high. Maybe fifty or more were on deck now. Mary wondered if that was all who were left of the four hundred. Surely not.

Letla was scrubbing her beautiful body with the harsh bristles of the swabbers' brush; after rinsing in a bucket of sea water, she stood to dry in the sun. Looking out over the rail at the great ocean, she dreamed of darkness and the comforting arms of her friend. Smiling, Letla turned in the direction of the stern, where Mary stood tall behind the wheel. Mary smiled back, noting at once the odd sensation in her face. She had quite forgotten what a smile felt like.

Captain Thomas swore heavily as he lurched up the stairs to the quarterdeck, whip in one hand, bottle in the other. The men shrank into their work. The black women slipped quietly back into the hold; a pit of anguish and torment now became a place of refuge. Mary leaned into her wheel. Her cold defiant eyes avoided him. The captain checked the compass and buffeted the master, who pushed Mary away from the wheel to make a small correction.

The sun was dropping to a level where no one could evade its blinding radiance.

Captain Thomas approached Mary. He was filthy. Mary could no more escape the suffocating odor of his presence or the ugly dark look of his face than avoid the setting sun. His codpiece was open as usual, exposing his clap-ridden member.

"So ye be still among us, Seaman Read. Perhaps ye be of further service to me yet, me pretty." He patted Mary's backside with his thick hand. Mary tightened her flanks and had turned to leave him when he wrenched her arm behind her back, pinning her in a muscle-tearing hold while he pushed her toward his cabin door. Both stumbled on the stairs. Mary broke free but could not escape his powerful pursuit. Bearlike he clutched her to him, his pistols cutting painfully into her ribs and breasts.

197

"Walk away from me, will ye? You'll not live through this, I'll warrant ye. You'll not live to see the the sun set, me pretty boy. I mean to cut off your balls afore I kill ye dead, then fuck thee after."

His reaching for her parts with one fat hand provided Mary with all the freedom she needed. Slipping his pistols from their brace, she fired directly at his groin, blasting away his erect member. She fired the second pistol point blank at his face. He staggered, then threw himself violently upon her. The weight of his body was too much for her and she had to endure the rape of his dying motions. She thought she heard more gunfire. Perhaps it was only her own shots reverberating in her mind. Rolling the dead captain off her, Mary staggered up to the quarterdeck. Startled to hear voices of Englishmen on the main deck, she looked to starboard and saw a large galleon tied there.

Pirates! She hastily located her sword and secured it in her belt. Her brow was on fire, her head pounding. With the captain's empty pistols in her hands, Mary emerged weakly to confront the pirate crew.

The capture of the *St. Job* had taken but a few minutes. The master had died defending his kingdom. The rest of the wretched crew knelt, quartered at sword point.

A tall man, garbed enitrely in black save for a scarlet plume in his hat, paraded up and down in front of his prisoners.

"Where be this damned captain?"

A few frightened words in Dutch was all he heard in response.

"Can no one speak the King's English?" he raved.

"I can."

When the tall man turned to face Mary, her eyes locked on a large cross studded with diamonds, hanging from a heavy gold chain looped ten times around his neck.

"Well, I await news of this captain."

"He be dead. I killed him."

"I see. And do ye mean to menace me with those ordnances?"

Mary let the useless pistols drop to the deck.

"Do ye desire to join us aboard me vessel or remain with this cursed ship? What say you, Englishman?"

Mary's eyes seemed drawn into the blackness of his own and, as if she were falling into a dark tunnel, she fell to the deck unconscious.

Princess Letla rushed boldly from her hiding place to Mary's side, weeping hysterically. The tall dark captain kicked her aside.

"Remove this man to our vessel and set fire to this hellish ship. The very stink of it offends these waters. Make haste, lads, afore the sun sinks. Lock these wretched sailors and the girl in the hold. Be lively, mates!"

It took two pirates to pull the screaming girl off Mary's body and drag her to the hold.

"Shall I check the cap'n's quarters for treasure, Cap'n?"

"No, leave it. There be no treasure here. We 'ave wasted good time in boarding her. 'Tis an accursed ship. I want no further truck with it. How many below?"

"Over a hundred poor wretches, Cap'n. More dead they be than alive."

" 'Tis a blessing to them then. Lock up the hold! Light your powders and let's away!"

Mary rocked fitfully in her hammock, images bursting in her head: charging horses, cannons blasting, a woman's head rolling in the sand. Her nightmare uprooted violent pictures, sending wrenching pains through her tortured body. Horrible anguished screams filled her throbbing head. Mary felt flames searing her arms and face. She sat up to escape the heat, coughing violently. When the racking fit subsided, she was drawn by a fiery orange glow to an open cannon port. Then she saw it. The *St. Job* in flames!

"No!" She raced up to the deck and grabbed at the rail, screaming in anguish, fighting against the two sailors who were restraining her.

"What be that bloody noise!" shouted the captain from the quarterdeck.

" 'Tis the new sailor, Cap'n. He be delirious with fever and is distressed by the burning vessel."

"Make away from that stinking ship. Handily, me lads,

199

handily. Douse that man in cool water. Give him brandy and tie him in his hammock lest he harm himself further.''

''She sinks, Cap'n! See there!''

A large explosion on the *St. Job* burst her seams. Across the waters, the screams of the hapless victims were but faint cries. Mary's own cries had become only a dull moaning sound as she watched the bow of the *St. Job* slip into its ocean grave. Racked with uncontrollable sobs, Mary sank to her knees on the deck, limp, useless and filled with measureless grief. A hand reached for her arm. She waved it aside. The sailors left Mary to her sorrow.

''A man's ship be a man's ship, however wretched she may be,'' said one of the pirates.

There was respect due a sailor who was determined to survive such perilous circumstances. There was awe, too, of one who had had the raw courage to kill the vile captain of the accursed *St. Job*.

Watlings Island, Bahamas: 1716

That same July when Mary was undergoing the rigors of the brutal middle passage, Anne Bonny was sailing the tranquil waters of the Bahamas with her African lover. Leisurely rolling down Exuma Sound, they in time stretched over to Watlings Island, where Tombay had been living with his immediate family: father, mother, sister, her husband and their five children. Except for a very old man who had lived all his days on the island, they were the only inhabitants.

It was entirely by chance that this small colony had come to this particular Out Island. They had been among a group of slaves being transported from Jamaica to the Carolinas when the sloop had encountered hurricane-force winds and had broken up in the heavy seas. The only survivors, they had drifted for days in the turbulent waters, holding onto bits of planking, crates and barrels until they were finally washed ashore on Watlings.

Since that morning on the beach Anne had been attracted to Tombay. She could not determine what it was about the man that charmed her. His face was not particularly handsome, but his lean and sinewy body was the most magnificent she had ever seen. Her body had longed for his and she had desired to be held in his powerful arms, yet there was something more. When she went to his boat the next morning, somehow she knew that he was the only man for her.

After mornings of fishing and turtling, they would make love in a quiet cove or on a deserted beach, a private paradise where they could enjoy the intimacy of each other in the midst of the vastness of nature. Anne felt a myriad of sensations as she wrapped up in his body, a world in itself; yet her eyes would span the bright blue sea and she would sense the vibration of the universe at the same time. The lap of a shore wave would reach out and touch her, stroke her—the fingers of God, as soothing and protective and sensual as Tombay's powerful hand upon her.

Days and weeks washed over them.

One day Tombay announced that he must take a journey to bring supplies to his family on Watlings. Anne went with him.

The north coast of Watlings was Tombay's home. Thatched huts snug among tall coconut trees dotted a sandy bluff, which overlooked both the northeastern tip of the island and the jagged cliff rocks that tumbled into the sky-blue sea. On the lee side, the old man's dwelling provided a view of the great harbor. At the edge of a ridge of land jutting to a point into the sea, the old man often stood looking out past the protective reefs.

"Who is that?" Anne was lying in Tombay's fishing sloop anchored in the harbor, watching the old man standing on the point. Of medium height with straight, stiff white hair, he had a face as creviced as the wind-eaten harbor side of the ridge. In perfect balance with his surroundings, he looked as if he were a part of the limestone.

"Dat mon a friend," said Tombay reverently. "You, Anne Bonny, his guest. My family too. All his guest. Cuffee de Lord Mayor of dis island."

"What did you call this noble lord?"

"Cuffee. We two weeks on dis island before he come speak to us. He watch us first."

"Bloody cautious bugger."

"He have reasons."

"Looks Indian to me."

"He is. Lucayan. Dese islands Lucayan islands."

"Why are there no Lucayans in Nassau then?"

"Cuffee may be de only one in all dese islands. Mattie teach him few words of English and he tell us de story of his people. See, one day de Spanish come. De Lucayans call dem gods from de sky. Dey welcome dem. Den de Spanish capture dem all and take from dese islands to Haiti and Cuba to work in de mines dere. Many Lucayans kill demselves. Most all de people die. Dat be two hundred year ago. Like what hoppen to my people now."

"How did this man escape slavery?"

"Cuffee's grandmother and grandfather hide in deep cave. He be the only survivor now. Anne, how old be he?"

"Oh, methinks five and sixty, perhaps."

"Far wrong."

"Older?"

"Yes. Over a hundred years."

"That's not possible! Tombay, he lies to you!"

"Dat mon not lie, you see. We best fish now or have no supper tonight."

They sailed past several large cays to the outer reefs, where Tombay cast his fishing lines and dived for conch while Anne held the sloop steady and looked after the fishing lines. The water was so clear that she could watch his naked body glide deep underneath the surface. He is beautiful, she thought, very different from other men. Most men abuse nature; this man is part of it.

Tombay tossed a large conch shell into the boat and his muscular body followed. He sat panting heavily, every muscle taut, his enormous penis dancing before Anne's eyes. She gave in to the impulse of the moment. "Leave those bloody fish and come into my arms."

"Let me put down de anchor," he grinned.

"Best do it handily and quickly too, lest we dash ourselves on those reefs there."

The heavy anchor dropped into the water and Tombay barely had it secured when Anne brought him crashing to the deck in a powerful tackle. Soon they were sliding around the wet deck, their passionate liftings almost in unison with the flipping motions of the fish trying to reach a last gasp at life.

The conch seeped out of its shell to expire slowly in the sun.

From the nearby ridge the old Indian watched the sun glance crystal rays from the bright waters. His thoughts drifted into eternity while the two magnificent bodies in the tiny sloop gracefully moved to the promptings of their passion.

Rolling gently in the calm waters, the sloop and its occupants were still once more. They listened to the distant thunder of the sea as waves broke over the outlying reefs.

"Are you happy, Tombay?" asked Anne, lying quietly in her lover's arms. Her index finger traced a course from the crown of his head to the tip of his manhood. She ran back and forth along the same path, again and again.

"Too much happy."

Anne moved slightly, readjusting her head on his shoulder, intertwining her legs with his and stretching.

"Tombay, we are going to have a child."

Excitedly, he disengaged himself in order to look into Anne's eyes.

"Be dis true?"

"Yes, it is true. Some five months hence."

His heaving chest preventing speech, Tombay smoothed his hand gently over Anne's slightly distended belly and put his ear to it, listening very intently.

Screeching sea birds flew over. A multitude of sounds assaulted his ears: waves pounding over the nearby reefs, sail lines slapping the mast, the ripple of water against the hull, the fitful tossing of the fish, even the breeze against his own face—but no sound of life from within the womb.

Tombay looked once again into Anne's eyes, eyes the color of the green sea, and there he saw the life in her womb. Laughingly she reached up to put her arms around him and drew him on top of her in a tender embrace.

"No," he said, not allowing his weight to rest on her. "It will hurt de babe."

"Oh, it will not. You need not fear to make love to a pregnant woman. I am a hearty Irish lass, not one of dainty English stock."

Nonetheless, Tombay was careful this time. He loved her gently, never allowing the full weight of his body to rest on hers. His tenderness made Anne laugh lightheartedly.

The sea is laughing, thought the old Lucayan to himself in wonder. He had listened to the sounds of the sea for over a hundred years but this was the first time he had ever heard it laugh.

Tombay's family had been so overjoyed to see him that at first they had not noticed Anne. Once their excitement abated, they looked upon the tall lighthaired beauty with astonishment. Then Eben threw Tombay a wry smile. Mattie had stared at Anne for a long time.

"Mattie, this be Anne Bonny, my Annie," said Tombay warmly. Anne, uneasy under Mattie's scrutinizing glance, had taken Tombay's hand. Seeing the loving exchange, Mattie had gathered both of them in her arms in welcome. Eben had taken Anne's hand in his and smiled. Marie and Dye had only nodded a somewhat aloof greeting. The children clustered about Anne, giggling and pointing their fingers at her light hair and white skin. Once everyone had adjusted to Anne's presence among them, the family settled back into its unhurried life.

Not content merely to help Mattie and Marie with household tasks, most afternoons Anne would hike and swim and she continued these activities well into her seventh month.

"Tombay," Mattie would scream, "dat child be born dead if you do not stop dat womon." But Anne was gone, marching down the hill path to the beach. "Crazy white bitch," Mattie muttered to herself. She had come to love Anne like a daughter and could not help her concern.

The brush was so overgrown and the shoreline so rocky in many areas that there were very few places to walk on the island. Anne would walk a stretch of beach on the east coast on those days when she most wished to be alone, stopping periodically to pick up a shell or to look at the sea. All too soon she would reach the bluff, at which point she usually turned back. Tombay had said that the bluff was impassable, but one day Anne decided to attempt it.

Climbing up, she made her way carefully along the edge of the cliff, prepared to turn back if the way became too difficult. Great chunks of limestone had broken off from the cliff and had fallen into the sea. Looking down, Anne saw the marvelous formations, the intricate root work which time had turned to stone. She studied the shapes, the patterns, the delicate natural cement casting of tree roots and branches, and was fascinated. Filled with the wonders of nature, she thought that not even this wondrous sight exceeded the fascination of the creation of life forming within her own body. No one on the island had seen what she had seen. And she was sure that no one really felt what she felt stirring within her.

The day was cooler when she returned. The men had come back with their catch and the little village was busy. Mattie complained about her husband's ''rum sippin' '' all the while she hacked away at the conch meat. ''Had to bring rum from Nassau Town for his Doddy. Dat ole mon do not need rum.'' Cutting away the conch's entrails, she tossed them aside angrily; the cats attacked the pile with relish.

The children squatted around her, waiting for Mattie to extract the long, clear, wormlike part of the conch. Each received a portion of the candylike substance and, running off with their little treasures, dangled the strange things above their mouths before sucking in their salty sweetness.

Lovingly Anne watched the old woman work. It seems that I have known this woman forever, thought Anne. ''Mother, you are beautiful.''

Mattie broke out in a toothless grin, turned her head a little and pushed it down into her shoulders, giggling. She was a small woman, but that was not easily perceived at first glance because she had enormous breasts which hung down over her belly. One would have expected the rest of her body to be proportionate, but it was not. Mattie usually sat comfortably settled on her wide bottom with her short legs stretched straight out in front of her, ordering the children about and slapping at the sandflies which bit at her ankles. But her hands were always busy and she loved to talk as she worked.

"I had seventeen children, Annie, did you know dat? Seventeen children all by dat same old mon you see dere. Tom and Marie de only ones lef' now. Tom, dat the name dey give him on de plantation. He call hisself Tombay in Nassau. He want everyone know he be free African."

"What happened to the rest of your children, Mother?"

"Most die from fever, some were born dead. Dot why I worry about you. Promise Mattie you be careful."

"I promise."

"Plenty children runnin' around dis yard now, Annie. Soon we have one more," she said, smiling as she patted Anne's belly affectionately. She looked about, surveying her domain. Tombay was fashioning an oar out of a piece of driftwood he had found on the beach. Marie's oldest sat next to him, working with a dull little knife trying to carve his own small oar. The thin twigs would snap under his rough clumsy motions. Undaunted, he would pick out another shaving from the ground, study Tombay's oar for a moment and fall to work again.

At dusk, Anne and Tombay were wont to climb up the narrow cut where Cuffee often stood lookout. The violence of the waves beating against the rocks on the windward side contrasted with the gentle waves lapping the beaches on the harbor side. The view was awesome. They stopped and looked down over the edge into the tiny coves and watched the fierce waves spurt up through arches in the rocks. Nearby underwater reefs were partially visible and sea fans broke the surface colors.

"Dis land signifies de nature of man," Tombay said after a long silence. "Peaceful and calm on one side and angry and violent on de other."

"Look out here." Anne pulled Tombay to the north tip

of the cay. "Look below. Tell me what you see in those waters."

Time had broken the cay in two. A river passed from the peaceful harbor across to the turbulent inlet.

"Well, what think you now?" Anne asked.

"De waters flow together here."

"And?"

"It be difficult to see, but de gentle wave undercuts de strong one, somewhere in dere," Tombay said, pointing to the center of the passage. He thought for a moment and then understood. "You be devilish clever, Anne Bonny." He took Anne into his strong arms and kissed her tenderly. At this moment they felt at one with the entire universe.

Walking back, Anne was startled by a circle of light blazing through a cloud that hung low over the cay to the east.

"Blast me eyes! What is that?"

"The moon," he said.

"The moon . . so low . . . so near! If I were to stand on that cay, methinks I could touch it. Such a magnificent moon! To think we have seen it so close."

The moon climbed far into the night.

"I love you, Anne Bonny. I hope you never tire of Tombay."

"That would not be possible. You might ask if I would ever tire of the colors of the Caribbean Sea or that moon up there or those trees over there. 'Tis not possible, my love. Forever. Anne Bonny is yours forever."

As Anne and Tombay approached the settlement they saw the leaping flames of the campfire. Food was hastily prepared and hungrily eaten. After dinner the little family sat quietly, listening to the sounds of the night creatures. Cuffee stared into the dancing flames. The mere presence of the old man gave Anne a feeling of security like that she had felt with Joe Buck. She could see Joe's wisdom in Cuffee and often wondered what he was thinking about during these moments of private meditation. No one dared speak. When Cuffee took up his pipe and lit it, that was the signal for evening conversation to begin. The children, who had remained silent entirely too long, suddenly converged upon the old Indian. He puffed solemnly.

"Cuffee, tell us de story of your people. Where be dey, Cuffee? Tell us! Tell us!" they clamored.

"Can you not leave dat mon in peace?" said Eben. "You children bad."

"My people Arawak. Peaceful people, like you. Gentle like you. We love our home, our children, our garden and da sea. Carib Indian come from south, capture and eat us."

"What!" screamed Marie.

This was evidently a new installment to Cuffee's story of his people, and the startling twist surprised everyone.

"Cannibals?" asked Dye.

"Eat all boy children. Like best. Very tender."

The children erupted into an hysterical uproar, scrambling away into the laps of the women.

"Come at night in big canoe and slip into da harbour. Attack us in our beds, carry everyone off. Eat males only, keep females for breeding."

Eben interrupted. "What about de Spanish? I thought dey carry off your people."

"Come later. Hunt down Arawak. Dogs tear to pieces. I see and hide in cave. Almost starve, but safe. Others, not eaten by dogs, go 'way in big canoe. Never see again."

"Dis story make me uneasy—I do not like to hear of dis," said Tombay.

"Mattie," said Eben, " 'member in Africa when we first taken, we all tink de white mon want to eat us. Even when we come Jamaica I tink 'bout dat. Worry 'bout dat for long time."

"Dear God!" said Anne.

"Stop dat foolish talk," said Mattie, noticing Anne's distress. "Dose days behin' us now. We be free. Dis our home. No one both us here."

"You be wrong, Mother," Tombay said fearfully. "In Nassau I hear about Spanish raidin' party and pirates who hunt dese islands to capture de black people and carry dem off to sell."

"I will not live to see dat happen again," said Cuffee.

"Children, to bed," Mattie said loudly, putting an abrupt end to the conversation.

A sleeping child was lifted from Anne's arms.

"Come to bed, old mon."

"Soon, Mattie. You ever see a mon fly, Annie?"

"Only as they are tossed from a tavern."

All laughed except Cuffee, and the tension was broken at last. Tombay got himself into a fit of laughter and couldn't stop.

"Disgustin' boy," Eben muttered. "I did, I see a mon fly over de water. In Jamaica, I see mon do dat. He be Obeah mon. He tell us many time how he goin' to fly back to Africa. An' in de dark light of de wastin' moon I see him do dat. He falter at first but den he take off like bird over de ocean. In de mornin' de overseer look everywhere, but cannot fin' him. Dey set de dogs on his belongings, den go after him. The dogs run straight down to de beach, den dey nearly go crazy crawlin' all over each other at de water's edge. Dey mus' conclude den dat de mon walk into de ocean and drown hisself. But I know de truth of it."

"Old mon, come to dis hut afore I come out to fetch ye!" Mattie shouted. "No one can soleep wid your mouth goin' on like dat."

"In one minute!" he shouted angrily. "I do not know why I put up wid dat old womon. Never leaves me a minute's peace."

"If you do not need her, sell her," said Dye jokingly.

"I need her to clean conch," Eben shouted. "An' I not need you to tell me what to do. She helps me!" His voice softened. "She helps me." The old man went to his hut and Dye to his. Tombay took Anne's hand and lifted her to her feet; they wandered off in the direction of their hut. The old Indian lay down by the fire, drew up his knees and drifted into sleep.

Awakened by a woman's screams, Cuffee scrambled to his feet. Tombay placed a reassuring hand on the old man's shoulder. "De baby. De baby come."

But the baby took its own time in coming. As the pains worsened, Anne ordered Tombay to wait down on the beach. Everyone in the little village was sent away. Only Mattie remained by Anne's side.

"Forgive me, Mother, but I needs must curse or I shall never survive the rigors of this confinement." A hard pain came. Anne arched her body and clenched her teeth against the flood of obscenities at the tip of her tongue.

"I do not want to offend you or your son. Forgive me, Mother."

"Den curse, womon, but bear down. I want dis baby be born alive. If cursin' bring him soon, den curse."

Anne did just that. Mattie shut her ears against the strong language and concentrated on the action of the baby, while urging Anne to bear down. Her prayers mingled with Anne's grunts and curses.

Tombay walked the beach, viewing the sunrise. He walked as far as the rocks which jutted out into the water and back again. A small round piece of dry sargassum weed was blowing along in the breeze. He looked along the trail of seaweed for a seabean for luck and protection. He searched and searched but could not find even one dry, gray-brown ball, which should have stood out sharply against the wet, rusty orange sargassum.

Once at the path up to the village he paused, restraining himself against the urge to go up the hill. Now the children were playing at the edge of the sea. He could see Eben, Marie and one of the older boys out fishing. Old Eben was sculling against the billowing waves, standing stronger in the rolling boat at this moment than he could stand weak kneed on the shore.

Squatting, Tombay watched a crab scamper into its hole. Tiny grains of sand tumbled down after it. He thought the crab lucky to be able to hide in a hole and pull the earth in on top. I wish I could hide like crab in hole, he thought, but I cannot. I be a father now. I have duty to my child. I be responsible for all de people on dis island, old men and young, women and children. But if trouble come to us dis moment, I could not lif' even one arm to resist it. Anne—Anne de strong one. I be shamed I cannot bear dis pain for her. I gladly do dat.

Tombay looked up at the high dunes. Springs of tall grass grew in spots and the harsh northeasterly winds had swept deep gouges along the steep cliff. He walked on and on until he felt a thrill course through his body. Suddenly he turned back.

Accompanined by a torrent of vile words, a boy had broken from Anne Bonny's womb.

Once past the rocks, Tombay ran toward the settlement. Seeing him, the children jumped up and down waving their arms and, not waiting for him to catch up to them, ran up the hill to the village. Tombay raced along the path. Mattie was waiting to place the tiny, naked body of his firstborn in his strong hands.

"My son." He looked down in amazement and wonder. "Annie! How be Annie! Be she all right? It be so long a time!"

"Annie be fine. Resting now."

Standing at the door of the wooden shack, Tombay looked in on the sleeping mother and wept tears of love and gratitude.

Six weeks passed. The child grew pudgy, and Anne was nearly recovered, spending active days swimming, fishing, sailing, turtling, as well as wonderful private moments with her child.

Anne and Tombay decided to take a holiday for a few days and explore the south end of the island. Loading the sloop with provisions, they sailed out of the harbor and ran down the lee side of the shore.

The sea was a spectrum of blues and greens. Watlings was a pleasant intermixture of hills and valleys. Inland, the lush green hills built higher as they approached the southern tip of the island. The dense brush and tall trees sheltered thousands of birds, varieties as endless as the fish that inhabited the sea. Crabs, lizards, insects—there was abundant life here, but no people. Anne wondered if she could be content to spend all her days on this quiet island with her little family. She buried these thoughts deep within herself.

As they rounded a sandy point, the sea was rougher and it took some expert maneuvering to sail the tiny vessel into the harbor at the south end of Watlings.

They drew the sloop up onto the beach and rigged a tent out of a sail before beginning their explorations. Wandering about the cliffs, they discovered a deep cavern, as well as many sink holes with large trees growing up in them. Many of the trees bore luxuriant airplants which Anne had never before seen.

Exhausted from their day of wandering, they built a fire on the beach and cooked the fish they had caught on the way. Streaks of burnt orange splayed across the sky.

"Look, Tombay, the sun!" The sun flashed all green; then it was gone. It vanished into the ocean as if sucked down by some powerful magnetic force.

"What are you doing?"

By the light of the fire, Anne watched Tombay scraping at a piece of turtle shell. The fine powder drifted into a bowl of coconut shell.

"I am making a potion."

"Are you ill?"

"No."

"Then what kind of potion are you conjuring there?"

"Love potion."

"Do we need it?"

"Dis be a holiday. Dis for me, not for you. I soak dis turtle shell in sour lemon for three day. Now it be ready. You see. Have some wine."

Tombay took the powder, washed it down with two sips of wine and waited.

"Well," said Anne, drinking her wine, "what's supposed to happen to you?"

"You see."

The night and the sea were black, the moon new. Its dim

light sometimes caught the top of a wave and illuminated an edge of white. Listening to the ocean beating a steady rhythm against the shore, Anne was soon asleep.

Hours later, gentle nudges, tender kisses on her full breasts and on her neck and eyes, and deft fingers prying at the folds of her vagina urged Anne from sleep. Squirming in delight, she awakened completely only when the enormity of his maleness thrust into her. Tombay was slowly riding her, delaying until he was sure that Anne had sufficient enjoyment from his movements and was ready herself.

He made love all night. He was indefatigable. He burst forth into every crevice of her body. Spurting his seed into the cleavage of Anne's breasts raised her to new heights of ecstasy.

They slept till the sun was directly above them.

"The day is high," Tombay said, standing and stretching his muscular body.

Anne broke into an outrageous fit of laughter. "The day is high . . . look at yourself."

Tombay's penis was pointing to the sky. Anne rolled in the sand, laughing uncontrollably.

"Laugh. Go on, laugh. You be de one to suffer, Anne Bonny."

Tombay leapt on her but Anne had deftly rolled away. She scrambled up and ran into the ocean and was soon lost in the high waves. Tombay dived in after her. They swam, bathed each other and made love in the clear cool white water.

After breakfast they set out to walk around the point. Arm in arm the couple fell into a steady rhythm and soon approached the grotto cliffs.

"Turtle powder, eh," said Anne, chuckling to herself and looking at his erect penis. "How long will you be this way?"

"Three day."

"Three days, God's Blood! You will fuck the very life out of me. How will I survive it?"

Tombay maintained an erection for three days as he had promised, and for three days they walked the beach, climbed the cliffs and made love. For three days the two celebrated the wonder of their bodies as well as the wonders of the island.

Later they sailed around to the bay on the southeasterly side. The water of the inlet was clear and smooth, protected by large cays. Small fish and various sea urchins swam and moved about, unaware that anyone was watching.

To Anne and Tombay this ocean bay was their second womb, where they both were conceived again and reborn, regenerated, locked in an intimate embrace, each a part of the other and of the sea and of the gentle breeze.

On the fifth day, without a word spoken between them, Tombay hoisted the sail on their little sloop and they departed the sheltering waters of the bay to work their way north along the east coast of the island back to the village.

By sundown they had reached home. Eben and Dye laughed about the turtle powder. Mattie saw the glint in Eben's eye as the men talked among themselves.

"I know what you tinkin', old mon, and you just put dat out of mind. I have plenty trouble wid you as it is."

"Jus' once more, Mattie, before I die, I like to try it."

"It would be de death of you, dat for sure. An' me too, mos' likely."

Tombay slept throught the next day. Anne was content to play with Nditi. She still marveled at his bright brown skin, his fair hair and blue eyes.

Out on the edge of the north cay, Cuffee stood, keeping his eternal watch against the gusty January winds. He could see everything from this point, all time, all space, all worlds: everything that mattered became one with him at this spot.

Calm days stretched before Anne like a glassy mirror reflecting more peaceful days with her island family. Tombay wanted to carry the baby with him everywhere he went, much against Mattie's protestations. Each morning they would argue over him. Mattie and Marie usually received custody for the day. The hot sun on the water was no place

215

for a baby. But in the cool evenings Tombay would carry his son and go for long walks with Anne. The boy slept between them on the straw mat on the floor of their hut. Anne would lie on her side and watch the sleeping father with the infant lying in the crook of his powerful arm.

If there is any other man to equal this one for me, I will never find him. And this child born of my body. What of him? What is his destiny and what is mine?

When Anne thought about the future she realized that this island was the only place she and Tombay and their son could live together and be accepted. The thought imprisoned her. She looked past her sleeping loves out to the warm glow of the fading fire in the yard.

We have no future. Now is all there is.

One morning Anne had gone alone to work a field some distance removed from the village. It had been neglected for a long time, and Anne was feeling energetic and ambitious. The men had gone fishing and Mattie and Marie were doing household chores while the older children watched over the baby in the yard.

It was well past midday before Anne decided to return. Her arm ached from wielding her cutlass, but she had made a deadly assault on the weeds in the cabbage patch and cleared a new section for planting. It had been a full day's work and she was tired to the bone.

A quarter of a mile away from the village she began to smell food. Having worked up a healthy appetite, Anne quickened her pace and ran up the hill. Sweat poured down her face, the salt burning and blurring her eyes.

Strange men, seven of them, were sitting around the fire stuffing their faces with fish and lobster and rice. Anne quickly looked around, but saw no one of her family.

Where is everyone? she wondered. Who are these men?

Anne watched them closely. They were not dressed as pirates but were richly garbed in heavy brocaded doublets. They were smiling, grossly dribbling food out of their mouths and beckoning her to join them. Anne's blistered hand gripped her cutlass tightly as she approached, her body numb with fear.

"Where is my husband?" she asked. "And my child?"

They looked around, bewildered, jabbering to one another in Spanish and gesticulating questioningly.

"My child?" she asked again, holding her hand about a foot above the ground.

They shrugged their shoulders, all the while forcing great quantities of food into already bursting cheeks. Grinning broadly, they swept their eyes over Anne's body.

Cautiously she moved around toward one of the huts. It was too quiet. The incessant noise of the children laughing and playing was ominously absent.

She tripped over a long tangled vine and fell into the soggy dirt. Blood! Anne looked amid the low bushy plants and saw in a heap of small decapitated bodies a tiny blond head. A quick stabbing pain pierced her chest, stopping her breath. A thousand icy fingers grabbed her throat. Trying not to tremble, she forced three deep breaths into her heaving lungs and turned toward the group of men. With great effort, she smiled.

The men who had been watching her horrible discovery were apprehensive, but seeing her seemingly warm smile, they began to laugh and gesture to her to join them in their feast, offering rice and lobster claws with grimy, fishy hands.

Anne approached slowly. When within range, she struck, decapitating two men at once. The rest were dispatched in rapid order. Surpised, not one man had had time to lay his hand on a weapon. Anne hacked and hacked at their lifeless bodies until she could no longer raise her cutlass. Then she fell away sobbing, covered with blood, with the cutlass still locked in her two hands. As she rolled back and forth on the ground, her cutlass slapped the dirt flatly.

Exhaustion stilled her rocking motion, and her sobs ceased, but she continued a steady deep moaning for some time. She lay on her side, both arms extended, bloody hands clutching the cutlass. Tears had washed some of the blood off her face.

The others! What has happened to the others? Although she wanted to believe differently, she knew they were dead. But she did not have the the strength to search for them. Not yet.

She would bury the children first. Anne laid a gentle hand on the small blond head. So here you are, my love. And here you will stay forever. Pouring great bucketfuls of sand on the small mound, Anne murmured an old prayer she had learned as a child. The words came flooding to mind, although she thought she had forgotten it:

Four corners to my bed,
Four angels round my head:
One to watch and one to pray,
And two to bear my soul away.

Where are your four angels, Nditi? Did they bear thy soul away?

Her task completed, she saw the tiny rough-hewn oar lying in the dirt and stuck it on top of the hill of children.

She dared not go into Mattie's hut. Not yet. Tears came up quickly again and she forced them away.

Anne decided to go in search of Cuffee. Perhaps he was alive, hiding somewhere. Once near the point, she saw him—what was left of him. His head was stuck on the tip of a Spanish spear; the spear's shaft had been driven into the hard ground. Looking below, she saw the old man's body being beaten against the rocks by the angry sea.

Anne studied the Indian's head. His face was peaceful, eyes open, without fear, ever watchful. So Columbus's people finally took you too, eh, Cuffee? A full turn of the wheel. Anne seemed to draw some unseen strength from the face of the old man, enough to enable her to go back to the village. She left the Indian as he was, sentinel of the island.

At the village, Anne found Mattie and Marie hanging naked in one of the huts. Their breasts had been cut off and their bodies were slit from their privates to their noses. Anne cut them down and carried them to the beach in order to bury them in the soft sand. That task completed, she went down to the water's edge.

The Spaniards' piragua was pulled up onto the beach next to Tombay's sloop. It took all her courage to approach the tiny vessel. The bodies of Eben, Dye and her beloved Tombay were lying on the beach; the tide was attempting to carry them out to sea.

Anne pushed the Spaniards' piragua into the water and left it to break up on the shoals and reefs. Eben, Dye and Tombay she placed in her sloop and she set out to sea.

Once in deep water, she wrapped Eben and Dye in pieces of sailcloth and sent them to their grave in the deep. This is where they would want to be buried, in their fishing grounds, near their home. But she could not yet bring herself to relinquish Tombay's body to the sea.

Anne rounded the north end of Watlings, sailed over to Little Island and put ashore there for the night. The sky was blanketed with a thousand stars. All at once they seemed to descend and smother her.

Totally exhausted, she slept. She dreamed of nothing, no previous star-filled nights, no other beaches, no earlier sailing journey. Yet when she awoke her cheeks were wet.

Anne bathed herself and washed her clothes before setting out again. The sight of Tombay's body in the sloop startled her. She had not been convinced at heart that he was really dead. He looked so strong there one would think he was asleep, but for the great gash in his belly and the gray color of his skin.

Where are you now, Tombay? Are you with our son? Find him. It would please me to know you are caring for him. It would make it easier to be alone.

There was no way to stop the tears from coming. On shore, she gathered flowering weeds from the dense ground cover and placed them in the sloop. Pushing off, she sailed into Exuma Sound, heading north to New Providence.

When the sun was high she lowered the sail and drifted.

Removing Tombay's clothes, Anne washed his body, kissed his lips tenderly, then wrapped him tightly in a piece of sailcoth. Tying rocks as ballast to the foot of this precious package, she eased it over the side.

Tombay's body slipped from her sight slowly but she knew he would never leave her. His memory would remain in thoughts of love and tenderness as long as breath was in her and after, yes, long after that.

Anne let the withered flowers drop from her hand and watched them float away as she hoisted sail and glided off.

That night Anne pulled her sloop ashore at one of the smaller islands in the Exumas. There she burned Tombay's clothes and buried the fishing knife he had made himself, which she had found still tied to his makeshift hemp belt.

You never had a chance to use this weapon. Probably you did not even think to use it. I can see you standing there offering a share of your day's catch to those you thought were hungry mariners, until flashing steel cut your guts. Only then, perhaps, with your insides spilling out onto the sand, did you learn not to trust people. Did you learn that, Tombay? At that moment, did you think it? I have learned it. And the lesson has cost me dearly.

Anne needed time alone to purge her heart of bitterness. Several days passed before she sailed the sloop up the Sound to New Providence. She had nowhere else to go.

The Caribbean Sea: 1717

Mary Read stood staring at the red deck of the *Royal Fortune,* trying not to think. The early morning breeze pulled fine strands of hair free from the tie and whipped them around her tanned face. Her full white blouse flapped and billowed like the topsails. Walking to the railing of the quarterdeck, she looked out over the Caribbean Sea and watched the pale yellow sun rise clean and fresh on this brisk January morning.

Mary had been at sea over six months now. To her the months seemed more like weeks. The deeply maturing experience on the slaver had changed her, but only work would prevent her from dwelling on those bitter memories.

She was a diligent seaman, just as she had been a diligent trooper. In this way she attracted the attention of the captain, who issued her responsible duties. For whether it was her intention or not, Mary stood out among the indolent pirate crew of the *Royal Fortune.* They, like other pirate crews, were addicted to drinking and whoring, dancing and singing, cursing and fighting, in that order.

The *Royal Fortune* had been cruising the coast of Brazil for nine weeks, out of sight of land and without sight of another sail. Yesterday they had decided to beat up to the Lesser Antilles and careen at one of the smaller islands there.

Black Bart, the most dreaded pirate captain in all the Spanish Main, came up to the quarterdeck. He acknowledged Mary with a nod and snapped out his glass to scan the empty ocean to leeward. He wore dark green breeches and black boots polished to brilliance, their soft leather tops folding over just below his knees. His white tunic was open to the waist, revealing the diamond cross which hung in the thick black hairs of his chest. All was darkness about him, his clothes, his complexion, his hair, his eyes, all but those diamonds. She could never forgive him for having sent Letla to such a horrendous death, or herself for not having had the strength to try to prevent it.

The often backbreaking labors of the day kept those painful memories from seeping into her conscious thought. But even now images of the burning *St. Job,* and her friend drowning in the crowded, blazing hold, flooded her dreams.

For two weeks after her rescue Mary had been consumed with fever, but somehow, in spite of her hideous dreams, her hatred for Captain Roberts had burned away. And although she had seen him perform barbarous cruelties upon hapless victims, she did not fear him as most of the others did.

Once her bowels were purged of hatred she had begun to view him with detachment. He had saved her life; she owed him a certain loyalty. Although she never signed the articles, she obeyed them. Roberts never pressed her to sign them and Mary respected him for that.

For the past four months pirating had been her occupation, and Mary had had to learn it, just as she had learned the arts of war. The articles were clear and Mary, being used to the military, had no trouble adapting to them. There was to be no gaming at dice or cards, one's pieces were to be always kept clean, musicians were to have rest on the Sabbath, to desert ship was punishable by death or marooning, any quarrel was to be settled on shore with sword and pistol, and there were to be no boys or women among them. This last rule Mary viewed with amusement, thinking her hidden defiance of Captain Roberts on this account would suffice as a daily dose of revenge.

The *Royal Fortune* was a galleon of forty guns. Roberts

was an expert seaman and Mary, rather than indulge herself in the favorite pirate pastime of drinking, spent long hours with the teetotaling captain learning the art of sailing. Although she had yet to take the helm in a storm or during a chase, she was a respectable helmsman and her sobriety indicated that she was the best man for long-distance navigation.

The *Royal Fortune* had a crew of almost two hundred men, of whom forty-five were Negroes. Slaves were prime candidates for piracy. At least in this society they were free and had a vote the same as the rest.

The crew began to tend to their morning duties.

James Skrym, a courageous fighting man, was the quartermaster of the *Royal Fortune*. The surgeon, Peter Scudamore, who knew the Angolan language, served Roberts well during his adventures on the African Coast. Scudamore boasted that he was the first surgeon ever to have signed the pirate articles, and the fact that he possessed a backgammon table made him a popular man with the crew. The bully John Mansfield wore the silver call about his neck, the symbol of the boatswain. Mary also made the acquaintance of a Fleming, Michael Maer, from Ghent. They spent many hours talking of the Lowland wars.

Besides Mary, Captain Roberts had collected other strays. There was a stocky Polynesian man whose name Mary could never pronounce. She called him Koo. This Koo was covered in tattoos, pictures of ships, flowers and palm trees. John Walden was a giant of a man from Whitby. He carried a pole ax which he used on everything: boxes, doors, anchor cable, even heads if they happened to get in his way. He was deadly in close fighting, for his temper was short and brutal. The other pirates called him Miss Nanny.

In the crew were four musicians who were in constant demand, for the pirates, always a happy lot, dearly loved singing and dancing, especially when they were drinking. Pirates were suspicious of anyone who did not drink with them. Mary soon discovered ways to make it look as if she were drinking as much as the rest, but she would never allow herself to drink to the point of intoxication for fear of revealing her sex.

Now she watched a school of whale fish off the starboard rail, and was thoroughly absorbed in their graceful motions when the watch in the topsails lifted his voice in the long-awaited shout, "Sail ho!"

Robert's commands were sharp. "Helmsman, approach that bay and lay to. We will have a closer look at this sail." The master, Harry Glasby, came to the deck with the quartermaster and the boatswain. After looking at his charts, Roberts decided they should be near a bay called Los Todos Santos, just off St. Salvador.

"Canst see their flags?" shouted Glasby.

"They be Portuguese, 'tis certain, Cap'n," said James Skrym.

"I count forty-two sail," said Roberts. "Bound for Lisbon, I'll warrant, weighted down with bullion. We've fallen into a fuckin' gold mine, mates."

"God's Eyes! Cap'n, we cannot take 'em all," said Glasby.

"We can get the richest!" said Roberts. "But we have no time to waste talkin'. Look there, two ships of war. This fleet do but wait upon their convoy. I go below. Do nothin' yet. Wait upon me. I must think."

The Portuguese fleet was laying to outside the bay. The convoy deep within the bay was making ready to sail. Roberts came to the deck wearing his crimson damask breeches and waistcoat and his hat with the red plume. It was certain now that he would take this prize; his clothes bespoke it.

"Cap'n," said Mister Skrym, "Ye cannot take on so large a fleet. Each guardship is sure to have seventy guns. 'Tis foolhardy!"

"Enough! I be captain here and king in me own right. Ye'll do me biddin' or I'll blow yer brains out. 'Tis a merry life and a short one, remember that. Be ye pirates or bloody cowards? What be ye, mates? Think on the riches of this fleet. I'm for't! Do as ye please, but I'll make a dead man of 'im what tries to stop me. Helmsman, sail into the fleet and come up close to the last one to windward. Men, prepare to fight! Hide yerselves til I give the order."

The crew scurried around, loading cannons, fetching boarding axes, handspikes, pistols and grapples.

"Hold, luff here, helmsman," said Roberts, in a deep but quiet voice. He got the attention of the galleon's Portuguese sailors, who were very much surprised to see such a dazzling figure in their midst.

"Send thy master aboard this vessel," called Roberts, "and quietly too. If there be any resistance or signal of distress given, we will give no quarter. Men, show thy force." There was a sudden flourish of cutlasses, which surprised the Portuguese even more. They gave no word of resistance and quickly sent their captain aboard the *Royal Fortune*. Roberts saluted him civilly, as one captain to another.

"Sir, as you see, we be gentlemen of fortune," Roberts said, looking around at his shabby crew. "Now, senõr, simply tell us which of these sail be the richest prize. If you direct us right, no hurt will come to thee, but rather we will restore you to your vessel as safely as a baby to his cradle. Otherwise 'tis certain death."

The captain understood him well enough and pointed to a ship of greater gun and more men than the *Royal Fortune*.

"Must be sixty gun!" said the boatswain.

"No matter, mates, if she be bigger; she be Portuguese and we be English, and bloody pirates too. Steer for her, and handily, too, mate."

Mary was ready for a fight. Certainly this vessel would not give up her riches without a battle. They were so close that, even crouched on the deck, she could see the Portuguese sails flapping in the waiting breeze.

"We be nigh. Master, bid the captain invite you on board," said Roberts to his Portuguese hostage. "Say you have a thing of consequence to impart to him. Once aboard, say to the captain that if he offers us no resistance, there will be no bloodshed here. But if he gives us a show of arms, we will retaliate in kind and give no quarter. Believe it! Tell him that. Go on, ye lout, afore I slit yer nose!''

After the hostage captain was aboard, the pirates heard a bustle and Roberts perceived that they were preparing for close fighting. He ordered his men to board the vessel. Mary tossed her grapple line and was the first to board the enemy ship, slicing at the Portuguese resistance savagely. None of the pirates uttered a sound, only relentlessly slashed away with their cutlasses. Many Portuguese fell in the brief dispute, but the pirates lost but two. Although the battle was short, the fleet was alerted and guns were fired to give notice to the men-of-war which were still riding at anchor in the bay. The warships prepared for battle, but neither would venture after the pirate vessel alone. Roberts raised his colors on the *Royal Fortune* and opened fire on the fleet. Although his prize sailed heavy, Roberts was able to move it away from the fleet before the warships gave chase. Tarrying too long, the guardships lost both the pirate's vessel and their richest galleon.

Besides jewels and chains of considerable value, they counted ninety thousand gold coins, Portuguese moidores. One particular trinket was of exceeding beauty and richness, a diamond cross which had been designed expressly for the King of Portugal. Roberts decided that he would present this as a gift to the Governor of Guiana, to whom he was obligated for many past favors.

The crew transferred all the booty to the *Royal Fortune;* then, cutting all the lines, they set the heavy-bottomed prize ship adrift to be picked up by the fleet. Roberts and his officers decided that now it was fitting to turn themselves to gross wantonness, and they selected a course for their playground, Devil's Island, in the River Surinam off the coast of Guiana.

That night, after the coin was divided, the ship's crew caroused full measure. As a member of the boarding party in the day's activity, Mary was awarded two hundred moidores, more money than she had earned by honest labor in her entire life.

It was in the articles that the lights of the candles be put out at eight o'clock at night. Any drinking thereafter would have to continue on the open deck. Roberts had hoped this would curtail the crew's debaucheries. It did not.

Mary, having gone far beyond her usual measure of ale, was leaning against the port railing; the entire scene was swimming before her eyes. It was near midnight and most men had already retired below deck; others were passed out on the deck and would spend the night where they lay. A few insolent seamen were gambling with dice behind the crates of tobacco stacked on the forecastle.

Roberts came to the main deck, stone sober and irritated by the noise; the pipers piped on as he roamed among his men. Hearing shouts that only a winner at gaming would make, Roberts swung to the forecastle, hauled up the offender and threw him down to the main deck.

Angered, Arnold Cockrane raised himself from the deck and drew his sword.

"Dost draw on me, Mister?" Captain Roberts' eyes flashed.

"Why canst ye not leave me be, Cap'n? I bleedin' well harm no one by gaming."

" 'Tis against our rules!"

"Blast the rules! And blast ye too! I am fuckin' weary of your bleedin' articles."

"Watch your tongue, Mister; ye go too far."

"Fuck you, Mister, and the blackest devil carry your black heart to hell!"

Roberts pulled out both pistols and, in the heat of uncontrollable rage, fired on the man, killing him on the spot.

One Godfrey Jones, hearing the noise, came up to the deck and, seeing his friend dead, rushed at Roberts, who ran his sword at him, cutting him near the ribs. Jones was a brawny man and, undaunted by the wound, he threw Roberts over a cannon and beat him soundly. The crew on deck burst into a violent uproar, some men taking Jones's part and some the captain's. A general battle was about to break out among them when James Skrym, the quartermaster, rushed up to the deck to serve as mediator in the situation, a task which was indeed the main responsibility of his office.

"The cap'n's is a post of honor; he should never suffer to be beaten by one of his crew. It be mutiny!"

"But the cap'n did kill a man aboard ship. 'Tis against his own articles," said the pirate orator Valentine Ashplant.

"The man Cochrane were dicing," said another.

"Come on, we all do it, man, when we get the chance. An' here this day we divided a great prize. What else can a man do aboard ship with gold coin burnin' in his pocket?"

"Nonetheless, the man Jones fought aboard ship, which is likewise against our rules. He must be punished for't," retorted the quartermaster. "The cap'n must be supported in this!"

Several "ayes" were heard, and soon it was decided that Jones would receive two lashes from each member of the crew when he was recovered from his wound. The man did not flinch, he just stood holding his bleeding side, panting heavily and staring down desolately at his friend. The captain was unconscious and had to be carried to his cabin. All the pirates dispersed except Mary, who was too stunned by the action and the sentence to move. A few men tried to carry the dead man away but Jones put them off angrily.

"Leave him be! Don't any of you bastards lay a hand on him!" he shouted, raising his fist again. Everyone departed quickly.

Jones sank to his knees next to the dead body and gently touched the man's bloody chest. Thinking he was alone, he gave way to great heaving sobs. Mary, watching from a dark corner of the deck, listened to the horrible gasping cries which issued from him. Never had she heard any man weep in such a despairing manner. She wanted to go to him and comfort him but restrained herself, knowing he would have been embarrassed and angry that anyone should see him in such a wretched condition.

I know thy suffering, mate, she said to herself. Cap'n Roberts killed my friend too. I be thankful that ye has beaten

228

him for it. The man does not know what 'tis to love a friend.

Mary fell asleep on the deck. When she woke the next morning she found Godfrey Jones asleep on the deck, but his messmate was gone. Godfrey's shirt was soaked in blood. Mary tried to rouse him, but could not. When she saw the empty flagon of rum lying nearby, she realized why he would not stir. Well, she said to herself, if I cannot get thee to the surgeon, I shall have to fetch the surgeon to thee.

Peter Scudamore was suffering from his indulgences this morning also and was most reluctant to follow Mary anywhere. She gathered his bandages and helped him up the stairs, where the bright sunlight nearly drove him back to his cabin.

"Fuckin' sunshine," grumbled the surgeon. "I'd like to wake up to a bleedin' raincloud one day, just one day! Bloody Caribbean! I would this expedition went to Newfoundland; the gray north suits me better."

"Here is the man, Mister Scudamore."

"Blast me eyes, what happened to thee, man?" he growled, slapping Godfrey's face to rouse him.

Godfrey woke up, swinging wildly, until a pain in his side reminded him of his wound.

"Easy, lad, it be only old Scudamore come to patch thy wounds."

"Leave me to die, you old pisspot. Get away from me, man."

"Hey, watch your tongue, Mister. I be in no good humor this mornin'. Besides, you won't die for a long time, man, leastwise not from this pissin' wound. 'Tis only a scratch."

The surgeon washed the wound and bound it, then went directly down to his breakfast.

'Twould be better for Jones if the wound were grievous. He is like to be beaten to death all the sooner, Mary thought. The man leaned listlessly against the railing. He didn't seem to care one way or another about his fate.

"Godfrey," said Mary gently, "didst commit thy friend to the deep?"

"Aye, mate!" He managed to hold back the sobs, but tears gushed from his eyes anyway.

"I be sorry for thee."

He nodded. As sobs broke forth he waved her, and the world, away.

Mary left him and took her turn at the helm. Winds were astern and the *Royal Fortune* did ride a great road. Mary loved the feel of sheer power in her hands when the vessel was sailing large. Robust and healthy now, she had developed powerful forearms and shoulder muscles, while her hips were slim and her legs were lean and hard. Her face had lost its boyish look, making her even more handsome, and only a few tiny lines had creased the corners of her magnificent eyes.

Her physical stature commanded respect from her fellows, for at five feet eight inches she was taller than most of the pirates in Roberts' crew. Fear of discovery was not as much a concern to her now as it had been in the Marlborough wars.

On the day of their arrival at Devil's Island, the ship's company was called to the main deck. Godfrey Jones was stripped to the waist and tied to the capstan. The whip whistled through the air as the boatswain issued the first two strokes, then handed the whip to the master. On and on it went. Mary unobtrusively retreated to the rear of the company.

The whistling, snapping and cracking sounds threatened to drive her to madness. Clamping both hands over her ears, she paced the deck behind the dwindling group of men until a hand grasped her shoulder. When she turned, a seaman shoved the whip into her hand and pushed her nearer the capstan. Mary took one look at the great red welts and torn bits of flesh barely hanging from the man's ribs and turned away.

"Read, stand your ground. Do not dare to move away!" shouted the boatswain.

"Mister Scudamore, see if that man be dead or no," said the quartermaster.

Dead or not, thought Mary, I will not raise my hand against him. I can do most things but this I will not do.

"He be dead, Mister Skrym."

"Aye, then there be no more need to stripe his dead body. What say the rest of you men?"

The pirates agreed that the punishment should cease.

"You there, Read, Maer, Walden, toss his bones to the sharks."

They tied small sacks of bullets to his ankles and threw the body overboard. Mary walked away from the railing, her clothes saturated with blood.

In a few hours the *Royal Fortune* put into Devil's Island. They were greeted by the self-appointed governor, who kept three cannons at his door for the express purpose of saluting his friends. The governor was an old buccaneer, Roche Brasiliano, who in his youth had been cruel and barbarous, especially toward the Spanish. He had roasted one alive, skewered on a spit, for no other reason than that the man had refused to tell him where he kept his swine. Now near seventy and much less dangerous, he was called "Crackers" by the islanders. He kept the best inn on the island and he enjoyed life, especially when his friends came to visit.

The night the *Royal Fortune* put in, Crackers pulled out a pipe of wine and bid everyone drink. The same thing happened the following night, and for many nights after that. Even after a month of carousing with Roberts' crew the man never seemed to tire of his wild company.

The pirates grew restless. They had refreshed themselves, repaired their vessel and drunk rum, which was more plentiful here than water. Mary, beside herself with boredom, was brooding as she stood by a tent which she had fashioned from an old section of sailcloth, and staring out into the blackness of the sea. She was about to lie down on her bed of soft pine needles when someone came up behind her. Clasping a firm hand on her buttocks, he whispered, "Read, me love, I've come to your bed, you lucky devil." Mary turned, drew and sliced at the hand before she even looked into the man's face. He stood there dumbly bewildered for a while, looking down at his hand. "My . . . fingers . . . . Where are they? God . . . ." He stooped down. Mary saw the blood dripping from his hand onto the brown pine needles. The man had yet to feel any pain, he just searched the ground for his missing fingers. "Jesus! There's one. God! Another . . . and another . . . Christ! . . . Christ!" Clutching the three fingers of his right hand in his left, he picked himself up and ran off, calling for the surgeón at the top of his lungs.

Buggering fool, muttered Mary, as she moved her tent away from the blood. Serves him right. Next time he'll be more cautious where he puts his hands. I be not a toy for any man's wanton pleasures. Calm thyself, Mary. Thee be too bleedin' irritable, that's what's the matter with thee. I need a change of company. Perhaps some advantage will show itself soon. I am entirely too out of sorts. 'Tis a wonder I did not kill the man.

A week passed and Mary waited for the fingerless pirate to challenge her, but he never did. Roberts and a few others rowed over to Dutch Guiana to trade for munitions and other necessaries. Since Mary and Michael Maer spoke Dutch they were ordered along. The "House of Lords," a governing body made up of the oldest pirates, had declared that within a fortnight the *Royal Fortune* would stand off for Sierra Leone on the Guinea coast. Mary was at the point of complete despair, for Africa was the last place in the entire world she wanted to go.

As the trading party returned, they heard Crackers' guns firing and knew another pirate vessel had put in. This gave Mary a glimmer of hope. She went straight to the tavern and discovered that the pirate captain Charles Vane had just put in. He and his quartermaster Jack Rackam were sitting with Crackers at a table in the corner. Mary watched and waited for an opportunity to speak with them.

Vane was a small man, wiry of build, with a very ordinary face. The man's eyes were frightening. There was something about him Mary did not trust. In a way he reminded her of Giles Deegan. The quartermaster was a pleasant-looking fellow, of medium height and build. He seemed uninterested in the conversation and was looking around the room, smiling at the native women.

Wonderful smile he has, thought Mary, and an affable personality, to be sure. Rackam excused himself and came to the bar to order three rum punches. He took out a long clay pipe and began to fill it with a sweet-smelling tobacco.

He certainly strikes a colorful figure, thought Mary; his clothing be all stripes. She went over to the bar and introduced herself as helmsman to Bartholomew Roberts. Rackam seemed duly impressed and they began to talk.

"Where sail you next, Mister Rackam?"

"New Providence, our home, if ye can call it that. At least it be dry land, and has pleasant company. We have been at sea nine months now and are weary of it."

"Be there many people on New Providence?"

"Aye, Mister Read, very many. 'Tis a growin' thrivin' community. Be ye interested in comin' with us, sir? We have need of a tiller, our man has been taken with the bloody flux and has not been himself for some months. We could use you, Mister Read."

"Matt."

"Aye, Matt."

"I be bound to Cap'n Roberts."

"Hast signed the articles with him?"

"No."

"Well, perhaps we can negotiate a trade. I'll speak with Cap'n Vane about it." Rackam smiled and, taking up the drinks, swaggered back to the table. Crackers had taken leave of his company in order to arrange for water to be transported to Vane's sloop. Mary stood at the bar, sipping her ale. She glanced at the table and knew Rackam was speaking to Vane about her, for they were both looking her way now. Then Rackam smiled and beckoned her to their table.

"Matt Read," said Rackam in a formal tone, "this be Cap'n Charles Vane."

"How do, Mister Read," Vane said. "Mister Rackam here tells me you be a tiller artist."

"I be tolerable at the helm, Cap'n."

"No need for modesty, Mister Read; if ye be helmsman to Roberts' galleon, you be tiller artist for our sloop."

"I cannot desert him, Cap'n Vane. It be certain death for me. He be a man who lives by his articles."

"Speak of the black devil and he be here already," said Rackam, smiling.

Roberts looked over to them and, seeing Mary, his face darkened. He sat down at a table in the center of the room, facing them, and waited for his tea. Rackam threw him a smile and Roberts scowled back, then pulled out a pistol and slammed it on the table.

"I will go and speak with him. Perhaps we can bargain," said Vane. "Though it looks like the sight of you sttin' here with us has put him in a dark humor."

"I fear it has," said Mary.

Vane walked over and sat down at Roberts' table. After Roberts had been served his tea, he spoke. "Mister Read would like to sail with us to New Providence, Cap'n Roberts. Can we discuss a trade twixt you and me?"

"Let me ask thee a question, Cap'n Vane. Who be the first man to board any prize in close fightin'?"

"Why, the quartermaster, be he brave or no, he must do it."

"Didst know that Mister Read there were the first man to board a Portuguese galleon of eighty gun and over two hundred men who were waitin' to fight him?"

"God's Eyes! He be a bloody fuckin' brave man if ye ask me!"

"Aye, sir. Now I put this to ye: if he have balls enough for that business he can bloody well come over here and talk to me personally!" Roberts raised his voice louder with each word. Vane coughed nervously and excused himself to go back to his own table, passing Mary on the way.

Mary sat down and waited for Roberts to speak first. Many tense moments passed.

"You know we go to Sierra Leone?"

"Aye, sir. I like not to go to Africa. You know my reasons."

Roberts waited before he responded. "That girl?"

"Aye, sir."

"Well . . . the articles. . . ."

"I know, sir. I have practically all my money, over one hundred and ninety moidores. I will give it all to thee for my freedom."

"One hundred and ninety moidores—that be quite a sum. Dost know most of my men have not even shirts for their backs?"

Mary nodded.

"Well, keep your money. Thee didst earn it. Besides, ye'll need it. Ale comes dear in Providence these days."

"Then you mean I be free to go, sir?"

"That be right, Mister Read. You ne'er did sign the articles, and so you are in no way bound to me. However, I like not the fact that I have instructed thee in the ways of the sea for another cap'n's benefit."

"Nonetheless I do thank you, sir."

"You be a man of sobriety and uncommon courage, Mister Read. Ye has earned my respect. Luck to thee."

"Good fortune be with you, sir." They shook hands. Vane and Rackam sat amazed. Roberts put his pistol in its sling, took up his red plumed hat and quit the tavern.

The water kegs were loaded upon the *Condor,* a sloop of twelve guns and sixty men, belonging to Captain Vane. Mary gathered her few belongings and in the morning, with a fresh land breeze, they set sail for New Providence.

New Providence: 1717

At eighteen Anne Bonny had experienced more than most women suffer in a lifetime. When Henri saw Tombay's little sloop putting in practically at his front door, he ran down the beach to help Anne. Overjoyed to see her, he babbled words of greeting. But when they had finally pulled the sloop ashore and he took her in his arms, Anne's silence gave way to tears. He let her cry for a long while, stroking her hair and hugging her tightly.

"Thank God I am with someone who loves me," she finally said. "I need that now."

Henri did not press the griefstricken girl for news of her adventure in the Out Islands. She would tell him when she was able, and in good time she did.

"I do not think I shall ever love like that again," said Anne.

"Perhaps not, but how wonderful to have had such a beautiful love. Henri, he has never had love like zat. But zis does not mean he never will, or zat you will never love again."

"You know, Henri, Watlings Island was like no other place."

"How do you mean?"

"It was so apart from the rest of the world that I lost all sense of time and place there. A piece of land lies to the north of the island, a small cay surrounded by water. Standing on that spot you know the ground is but a speck in all the world of land and sea, but you feel a part of every-thing—all the world and the heavens too.''

Nights were hardest for Anne. She and Henri would talk for hours, for she never wanted to go to sleep. Her dreams were heaped high with mounds of headless children, all with the same face, that of her precious baby, Nditi. The image of his severed head was the most difficult to wipe away. Many nights she would awaken screaming in horror and pain. Henri would come to her and hold her in his comforting arms.

Anne soon discovered that when she was busy she did not think as often on her tragedy. After almost two months she became herself again, somewhat subdued but no longer morose. She and Henri had begun to invite people in for dinner and to visit the inn on occasion. Anne felt better from being in friendly company once again.

When Charles Vane sailed the *Condor* into busy Nassau Harbour in early March of 1717, he found New Providence much different from the town he had left a year and a half before. Now the island was a full-blown pirate colony, a second Madagascar.

Nassau was a crowded and lawless town now with a population of over two thousand souls. Thatched stalls lined the congested streets where people mingled, dodging live-stock, knocking down beggars and trying to bargain for the necessaries and not so necessaries of living. A band of sailors calling themselves the Flying Gang extorted money from the inhabitants and the infrequent travelers. Women fought in the taverns and the pirates wagered on the winners.

Captain Jennings had expanded the King's Head Inn in three directions—east, west and north. All three sections were outdoor patios thatched with palm. It was here that Captain Vane and his crew came that first night of their arrival to refresh themselves after the fatigue of the sea.

Vane's group sat at one of the larger tables inside the tavern. With him were Jack Rackam, Mary Read and George Fetherston, boatswain of the *Condor*. Nicole was perched on Vane's lap. She was beautiful, with her tiny

237

waist and large creamy brown breasts escaping from her tightly laced bodice. Her hair was extremely long and was twisted around her head several times before falling in a single long curl down the middle of her back. Her deep brown eyes were very large and slightly bulging. Right now they were closed as she kissed Charles Vane's neck. Her ever present cutlass was gripped in her right hand and hanging by her side.

Rackam signaled to Nicole with his pipe and jerked his head toward a small room at the rear of the tavern. Nicole kissed Vane on top of his balding head and left with Rackam. Vane did not seem to mind.

"Mister Rackam likes to indulge himself," said Fetherston to Mary. "'Tis a foul-smelling weed they smoke, a drug of some kind."

"Aye, I understand ye. The woman too?"

"Aye, she doth keep at it all day, they say."

"Does Vane partake?"

"No, but he likes Nicole to do it, especially afore their nights of love. Tis said he likes to be hurt during love-making, an' she be just the woman what can pain him. They say it of her, anyway."

Just then Anne Bonny entered the tavern with Henri and sat down at one of the smaller tables at the door. Anne was wearing men's clothes, green velvet breeches, knee boots, and a white tunic which was not tied in front. As always, her breasts were exposed; she no longer made any attempt to disguise the face that she was a woman. She wore a rapier, and Henri wore a thick leathern belt decorated with small silver daggers. Since her return from Watlings, Anne never felt safe enough to go out of doors weaponless.

Vane, Fetherston and Mary were all looking at Anne Bonny. Henri was talking very quietly to her and looking around the room. When Anne turned to look at Charles Vane, Mary saw her face in the glow of the lantern light.

How lovely! she thought. She be more beautiful even than Madame Beaulieu. 'Tis no wonder all eyes in the room be upon her.

Henri took another quick look around the room before

taking Anne by the hand and escorting her to Vane's table to introduce her.

"Captain Vane, zis is Anne Bonny."

"How do, Mistress Bonny," said Vane, lifting his buttocks up slightly before plopping himself down again. "Bonny in face and form as well as name, I see."

"Thank you, sir."

"And zis is George Fetherston."

"Mistress Bonny," acknowledged George, somewhat shyly. He did not get up; he only looked down at the table top.

"And zis is. . . ."

"Matt Read," said Mary, standing. "Mistress Bonny, 'tis a rare pleasure to make you acquaintance." She took Anne's hand and kissed it.

Almost compelled to look into each other's eyes, the two women stood facing one another for a moment longer than the situation warranted.

Henri, taken by the handsome stranger, was anxious to introduce himself. "Henri Duplaissez, *à votre service,*" and he bowed low.

"Likewise, Monsieur," Mary replied, returning the bow, not as grandly, but as gracefully as Henri had done.

"You speak ze French, monsieur?"

"*Oui,* monsieur, and Dutch."

"Read is a man of many talents," commented Vane.

"Oh, I hope so." Henri ogled Read's handsome frame.

"Come here and drink with me," shouted Vane. He poured them a rum punch and they excused themselves and went to the other end of the table. Henri was still nervously looking around for any sign of Nicole. He would not allow Anne to sit at Vane's table. They stood and sipped punch. Henri looked around the room, then at Mary, and smiled. Mary smiled back.

"I fear Henri Duplaissez has taken a fancy to you, Mister Read," whispered George.

"You surely do not mean he. . . ."

"Aye, he be one that doth navigate the windward passage, if thee catches me meanin'."

Mary burst into laughter and was laughing still when Rackam and Nicole returned to the table.

Vane stood up now and, restraining Nicole, who was practically breathing fire in Anne's direction, introduced Rackam. "Mistress Bonny, my quartermaster, Jack Rackam."

"How beautiful!" Rackam took Anne's hand to kiss it. "A pleasure, Mistress." He put on his most charming smile.

"Nicole, say *bon soir* to Mistress Bonny," prompted Vane. "She speaks only French and forgets her manners, too."

"Bon soir, Nicole," said Anne. *"Je suis enchanteé de faire votre connaissance."*

Vane was straining with all his might to keep Nicole's arms locked to her side when she spat in Anne's face and a torrent of foul French words issued from her. Enraged, Anne drew her rapier.

"No!" shouted Henri.

Because the woman's arms were still pinioned by Vane, Anne was forced to exercise patience.

"Sit down, you she-devil!" Roughly, Vane threw Nicole into a chair. "I'll tie thee down if I must." She sat quietly, her cold eyes never leaving Anne's face.

"I am sorry for this show of rudeness, Mistress Bonny. Nicole be a woman of inordinate jealousies."

"Best keep her indoors then, away from me, Captain Vane. I am a woman of small patience." When Anne and Henri turned to leave, Nicole sprang across the table, grabbed the back of Anne's collar and tore her tunic off her body.

Anne turned, drawing on the woman, who now held everyone at bay with her swinging cutlass.

"Mon Dieu! I knew it would come to zis."

"Henri, back away."

"Cherie, she will kill you!"

The onlookers quickly moved the tables to the edges of the room and the duel began. At first Anne had all she could do to ward off the powerful cutlass. But soon tiring from the heavy weapon, Nicole gave up her relentless offensive and began to dodge Anne's attack.

Henri fainted. The strain of watching his dearest friend in danger when she had forbidden him to help her had been too much for him.

Nicole was tiring but uncontrollable passion drove her on. Mary was amazed at Anne's swordsmanship; the grace and precision of her assault were astounding. She had never seen anyone use a sword with such exactness.

She be bold to fight barebreasted, giving no thought to her nakedness. 'Twould be the ultimate in freedom, Mary mused.

Barely able to swing the heavy cutlass, Nicole managed to bring it down once more upon Anne's rapier, this time snapping the lighter weapon in two. Ripping off what was left of her tattered shift, Nicole wiped the blood from her face and renewed her charge with inhuman strength. Several times Anne dodged the cutlass, looking for an opportunity to move in and disarm the woman, but could find none.

"Mistress Bonny," shouted Mary, "catch!" She threw her sword to Anne, who caught it just in time to run the woman through; another second's delay and she herself would have been dead.

Anne looked down disgustedly at the woman's naked, lifeless form. Finding her torn tunic, she wiped the blade of Mary's sword. Lost momentarily in the confusion of these events, Anne stared at the blade and seemed to study the intricate work in the hilt.

"Mistress Anne," said Mary softly, bringing her back. " 'Tis done." Anne looked into Mary's calm eyes, finding strength and reassurance. She was herself again. Returning the weapon, she said, *"Merci, Monsieur Read."*

" 'Twas an honor for me to commit my humble sword to such capable hands. You be an admirable swordsman, Mistress Bonny."

"I am sorry, Captain Vane. I did not want to kill her."

"You could scarce avoid it, Mistress."

"God, what a wench!" Rackam could not contain his excitement. "She be an entire army!"

241

"Where is Henri?" asked Anne, suddenly concerned.

"He be here on the floor, Mistress," laughed Fetherston.

"Oh, God, what happened?"

"Swooned, I suspect."

"You'll not laugh at him," Anne warned. "He is my friend and I will suffer no one to insult him."

"No offense intended, Mistress Bonny."

"Henri, wake up! Wake up!" Anne slapped him about the face and rubbed his palms, and slowly he came to. With her help he stood up.

"Oh!" he gasped, as he saw the mutilated body of the dead woman lying on the floor. "You, Anne Bonny, have done zis. *Incroyable!*"

"Let's go home, Henri. You've had quite enough excitement for one evening."

Henri looked over at Mary. "Oh, I feel weak, Anne. Ask ze gentleman, Monsieur Read, if he will help you to get me home."

"Oh you be devilish, Henri. I do believe you will proposition St. Peter at the gate of heaven."

"Only if he is good looking. But zis man, he is beautiful. Look at him, *cherie*, so tall, so handsome. I am in love. Zis time it is love."

After wrapping Henri's cloak around Anne's shoulders, Mary helped them home. From time to time Henri waved his handkerchief at his face, feigning illness and leaning heavily on Mary's shoulder. Sensing his intentions, Mary bid them both goodnight and made a hasty retreat before there were any further incidents.

During the following weeks Rackam pursued Anne with generosity and fervor, and she found she could not refuse his smiling persistence. Jack Rackam was a man of medium height and build, with a handsome face, large brown eyes, and thin black hair which was graying slightly at the temples. Lacking grace, he was flashy rather than debonair; he was so highly kinetic that, even sitting, he had the irritating habit of shaking his leg up and down. Calico Jack was always laughing, a natural display of his sanguine temperament. To him everything was fun, or it ought to be; if it were not, 'twere best to smile and go on to other things.

Mary, starved for conversation, had accepted Henri's frequent invitations to visit his house. Fully aware of his ulterior motives, she had made it clear as graciously as she could that she would not bed him. Henri was heartbroken, but, always a gentlemen, did not abuse the growing friendship.

Although she enjoyed the company, Mary had become acutely aware of her own loneliness. Anne had Jack, Henri always had somebody, but she had no one. The idle days ashore had only served to deepen the hollow of emptiness within her. At times, even in the presence of the others, her mind would drift off, carried away by the intensity of her own desolate feelings.

Anne was reasonably happy now. She did not feel for Jack Rackam the same intense passion she had felt with Tombay, but he was pleasant, easy company, and could always make her laugh; Anne needed to laugh.

Henri and Anne were curious about Matt Read and discussed him over breakfast, their own private time of day.

"You know, zer is something unusual about zis Read. I do not know exactly what it is but zer is something."

"You are just jealous, Henri, because you cannot get him into your bed."

"No, no, *cherie,* somesing else."

"He is a gentleman of excellent appointments, anyone can see that. 'Tis certain he is no criminal like the rest of these sea rovers."

"Zis be true. He have not zat look about him. But zere is somesing, some deeper secret zat he be hiding. You know, *cherie,* one day Matt, he brings me zis rag, some faded Guinea cloth, and he want Henri to make him a vest."

"He was taken by pirates from a slaver. That vile rogue Bartholomew Roberts saved him. At least we needs thank the man for something. Perhaps he got the fabric from the slave ship."

" 'Twas not new. I tell thee it be old and worn."

"You showed him your fabrics, I imagine?"

"Certainement! But Matt, he will have none. So Henri, he try. I use ze leather, ze brain trim, everything else I can sink of."

"I've seen it, I think; he wears it often under his coat."

"Zat is ze one. *Cherie,* I never see zis man so happy. He wanted to pay Henri twice ze price. But I give it to him."

"A very strange man, Matt Read, no doubt of that."

"Zere is somesing of deep emotion in zis man and somehow it has to do wiz zat fabric. *Cherie,* I know I am right in zis."

On September 5, 1717, George I issued at Hampton Court a proclamation for the suppression of piracy. It was mid-November before the mandate reached New Providence. Alfred Butler read it grandiloquently at the King's Head Inn to all who were gathered there:

". . . .we have thought fit, by and with the advice of our Privy Council, to issue this our Royal Proclamation, and we do hereby promise, and declare, that in case any of the said pyrates, shall on, or before, the 5th of September, in the year of our Lord 1718, surrender him or themselves, to one of our principal Secretaries of State in Great Britain or Ireland, or to any Governor or Deputy Governor of any of our plantations beyond the seas; every such pyrate and pyrates so surrendering him, or themselves, as aforesaid, shall have our gracious pardon, of and for such, his or their pyracy, or pyracies, by him or them committed, before the fifth of January next ensuing. . . ."

King George also promised certain awards of money for the capture of captains, masters, boatswains and officers of any pirate vessels.

"Fuck the king's proclamation!" was the unanimous response of all present.

"We have time enough! Piss on't til then!"

Several pirates took this suggestion literally, and Commodore Jennings had to hang the edict behind the bar to dry. Vane and Rackam immediately sat down to plan an expedition against the Spanish, one grand prize before January 5, 1718. As Rackam's lieutenant, Mary was included in the strategy meetings. Later, when all was resolved, Rackam asked Anne to join them.

They decided to lie off the Caymans and wait for a vessel bound for Havana from Cartagena. Vane felt certain they would encounter a rich galleon unescorted on this road.

With forty good men the *Condor* set sail for Grand Cayman, which lies thirty leagues to the leeward of Jamaica, and cruised between that island and the Isle of Pines for a fortnight without sighting a vessel. They then decided to run down to Cartagena and have a closer look.

Midway between Cuba and Cartagena was a place called Seranilha, an area of unknown shoals. Mary's prowess at the helm was put to the supreme test. Vane had misjudged his course; they were too close to the dangerous waters of the hollow sea. It was here that they spotted a sail to the windward. The *Condor* gave chase, bearing away from the rocks and shoals and into the open water again. She was a large vessel and Spanish. Mary gave the wheel to Fetherston and armed herself for close fighting, while the crew loaded cannons and prepared for battle.

Gaining fast, the sloop fired broadside at the galleon, and once grapples had been hurled, Anne and Mary climbed across the ropes onto the deck of the galleon, leading the others.

"Spanish scum!" shouted Anne. "Bloody bastards, murdering pricks! I'll show ye. I'll cut the balls off each and every one of ye and throw ye to the sharks as well!" Using a cutlass and ax, Anne slashed throats, split heads and disemboweled nearly twenty of the enemy.

"Ram 'em through the scuppers!" shouted Mary, who was equally devastating as she fought beside Anne.

The fighting lasted nearly an hour before the crew of *La Santissimo Trinidad* surrendered. Mary had killed the captain. The crew, disheartened to see their leader dead, begged for quarter.

Rackam came to the deck, ordering his men to unload the strong room. Vane was busy executing the Spanish officers by hoisting them by the neck up the yardarms. The dead and wounded were pitched overboard.

Besides a bucket of pearls there were five small casks filled with various gem stones, and over 200,000 pieces of eight. Taking a few bolts of fine fabric back for Henri, they left the crew tied, lowered all the sails and set *La Santissima Trinidad* adrift.

As the *Condor* sailed away, Mary observed the floundering vessel with its ghastly ensigns. Looking at Vane, who was standing on the quarterdeck watching the bodies of the Spanish officers sway in the yardarms like puppets, she wondered, when had that been done? I heard no order given for their execution. Why did not Mister Rackam contradict it?

The next day they sailed to Nassau and lived as befitted their wealth. Anne purchased new furnishings for Henri's house, trading gem stones for plate and chairs and tables. He made her an exquisite new wardrobe: coats of satin, taffeta and silk, elegant gowns laced with gold, plumed broadbrimmed hats.

From Captain Jennings Mary rented a small house with a view of the sea and she lived quite comfortably during this pleasant time ashore, but she was reluctant to spend any money on herself. Finally she gave in to Henri's persistent campaign. He dressed her tastefully in brocaded waistcoats trimmed with gold and silver, in deep rich colors: wine, royal blue and rich brown. He also made for her loose linen shirts, tight satin breeches, and cravats and ruffles of Mechlen lace, and found for her handsome boots of Cordovan leather.

In April of 1718 various reports came in to Nassau that the government of Great Britain was sending a governor to New Providence to enforce the pardon. Woodes Rogers was coming to expell all pirates from the Bahamas. Pirate captains assembled from all parts of the Caribbean, arriving at Nassau as if hearing a mysterious silent call of danger.

Once again the New Providence "House of Lords" gathered at the King's Head Inn to determine what might be done should the king's threats materialize. Anne, Mary, Rackam and Henri came to listen.

There was great contention among the pirate captains. Those present were Benjamin Hornigold, Edward Teach, Thomas Burgess, Oliver la Bouche, Charles Vane, Nicholas Brown, James Fife, Richard Sample, John Martel, Christopher Winter, Major Penner, Edward England and Charles Bellamy. All were speaking out at the same time and Captain Jennings, who presided, could bring no order to the meeting.

Finally Teach drew a brace of pistols and shot into the air. He now had the floor. "What be ye afraid of? Be we bloody pirates or no? Mount guns in the fuckin' fort and arm yerselves for battle!"

"Nay, we cannot fight the king's man," shouted Richard Sample.

"And why not?" roared Teach. "We do it every day. Fear ye a man-o'-war what can't even get its fat hull into the harbour here? Where be your sense, man?"

"It be more'n that, Teach," retorted Hornigold. "It be not one or two men-o'-war—it be the bloody empire, man. They will keep sendin' vessels till they squash us."

"Ay, go fart, Hornigold," thundered Teach. "Ye be too old and fat to fight, face that, man!"

"I be man enough to whip thee, Teach," Hornigold challenged, raising a hand against him.

"Cut it, both of ye," warned Jennings. "We will never resolve these matters if we fight each other. We must try to make peace with the Commonwealth."

"Fuck you, Jennings," bellowed Teach. "Ye be established here and can well afford to talk of peace, but look around ye, man, and tell me what ye see. Dost see any carpenters, farmers, or log-wood cutters in this company?"

"But we cannot fight the king's government!"

Bellamy rose to his feet. "Damn my blood! Damn the king's government, and damn ye altogether! Wilt submit to be governed by laws which rich men have made for their own security? Damn ye! I be a free prince, and I 'ave as much authority to make war on the whole world as he who has a 'undred ships at sea, and an army of a 'undred thousand men in the field.''

There was a silence. Regardless of these arguments, each captain would ultimately have to make his own decision. At length Jennings rose. "I will take the king's pardon."

"Well, I won't," shouted Vane, and he got up and left the tavern. Rackam followed him to discover his intentions. Several of the other captains followed Commodore Jennings because he always bore great sway among them. Teach went back to Carolina, and Bellamy took his leave and sailed to New England to continue his private war against the forces of hypocrisy.

Angry, Vane determined to menace all vessels bound to New Providence. Rackam went with him, but promised Anne that he would return before any king's authority arrived.

Off Rum Island, Vane captured the sloop *Diamond* belonging to Bermuda. He cut away the masts, drank toasts to the damnation of King George, beat all the crew and hanged the captain, who miraculously lived to issue a deposition to the Board of Trade. He continued these barbaric activities through the months of May, June and July.

During the few months remaining prior to Woodes Rogers's arrival, both Anne and Mary had given much thought to what future course they might pursue. Both had been happy in Nassau for almost a year and a half. Anne knew that life restricted by the rules of government was not for her. She envisioned this new governor as a replica of Judge Trott, or perhaps worse. Mary was almost tempted to stay; perhaps she could be of service as an officer in the king's battalion here. But she needed only to recall her dull experience in Flanders as a peacetime soldier to dispel that thought. Why break her backside building palisadoes in the scorching sun when she might feel the fresh sea breeze against her face? They would trust to time; some path of action was sure to show itself. In the meanwhile it was best to enjoy life and not worry.

One afternoon while boar hunting Mary reinjured her left shoulder. She had stabbed the animal, but then she fell against the spear handle and struck her shoulder very near her old wound. Anne lured the animal away from Mary by encouraging it to charge at her, and then she killed it with her spear. When she discovered that the injury was serious, Anne helped Mary back to Henri's house, where both of them fussed over her. Although her pain was still intense, Mary protested that she was fine. She insisted that Henri help her mount and she rode off toward her hut, leaving behind her puzzled friends.

Later that evening Anne came to her hut bringing a soothing balm. Mary was stretched out on her cot; her shoulder was severely bruised but the pain had lessened somewhat. When Anne walked in Mary quickly pulled her greatcoat up under her chin.

"I brought you a salve for your shoulder."

"I thank thee, Mistress Anne."

"Wouldst like me to apply it to thy bruise?"

"No, no, I will do it later. Please lay it aside. The wound pains me too much now to touch. The blow aggravated an old war injury."

"Didst fight in the wars, Mister Read?"

"Aye, Mistress, the Flanders wars."

"I did not know you were a soldier."

"The Dragoons, Mistress."

"Well, 'tis no wonder you ride so well then."

"I thank thee for the compliment."

"I did fear for thy life today, Matt."

"I am thankful ye are a woman of raw courage or I would be dead now."

"Oh, I think you would have found a way out if you had been alone." At length Anne asked, "Will you take the pardon, Matt?"

"I think not, Mistress. I am easily bored with life ashore. Besides, I be Mister Rackam's Lieutenant and I feel guilty that I have not been with him these past months. Will you leave New Providence with us when the governor comes?"

"I think I must. I also am bored on land but I may have no future opportunity to go once Vane and Rackam are gone."

"Then we shall be pirates together."

"Aye."

Anne had to pull away from Mary's intense eyes. Mary blinked, realizing that she had been staring too hard at the other woman.

"I will leave thee to thy rest, Matt. Apply the balm, it will soothe thee. Oh, and here—" she pulled a batik scarf from her blouse—"Henri sent this along to tie up your arm. Ye needs must rest it a few days."

Anne was beginning to take a more than casual interest in Matt Read. She went to the inn and sat down at one of the tables outside and watched the sea. I must examine my feelings closely, she thought. Anne Bonny is used to having anything she wants. Do I want Matt Read simply because he cannot be had, or have I some genuine feeling for the man?

"Mistress Bonny."

Anne turned and gasped in shock at the black man standing at the table.

"Who are you?" she asked, astonished.

"My name be Black Robin, Mistress. Forgive me if I startled ye. May I sit?"

"Yes, of course."

When he sat down and was in the direct light of the lantern on the table, it became clear to Anne that the man looked nothing like Tombay. He was the same size and build but there was no facial resemblance and this man's skin was much lighter. Still, he had given her quite a start, and it was a few moments before she could speak.

"You work for Captain Jennings, Robin?"

"Aye, Mistress. I had a sloop out of Philadelphia and pirated along that coast for a time, but I came here to take the pardon. I have no stomach for such business any more. I be a fisherman. I have news of Cap'n Bellamy; Cap'n Jennings said ye might like to hear it. 'Tis not pleasant news, however.''

"What of Bellamy? Tell me; I will hear it.''

"Well, just this past July 3rd he were shipwrecked on the shoals of Cape Cod and killed. What men escaped drownin' were taken to Boston and hanged. They say a preacher fellow there, Cotton Mather, railed so against not only pirates but Anglicans, Quakers and witches that the whole city got up in arms and they gave the drowned men decent burial only for the sake of their own health.''

"Poor Bellamy. All his life he fought hypocrisy; only to have his eulogy spouted by some pulpit thumper. There be no justice in this life, 'tis sure. I thank thee for thy news. I am weary from the day's exercise or I would stay and talk longer. I beg you excuse me.''

On July 24, 1718, Vane returned to New Providence in a fast sloop of fourteen guns which he had named the *Port Royall*.

He was accompanied by a French ship of twenty-two guns filled with barrels of brandy which were quickly unloaded and taken to the King's Head Inn. The inhabitants of the island caroused full measure, all that day and the next. The end of their idyllic existence was near; they knew it was only a matter of days now. Mary and Rackam helped Anne carry her belongings to the sloop. They had to be ready to leave at a moment's notice. Henri was despondent; he would miss them all terribly. Their only hope would be the possibility of Vane and Blackbeard's gathering a force large and strong enough to recapture the island, a feat which seemed hopeless. Vane had made his intentions clear, and anyone who wanted to sign on with him could do so. Black Robin made his mark on the accounts.

Empty brandy kegs were put back aboard the French vessel and Vane left a small crew there with instructions to set fire to the ship if a man-of-war came into the harbor.

On the evening of July 25th, *H.M.S. Rose* eagerly put

into Nassau Harbour. That night Vane set fire to the French prize, forcing the *Rose* to cut her cables and run out in the night for fear of being burned.

The next morning Woodes Rogers arrived and sent the *Milford* and another ship to chase Vane, who raised his black flag in defiance and under blazing guns sailed out of the narrow easterly channel of the harbour. The *Milford* ran aground and the other ship of war was not fast enough to catch the *Port Royall*. Vane and about ninety men escaped; His Excellency Woodes Rogers set his authoritative presence on New Providence.

When Vane was two days out he fell in with a trading vessel, the *John and Elizabeth,* bound for Providence with a quantity of Spanish pieces of eight aboard. Later Vane took a ship belonging to Ipswich. It was loaded with logwood, but he forced the crew to throw the logs overboard, then decided that he didn't want the vessel after all and sent them on their way without their cargo. In this manner Vane menaced the coast of America for almost two months, sailing as far north as Long Island.

In mid-September Vane's sloops successfully blockaded Charleston Harbor for ten days before sailing north to Cape Fear. The governor was obliged to fit out a force against him. Two sloops of war commanded by Colonel William Rhett scoured the rivers and inlets to the southward but, unable to find Vane, steered for Cape Fear. Rhett did not sight Vane's vessels there either, but upon entering the Cape Fear River he found a sloop of eight guns and fifty men, commanded by Major Stede Bonnet, who also had with him two prize sloops from New England.

When Bonnet saw Rhett's vessels he endeavored to get away, but all three of his sloops ran aground on the river shoals. Just as Rhett gave the signal to board, Bonnet raised the white flag and surrendered on Colonel Rhett's promise that he would intercede for mercy. All the prisoners were turned over to Judge Trott in Charleston to await trial.

Because of swelling seas, Vane was unable to navigate

the treacherous Frying Pan Shoals and had to steer away from Cape Fear; he therefore had no knowledge of Bonnet's presence there. Anne did not know how close she was to meeting her lover again and having an opportunity to save him.

Vane bore away north to Ocracoke to engage in riotous living at this favorite pirates' rendezvous. When Vane arrived he saluted Blackbeard with great guns, as was always the custom when pirates met.

Vane's arrival in October caused a large festival to be held at Ocracoke. Lying at the southern tip of Cape Hatteras, this small island was sometimes called Thatch's Hole because it was Blackbeard's favorite channel on the Carolina Coast. Other pirate captains came and went and the inlet was crowded with vessels, many of which displayed the death's head in their sterns. But as long as Teach's *Revenge* rode at anchor among these frightful ships, the people of the Caroline coast felt safe. Fishermen came to trade. Knowing they would get a good price, some brave souls from the mainland brought beeves to sell. The corsairs always had fresh provisions.

One such provider was Joe Buck, who was as surprised to see Anne as she was pleased to see him again.

"What news, Joe? How does my father?"

"Fairly well. Be you a pirate, Annie?"

"Aye, Joe. I am a lusty pirate now."

"You father feared ye had turned pirate, but I scarce did believe it."

" 'Tis true. How is he, Joe?"

"He misses thee, Annie."

"I miss him too, greatly. Dost see him often?"

"Now and again. The house is not as lively as it was when you were there. He needs very little game now."

"Do not tell him you saw me here. Promise?"

"I promise, Anne." He stared at her for a time. "Thee be a woman now, 'tis certain, somewhat more settled than before."

"Aye. I think of thee, Joe, and oft ask questions of thee in my mind."

"Dost get answers?"

"At times."

"Ye dost follow the dictates of thy own heart, then, because, having taught thee, I be a part of thy thought." Looking into her eyes, he had to ask, "You have lost a great love, have you not?"

"Aye. Will I ever love that way again, think you, so fully, so completely?"

"Perhaps. Thee must leave that to time. There be time enough yet for thee. Have patience."

"Look after Father for me, will ye, Joe?"

"Aye. Who looks after thee?"

"That handsome devil there," she said, pointing to Rackam, who was playing cards with three other men under the shade of a pine tree.

"He does not look like the man, Bonny, your father described to me in such vile terms."

"He is not Bonny; this man is Jack Rackam. James Bonny is no longer a part of my life."

"What do you for entertainment here? Ye must be out of patience by now, I think, knowing thee."

"The nights are lively."

"I wager they be. I know there be wild ponies somewhere on the plains of this island. Let us see if we can catch one for you to ride."

Rackam looked up from his cards just as they went off. He had grown suspicious and jealous of late. Anne is too beautiful and knows too many people, he thought. Who be that Indian she has gone off with now, I wonder? It be a good thing there be many women here. I'd not like to have to share her with these other men. I do not understand her; we be lovemaking every night. What is she doing with that Indian? Then he shrugged, lit his pipe and smoked himself into a state of euphoria.

Mary was aboard the *Queen Anne's Revenge*, playing cards to pass the time. Besides Mary and Blackbeard, Israel Hands and Joseph Curtice were sitting at the table in Teach's cabin.

Mary's losses were heavy and she was weary of cards,

but she could think of no graceful way to leave the company. She observed the group at the table. Israel Hands had been a London beggar before he joined Teach's company. Now he had wealth enough to gamble and he earnestly applied his scattered brains to the strategy of the game. Joseph Curtice, his tongue between his teeth, was likewise intent. Blackbeard was getting bored waiting for his mates to decide on a play. He put both hands under the table. Mary was suspicious. Israel issued grunting sounds of indecision while Joseph chewed on his tongue. Mary heard small clicking sounds and forthwith got up from the table and walked out on to the deck.

Moments later she heard gunfire and rushed back into the captain's cabin. Curtice, cards still fanned out in front of him, had his mouth open now and his head cocked at an odd angle, staring blankly at the two small pistols on the table. Israel Hands was screaming in pain and clutching his leg. Teach drew a card and was studying his hand. Just as Mary left the room Teach had closed his eyes, crossed his arms, and, with a pistol in each hand, fired, missing Curtice but shattering Israel Hands's kneecap. Mary saw a piece of shot lodged in the back of the chair she had been sitting in. Joseph Curtice looked dumbly under the table, then at Teach and then back at Israel. Finally the silence was broken as Teach's quartermaster, Thomas Miller, questioned him about the meaning of his action.

"Why? Ye needs a reason for everything, eh, quartermaster?"

"I must protect me men, Cap'n."

"God damn yer eyes! I'll give thee reason, then. If I did not kill someone now and then they would soon forget who I be!"

Nights at Ocracoke were lively, with music, dancing and other revelries. As the host, Teach dressed up for his evening barbecues in bright-colored waistcoats which clashed with the gaudy breeches he wore. He loved to dance. His feet, clad in heavy knee boots, pounded the ground savagely.

255

"I'll dance the heart out of ye!" he shouted to the unfortunate wenches who huffed and puffed to keep in step with his erratic timing. Afterward he would quench his thirst with a special punch of his own making. Concocting a mixture of gunpowder and run, he would set the bowl afire and guzzle down the entire contents.

Each night Mary walked further and further away from the village. Stopping often on the beach, resting against the grassy dunes, she would gaze at the stars or out to sea. Then, spreading out her colorful sash, she would sleep in the peaceful protection of the dunes.

Pirate vessels put into Ocracoke every day and captains sat around with rum and pipes, discussing the news of the world. In late October Oliver la Bouche, captain of the *Rising Sun*, recently come from Charleston, brought rather startling news.

Since he was highly excited, la Bouche's French was too rapid for Mary to translate. Vane was cursing; Teach was raving. Amid the shouting and confusion only one word was understandable. "Bonnay." Thinking he wanted Anne, Rackam sent Black Robin to fetch her.

"No, no," la Bouche shouted at Teach. "Bonnay, Bonnay!"

"Fuckay voo!" roared Teach. "Can't ye learn at least to speak the king's English afore he hangs thee?"

When Anne arrived, Mary introduced her as Madame Bonny.

"Non. Non."

Teach's eyes turned coal black in anger.

"Bonnay," repeated Oliver tearfully.

"Aye, Bonnet!" shouted Teach.

"Bonnet!" repeated Anne, startled.

"Aye, Bonnet! Fuck me eyes! Ol Bonnet. Bird spit. Thee remembers him, Anne."

"What of him, Oliver?"

Oliver pantomimed hanging from a noose.

"Oh, *Mon Dieu!* It cannot be. Stede Bonnet? Does he mean Stede Bonnet?"

While Anne was confirming the identity of her lover with

Blackbeard, Mary tried to get the details of his story.

"Mistress Anne," said Mary, "Monsieur Bonnet be not yet dead. He was captured at Cape Fear, late September last."

"The governor's soldiers were after us, I warrant," said Rackam.

"No doubt of it!" Vane was pacing now, anxious to hear the details of Bonnet's capture.

"Anne, help me, please," asked Mary. "I be getting conflicting stories."

Anne be distressed at this news, thought Rackam. This Bonnet means something to her. I wonder what manner of man he be. I'll ask Teach.

Anne was certain that la Bouche said that Bonnet had escaped. Mary thought he said that he had escaped but had been recaptured. She hoped for Anne's sake that she was wrong.

Joining Teach and the others, Anne and Mary delivered all the news. It seemed that Benjamin Hornigold was chasing pirates in the Bahamian waters. Woodes Rogers obviously ascribed to the theory that it takes a thief to catch a thief.

"Why, that old fart turned fuckin' traitor!" bellowed Teach. "God's Nails! He best not come up here. He best keep his fat arse in the Caribbean Sea or I'll blow his balls off!"

"Ned, why did thee not tell me Bonnet had turned pirate?" asked Anne.

"Ye never did ask, girl." Teach could see Anne was in no humor for his flip tongue, but this knowledge served only to press him on to further mischief. "Didst know that Bonnet did buy a vessel to go a-pirating?" Teach chuckled derisively. Rackam was rolling on the ground laughing. Even Anne could not suppress a giggle. "He be the only pirate I know didst ever purchase a vessel. Why, he don't know stem from stern, port from starboard, tiller from capstan, leeward from windward. He may be a lover and a poet, but he be no sailor, that's certain. Bold he be, though.

He have taken many prizes. Now he must hang for't, I fear.''

"God's Death! He be in Charleston; that be under Judge Trott's authority. Jesus fuck! The man will preach him into his grave.''

"Be there no chance of acquittal if he come to trial?'' asked Mary.

" 'Twould be like getting a fart out of a dead man.'' Jack was laughing hard.

"What manner of man be this judge?'' asked Mary.

"Naught but a hog in armor!'' Anne got up and waddled among the group, imitating him. "Where be this villainous pirate?'' said Anne in a deep voice, mimicking Trott. "Come to trial, sirrah!'' She kicked Jack in the buttocks.

She took up an old piece of tarpaulin and tossed it around her shoulders, and turned her hat inside out. Then she climbed into a tree. Black Robin addressed the entire assembly.

"Harkee! High and mighty Judge Trott doth sit in his high and mighty place and attend this high and mighty court.''

"Let the prisoners be brought in,'' shouted Anne to Black Robin. "Blackbeard, as Attorney General ye are bound to bring the charges against these men.''

Black Robin and a few other pirates tied up some of their fellows and brought them before the judge. The jury sat on one side, holding handspikes and axes instead of tipstaves and wands as symbols of the court. Among the "prisoners" brought before Anne were Mary, George Fetherston, Robert Deal, Owen Roberts and other members of Vane's and Blackbeard's crews.

Blackbeard pulled Rackam out from the rest and addressed the mock court. "Your lordship and ye gentlemen of the jury, this fellow here before you be a sad dog, a sad, sad dog, and I humbly hope your lordship will have him hanged out of the way immediately.'' After a pause, Blackbeard prompted the jury, "Well, what say ye?''

Popping up one after the other, each man in the jury

shouted out his "Aye!"

"Hold!" said Anne. "I will hear some charge against this man."

Blackbeard once again addressed the court. "This man hath committed piracies upon the high seas. An' we shall prove that he, this sad dog before you, hath escaped a thousand storms. Aye, he hath got safe ashore even when his shap has been cast away, which be a certain sign that he were not born to be drowned."

Mary had dropped to her knees, weak with laughter. Anne was laughing so hard that she fell from the tree. Black Robin helped her back to her lofty seat. Every time Rackam smiled, Blackbeard poked him with the butt end of his pistol and murmured, "Look sad, ye sad dog!"

"Furthermore, your worship," continued Blackbeard, "This fellow, not havin' the fear of hangin' afore his eyes, goes about fresh piracies: robbin' and ravishin' man and woman, plunderin' ship's cargoes fore and aft, burnin' and sinkin' ships, bark and boat, as if the devil be in him.

"But this be not all, your worthiness. He hath committed worse villainies than these. We shall prove, here and now, once and forevermore, that this man, this sad, sad dog, hath been guilty of drinkin' small beer. And your holiness knows there never was a sober fellow what was not a very rogue.

"For meself, I should have spoke finer, but your lordliness knows all our rum be out. How should a man speak good law that has not drunk a dram? However, I hope your loftiness will order this fellow to be hanged straight away."

"An't please your worship's lofiness, good my lord," interrupted Rackam, "I am as honest a poor fellow as ever worked between stem and stern, and I can clap two ends of a rope together as well as any man what have ever crossed salt water; but I was taken by one Anne Bonny, a notorious pirate, as sad a rogue as ever was unhanged, and I was forced into service."

"Enough talk, sirrah! Gentlemen of the jury, proceed to judgment."

"Right, your worthiness," said Teach. "If this fellow

should speak, he may clear himself and that would be an affront to the court.''

"But I hope," interjected Rackam, "your loftiness will listen to some reason?"

"Dost hear this fellow prate? What have we to do with reason? I'll have thee know, rascal, we do not sit on the bench to hear reason. We judge according to law!" Anne sniffed the pungent odor of the evening barbecue and addressed Robin. "Be our dinner ready?"

"Aye, your worship," Robin replied.

"Then hark, ye rascal at the bar. List me, sirrah, and list well. Ye shall suffer hangin' for three reasons. First, because it be not fit that I should sit as judge and nobody be hanged; secondly, ye must be hanged because ye have a damned hangin' look; and thirdly, ye must be hanged because I am hungry. Know, sirrah, that it be the custom that whenever the judge's dinner be ready afore the trial be over, the prisoner must be hanged. There's law for ye, you dog. Gaoler, take him away!"

Rackam lifted Anne out of the tree and the group applauded her fine performance, then all went off to eat and drink and watch the sun set over Pamlico Sound.

Unusually quiet, the band of corsairs chewed their beef while staring out over the water. Anne was lying on her back with one arm flung over her eyes. Jack knew she was crying over Stede Bonnet. Sullenly he swilled down his rum. There was always plenty of rum at Ocracoke, enough to drown the entire population. Everyone was out of sorts tonight and rum was more than welcome.

Mary felt a dire longing within herself. I must love someone again before I die. There must be someone in this company who cares about me. God, how I long to be held in someone's arms again; just that, nothing more. To think I may die alone be a frightening thought to me.

Momentarily overwhelmed with fear and loneliness, Mary puffed on the pipe handed to her. Usually she passed it on. Moments later she felt strangely lightheaded. Slowly the thoughts of trials and hangings drifted away.

Blackbeard, who was consuming large quantities of rum, remarked that the smoke of the hemp plant spoiled the taste of his liquor. Everyone was lying around the fires drinking and smoking; no one spoke. The aloof and doleful sound of the hautboy and virginal seemed apt accompaniment to their sullen mood.

Finally, Teach spoke what everyone was feeling at the moment. "Somehow this news of Bonnet's trial has chilled me blood and turned the very soul within me." Silence prevailed a long time after he spoke.

"His capture be just the beginnin'," said Vane ominously. "The governor means to hang us all, I warrant. If't be not now, 'twill be some future time. But 'twill come."

"I'll not hang," retorted Teach. "I will not suffer meself to be laughed at whilst I dance on a bloody gibbet. My lad Caesar here hath the order to set a match to the powder room the moment the king's men board us. I'll bleedin' well take 'em to hell with me, that's certain."

"If something should perchance to happen to thee, Teach," asked Vane, "dost your wife know where your money be hid?"

"Only myself and the devil know where 'tis and the longest liver take all!"

Mary seemed to be overwhelmed by gravity. She stared at Teach and envisioned horns growing out of his forehead. When he stood up he appeared to her to be ten feet tall and his voice reverberated within the hollow of her head.

"Come, lads!" roared Blackbeard, about to initiate one of his bizarre games. "Since we needs must die and go to hell, let's make a hell of our own right now. Let us go to me ship's hold and fire up some pots of brimstone; then we'll close down the hatches with us inside and see who can bear hell the longest. Come, who's with me in this contest? Two barrels of rum to the man what can stay the longest!"

Several men accompanied him as he headed for his ship. Mary crawled away into the night. She wanted nothing to do with this evening's entertainment. Slowly she made her way along the beach on the ocean side of the point. As she passed Jack's tent she heard him and Anne exchange oaths. She walked faster, leaving the sounds of their argument behind.

"What are ye raving about, Jack Rackam!" shouted Anne. "You have not been wronged by me. Stede and I were lovers long before I ever met you. I am with *you* now, not him."

"Ye loves him still, dost thee not? I see it in your eyes. Don't lie to me, woman. I know thee too well."

"You know me not at all, Jack Rackam. If ye did, ye would give me a word of comfort now and not be shouting at me."

"You be my woman, Anne Bonny, and I'll not share thee with anyone else, alive or dead."

"I am no man's woman, Jack. I am my own woman or none."

"Fuck thyself then."

"Aye, an' ye can screw your cock into that rum bottle for all I care. Ye spends more time caressin' it then me."

"Wilt foreswear my bed, then, too?"

"Jack, listen. Every night ye come in here and mount me as if I were a dog, and when ye are through ye roll away and sleep. A woman needs tenderness, Jack. 'Tis even more important than swiving."

"A tender man be no true man."

"Ye be wrong there, Jack."

"Your Stede Bonnet, be he a tender man?"

"Aye."

"Well, he'll hang for all that."

"Perhaps he will. Ye know how to cut, Jack."

"I'm sorry. It be the rum. Come to my arms, Anne Bonny."

"Not til you are sober. You'll not bed me again when in your cups, believe it! Best think on what I say, Jack."

Anne left the tent and walked down the beach away from the village. Jack Rackam fell deep into his bottle.

Mary, lying with her back against a sand dune, was

staring out over the water. Not quite herself yet, she felt as if she were floating on the rolling waves. No one came to this, her private place, and she was grateful because she was feeling completely relaxed and defenseless now. Giving way altogether, she allowed herself to drift upon the sea of her fantasy.

Anne, walking slowly, came quietly upon her. Anne stood back and watched and thought to herself, Matt Read is unlike ordinary men. 'Tis true he is handsome, kind, compassionate and gentle, yet he is also bold, daring and courageous. Why is he always alone? He will allow no intimate contact with either women or men. I have watched many approach him only to be rejected. He doth it courteously yet 'tis rejection all the same.

Well, Anne Bonny, rejection is the worst that can happen to thee if ye try him. Canst take rejection, girl? That needs yet to be proved. The November night is cool and I did leave my tent without a wrap. Wouldst seek warmth, then, Anne? God knows, thee have need of't.

Anne sat down on Mary's thick sash and rested her hand on Mary's thigh. He is asleep, thought Anne. How beautiful he is. The breeze stirred wisps of fine hair about Mary's handsome face. Anne traced the curve of her throat, and noticed the Buinea cloth vest buttoned tightly across Mary's chest. Anne felt the rough material, trying to gain through her fingertips an understanding of its origin. Taking Mary's hand in her own, she kissed it tenderly. Still Mary did not awaken. With feathery strokes, Anne touched every part of Mary's face and neck. Her touch became heavier as she gripped the strong muscles of Mary's arms and shoulders. Rolling half on top of Mary, Anne began to kiss her face and neck.

God, how strong his body is. Anne felt along Mary's legs, arms and shoulders and she kissed her lips tenderly. Oh, God, I am undone, murmured Anne, unable to quell the throbbing heat of her body.

Thinking herself in a dream, Mary wrapped her powerful arms around Anne and responded to her kisses as their bodies dissolved into a passionate embrace. For Mary, the feeling was blissful; she did not even care to know if she dreamed or who this person was who initiated such rapture.

Mary's response prompted Anne's fervor. With growing passion their kisses deepend. Not until Anne rolled onto her, pushing her soft full breasts into her flattened chest, did Mary know that her lover was Anne Bonny. But it was too late to stop her now. Anne's lovemaking was so urgent and breathtaking that Mary's entire body weakened. She had no power to resist or even to speak.

The sensuousness of Anne's orgasmic movements and the passion of her kisses brought Mary to incomparable heights of love. She drifted off, away into the heavens somewhere. When she came back, she tightened her arms around Anne in order to get a sense of reality. Struggling for breath, she tried to speak, as Anne was untying her codpiece, but could not.

Matt's arms felt as wonderful to Anne as she had known they would, and now she longed for the ultimate connection with this attractive man. I'll not be rejected, for I can sense the strength of his feelings, Anne assured herself. Mary lay still under Anne's groping fingers. The movement of Anne's hand became furtive once she encounted the wetness of Mary's private place. Mary could feel Anne's bewilderment in the touch of her hand, but she could not speak.

Not believing that she could have been so thoroughly deceived, Anne unbuttoned Mary's tight vest and uncovered her beautifully rounded breasts. There was no doubt in Anne's mind now. Matt Read was a woman. Anne felt Mary's body shake as if she were crying and, reaching up to touch her face, felt the tears.

"I be sorry to disappoint thee, Anne."

Laughing, Anne said, "Just like a woman to cry! What a grand joke on all of us. Ye had me fooled, and Henri; you had him almost crazy.

Both women were laughing now. Tension released, Anne put her arms around Mary and embraced her warmly. Mary responded in kind.

"Poor Henri," chuckled Anne. "How disappointed he

will be in thee. Oh, how he pined.''

For a few moments they lay still.

''What is your name, then, Matt Read?''

''Mary.''

'' 'Twas my mother's name.''

Mary was holding Anne's hand tightly. It seemed to her that if she loosened her grip even for an instant she would lose something very precious. Anne's hand was her anchor; she would be adrift without it.

Although her feelings were intense at this moment, Mary could not help chuckling at the irony of her discovery.

''What is it?'' asked Anne, confused by Mary's laugh and the grip she had of her hand.

''I cannot help thinking, I have kept this secret from entire armies and hordes of pirates, only to be discovered by one woman.''

''Relax, thee has my hand in a death grip. Dost know it? Your secret is safe with me, Mary. No one will learn of't from me, believe it. This deceit has been hard on thee, has it not?''

''Aye.''

''It cannot be an easy thing to play a part all the time. Canst never be thyself. Always thee must be on guard.''

''Aye, 'tis difficult, even desperate at times.''

''And tonight, dost always sleep so soundly? If so, it should have been a danger to thee before this time.''

''I did partake of the heavy smoke. I thought myself in a dream somewhere.''

''Didst know me?''

''Not at first, and when I did my limbs were weak, powerless to resist.''

''Didst want to resist? Be honest; thee can answer me.''

''I . . . I be desperate lonely and longed for a loving touch . . . to be held in comforting arms . . . I . . . . And what of you, Anne? Why did you come to me this night?''

''I was troubled in my mind. I do confess that I have been attracted to thee for a long time now. 'Twas fear of rejection that kept me away. I came here and found thee asleep and, quite truthfully, I took full advantage of the situation. So ye see I well deserve what I got."

"What did you get?"

"That is the most surprising thing of all. My feeling is as strong now, knowing you are a woman, as when I kissed thee and held thee and touched thee, thinking ye were a man. I feel no shame at that, do you?"

"None. I be surprised at that too."

"I have felt deep genuine love for only one man in my life. This feeling I have with thee be akin to what I had with Tombay, my lover who was killed by the Spanish. Remember, I told thee of him."

"Aye."

"I never thought I could love anyone again, not like that; and I never did think I could ever love a woman. Didst ever have a lover, Mary?"

"Aye. I buried my husband in Flanders almost three years ago. I loved him well, and lived as a woman the six years we were married. 'Twas the only time I did so."

"Six years? I didst have my Tombay only a year. Didst have any children?"

"No, we were never blessed with children. I know not why. And you?"

"A son . . . a sweet brown baby boy. . . ."

Mary knew by Anne's quiet sobs that the baby was dead. She drew Anne closer into her arms and held her tightly until the pain of her memory passed.

"Tombay was a free African?" asked Mary.

"Aye."

"Before I was picked up by pirates, I was aboard a slaver where a young slave girl kept me alive after I was nearly whipped to death."

"What happened to her?"

"Captain Roberts had all the people locked in the hold and burned them alive in the vessel. And I, poor bastard, was taken unconscious to Roberts's vessel. I would have fought to my death to save that girl. Very few people in my life had ever been kind to me."

"She gave thee this vest, did she not?"

266

"Aye, when my shirt had been stripped from my back, she gave me this, her only garment. 'Tis strange I should think of her now. I did love her. It felt simple and natural to do so. Somehow it was like what I felt with thee earlier. 'Tis difficult to explain."

"There be some affections women feel only with other women. A special kind of love, a tenderness and comfort which men do not provide. I understand thee very well, Mary. Ye need never be lonely again. I am your friend. Ye can tell me what ye have never told to anyone before. If ever ye need comfort, I will come to thee."

"Thank thee, Anne. If ever you have need of me, I will be with thee also, believe it."

She drew the long woolen sash around Anne and herself. The women stared up into the starry night and listened to the waves lap the shore.

The next morning Rackam found Anne sleeping in Mary's arms and he went nearly wild with rage.

"Bitch! I'll kill thee for this. I knew I'd find thee in another man's bed."

Anne confronted Jack first to allow Mary enough time to dress.

"Jack, this is not what it seems."

"Oh no? Look at thee, naked as a jay. If ye were not fuckin' with this man, what were ye doin'? Tell me, hell-kite!" He drew his cutlass.

Not bothering to tie her shirt, Anne stepped into her breeches.

"Jack, calm thyself, please. You are too hot!"

"Not hot enough, I warrant. I'll whip myself into a frenzy yet and kill the both of ye. See if I don't."

"Ye have no cause for thy jealous ravings. I was cold last night and Matt shared his blanket with me, that is all."

"Woman, dost think me stupid? Naked abed and he did not fuck thee. Hah! Draw, Read!"

"I do not want to fight thee, Jack," said Mary, refusing to draw her sword.

"I'll kill thee anyway." He lunged at Mary, who drew

267

her sword and caught his cutlass, turning it away from her breast. They fought in the foamy sea wash. Mary took a defensive posture against Jack's wild blows but he was no real threat to her.

"Ye looks foolish, Jack. You know Matt is the better swordsman. Stop this now before ye get hurt."

"Don't pretend to care about me, bitch! I know thee doesn't."

"Matt, don't hurt him!" warned Anne, perceiving that Jack's assault was beginning to anger Mary.

"Rackam, damn thee, man, back off!" shouted Mary.

"I will fight thee to the death, damn your blood! I'll teach thee to bull another man's wench."

Jack's cutlass slit Mary's vest open and the blade nicked her chin.

"Stop it, Jack," screamed Anne in fear. "You have drawn blood now; 'tis enough. Leave off!"

"Damn him! Not til I've killed him."

"Damn thee, Jack," shouted Anne, "stop long enough to look at your opponent."

Mary's chest was completely uncovered. She looked at Anne in despair, blood running down her neck onto her naked breasts.

"Forgive me, Mary. I cannot let him kill thee, and I know you would not hurt him for my sake."

"Damn me eyes, Matt, thee has teats!" Rackam gasped in surprise.

"You foolish bastard!" said Anne. "Why did thee not listen to me? Matt is a woman; her name is Mary."

"Lucifer's balls! When did this happen?"

"Beef brain! You'll not say a word of this," warned Anne, "or I'll slit your throat. You keep your drunken tongue still. Swear!"

"Jack, you must vow to say nothing of this," said Mary.

"I'll not say a word."

"Swear on Mary's sword," demanded Anne.

Jack put his hand on Mary's sword hilt. "I swear! I be sorry I did hurt thee, Read."

"I think no ill of't, Jack. Just remember your promise.

268

You and Anne be the only people in the world who know of my true sex. If you let slip the knowledge I will have to kill thee to deny it—and I will, believe it.''

"Aye, I understand thee well. Your secret be safe with me.'' He left and walked back to the village.

It took almost a half hour for Anne to stop the bleeding of Mary's chin, which had been cut to the bone. Anne applied a certain moist leaf to draw the skin together. There was also a hairline scratch from Mary's throat to her navel.

"Thank God this cut on your chest is not deeper.''

"Thanks for. . . .''

"Don't talk, Mary. I don't want your chin to open again. We'll go to the *Revenge*. Wear my tunic; I can wrap up in your sash.'' Anne helped Mary out of her bloody garments. "I'll get the blood out of this vest and repair it for you.''

"Thanks. . . .''

"No, don't speak. Best throw this shirt away. Oh, dear God!'' Anne was shocked at the sight of Mary's scarred back and stared at it for a long time. "Jesus! I hope you killed the man who did this to you.''

Mary nodded.

"Here, get into this.'' Anne helped Mary into the tunic. "You go ahead. I'll follow after and meet thee at the *Revenge*.''

Mary touched Anne's face gently in gratitude and began to walk toward the pirate village.

In November of 1718 there were nearly two thousand pirates out menacing the seas. Vane and Teach were the most sought-after captains. Colonial governors feared pirate threats to take over New Providence. There was continued destruction of trade in the West Indies and the Main of America.

Vane made hasty preparations to leave Okracoke, knowing full well that if he stayed he could be captured along with Teach. Blackbeard was determined to remain in his hole. Surely his friend Governor Eden would not betray him. Teach bid fond farewell to his friends, firing off

269

three brace of pistols into the air, his hat pulled down over his face to hide his tears.

The *Port Royall* sailed north, and Vane cruised the New England coast for several weeks without sighting any other vessel. Finally, in late November, near Delaware Bay, Vane took a small brigantine, the *Protestant Caesar,* bound from Charleston to Salem. Vane's crew was drunk and the *Port Royall* suffered a broken bowsprit during the boarding. Angered at this loss, Vane was provoked to considerable mischief.

"By Christ, ye'll pay for me damaged vessel, ye whoreson knaves. Where be yer money hid?"

The officers of the *Protestant Caesar* were silent.

Vane beat the master, John Shattock, about the deck with the flat of his cutlass. "Speak, man; where be your money?" The man was in too much pain to speak. Vane continued to beat him. "Speak, I say, or I'll throw you overboard with a doubleheaded shot round your neck! Hear me, man!" Finally the master pointed to his cabin. "Ye best be tellin' the truth, Mister, or I'll cut off yer lips and boil 'em before yer fuckin' eyes!" He left the man groaning on the deck and beckoned Robert Deal to come with him to the master's cabin.

"I hate these barbarities, Jack," said Anne, as she helped him tie up the crew of the brigantine. "Canst go against him in this?"

"I look for overthrow every day. Be patient, Anne. Our. . . ."

Vane stormed back to the deck. "Nothing, not one farthing. You're a bleedin' liar, Mister."

Shattock crawled away, whimpering. "Please, give me but a moment to beg forgiveness of my sins."

"Damn thee, man," shouted Vane, drawing his pistol, "this be no time to pray!" And with that he shot the man dead.

"Deal, bring the quartermaster and the rest of these officers between decks. We'll try a sweating. Perhaps that will loosen their bleedin' tongues. Rackam, get thee below with us. Read, stand the watch. Come! We will have music.''

"Anne," said Rackam, "stay on deck with Read. Don't come below. Vane be in a foul humor; no telling what he'll do next."

"Aye, Jack. Be ye careful of thyself."

Between decks, Robert Deal tied candles around the mizzenmast. Vane's crew, armed with knives, swords, forks and dividers, formed a circle. One by one the officers of the brigantine were brought in. Each unfortunate man was made to run around the mizzenmast to the accompaniment of the music and was jabbed by the sharp instruments until he could stand no more. The sweating continued.

On deck Mary listened to the groans of the tortured crew.

"God, what are they doing to those poor men?" asked Anne.

" 'Tis a cruel kind o' dance."

"I am weary of this Vane and his brutish games. Yet I dare say he will outlast all the other pirate captains."

"Aye, one at any rate."

"Why, what mean you?"

"I have bitter news for thee, Anne. I like it not that I needs must be the one to learn of it and I know no gentle way to tell thee."

"What is it? If't be bad news give't me quickly. That is the kindest way."

"On November 12th Stede Bonnet were hanged at White Point. This vessel has just now come from Charleston. The man I spoke with was present at the trial and execution."

"Where is this man now?"

"Below at the sweating."

"Christ!" Anne smashed both fists down on the railing. "I thought Stede had escaped."

"He did. He and David Heriot got away to Swillivant's Island but were captured again by Colonel Rhett and taken back to Charleston to be tried by the court of the Vice Admiralty. Bonnet asked for the king's pardon and begged to be tried before His Majesty in England, but Judge Trott refused to let him go."

Anne buried her face in her hands and wept. Mary had also learned that Bonnet had pledged to cut his limbs from his body, leaving only his tongue to pray for God's mercy the rest of his days, if the court would but spare his life. Knowing that Anne would be disgusted at this faintheartedness, Mary withheld the news of his cowardly pleas. Saying nothing more, she held Anne close.

Rackam opposed the wholesale execution of the crew of the *Protestant Caesar*. Vane did not have unanimous support so he could not challenge his quartermaster. Instead he put all the captives aboard the damaged *Port Royall* and, cutting away all her lines, set her adrift.

On November 23rd Vane fell upon a large vessel which he had fully expected would hoist black colors as soon as he struck his. Instead, she discharged a boardside upon the small brigantine, hoisted colors showing her to be a French man-of-war, and, setting every inch of sail, gave chase to the brigantine.

"Trim up and stand away from that vessel!" Vane shouted. "I have nothing further to say to her!"

"Challenge him, Jack," said Anne. "He may miscarry in this and we will have what we need to overthrow him."

"Why run away?" said Rackam. "Though she have more guns, we might board her and let the best boys carry the day."

Rackam was seconded by several others.

" 'Tis rash," said Vane. "The man-o-war be twice our force and may well sink our brigantine afore we can reach to board her."

Robert Deal and several others were of Vane's opinion, but the majority of the men were against him. Captain Vane, whose authority by pirate law was absolute in matters of fighting, chasing or being chased, decided the dispute. And so his faster brigantine soon ran away from the mighty man-o-war.

The next day, however, Vane's behavior was put to the vote. Branding him a coward, the crew overthrew Vane and voted Rackam captain in his place. Along with the fifteen men who had voted not to board the French vessel, Vane and Robert Deal were put upon a piragua with some provisions and ammunition and turned out of the company.

Captain Rackam headed south again. At Okracoke he addressed Blackbeard with blasting cannons, but received no answer. Sailing the brigantine around to the inlet, they saw the *Revenge* broadside to the shore. The pirate playground was deserted.

The *Protestant Caesar* dropped anchor. There was much speculation as to events that had taken place here since their departure. Jack left most of his men on the brigantine, and with Anne, Mary and two others rowed into the Pamlico River toward Bath Town.

It was dusk when they neared the inlet and, seeing a sloop of war anchored in the river, quickly beached their craft. Rackam left the two seamen to guard their small boat, and with Mary and Anne he headed toward the town.

"A sloop of war, here at Bath Town," said Rackam. "Something be amiss, surely."

"Wait," said Anne, stopping them. She listened intently.

" 'Tis only a bird," said Jack.

"Nay, Jack, 'tis my friend Joe Buck." Anne answered the call; a few minutes later Joe Buck leaped onto the path in front of them. Jack drew his cutlass and Mary her sword.

"Hold," said Anne. " 'Tis only a friend. Joe, what news?"

"Ye must leave here at once. There be troops in the town."

"Why? What is amiss? Hast anything to do with Ned Teach?"

"Aye. Lieutenant Maynard killed him and caused his head to be severed from his body and lashed to the bowsprit of his vessel. He put twenty-five wounds in Teach's body afore he finally dropped."

"Twenty-five wounds!" said Mary.

"Aye," said Joe. "One of his men told me that Teach's body swam around the sloop three times afore it sank."

"I can well believe that," remarked Mary.

"You cannot go near the town, Anne. Ye must go to your vessel now and make way."

At first light Captain Rackam sailed the *Protestant Caesar* out of Ocracoke Inlet.

Blackbeard's death was a decided turning point in the Great Age of Piracy. Lieutenant Robert Maynard sailed into the James River and arrived at Williamsburg with Blackbeard's head still swinging from his bowsprit. He was the hero of the day. Thirteen of the fifteen members of Teach's crew were tried and hanged in Virginia. The two spared were one Samuel Odel, a forced man, and the disabled Israel Hands. Hands was condemned at the trial but, just as he was about to be executed, a vessel came to Virginia with another proclamation from the king extending the time of pardon.

Rackam was eager to sail to the Caribbean Islands, far away from the king's forces in America. He stopped to careen at Green Turtle Cay on the windward of Abaco Island. While resting comfortably on the pleasant little cay, which was also dangerously close to New Providence, Jack questioned members of his crew concerning surrender.

Mary was attacking the wormshells in the hull of the *Protestant Caesar* with a vengeance. A tune she had once heard in Plymouth would not leave her head and she sang it softly to herself over and over as she worked:

"If I swing by a string
I will hear the bells ring.
An' that will be the end of poor Tommy."

Jack was curious why a woman would masquerade as a man and pursue the life of a pirate. He made bold to ask her. "What pleasure do ye take in these dangerous enterprises, Mary, where your life be continually in danger?"

"I be used to that, Jack. I were a soldier once."

" 'Tis not only that. Ye must needs suffer shameful death if taken alive. What think thee of hangin'?"

"That be no great hardship. If't be not for the prospect of hanging, every dastardly fellow would turn pirate and so infest the seas that men of courage might starve. 'Tis fear, Jack, that keeps cowardly rogues honest."

"Aye, 'tis true."

"Many a knave who now cheats widows and orphans and victimizes his poor neighbors would then rob at sea, and the ocean would be as packed with rogues as the land. No merchant would then dare to venture out and soon the trade would not be worth following."

"Thee hast thought this out well."

"Aye, 'tis my habit to reflect afore I do a thing."

"Wouldst consider taking the pardon?"

"Perhaps, if the majority be for't. Dost begin to feel closed in, Jack?"

"Somewhat, aye. I will question the rest."

"Do that, Jack. I can learn to plant peas as well as any man, I warrant."

The crew voted to return to Nassau. With Bonnet hanged and Blackbeard dead, all hope of assembling a force large enough to fight the king's provincial government seemed lost.

The next day, December 5th, Rackam sailed into Nassau Harbour, flying a white flag, and surrendered himself and his crew to the mercy of the colonial governor.

In the autumn of 1718 Woodes Rogers had been appointed Captain-General and Governor-in Chief in and over His Majesty's Bahama Islands in America. A Bristol man, he was intrepid and possessed of both great physical toughness and a keen sense of humor.

In 1708 he had sailed around the world in two frigates, the *Duke* and the *Duchess*. Under letters of marque, he was commissioned by Prince George of Denmark, Lord High Admiral of England and husband of Queen Anne, as a privateer against the Spanish and French in the Pacific.

Once, after two days and a night of fierce battle, Rogers had lost a rich prize ship, as well as parts of his upper jaw and his ankle. But he had successfully captured twenty other prizes, sacked the city of Guayaquil, and seized the ultimate prize, the Manila galleon. Rogers returned with treasure valued at 800,000 pounds; his voyage had been a success.

On July 27, 1718, Rogers and one hundred soldiers had

disembarked from His Majesty's warship *Delicia* and set foot on New Providence to take over the fort. An eleven-gun salute from the *Rose* was answered by ragged musketry. Of the two hundred destitute inhabitants and nearly six hundred pirates remaining in Nassau, three hundred people gathered at the fort to greet the new governor. His Majesty's commission was read and two hundred pirates immediately accepted the Act of Grace.

Rogers had high hopes for the colony. Desiring to establish sugar plantations on New Providence, he discovered that the land was more suitable for cotton and indigo. But the most profitable industries, he thought, would be salt racking, whale fishing and wood cutting. However, he soon found that the inhabitants were exceedingly lazy. Preferring to starve rather than work, the islanders did nothing except wait for wrecks and pirates. Farming was mortally hateful to them; they were content to live from the sea rather than raise cattle.

People were leaving New Providence in droves. Of the four hundred men on the island when Rogers arrived, only two hundred remained, and more threatened to leave every day. Rumors of Spanish invasion kept new colonists from settling on the island.

The garrison was weak. His Majesty had sent no support of ships. Rogers, realizing his large vessels were no good for chasing pirates in Bahamian waters, had petitioned His Majesty to send small cruisers. Rogers had also petitioned Governor Lawes of Jamaica for thirty or even twenty soldiers.

But Rogers had a few faithful men among reformed pirates. Hornigold was sent out again after Vane. Because the inhabitants were such friends to pirates, Rogers feared he might have to receive pirates should they come to New Providence, even though the period of the King's Grace had expired. He justified his proposed amnesty by the fact that, since no king's ships had yet come, he would need the pirates and their vessels to defend Nassau against the Spanish.

An armed guard was stationed on the beach to greet Rackam's brigantine the moment it put in to the harbor. Jack, Anne and Mary rowed ashore in the small boat. Already a large group of the inhabitants had gathered. Anne looked for Henri but did not see him amid the cheering crowd. Jack was confronted by Captain Wingate Gale.

"Be ye cap'n of that brigantine, sir?"

"Aye. Cap'n Jack Rackam be my name."

"Cap'n Gale, here. I come to bring ye afore the Vice Admiral."

"Aye. We thought as much. We would desire to speak with the governor on our own behalf."

"Hand over your weapons and come along with me."

They made their way to the guardhouse at the fort. As they walked along Anne saw Emma. "Emma!" she shouted.

"No speaking to the islanders, Mistress, not til ye has seen the gov'nor."

"Aye, Captain."

Anne caught Emma's eye and jerked her head in the direction of Henri's house. Emma understood and hastened away.

Rogers was seated at a wooden table in the guardhouse, writing one of his many fruitless petitions to His Majesty. When he looked up they noticed that the right side of his face was sunken in. The absence of a portion of his upper jaw affected his speech.

"Your honor," said Gale, "this be Cap'n John Rackam, who has just now put in to the harbour in a brigantine flying a white flag."

"Ah, sir," said Rogers, "dost come here to surrender yourself to the king's justice, Captain Rackam?"

"Aye, sir."

"Who be your companions here?"

"One Anne Bonny and Matt Read, sir."

"Mistress Bonny, what be a woman doin' out pirating?"

"She were taken hostage by Cap'n Vane, your honor," said Rackam hastily. "In fact, sir, we are all forced men."

"Captain Vane—I greatly desire news of him, if thee has it."

"Aye, sir. You see, bein' forced, we could do nothin' to prevent our leavin' here that day of your arrival. We could but look for an opportunity to mutiny."

"Didst put Vane out, sir?"

"Aye. He and fifteen others were put off in a long boat and we bid them go to the devil."

"Couldst not destroy him utterly?"

"Sir, we be not cruel like him. We could not do it. Then we came straight here, sir, to beg the king's grace."

"The pardon be out. 'Tis too late. Thee must hang for't."

Anne took this occasion to faint into Mary's arms. Everyone was distracted.

"Fetch some water, Captain Gale," directed Governor Rogers. "Be this woman ill?"

"Very likely, sir. We were a long time at sea. Anne, Anne, be thee all right?"

Anne was regaining consciousness. She took a few sips of water. Then Mary dipped her kerchief in the cup and pressed cold water to Anne's forehead and neck.

"What ails thee, woman?" demanded the governor.

"I think . . . I think, I am with child, sir."

"Anne, be this true?" asked Rackam.

"I fear 'tis, Jack."

Mary was not sure, but she thought that Anne might be feigning illness. She helped Anne to her feet. Captain Gale offered her a stool to sit on.

"Governor, please, you must believe me," pleaded Jack. "We were forced and have been at sea since July last and had no opportunity to take the pardon afore this time."

"What have you to say to this?" Rogers said, addressing Mary. "Were ye forced into piracy like Captain Rackam says?"

"Aye, sir, circumstances being what they were, I had no other choice."

"Where do you come from, Mister?"

278

"Read, sir, Matt Read of Plymouth Port. But more lately from Flanders."

"What occasioned thee to be in Flanders?"

"I was a trooper in the Duke of Marlborough's Dragoons for almost two years, sir."

"Well, we must chat some time about your adventures in the army, Mister Read. Well then, Captain, how many men aboard your brigantine?"

"Some sixty or so."

"Very well, sir. I grant you the king's pardon. Return their weapons, Captain Gale. But I will take your ship, and your men must work for at least six months on the rebuilding of this fort. I will pay them, of course."

"Aye, sir, thank you, your honor," said Jack.

"Aye, sir," said Mary. "We thank you."

"As for you, Mistress, get thee into woman's dress. 'Tis not fitting ye should walk the streets in breeches."

Anne bit her tongue. "Aye, your honor, sir."

They walked out of the damp guardhouse into the afternoon sunshine—free. Henri was waiting for them.

Anne was pregnant; she was sure of it. Henri fussed over her all the next day. Jack was elated. Mary was concerned and urged Anne to see the doctor.

Anne swore, "Christ's Balls! No piss prophet will touch me!" She knew she was healthy. Mary said no more.

The evening of December 8th, in defiance of Governor Rogers's order, Anne arrived at the King's Inn wearing breeches and a coat of cobalt blue satin. A wide crimson sash was tied around her waist. Anne, Jack, Mary and Henri dined with Henry Jennings and Emma. A huge punchbowl with the elector of Hanover, King Geroge I of England, pictured on it rested in the middle of the banquet table, which was lavishly set with fine delftware. The platters and glassware were decorated with pictures of various royalty and the Duke of Marlborough.

"Christ, Jennings, are ye a bleedin' ambassador or what?" remarked Anne.

279

"Nothin' be too good for me friends," he commented wryly. "Besides, it does no harm and a hell of a lot of good to purchase Rogers's pottery."

"This be his business?" asked Jack, serving a glass of punch around the table.

"One of them. The man has his fingers in a dozen pies. He be a partner in a pottery works in Bristol."

"God's Eyes, Jennings, if ye are so in love with the man, why did ye not invite him to dine with us?" Anne asked sarcastically.

"*Cherie*, stop zis. You must remember we must live here wiz him. Now zat you be back among us, you must learn to get along wiz him, too. 'Tis not Jennings's fault Woodes Rogers be here."

"I am sorry, Henry. I fear I am making rash judgments about the man. But something tells me we are going to clash swords afore long."

"Come," said Emma, "let's eat and drink to yer homecoming. 'Tis a long time, 'Enry, is it not, since we 'ave so many at our table?"

"Right, Emma! I propose a toast to the happiness of all present."

Emma, sitting next to Anne, placed her hand over hers and said in a whisper, "Be this news true, Anne? Jennings said ye fainted t'other day at the guardhouse. Be ye with child?"

"Aye, Emma."

"I be glad ye be back among us. We can care for thee proper 'ere."

Anne squeezed Emma's hand affectionately.

Sopping up her gravy with a piece of bread, Mary uncovered the likeness of General Cadogan on her plate and pushed it aside without finishing eating. Reminders of the time when she had known him were disquieting. Her actions were honorable then; now she was no better than a common criminal.

Rackam and Jennings engaged quietly in a private conversation at the end of the table.

"Where be old Hornigold?" asked Rackam.

"Out looking for you, I'd wager. He has a sloop, the *Willing Mind,* with fifty good men. He have been busy. There be ten prisoners confined on the *Delicia* this minute. The council have ordered that an admiralty trial take place but Rogers have not approved that yet."

"Who are they?"

"John Augur, Dennis McKarthy and some others who did mutiny last October with Phineas Bunce.

"What think ye, means Rogers to keep those men locked up forever? He must do something soon."

"Aye, but it will go hard with the mutineers, I can tell thee that much. Rogers did trust those men, and he be a hard man when crossed. Well, speak of the devil. Here be old Rusty Guts now."

Woodes Rogers limped into the room and took his customary seat at a table reserved expressly for him. Henry Jennings left his party and went over to serve him. Emma got up to attend to a problem behind the bar. Two waiters were arguing; one of them had a wooden mallet raised over the other man's head. Rackam urged Mary to go talk to Rogers, search him out, test the kind of man he was. But Mary didn't feel like talking just now.

"Jack, leave Matt alone, will ye," said Anne.

"All right, all right!" Getting up, he strutted over to the bar. Flashing one of his warm smiles at Emma, he pinched her cheek while she giggled and beamed before bringing him an ale.

When Mary looked over to the table where Rogers was sitting, he beckoned her to join him.

There be no escaping now. I should have gone home long ago, she thought. I am in no good humor for company, pleasant or otherwise. But I cannot insult His Excellency by showing rudeness.

Mary downed her punch, excused herself to Anne and Henri and went over to Rogers' table.

"Always ze gentleman," remarked Henri.

Anne laughed. "Come, Henri, let's sit at a smaller table.

I have something to tell you about our gentleman friend Matt Read.''

''Read, Read,'' said Rogers, searching his mind for the remembrance of someone in his past. ''Me thinks I should know that name. Was thy father a sailing man?''

''Aye, one Alfred Read.''

''Alfred Read. No, that be not the man I know. Oh, now I remember—'twas John Read. No kin to thee, I trust.''

''No, sir, not that I know.''

'' 'Tis well, because this John Read, if I remember myself, was killed by a shark.''

''Gramercy!''

''Hast e'er been to the South Pacific?''

''No, sir.''

''Oh, 'tis as wondrous as it be dangerous, if thou dost love the sea as I do.''

''Aye, sir, I do.''

''We did sail around Cape Horn. Oh, Mister Read, ye have never encountered seas like the cape, I warrant ye. Ye be standing there up to yer chest in pounding green water. Ice cold it be. The wind be so violent, belike to tear the words from yer mouth. Oh, a treacherous sea, Mister Read, bloody treacherous. But then, sir, there be islands like the Galapagos—enchanted they be.''

''Enchanted?''

''Aye. 'Tis a place what has strange currents running by. But mainly 'tis a feeling that be there—ageless, endless, like the turtle which abound there. Perhaps ye might go there some time, Mister Read?''

''Aye, sir, perhaps one day.''

''If there be war with Spain again we will be sending out privateers. Wouldst consider that, Mister Read?''

''Aye, sir, I will give it thought.''

''I think the old fart be like to talk poor Matt's ears off,'' remarked Anne to Henri, who was looking over at Mary.

''You said you had something to tell me concerning Matt. What is it?''

Anne was not betraying a confidence. Mary felt Henri

had the right to know and Anne had assured her that he could be trusted to keep her secret.

"Well, *mon ami,* I will put it straight to you. Matt Read is not Matt Read but Mary Read."

"No! A woman, no! *Impossible!*"

"I know it sounds incredible but 'tis true all the same."

"How did you find zis out?"

"One night I tried to make love to her and found she had no part. . . ."

"Oh, how exciting! You must tell me everything that happened."

Anne related the story of her encounter with Mary that evening at Okracoke, complete with amorous and sensuous details. Henri responded by laughing and clutching his penis, which throbbed in agony.

"Oh! Oh! How wonderful! Zis story she makes me laugh and cry."

"Cry? Why do you cry? Are you disappointed Mary is not a man?"

"Bien sur! And I weep for you. But most of all I laugh at ze both of us, each loving ze same person, sinking her a man. 'Tis funny, no?"

"No! 'Tis not funny at all."

"Why are you angry wiz Henri? Do you not sink it ze grand joke on both of us?"

"I am not angry, Henri. I only tease you. I laughed too, at the time. You won't laugh at me for what I must tell you now. I love her."

"Henri laugh? What is zat to laugh about? You love her. Of course you love her."

"You do not think that strange?"

"Strange? If you did not love her, zat would be strange."

Jack Rackam stood at the bar, studying the black flags decorating the walls and ceiling, and thought to himself, I was a pirate cap'n, too, like those men—only for a few days, but nontheless a cap'n. What should be the ensign of Cap'n Jack Rackam? I will think on't. Perhaps I'll even have Henri make it up for me as a souvenir.

James Bonny sidled up to the bar next to Jack. He was extremely out at the elbows.

"Be you Calico Jack Rackam?" he whispered in a harsh voice.

"Aye, Calico Jack be my name."

"Buy me a drink."

"And who be you that I should buy you a drink?"

"James Bonny."

"Oh, James Bonny, eh? Waiter, bring Mister Bonny here a small beer." Rackam started to walk away.

"I would have a word with you, sir," said Bonny, putting a restraining hand on Jack's arm. "Hast been swiving me wife, hast thee not?"

"That be none of yer business."

"Aye, but 'tis my business, sir. I be her lawful husband."

"So?"

"Well, sir—" he lowered his voice—"I will sell her to thee. Wilt buy her?"

"What! Buy what I already have? Ye must be a bleedin' madman. Why, you scum, dost know what will happen to thee when I tell Anne this news?"

"No, please, don't tell her. Forget it, man, forget it!"

"She would break yer balls, man; tear those nutmegs out by the roots and feed them to the fishes."

Bonny looked around quickly and fled out the back way.

"Slimy, sneakin', scummy fellow," muttered Jack to himself as he ordered another punch. "What in the name of God did she ever want with him in the first place?"

James Bonny was an informant in the employ of Woodes Rogers, a position which suited his talents. He had hoped for rapid advancement in this new government but that had not happened yet. Now and again he would take bribes to withhold information from the governor. Recently he had concentrated his efforts on petty vengeances and household disputes.

Rogers be an upright man, a man of morals, thought Bonny. Surely once he hears how I have been wronged by Anne, he will deal justly with her and that bastard Rackam.

Very late that night Bonny found Rogers working on his papers in the guardhouse and told him everything.

"Dost say she is thy lawful wife?"

"Aye, sir."

"Somehow I did never connect the name. She boldly uses thy name and fornicates with this Rackam?"

"She have used me, sir, most abusedly. I am the laughing stock of me friends. She doth parade on the arm of Calico Jack Rackam and brazenly consorts with him most lewdly before me very eyes."

" 'Tis disgraceful. Dost want the baggage? I mean, wouldst sell her?"

"Aye, sir, but Rackam will have none of't. Says Anne be his already."

"Outrageous knave. Bring them before me!"

"Ah . . . sir, I cannot do it . . . alone."

"Find Richard Turnley; he'll help you. Take a half dozen men if ye needs them, but bring this pair before me this night. Didst know she be with child?"

"No, I did not, sir. 'Tis not mine, that's certain."

"Must be Rackam's bantling. She will pay for her loose ways, I warrant ye. I will make an example of her afore the town."

Rousing Richard Turnley, Bonny assembled three other men whom he knew to be sober and went to Henri's house. Mary was staying in a hut rented from Jennings, and this night Henri had remained in town with a friend. James Bonny had discovered that Anne and Rackam were alone in the house, asleep in a bedroom on the third floor.

"We must work fast," cautioned Bonny. "The woman is a veritable hellkite. I'll take Rackam. Turnley, you and the others take the woman."

"Four men to seize one woman? Come on, man."

"You will see; she be the devil's whore when roused. She be more fierce than any mountain lion."

Armed with guns, manacles and a quantity of rope, the raiding party quietly ascended the stairs and surrounded the bed. Bonny tore off the sheet and all five men pounced on the naked pair.

"What the devil!" shouted Rackam, going for his cutlass, which lay on the floor by the bed.

Bonny held a pistol to his nose. "Out of there, man, up, I say." Quickly he manacled Jack's hands behind his back.

There was a sudden flurry of activity on the opposite side of the bed. Anne fought and bit and cursed. All the while, Jack, held at bay by Bonny's pistol, was begging for his pants.

"You fuckers! God's Arse! Unhand me or I'll tear yer eyes out!"

Two men held her legs and two her torso and still she was jerking her body in all directions in an attempt to free herself.

"Now what?" said Turnley. "How the shit are we supposed to tie her?"

"Rackam, don't you move! I'll blow you apart!"

"Where the fuck am I supposed to go, man, without me pants?"

"Just stay there." Bonny took a length of rope and, starting at Anne's feet, began to wind it around her naked body until she was entirely clothed in hemp.

"Pissers! Damn yer blood, Bonny. I'll kill thee if I get my hands on thee. I'll bite off your prick and broil yer shriveled balls afore yer very eyes."

"What did I tell thee, man?"

"Shut it, Rackam!" Bonny put the thick rope across Anne's mouth. Unable to speak any more, she began grunting and screaming with frustration.

"My pants, God damn ye, Bonny. Give me my breeches!"

Jack stepped into his calico breeches and Bonny laced them for him.

It took four men to carry Anne through the streets. Such horrible sounds came from her that practically the entire town was awakened.

"Shut it, woman!" said Rackam. "I don't want all of Nassau to see us taken to the gaol. Have ye no pride?"

Mary entered the street. "Stop there, James Bonny!" she shouted, drawing her sword.

"Out of my way, Mister Read. Do not try anything. We have a greater force of arms and needs must kill thee."

Mary stepped aside to let them pass but followed to see where Bonny was taking her friends.

Once at the guardhouse, Anne was placed on her feet but was so tightly bound that she had to be propped between two men.

"I see what thee means, Mister Bonny. Canst take the rope from her mouth at least?" asked Governor Rogers.

"Sir, believe it, she be enraged still. Ye do not want to hear what she has to say. 'Tis a vile tongue she has when angered."

"Woman, ye have behaved yourself in a most unseemly manner and will be punished for't."

Anne growled a response.

"And you, sir, what have thee to say to this?"

"If James Bonny will sell his wife, I will buy her."

A series of grunts, howls and harsh gnarring sounds issued from Anne. Her face was beet red and her eyes flashed fire.

"Douse that woman; she be too hot!"

Richard Turnley threw a bucket of water into Anne's face. She coughed and choked but was otherwise still.

"Are you calm, now, Madam?"

The water had caused the rope to draw tighter across Anne's mouth, throat and chest. She was extremely uncomfortable and suddenly afraid.

"Can we untie you now?"

Anne nodded.

"She be naked, sir," said Bonny.

"I see. Well then, Madam, thee must needs wear thy hempen gown through the night. James, I can do no more with this business now. I have just signed the mandate establishing a court of the Vice Admiralty. The trial of the mutineers will take place here in the guardroom tomorrow. This business must wait. Untie that man and put him in the cell. Put the woman in a cage. You men stand guard outside. Let no one in unless I give the order."

Anne was placed standing in a narrow iron cage which was too short for her tall frame. The cage was hoisted up to the ceiling. The rope was so tight around her that no part of her body could bend and she could fit in the cage only by leaning on the diagonal.

By morning she was in intense pain. At noon the sun beat down mercilessly upon the thatched roof. Soaked in perspiration, Anne feared that the scratchy hemp would shrink, cutting off blood circulation altogether. Despairingly she gave herself up to death by strangulation.

At one in the afternoon the doors opened and, through sweat-filled eyes, Anne saw Emma come in with Richard Turnley. Emma had been allowed to bring food and clothes for her. Rackam was taken outside and allowed to smoke and have a few words with Mary and Henri, who were out there waiting for him.

None too gently Turnley lowered the cage, jostling Anne roughly. He placed her on the bench in the tiny cell and locker her and Emma inside, leaving them alone. Having no knife, Emma took some time to untie Anne.

"Oh, Christ! Thank God!" said Anne, relieved of her bonds at last. Horrible red marks laced her body and she was chafed raw in several places.

" 'ere, I brought an ointment. Let me apply it first. Onree made thee a loose-fitting shift. Matt Read told 'im how ye were bound most brutally."

"Dost believe it, Emma, that fucker Bonny means to sell me. Christ Almight!"

"Now calm yerself. Perhaps Rogers will release thee from thy marriage bond."

"That man, never! The bastard! I thought I was shut of James Bonny."

"That man'll do anything for a coin, and 'e 'ave the gov'nor's ear. That do make 'im somewhat dangerous."

"Oh," groaned Anne, "I am nothing but a walking wound."

"I think Matt Read be makin' plans for yer escape, should this business miscarry. 'ere, 'ave somethin' to eat. Onree prepared a chicken, and 'ere be beer as well."

"Thank ye kindly."

Turnley came back, bringing Jack Rackam, and opened the cell.

"The woman must be manacled," said Turnley.

"Canst wait til she 'ave eaten?" shouted Emma.

"No! 'Tis the gov'nor's orders."

Turnley placed manacles on Anne's wrists and legs and escorted Emma out of the cell.

"A warnin' from the gov'nor, Mistress," said Turnley as he departed. "They be bringin' the prisoners in 'ere for trial shortly. One word from you and the gov'nor will hang ye with those men. Dost understand?"

Anne spat in his face.

"Why, you bitch!" Turnley got control of himself. "Ye 'ave been warned. Say somethin'—one word. I'd like to see thee swing." He and Emma left the guardroom.

Jack and Anne devoured Henri's lunch.

" 'Tis a foregone conclusion that these men will hang. Didst hear Turnley say it?"

"Aye," replied Jack.

"What will happen to us, think you, Jack?"

"No tellin', with this new gov'nor. Mary be plannin' our escape in any case. We must trust this to time. She be lookin' for a sloop now."

"I won't be sold, Jack. I am telling ye now."

"All right, all right! We'll get out o' this somehow."

Woodes Rogers and the officials of the court came into the guardroom and sat behind the long wooden table. The ten prisoners were brought in shortly after.

"Keep yer mouth shut, woman, or we'll all hang," Jack whispered.

William Fairfax, Esquire, was elected Judge of the Admiralty.

The governor's commissions were read, giving him the right to establish this court under the intent of a late act of Parliament entitled "An Act for the More Effectual Suppression of Piracy." The prisoners were brought before the bar and accused of mutiny, felony and piracy. Witnesses were heard.

Benjamin Hutchins, sworn in for one prisoner John Hipps, who claimed to have been forced by the mutineers, said that Hipps had shed many tears when he spoke of his misfortune. Damning evidence against the rest of the men was given by John Carr and Richard Turnley, who had been left to starve on Green Key.

The court summed up the evidence for the king and prisoners. All were voted guilty except John Hipps. The sentence was read by William Fairfax: "The court having duly considered of the evidence which hath been given for and against you, and having also debated the several circumstances of the cases, it is adjudged that you, the said John Augur, William Cunningham, Dennis McKarthy, George Rounsivel, William Dowling, William Lewis, Thomas Morris, George Bendall and William Ling, are guilty of the mutiny, felony and piracy wherewith every one of you stand accused. And the court doth accordingly pass sentence that you be carried to prison from whence you came, and from thence to the place of execution, where you are to be hanged by the neck till you shall be dead, dead, dead; and God have mercy on your souls."

Governor Rogers appointed that the execution take place the following morning, the 12th of December, at ten o'clock. The prisoners begged for a longer time to repent and pray for death. Rogers reminded them that they had had since the 15th of November, when they were apprehended, knowing full well they would be condemned by the laws of all nations.

Black Robin was a member of the detail ordered to build the gallows. Anne watched him from the window while Jack paced back and forth in the cell. The trial had distracted her from her own predicament. Now she had time to think the matter out.

"That rascal Bonny—when I get my hands on him, I'll throttle him proper. Sell me, indeed! Let him try it; he'll not live to spend a farthing. Damn it, Jack, sit down. Ye will drive me to extremities with your pacing."

Jack sat on the bench and immediately set his left leg in motion. Anne glanced out the window. A scaffold and platform long enough to accommodate all nine men at once had been erected.

"Christ's Balls! Jack, look here."

"Fuck me eyes! Rogers means to hang them all at the same time." exclaimed Jack.

"Is there no way to save these men? Christ, man, McKarthy is my friend."

"Dost see where we are? There be nothin' we can do here, 'tis certain. Me thinks that be one reason Rogers left us locked up here. He could have settled our petty business long before this."

"Petty business! That arse worm means to sell me, and ye call it petty business. That milksop. Damn him! Double damn him!"

"Calm thyself, woman. I mean there be an expectation of a war with Spain. That be somewhat more important than domestic squabbles, I should warrant. I think that be why Rogers was so quick to execute those poor fellows. He must mount great guns and prepare for war. Look, why not go along with Bonny? We have plenty of money, more than we can use. Didst see him, poor bastard?"

"What? Poor bastard, indeed!"

"If a louse missed its footin' on his coat, it would break its neck."

Anne laughed. "His coat is threadbare, that's certain."

"So we pay him and have done with it."

"No. Ye'll not buy me, Jack, for I'll not be sold. I'll give the bastard all the money I have, but I will not suffer to be humiliated in this manner."

"Christ, woman, what do it matter, sold or not?"

"It matters greatly. I have pride. I'll not be yoked and led through the streets like an old cow to the auction. Christ, Jack, how can ye even suggest such a thing?"

Jack sank deeper into himself. Anne Bonny was not a woman like other women. He wondered if he would ever understand her.

I should 'ave bought him off that night at the inn, he thought. But I never did think 'e would bring the matter to the attention of the gov'nor.

"Come on, Jack, do not look so sad. Take me in your arms betimes."

"Here? Christ, woman, ye must be mad! Here, with the king's guard lookin' on? Rogers will surely hang us with the others tomorrow. God, I think I would sell me soul for a drop of liquor right now."

"Right, Jack. I do sometimes forget that drink is your true mate. Ye are faithful to her along."

"Oh, get off't, woman. Lucifer's balls! All ye seem to do lately is bitch at me like a bloody fen. Leave off, will ye!"

They were sullen. Jack paced and Anne stared despondently out the window, through the scaffold and out to sea. Emma was allowed to bring them a little supper. She pulled a piece of paper out of her bodice and gave it to Anne to read.

" 'Tis from Matt Read."

"Let me see it," demanded Jack.

" 'Tis in French," said Anne. "He be fearful the guard might see it."

"Well, what does it say?"

"Give me a minute. Matt plans to steal Haman's sloop."

"Good man! I knew he could do it."

"Wait, there's more. 'Fetherston, Corner and Black Robin be with us. I am looking for others. Henri is buying supplies to stock the vessel. Arms are difficult to come by just now. I will purchase all I can afford. Do not worry. We will look for the best advantage and rescue you both. Be patient, Anne.'"

"Oh, he doth know thee."

"Aye." Anne read Mary's closing endearing remarks to herself, grateful that Mary had thought to write in French, ensuring their privacy.

By nine the next morning, Friday, December 12, 1718, the area in front of the scaffold was crowded with over a hundred people. Rackam looked among the group for a friendly face but could find none. Guards were stationed below the window and would allow no one to get near.

Anne had been ill. She was not sure whether it was the

pregnancy, the prospect of the execution, or both. Deep down, rumbling in the pit of her stomach, was the memory of her own mother imprisoned before her birth, and Anne was unable to dispel these thoughts or the fears which accompanied them. Mary must get her out of here soon, she hoped, lest she go mad.

The prisoners were piniones and led by Thomas Robinson, Esquire, provost marshal for the day, to the top of the rampart fronting the sea. Several prayers and psalms were read. A stage had been erected under the gallows and was supported by three large barrels. One by one the condemned were called to the stage.

First John Augur, a man of forty years, who had accepted the king's grace and the governor's trust and betrayed both, took the small glass of wine offered to him. He raised the glass in a trembling hand and said, "To the good success of the Bahama Islands and the gov'nor!" Drinking it down, he remained silent thereafter.

William Cunningham had been Teach's gunner. He was very conscious of his own guilt and penitently walked up the ladder to the stage and stood next to Augur.

Dennis McKarthy mounted the stage with the agility of a prizefighter.

"Anne, look here," said Rackam.

"No, I don't want to see it."

" 'Tis Dennis."

Reluctantly Anne stood on the bench and looked out over the crowd to the gallows.

"He be dressed like a prizefighter."

"Aye. He doth cut a handsome figure," she said sadly.

McKarthy had put on clean clothes for the occasion. He wore long blue ribbons at his neck, wrists and knees. He looked cheerfully around him and said in a loud voice, "I knew a time when there were many brave fellows on this island who would not have suffered me to die like a dog."

The guards on the parapet cocked and pointed their muskets at the crowd nearest the scaffold. Although some of the spectators were sympathetic, they saw there was too much power over their heads to attempt any sort of rescue.

McKarthy pulled off his shoes and kicked them off the platform, saying, "I promised meself that I would not die with my shoes on."

"Dear Christ! I cannot take any more of this." Anne sank to the bench, put her hands over her ears and waited for the execution to be over.

William Ling and George Rounsivel were the last to mount the platform. The hangman fastened the cords as dextrously as if he had been a servitor at Tyburn.

Captain Burgis, one of the judges at the trial, spoke up. "Your Excellency, I hereby willingly offer my bond for the future conduct of George Rounsivel."

Rogers looked at Rounsivel. Sweat was pouring off the young man's face.

Burgis entreated further. "I be an old pirate, 'tis true; but I have served thee well, gov'nor, since the pardon, and that lad were a good and faithful seaman to me. What say ye, gov'nor?"

"Mister Robinson, untie that last man there."

"Aye, sir!"

"And prepare to execute the death sentence upon the rest."

There was some grumbling among the crowd, who had expected Rogers to show leniency to the other eight.

An ex-pirate, Rob Maurice, mounted a barrelhead and shouted, "Wilt stand for this, mates? Wouldst watch thy friends swing? Attack! We outnumber 'em. What be a few guns?" The crowd cheered and clamored in agreement.

Rogers shot the man and the mob was stilled. "Haul away those butts, hangman!" bellowed Rogers. The barrels, which had been tied together, were pulled away; the platform fell and the condemned were suspended.

"Christ Almight!" Rackam watched the men struggle for air. Hanging was a long, painful death. Afterward the guards dispersed the crowd. Rogers ordered the bodies to remain as an example to others who might have ideas of returning to their old habits.

"Is it over?" asked Anne.

"Aye, 'tis over. This be enough to encourage me to take up farming. Ye know, Anne, if we go out again, we can never return here. If we be caught we will all wear hempen neckties like those men in the yard."

Mary had visited John Haman's sloop several times. Haman lived on Hog Island with his wife and children and derived his livelihood solely from plundering the Spanish. His sloop was near forty tons and one of the fastest sailers of its kind. In fact, the islanders were wont to say of him, "There goes John Haman; catch him if you can."

Since Haman stayed ashore at night, leaving only two men aboard, the attempt would have to be made then. All was in readiness. Henri had loaded all necessaries into a small boat. This night of the execution had been chosen for the escape. The guard would be slack, thinking the townspeople were subdued. Mary would take care of the guards and Henri would be waiting at the parapet in the boat. They would row out to Haman's sloop, take it over and slip out of the harbor.

About four that afternoon, Woodes Rogers came to the guardhouse with James Bonny and Richard Turnley.

"Bring those two malefactors afore me!" demanded Rogers.

Turnley unlocked the cell and removed the manacles from Anne's feet, but left her hands bound.

"Well, Madam, hast considered with thyself? Wouldst consent to be sold?"

"No, I will not. I beg annulment."

"Annulment? On what grounds?"

"This marriage to James Bonny was never consummated."

James Bonny's face turned red and he put his head down and stared at the ground. Rackam looked at him, bewildered.

"That matters not," said Rogers. "Ye be married by law and married ye will stay unless ye be sold."

"Never."

"Stubborn still. We do not need your consent, Madam,

if Mister Rackam be willing.''

"I'll not buy her, for it doth offend her dignity to be sold.''

"Hast money enough to buy this man's wife, Mister Rackam?'' asked the governor.

"I do, but ye has heard her, has thee not? She will not be sold or bought. She speaks plain enough for thee, I trust.''

Rackam was getting hot. This surprised Anne, inasmuch as he had been lecturing her all afternoon to remain calm during the inquiry.

"Mister Rackam,'' said Rogers, "what sort of man be you to be ruled by a woman?''

"God's Death!'' Rackam sputtered and fumed. "I be ruled by no woman. I have never and will never be, Gov'nor!''

"Explain your behavior here, then, if you please.''

"Anne be a woman, a person like you and me.''

There was no need for Anne to say a word. She was proud of the way Jack spoke for her before the governor.

"Would you be sold, sir?'' Rackam asked the governor.

"I tell thee true, I would not.''

" 'Tis not the question before us, Mister. A wife is a chattel. That be the law, sir, and by ancient English practice may be sold at market.''

"Fuck the law!'' Anne yelled.

"One word more, Madam, and I'll have thee confined for a year.''

"No, sir. I do not agree with this law and will have no part of buying this man's wife.''

"That be your final word on't?''

"Aye, your honor, sir; 'tis.''

"Very well then. Mistress Bonny, one hour hence you shall be taken out, stripped naked and flogged publicly for your lewd behavior. And you, Mister Rackam, will execute the stripes upon her body.''

Anne's face turned to stone. She was pulling at her chains to keep from speaking out.

"What? I will not!" Rackam shouted.

" 'Tis the law!"

"F . . . I will not do't, law or no!"

"Then, Mister Bonny, *you* must. . . ."

"Ah . . . sir, I would rather not be the one."

"Then appoint someone."

"Richard Turnley, sir, if he will do't."

"With pleasure, sir," responded Turnley with a smile.

"Anne, will ye reconsider?" begged Rackam. "You be with child. Please! I cannot bear to see thee whipped."

Anne shook her head defiantly. Rogers left the guardroom. Turnley locked them in the gaol.

"Ye had better run, James Bonny," threatened Anne. "And run far, too. You likewise, Mister Turnley, for I mean to kill ye both."

In a matter of minutes, the whole town knew of Anne's sentence. Mary was determined to go and try to rescue her. "I must save her. I could not live with myself if I did not."

"What about tonight's plan? Will zey release her after zey whip her? Oh, *Mon Dieu!* I cannot bear to sink of ze whip striping her beautiful body."

"She will probably be imprisoned again. You must remember the plan. Be in the boat at the steps of the parapet at midnight."

"I will be zere."

"Take my sword. Stow it safely in the small boat."

"I will. Oh, I hope you can save her."

"I will try."

Mary kissed him on the cheek and ran off in the direction of the fort.

When she arrived, Anne was standing in the yard, surrounded by a crowd of people. Richard Turnley announced to the spectators that this woman was to be beaten for her lewdness. Then he tore the clothes off Anne's body and chained her to a post. He raised the whip and sent its stinging lash to meet Anne's back. Several strokes hit her before she sank to her knees. Her teeth were clamped shut; she uttered not a sound.

Mary fought her way through the crowd and threw herself on Richard Turnley, knocking him to the ground. They wrestled for some time before he got up and turned the whip on Mary, who was struck twice before she caught the whip and pulled it out of his grip. Then she went after him with her bare fists and pummeled him soundly before the guards were able to separate them. The crowd dispersed, Anne was unchained, and she and Mary were placed in the cell with Rackam.

Jack was beside himself with anger. Mary tried to comfort Anne as best she could. There were welts all over her body but no cuts. Anne wept not from pain, but from humiliation.

Around nine that evening, Emma came again with clothes for Anne and food. She could say nothing with the guard standing by, but handed a note to Mary. It was from Henri. It said that they should not worry; he would be at the fort at midnight.

Kissing Anne's cheek, Emma tearfully bid her boodby. Before she left she distributed bottles of rum to the guards stationed around the fort and on the parapet by the sea. Jack, Anne and Mary waited.

Henri arrived at the fort at midnight with Fetherston, Corner and Black Robin. The night was dark and rainy. Leaving Corner and Fetherston with the small boat, Henri and Robin crouched on the steps leading up to the parapet to coordinate their plan of attack. It had been Henri's idea for them to dress as women so that they could get close enough to strike and dispatch the guards silently and effect the rescue of their friends without alerting the town. Henri looked ravishing, but Robin looked ridiculous with his kneeboots showing beneath his wide skirt.

"You go in zat direction and I will go zis way. When we reach ze guardhouse, let me go up to ze guard first. Zen you come from behind and put his lights out."

"I'm with you," said Robin, clutching his mallet. "We be ready for this night's business."

"Oh, zis rain, she will ruin my hair."

Robin laughed, then leaped up to the wall. Sneaking up behind one of the soldiers, he whacked him with his mallet, then stealthily worked his way around the yard of the fort.

Henri, using the edge of his powerful hand like an ax, came down hard on the back of a man's neck. He poured what was left of a bottle of rum all over the soldier's clothes and went on to the next man, then the next, until he reached the front of the guardhouse.

As was usual, there was only one man outside; within the guardhouse there would be two more. Henri waited until it was so dark he could barely see the guard leaning against the door, swigging from the bottle Emma had given him.

"Who goes there?" he mumbled drunkenly.

"Only Bertha, sweet pillock," Henri answered in a high-pitched voice. Then he waltzed up to the guard and planted sensual kisses on his mouth.

God's Balls! Whence came this doxy? thought the guard. I thought I'd had 'em all but none the like of this hobby-horse.

Henri thrust his hand into the man's breeches and fondled him. Robin came down with the mallet upon the man's head.

"Oh, zis man will have ze sweet dreams while he sleeps. Remember, Robin, you must do ze talking inside. No one must guess who we are."

Robin knocked on the door.

"Who be that?" shouted one of the men.

"Only Bertha and Emily," called Robin in a falsetto, "come to see you sweet boys."

"Enter."

"Work fast, Robin; we have not much time."

Both men swished into the guardroom and ploped themselves on the guards' laps. It was all Anne could do not to ruin the escape by laughing. She watched Henri and Robin fondle the drunken men until they were weakened almost to the point of unconsciousness. Then Robin struck his man with the mallet and Henri pinched his man's neck in a vulnerable spot. Robin tied and gagged the now unconscious guards while Henri unlocked the cell.

"Christ, we are free at last!" whispered Rackam. "One more hour in this place and I would have been raving mad."

"Cherie, are you all right?" Henri asked Anne. "Zey did not hurt you, did zey?"

"I am fine, Henri."

"Come, we must leave this place," urged Mary. "The relief guard may come."

"Oh, *cherie,* I shall miss you." Henri hugged Anne tightly. "I will cry myself to sleep every night."

"Oh how I wish you could come with us, *mon cher.* I know, I know, that you cannot, but I will think of you often and pray you will not be lonely."

Henri kissed her and held her close. Then, kissing Mary on the cheek, he bade them farewell. "Jack, take care. Keep them safe from harm."

"I will, Henri. Do not worry."

Robin escorted the three from the guardhouse across the yard to the parapet. The rain had stopped and it was not as dark as it had been.

In the dim light of the moon Anne saw the shadows of the eight men hanging from the scaffold. The black flag flapped angrily in the dark night. She could see McKarthy's ribbons flying in the breeze. She was held transfixed by the ghastly scene she had sworn not to witness.

"Anne," said Mary, gently taking her hand, "come away from here." Mary pulled and Anne followed slowly.

"Christ, where are they?" whispered Jack harshly as he looked up to the parapet from the boat.

"Here they be," said Robin from the top of the wall.

Soon everyone was safely aboard the small boat. They pushed away from the parapet and rowed out to Haman's sloop.

Anne followed Mary below to where Haman's two men lay sleeping, while Rackam and the rest were busy hauling in the cables. The noise woke the men, who sat bolt upright in their bunks.

"One move to resist or one sound and I'll blow out your brains," Anne threatened.

Mary checked them for arms and tied their hands; then she and Anne brought them up to the deck.

Taking the helm, Mary steered the vessel through the

narrow eastern channel by Potters Key.

"Bring those men to the stern," whispered Mary to Anne. "I'll never get through this channel without their help. Jack, be ready to speak to the battery from the starboard rail. We sail by the redoubt soon."

Anne held her pistols to the heads of the two young men and ordered them to aid Mary, saying, "I, warn you, if this vessel goes aground, you are dead men. Understand me?"

"Aye."

The guard on the battery hailed the sloop and asked where they were going.

Rackam called back to him, "Our cable has parted and we have naught but a grapple, which will not hold us."

When they were clear of the harbor, they hoisted all the sail they had and stood to sea.

"You there, Haman's men," offered Rackam, "wouldst join our company or nay?"

Grateful that they had a choice, Haman's men declined to join Rackam's crew.

"Take this boat then and row back ashore. Tell Mister Haman we are much obliged to him and will return his vessel when we have done with it."

"Aye, sir, we'll tell him, Cap'n Rackam," was the response of the taller youth. The other lad grinned in agreement, delighted to escape impressment.

"Dost know my name, fellow?"

"We do know thee by thy calico breeches, sir."

"Ah, if ye be smart, canst tell me where Turnley and Bonny go turtling?"

"Aye. Cruise along here as ye would go to Harbour Island. There be a cay to the nor'east with a good anchorage. Ye should see Turnley's vessel there."

Haman's men were put out. Rackam held a brief consultation with his crew.

"I bear great spleen toward Richard Turnley," said Rackam.

"And I," seconded Anne.

"We would avenge ourselves against him. Are ye with us or no?"

301

"I for one am with you," said Mary. "I had not the opportunity to beat him properly."

"I be with you, Cap'n," said Black Robin.

"And what about you, Corner and Fetherston?"

"We be with you, Cap'n Rackam."

"Aye, then. Read, take the helm and steer for that cay. We cannot be far. All you men keep a sharp eye out for any vessel."

"Christ, I hope James Bonny is with them," said Anne. "I mean to send him straight to hell."

Nearing the cay, Robin spotted a vessel fishing about a league from shore.

"That's Turnley's sloop, Cap'n Rackam. I know it well," volunteered Richard Corner.

They boarded the vessel and learned, much to their disappointment, that Turnley and his son were on shore preparing to hunt wild hogs at the first light, and that Bonny had not come with them at all.

Anne did not believe them. Searching the sloop, she looked in every corner where a rat like James Bonny could possibly hide, but she did not find him.

"We'll go ashore and find Turnley," said Jack.

He, Anne and Mary rowed toward the shore but the surf was strong and they could not get the boat in. Jack and Anne waded in to the shore, while Mary kept the boat as near as she could.

Calling out, Jack got no response from Turnley who, seeing them coming, had hidden in the thick bush.

"Anne, we must give this up. He does not answer. The wood be too thick here to search for him in the dark."

"Aye, Jack. Let him rot here."

Wading back to the boat, they got aboard and rowed back to Turnley's vessel. After ransacking the ship for sails and other valuables, Rackam towed Turnley's sloop into deep water, cut the mainmast and sank her. Two of Turnley's hands, John Howell and John Davies, joined Rackam's crew. Rackam rejected the third crewman, one David Soward, who, though old and experienced in the ways of the sea, was crippled by an old wound. He was given a boat.

"Shift for yourself, man," said Rackam. "And tell Turnley," said Anne, "that I meant to whip his fuckin' hide off. Tell the bloody bastard that. I had better never see his friggin' face or I'll whip him to death and blow his head off after!"

From here they stretched over to the Berry Islands, where Rackam plundered several sloops and strengthened his company with more hands.

Practically under the nose of Woodes Rogers, Rackam sailed Haman's sloop by New Providence down the Exumas to Long Island. He was determined to menace any vessel in Bahamian waters, and he did. Off Rum Island he took a French vessel loaded with brandy, claret, silks and soap. Afterward he decided to stop and clean his sloop. Anne had been ill that morning and had not taken an active part in capturing the French vessel. Rackam knew of a large pleasant harbour at the north end of Watlings Island and gave the command to steer that way. Anne was not aware of their destination, nor did she particularly care as long as it was land. She needed time ashore. Late that afternoon Haman's sloop rode at anchor in the harbour at Watlings Island.

Jack helped Anne onto the deck. She gripped the rail, trying to maintain balance, as she looked around, stunned. She was not sure if she were awake or dreaming.

"Dost know where you are, Jack?"

"Aye, 'tis Watlings."

"Stand away from this island!"

There was a deadly earnestness in her voice which frightened him. Rackam did not know why but he knew better than to contradict her in this.

"Break ground!" commanded Rackam in a loud voice.

"Aye, aye, sir."

"Hoist your sails halfmast high! Man into the tops! What, is the anchor aweigh?"

"Yea! Yea!"

Anne gripped the railing, bracing herself against both the movement of the sloop and the turmoil within her. Her teeth were clenched against the cries tearing up from her throat, eyes shut against the ghastly images of her last day on this island.

"Helmsman, keep course for the Crooked Island Passage!"

"Anne, let me take you below."

"Leave me be, Jack," she said through clenched teeth.

"All right! All right! Let out your sprit sail! Move, you friggin' pricks! God damn yer eyes!"

Jack walked to the stern, checked the compass and said to Mary, "Give over the helm to me and see if you can get Anne below."

"What be the trouble, Jack?"

"I wish I knew. 'Tis something to do with this bloody island. Look at her face. 'Tis pained past recognition."

"Some bitter memory, perhaps."

"Aye, that's certain."

Mary stood beside Anne at the starboard railing. Their hands touched. Anne sighed, relaxing somewhat, then opened her eyes. They were heading south. She could see the sandy point where she and Tombay had spent their glorious holiday. Anne watched in stony silence until the island passed out of sight.

Anne felt Mary's hand next to hers on the railing and took it into her own, clutching it desperately.

"Wilt go below, Anne?"

"Aye."

Once below in the captain's cabin, Mary asked, "Wouldst rather be alone or wouldst like company awhile?"

"No, stay awhile. I need to talk."

Anne had not told even Henri the whole story of her experience on Watlings Island. She had kept the bitter details locked in her heart. To Mary she now told all. There were no tears. She discovered, in relating the events surrounding this period of her life, that she had many more beautiful memories than tragic ones. Lying on the cot securely held in Mary's arms, she found that much of her bitterness seemed to float away.

It was almost Christmas, and Rackam was looking for a pleasant place to go ashore and carouse. He decided to sail easterly toward the Caicos Islands. Also his ship was in need of fresh water.

The Caicos Islands lie in the form of a crescent opening to the south and are separated from each other by narrow passages. Rackam put in at one of the smaller islands near the northwestern part of the group. The company went ashore to put up tents among the pine trees. It was here that Rackam and his crew spent Christmas.

Anne was grateful for the time ashore and she felt sure Jack would not leave while he had liquor left. She swam in the turquoise sea and rested in the shade of the pines. Mary helped clean their vessel, walked the beach and scoured the island for fruit. Rackam was content to drink, smoke and gamble at cards and dice.

After a few days Anne and Mary decided to take the small boat and explore the nearby islands. As they sailed through the narrow cuts, it became clear to them that these islands afforded good hiding places. Mary felt sure a small sloop could run safely through any of the cuts. They coasted north on the ocean side until they came to the last and largest cay. Going near the shore, they saw an abundance of colorful parrots flying in the trees.

Off North Caicos Anne saw three small cays.

"Dost the chart name those cays?" asked Anne.

"They be called the Three Marys."

"Well, there be two Marys in my life, you and my mother, Mary Flanagan. What about you? Can we come up with three Marys between us?"

"My mother's name is Molly."

"That is Mary, too, you know."

"Aye, but it does not please me to think of her. I had a sort of mother in Madame Beaulieu. Her name was Marie. She taught me to read and write in English and French."

"Sounds to me as if Marie belonged to a House of Sale, from what you've said of her."

"You have guessed it. My mother put me out to work for her as a footboy when I was but thirteen."

"No! You can't mean it."

"I do. I was there three years, until one day Marie tried to seduce me and I ran away."

"Oh my, the story gets better and better. You must have been frightened in the face of discovery."

"Near out of my wits." Mary was laughing now and Anne giggled as she listed to the story of the day Mary was nearly raped by Madame Beaulieu. The women almost overturned their small craft.

" 'Tis good to laugh," remarked Anne. "You know when you first came to New Providence, I cannot remember that you ever smiled."

"I be happier now. More content, less lonely."

"Three Marys. I will laugh and cry a little to think on those cays."

"Why weep?"

"Oh, I weep sometimes to think of my mother gone. I weep for you sometimes, too. I fear I will lose you. I know not why."

" 'Tis a fearsome thought," said Mary. "I like not to think of a time when we must part."

Anne was sorry she had mentioned her fears and tried to bring herself and Mary out of this dark mood.

"If my baby is a girl I am going to name her Mary."

Mary was too moved to speak. She kissed Anne's hand and held it for a long time.

On the way back they stopped to explore the parrot island. Staying inside the coral shelf, they coasted near shore until they found a little cove where they could pull the boat onto the beach.

As they walked the beach the women watched the birds and studied the seashells. Anne saw a grassy area near the south point of the cay. Pushing their way through the tall grass they soon came to a clearing. Lying down, they scanned the sky and listened to the birds and the waves. Both women lay quietly all afternoon basking in the sun and the peaceful atmosphere of this pleasant cay.

Rackam had built a high tower of stones and had a man

posted to the watch day and night. George Fetherston had had information on good authority that immediately after Christmas a Spanish armada had left Havana for Hispaniola and Puerto Rico with money to pay the garrisons. Sailing via the Old Bahama Channel from Cuba, their ships could be spotted once they entered the Caicos Bank. The armada would pass between the Caicos Islands and the north coast of Hispaniola and would stop first at Porto Plata before continuing to San Juan. Rackam had resolved to remain in the area and molest the Spanish.

Anne and Mary sailed to the large island southward of the pine cay in order to establish a lookout tower there. Sitting on the beach with his arms planted in the sand behind him and his left leg shaking up and down, Rackam planned his strategy for attacking the armada.

Anne and Mary pulled the small boat into a cove on the lee side of the hilly, crescent-shaped island. Taking down the mainsail, they fashioned a tent. It was nearly dark. Anne built a fire and fried some conch they had brought with them. That, washed down by a few bottles of beer, constituted dinner.

The women chatted by the dwindling fire, exchanging stories of their early lives. Mary felt a kind of freedom she had never experienced just telling Anne the unusual story of her life. There were elements of it which she told to Anne that she had not revealed even to Max. Anne knew how to draw her out of herself. Deep secrets emerged painlessly. She no longer carried bitterness in her heart, not even toward her mother, who had contributed to years of frustration and suffering. May seemed to understand her life much better now. She was almost at peace.

"Are there other women like us, think you, Mary?"

"I know one—Mother Ross."

"Who is she?"

"Mother Ross followed the wars in Flanders. She was a sort of scavenger and a healer. She tended my wound and saved my life. Sometimes she dressed like a man, as I do. One thing—" Mary laughed to recollect it—"Mother Ross used a grand pissing device."

"A what?"

"A pissing device made of silver which was strapped around her waist and fit into her . . . well, you know where."

"Jesus God, now I've heard everything!"

"I can't tell you how often I have thought of that and wished for one myself."

"We'll have one made for thee!"

"Where? Not in the islands; 'tis impossible."

"We may get to London one day, or Carolina. Yes, we'll have one fashioned for thee."

"I doubt we'll ever see London."

"Dost ever wonder, Mary, what would happen if we were caught and brought to trial? Would you reveal yourself then, think you, if by doing so you could save your life?"

"I do not know what I would do. I always hoped I would die in battle, fighting bravely. I have lived by the sword all my life. I wish to die with honor like a soldier."

"I hope 'tis so for you. For me, I am not ready to die. Oh, let's leave off talking. 'Tis depressing. Wilt take a swim with me?"

"Aye."

" 'Tis private here; take off all your clothes."

Anne undressed quickly. Mary was hesitant and waited until Anne was in the water, then undressed to join her. The sea cove was lit by phosphorous. Mary watched the tiny bits of light swim about her. Under water she could see Anne's golden hair radiating electric colors all about her. Bits of colors streamed from her nipples and fingertips. The water was cool and Mary felt exhilarated and free, wrapped in the beauty of the phosphorescent sea.

The next morning Anne and Mary climbed straight up from the cove to a high ridge overlooking what appeared to be blue hills and the blue-white water of the Caicos Bank. For three days they did not see any sail. On the fourth they spied a fleet of fifteen ships.

Hoisting the sail on the small boat, they set out to meet Rackam. He had likewise espied the fleet and came to meet them. Before sailing out of the cut, he went over the plan of attack with his crew.

"We will cut across with the wind and take the last ship, board her, loot her and run back here to hide. A galleon draws too much water to come into these cuts. We will be safe."

Haman's sloop set out across the bank. The wind was fresh and astern.

"Keep her full!" shouted Rackam.

When they came near the fleet Rackam ordered the cannons to be loaded and bid everyone pray.

"Meet that last vessel at the nearest angle, helmsman. Fetch her up! Fetch her up smartly!"

The galleon fired upon the pirate sloop.

"Hoist our colors, God damn it! Bring dripping blankets! Splash the deck with water! We want no fires, lads. Give her a volley of small shot!"

Rackam's ensign, a white death's head cradled in crossed cutlasses on a black background, was hoisted to the mainmast and the black flag flew the mizzen peak.

"Prepare to board! Stand by with grapples! Spoil their tackles if ye can, lads!"

Anne and Mary stood at the bow ready to board.

"Fetch her up! Fetch her up! That's it, mates. Board her now!"

The fighting was fierce but quick. Rackam swung a deadly cutlass, Mary's sword was murderous. Anne's shirt had been torn off and she was fighting barebreasted.

What a sight! thought Mary to herself, finding a moment to catch her breath. The Spanish were likewise astounded to see a woman fighting in a such an aggressive and brazen manner. Anne took full advantage of her nakedness and slashed a gaping hole in a man's stomach to match the one in his face.

After fifteen minutes the Spanish crew called for quarter.

"Loot only coin and gold dust. Carry it to the sloop. We have no time to waste. We will set this vessel afore the wind."

Sizable chests were transferred to the sloop. The pirates cut the shrouds of the galleon's sails and hacked down her mainmast, sending her away before the wind.

One of the guardships gave chase to Rackam's vessel, but the sloop outsailed the heavy-bottomed galleon. Rackam slipped into a cut between the big island of the bluehills and a mangrove cay. Sailing westerly along the coast on the ocean side, he anchored in the cove behind a high hill, well hidden from the fleet.

Rackam stayed on that island and kept watch on the Spanish guardship, which rode at anchor in a large bay on the south side of the island. Soon wearying of this waiting game, he decided to leave the Caribbean and beat up to the Bermudas.

The blue water of the Sargasso Sea stretched before them as Haman's sloop pitched its way through the swells.

"Sail ho!" cried the man in the topsail.

Rackam snapped out his glass to have a look. "'Tis a galleon but she flies no colors. We'll give chase and have a closer look."

The fast sloop set every inch of sail but was unable to reach the galleon that day. She had altered course and tacked as near the wind as she could lie in order to keep her own until night.

"She will try to lose us in the dark," said Rackam to Mary. "We cannot weather her now. Stay with her if you can."

Mary and George Fetherston alternated helm duty throughout the night. The galleon's lights had been doused; she could not be seen at all.

Mary was weary of battling the heavy sea. In the morning Anne joined her at the helm. The galleon was nowhere in sight. By pursuing the galleon, they were now following a course which would take them to the Carolinas.

By noon they descried a sail. The sloop had the benefit of a fine topsail gale and in several hours they gained considerably and were within sight of the galleon's colors.

"British, bedad!" shouted Anne. " 'Tis the king's jack."

"Some merchant vessel," said Rackam. " 'Twill be a fine prize."

"We'll be swimming in tea," said Mary.

"Come, mates," said Jack. "'Twill be a stern chase and a hard one."

The galleon was relentless in her efforts to outmaneuver the sloop, but she could not get away and was finally forced to defend herself.

"Let her go a little more large," shouted Rackam to the seamen at the shrouds. "We must chase under her lee till we get broadside! Let fly our colors! Man the ordnances! Fire!"

Although Mary sluiced the cannons with cold water and vinegar, several of them burst on the second firing. Her face was blackened by powder.

"Board for close fighting."

Anne threw a granado onto the quarterdeck and boarded there. Mary was right behind her. She marveled at Anne's courage. Boarding a vessel was far more dangerous than charging trenches. Mary had had enough experience in both actions to know.

In a matter of minutes the pirates had the crew of the British galleon quartered.

Mary looked around suspiciously. "I like not the stink of this vessel."

Approaching the captain she demanded, "Be ye a slaver, Mister?"

The man said nothing.

"Answer me, you bastard!" Mary struck the man hard with the back of her hand. A thin line of blood ran from the corner of his mouth down his chin, but the captian remained silent.

"Open that hold! We'll see the cargo," ordered Rackam.

"I smell it already," remarked Anne. "Look at the stern, Jack. Here be their goods. Crates and barrels are stacked up everywhere."

"Some of you men put what we can carry aboard the sloop. Leave no rum behind, hear me!"

Mary's eyes were riveted on the opening of the hold. She had not really prepared herself for what she saw emerge from there. The chained figures were not slaves, but whites. Beaten and broken men and women stumbled up to the deck. They had been starved and tortured unmercifully. Clothes had been literally whipped off their bodies. Not one was a whole person. Each seemed to be missing some part: hand, leg, eye, ear, tongue, nose—something. All were hiding from the sun as if it were their mortal enemy.

"Lucifer's balls! 'Tis a hellship." Anne stared at the maimed creatures.

There had been no need to spare these miserable wretches and the hellship captains knew this. Criminals were not nearly as valuable as African slaves. Ugly, ignorant, penniless, these had been the dregs of society even before they were tried, sentenced, branded and shipped aboard the Newgate vessel.

It took Fetherson, Davies and Black Robin three quarters of an hour to unchain the lot. Robin carried up to the deck one man he had released from the rack. The man was so maimed and broken that he could not even put his arm over his eyes to shield out the painful light.

"Put that man in the shade," commanded Rackam.

Robin laid the man on a shady portion of the deck and went below again. Mary watched the man groan and twist in agony. His body had been stretched well beyond the limits of his tall frame. Every bone was cracked and every muscle torn. He was not a young man, about fifty she guessed, and had perhaps been handsome before his torture. She could tell by the cut of his cloth that he was no ordinary criminal.

Mary moved closer and, noticing the rosary of pain around the man's forehead, called to Anne, "Your knife, please, Anne."

Anne handed her the knife.

"Ask that bastard captain about this man for me, will you, Anne?"

"Aye, I will."

Mary tried but could not remove the metal stem used to

tighten the knotted length of whipcord which was bound around the man's forehead. Carefully she inserted the knife under the cord and began cautiously to cut. She did not want to injure the man further. Once the rosary was removed, the man sighed in relief and opened his eyes to look at Mary.

Looking into this man's eyes was like gazing into her own. The intense depths of her dark eyes were reflected in his. Startled, she backed away.

The man seemed to reach for her arm but grasped her sword hilt instead. Blinded by the light and pain, he could not see it at first but he seemed to know the feel of the weapon. Mary started to pull the hilt out of his hand, but as she watched his fingers grope for knowledge, she sensed that the man knew her weapon or one like it.

Painfully he tried to raise himself. Anne returned and helped Mary lift him. His breathing was labored and his body weakened by pain but he had to see the sword.

"*Mi* . . . ." He tried to speak but could not.

Finally he removed the sword enough from the scabbard to touch the etched initials. Excitedly he raised up further to look at Mary and said, "*Quien*. . . . Who . . . who are you?"

"My name be Read."

"A. . . ." The man coughed violently, then reached up and touched Mary's face, and whispered, "*Mi hijo* . . . my son, my . . . son."

He fell back into Anne's lap; a horrible gurgling sound came up from his throat and was followed by a final whisper of breath. The man was dead.

Mary stared down at the man, bewildered. "What did he say in Spanish?"

"He said, 'My son,'" replied Anne, greatly disturbed by Mary's reaction to the man's dying words.

"Who be this man, Anne? I must know. Do you see—he does resemble me. Could this Spaniard be my father, or did he mistake me?"

"The captain said he was a political prisoner, one Miguel Rivera, alias Miles Randall. Does the name signify?"

313

Mary looked at the man's hand locked on her sword hilt and shook her head.

"M. R. . . . M. R.," she murmured. Leaning down, Mary kissed the fingers which were entwined in the hilt of her sword. Tears streamed down her face. She touched the dead man's face and, after taking one last look into the brown eyes, she closed them.

"This man must be my father, Anne. Canst believe that? And now he be dead. He recognized his sword that I have carried with me for so long. How can he be gone from me so soon?"

As Mary fought to hold back her sobs, the pinched look of her face brought her cheekbones into prominence. Anne was startled to see before her a living replica of the dead man's features.

Mary pried the man's fingers away from the sword hilt. Anne wound a piece of sailcloth around his body and tied stones to the foot of the package. Mary lifted his body over the railing, committing her father to the Sargasso sea.

In April of 1719 Rackam and his crew cruised in the neighborhood of the Cayman Islands, taking small fishing sloops and recruiting men to strengthen their number.

By mid-April they stretched up to the Isle of Pines to clean their vessel and celebrate Anne's twentieth birthday. By this time she was big with child but she still refused to be delivered over to the old women at Zagua, a village in Cuba where Rackam kept a kind of family. Even Mary's entreaties did no good.

Rackam and his crew of nearly thirty men beat up to the Tortugas, off the tip of Florida. These small islands were in the path of the flota sailing from Vera Cruz to Havana. The route chosen by the Spanish was occasioned by the trade winds. Rackam was looking to snatch a prize galleon from the flota and present it to Anne for her birthday.

After a week of waiting, Rackam saw his opportunity. Using the same strategy as had been successful against the armada in the Caicos Bank, he cut off the last ship in the fleet and boarded her. Turning the Spanish crew out in a longboat, Rackam waited until the fleet was far ahead and, under cover of night, sailed through the Old Bahama Straits. He planned to take the Mona passage between Hispaniola and Puerto Rico and cruise the Leeward Islands.

The galleon proved a fine prize; its strongroom was filled with Mexican silver. Anne was installed in the great stern cabin and Rackam, taking his original crew aboard the galleon, left the English sloop in the capable hands of one Roger Scot, a stout Newfoundland seaman.

On the galleon, Rackam appointed officers in the tradition of the British Navy: George Fetherston, master; Richard Corner, quartermaster; Black Robin, boatswain; John Howell, gunner; and John Davies, gunner's mate. Mary was the pilot.

Days passed into nights.

Mary often spent the quiet evening lying on the quarterdeck listening to the tinkle of the ship's bell.

Time passed.

The weather thickened.

"The wind veers; settle your main topsail!" shouted George Fetherston.

The sea grew large.

"Matt, fetch the commander to the quarterdeck," requested Robin, who was helping his men struggle with the mainmast shrouds.

"Aye, Robin."

Jack was below with Anne. Mary knocked softly on the cabin door. There was no answer. She knocked louder.

"Enter!" shouted Rackam impatiently, as he lifted Anne onto the bed. She was unconscious.

"My God, what happened?" demanded Mary.

"She fell."

"Christ, no! Be she all right?"

"I know not. I found her here on the floor when I came in. She has fainted or fallen from the bed. I know not which. We must secure this vessel against the storm; the sea be getting mightier by the hour. Stay with Anne; she must not be alone. She did complain of pains earlier. I pray God the baby come not now."

"I hope not. 'Tis not her time yet. But I will gather what I need now while I be able to move about the ship."

"Here be a mixture of opium which she may need later. I must go to the deck and see how best to make our way out of these seas."

Mary put the vial in her vest pocket. "Canst descry a place to put in?"

"I cannot put a man up to see; he will be blown out of the tops."

"Do the best thing, Jack, and do not worry. I will take care of Anne."

Anne was moaning softly as Mary wound a sheet around her, sling fashion, and tied it to the headposts of the bed. Mary was not sure if Anne was experiencing labor pains or had hurt her head in the fall. She fetched a quantity of clean cloths and bathed Anne's burning forehead with cold water.

On deck Rackam's commands were loud and urgent. His men leaped upon the shrouds like leopards.

"Shorten sail! Lash the ordnances! Helmsman, put her right afore the wind. She will roll but she will not strain anything. Lower the foresail!"

The galleon scudded all that night under bare poles.

By morning the winds had increased and Anne was wakened from her delirious sleep by fierce pains.

On deck high waves broke upon the poop. Two men were washed away from the helm but were saved in the netting.

When Mary untied Anne's legs she noticed that the bed was wet. Lashing rope around her own waist, Mary tied herself between the footposts of the bed and braced herself against the movement of the sea, waiting. With each pain, Anne gripped Mary's hand in a grinding hold. Mary whispered comforting words and urged Anne to breathe deeply.

Blasts of lightning flashing through the cabin were followed by incessant claps of thunder.

Anne's pains quickened.

"Breathe and push!" shouted Mary over the howling wind. "I'm here with ye, Anne. Ye have nothing to fear. Come now, with the next pain . . . that's it, breathe. Now push down. Let the child come, Anne. Ye be wide enough for two babes now.''

The wind was shifting around the compass, making a short and angry sea. Oakum was spewing out of the seams in the bow.

''Try the pumps!'' Jack roared. ''All hands to the pumps. Push, lads!''

The big sea smashed the great cabin windows at the stern, showering glass all over Anne and Mary.

Above and below, the ship rang with blasphemies. Curses loud enough to drown the uproar of the warring elements boomed from the voices of the rain-battered men as they struggled desperately for life in the very face of death. But there was little hope of safety.

The mainmast tore away from the boom.

At last Mary's hands brought the babe from Anne's womb. She stared in wonder at the lifeless form she held. 'Tis blue. Dear God, this cannot be. The child must live.

Mary cleaned the film and blood away from the baby's mouth, tied off the cord, then cut it.

Anne, suddenly aware that she had heard no sound from her baby, directed weakly, ''Slap it.''

''Aye,'' responded Mary, taking the child's feet in one hand and slapping it on its backside.

Still no cry was heard.

Mary whacked the babe several times with no response. Anne slipped into unconsciousness. Mary cradled the tiny baby in her arms and talked softly to it. ''Don't ye be dead, little Mary, please, please, don't ye be dead.''

On deck, Rackam was forced to order the mainmast cut away. The galleon lost in the rolling sea, he tied himself to the helm and gave way to despair. Below, Mary clutched the dead baby to her bosom and wept.

Anne had passed the afterbirth and the heavy bleeding hd stopped but she was still in a great deal of pain. Mary had forced a small dose of opium between Anne's lips before she washed and wrapped the baby in clean cloths and placed her in a heavy chest. The ship was rolling in the swelling sea and rain beat through the stern windows. Mary had canopied the bed to keep out the weather and had tied Anne and herself in the bed.

All that night Mary lay beside Anne, listening to her breathing and to the hollow roaring of the wind.

The next day the wind finally abated its fury and was decreasing hourly. When all was calm again, Mary brought the tiny bundle to the deck.

Jack, distraught and weary, rushed to her excitedly. Upon seeing the sadness in Mary's dark eyes and the child bound tightly in a winding sheet, his face darkened. Taking the bundle from Mary, he tied ballast to it and committed his and Anne's child to the deep. Jack Rackam stood for a long while at the railing and wept.

The vessel had taken on a great deal of water. Seamen manned the pumps constantly to keep the ship afloat. All they could do now was wait and pray they would sight land soon.

Mary went below again. Anne was awake but somewhat groggy from the effects of the drug. She refused to eat and asked only for a sip of water.

"Hast much pain now?"

"Aye. My breasts ache fiercely."

"Wouldst like more of the drug?"

"No, please, no more. Come, hold me."

"Aye."

"Why is my babe not here? What have you done with my child?"

"Anne, the baby . . . be dead. The child would not breathe and I could do nothing."

"Was it a girl?"

"Aye, a girl."

"Little Mary."

"Aye, little Mary be gone from us now."

"And Jack? What of Jack?"

"He did grieve to give her up."

"Aye, Jack be a good man in his way. Aaah . . . I had hoped this pain would abate with the wind but it has not."

"How can I help you?"

"I have an ointment of the aloe plant in my chest. Fetch it please. 'Tis clear in color.''

Mary found the ointment and applied it to Anne's privities. Her pain eased somewhat and now she was sobbing. Mary knew Anne was weeping not just for this lost child but for Tombay and Nditi as well.

"Do not weep, Anne. 'Twill only hurt thee more."

"I cannot help weeping. Canst say you have not wept? I know thee better. Ah, these breasts, they will burst from this pressure. Canst ease them? I can bear this pain no longer."

Anne pushed the bedclothes away from her throbbing breasts and, reaching up, drew Mary to herself.

"Land ho!" cried the man in the tops.

Rackam packed all the supplies and valuables he could hold into the longboat. Robin carried Anne to the deck. There had been no sign of the English sloop and Rackam assumed that those men had perished at sea. In all, he had lost seventeen men during the fierce storm. Leaving the galleon to flounder at sea, they hoisted a sail on the longboat and made for safe harbor on the north shore of Hispaniola.

Besides Rackam, Anne and Mary, only ten of the company remained. They looked for a quiet cove. So numerous were the inlets on the north coast of the island that it had become the refuge of over one hundred pirates who, using piraguas, robbed only in that neighborhood. Much of French Hispaniola was covered with high mountains which fell abruptly into the sea. Rackam found a pleasant beach cove which seemed to have been scooped out of a blue-green mountain. Here he and his tiny band would spend nearly seven months recuperating from the rigors of the sea.

Hispaniola: 1720

In January of 1720 Anne was healthy again and eager for action. She and Mary had hunted fowl, climbed mountains, dived the sea gardens in the gulf of Logane and explored the grassy channels of Cape Samana.

Jack had been occupied in operating a rumrunning business. Having stolen an English sloop in Bay Real, Rackam had increased his crew with five good men: Thomas Earl, Patrick Carty, James Dobbins, Noah Harwood and Jason Presgrove. They had been only too eager to join. Nearly half his crew now were Negroes. Recruited by Black Robin, these were hardworking men and not superstitious about having a woman aboard ship. It had been difficult for Rackam to enlist men because most seamen believed that a woman on a ship brought bad luck.

Mary had accompanied Rackam on several occasions, piloting the vessel into St. Ann's Harbour and Plumtree Point, two inlets on the northern coast of Jamaica. Most of the time Rackam and his chief officers, Fetherston and Corner, had made the tedious runs.

One afternoon Anne and Mary were swimming along the shoals off Monte Christi, on the north coast of Hispaniola, when they spotted the narrow stern of a French pink a little way out in the bay.

"Canst see the name of that vessel?" asked Anne.

"It cannot be what I think it be," replied Mary.

"Come on, say. I think I see it too."

"Maryanne?"

"Aye, I think so. What is she doing?"

"Fishing."

"Let's take her!"

"What, here? Now? We have no weapons. And look at you, stark naked!"

"I am not naked, I have my breeches on. How many men are on that vessel, think you?"

"Four or maybe six—no more."

"We can do it. We'll pretend we are drowning and call for help. Surely two or three men will come to rescue us. We can render them unconscious while they try to save us and then we can swim to the pink. Think of it, our very own pirate vessel."

"Aye, and once aboard you bounce those melons afore their eyes and I'll put their lights out with my bare fists. Oh, Christ, this be madness! 'Tis rash. Let's think on't awhile yet."

"No, we'll never do't if we think on't too long. Start screaming."

Anne and Mary set up a hue and cry that would have alerted the British Navy had they been in the bay. Two men from the pink dived into the water and swam toward them. Pretending to panic while drowning, Anne and Mary managed to deliver their rescuers several hard clouts to the chin, rendering them unconscious. Then the women swam out to the pink.

The three men on board, thinking their companions had returned, helped the women into the vessel. Once on deck all three men immediately locked their eyes on Anne's firm round breasts. Mary gave one man a paralyzing blow on the back of the neck. Once shaken out of their shocked incredulity, the men began to resist and hand-to-hand combat ensued. Anne wrestled the master and flipped him into the sea. Mary battled the other two with her fists until they dived overboard and swam for shore.

The pink was in need of repair and, since there was no

carpenter among the group, Rackam was for sinking the vessel, but Anne was determined to keep it. She felt that once they were at sea again they could press a sea artist into service at the first opportunity. Everyone worked on the pink to make her seaworthy for the expedition. Only so much in the way of repair could be accomplished because the vessel was iron sick.

Rackam installed twelve good men and his best officers on the *Maryanne*: George Fetherston, Richard Corner, Jason Presgrove, Black Robin and Matt Read. Anne was now captain of her very own pirate vessel. She traveled in consort with Rackam's ship, a fast, sturdy sloop of nine guns named the *Invincible*. Commander Rackam and his pirate band set out to menace the seas once more.

It was February, 1720, and England was at war with Spain. The war was brief, but war nonetheless. Commander Rackam had resolved to stand for the Leeward Islands in the Caribbean Sea. All ships bound for Jamaica or for the plantations in America were obliged to get to Antigua in order to fall into the trade winds and so bear away west.

Jack felt danger in the very winds. He wondered if it had been wise to give up his distillery business and initiate piratical activities again. But he had become weary of the mountainous country and had longed for the sea. Rackam knew they would have to be clever and careful this time in order to avoid being captured by the king's men and thereby share the fate of Bonnet, Teach, John Augur and the others hanged at Nassau.

Rackam gave strict instructions for the boarding and taking of any merchant vessel. No one was to call any of their company by name. Everyone would wear masks to disguise his identity, and if their vessels were chased by any warship they were to throw their colors into the sea.

One afternoon just off St. Christopher, the pirates sighted an English snow and, hoisting English colors, hailed her in the manner of the sea. Once aboard, the pirates surprised the crew with a flurry of cutlasses which would have terrified even a hundred men. Rackam's men had had months of practice on Hispaniola. He had impressed on them that the initial boarding pattern with a splendid display of weaponry, followed by a brave assault, would make short shrift of their work.

The officers of the snow stood quartered.

"What vessel's this?" shouted Rackam.

"The *Cadogan*, snow from Bristol," answered the master.

"The *Cadogan*," murmured Mary.

"Hast gold, sir?"

"No, only passengers."

"Let me see 'em. You—" he touched Richard Corner's shoulder—"follow this vessel's boatswain below. Mate," he said, addressing Robin, "search the cabins."

"Aye, sir."

The *Cadogan*, thought Mary as she expelled air rapidly, almost snorting her indignation. Jesus God! 'Tis not a joke any more. Methinks the man haunts me. William Cadogan, you old pisser, why can't ye leave me in peace?

"Pirate captain," said the captain of the snow, "didst know England is at war with Spain?"

War! The word blasted into Anne's head. She looked at Mary, who stood tall and proud, sword in hand. Her face was expressionless now and looked as if it had been chiseled out of marble.

Mary is suffering inside, battling her own private war, Anne thought. There she stands, one of Great Britain's soldiers, and child of a Spanish father.

"Well, pirate captain, think on what you do now," warned the captain of the *Cadogan*. "You have interfered with one of the king's couriers. It will go hard with you when you are caught."

"Enough talk, Mister! All this palaverin' won't save yer bacon if I have a mind to send you headlong to hell."

The prisoners were brought to the deck; about six men in all, no women.

"No chests of gold," reported Robin. "A few purses only. I searched their belongings."

"Tell this nigger to take his filthy black hands off me!" commanded a disdainful young man, elegantly dressed and powdered from head to foot.

"What?" said Anne. Jack put a restraining hand on her arm.

"My hands be not dirty. Huh, Mister, look 'ere, see, white on the inside, black on the outside, just as they should be." Robin was waving his hands in front of the young man's nose.

"Really, Captain, must I listen to this?"

"Aye, you'll listen to whatever he has to say to thee, fellow."

"I've done, Cap'n," said Robin. "I have nothin' more to say to this pup. In fact, sir, I will step away, for I like not the smell of him."

"I warn you, pirate captain, I'll not suffer abuse from this nigger."

"Oh, be that so? And who be you, sir, something special?"

"I am Temple Lawes, son of Sir Nicholas Lawes, Governor of Jamaica."

"Oh, well now, isn't that something, eh, mates? Strip!"

"What?"

"You heard me, strip! All of you, strip or I'll blow yer brains out. Search their clothing! We have tarried with these fools long enough."

The pirates found only a few gems and a little money on the passengers. Rackam was annoyed; once again he turned his attention to the governor's son, who was looking ridiculous, clothed only in a long curly wig.

"Now mates, lookee 'ere. Doesn't look like much, does 'e, lads? You be a foolish boy to brag so. Didst know I can take you and hold you for ransom? Huh? Didst know that? Now, lads, this puppy has nothin' to say, when a little while ago here were all mouth."

Jack knew it was a dangerous proposition to take the governor's son but he was determined to make the boy sweat a little.

Anne looked at Mary, who was now staring at a tall,

well-built man. He was handsome in a rugged way. His eyes were green, his hair had been bleached almost white, and his skin was tanned deep brown by the sun. The man wore a heavy canvas apron and held a chisel and hammer in his hand, the tools of a sea artist.

Anne went up to him and grabbed the hammer out of his hand.

"What, sirrah! Dost hold weapons against us?"

"These be only tools, mate. I am no fighter, Mister, just a poor carpenter."

"Say true, mate? Cap'n, here be a man more useful than that snivelin' puppy."

Jack came over to her and questioned the tall carpenter. Anne winked at Mary, whose face flushed red.

"Your name, sir?"

"Tobias Sampson."

"And be you a good artist, Mister Sampson?"

"Aye, sir, tolerable, tolerable."

"Wilt come with us?"

"No, sir."

Anne nudged Jack.

"Well, that be too bad. You're comin' anyway. We have plenty of work for thee. Gather yer tools and go aboard that pink."

Jack once again turned his attention to Temple Lawes.

"Well, sir, gov'nor's whelp or no, I daresay ye won't fetch much," he said, looking at the young man's scrawny frame. "Tie them all up, lads, and spoil their rigging. We must stand away from this vessel."

In early April the pirates beat down to the English island of Tobago to careen and repair the *Maryanne*. Cruising the Windwards during the past two months had been an unprofitable but beautiful voyage. Mary listened to the music of Anne's voice as she recited the islands by name, and remembered the time in Liverpool when she had first heard mention of the Caribbee Islands. Now she was actually seeing the spectacular mountainous scenery of the fabled Windwards.

"Dominica, Martenica, St. Lucia, St. Vincent, Grenada and now Tobago."

The great cabin was quiet for a long while, then Mary heard the sound of hammering coming from the deck. During the past two months Mary and Tobias had become what seamen term messmates or strict companions. She found him attractive, strong of mind and body, and honest as well. He could never lie, not even to himself. Because of his honesty Mary found it difficult to reveal herself to him. She had lived a lie all her life and she felt that Tobias would be disappointed in her.

She wanted to talk to Anne about her feelings, but when she tried to speak her thoughts the words seemed wrong in her head and she knew they would sound even worse. Deep inside herself Mary felt that she had somehow been unfaithful to Anne, if only in her thoughts.

Tobias Sampson had captured the heart of Mary Read, thought Anne. Not an easy thing to do, but the man has done it. My friend is in love, but will not speak of it to me. Why, I wonder?

"Mary, are you in love with Tobias Sampson?"

Mary did not say anything.

"Have you told him who you are?"

"No."

"Why?"

"Anne, you ask too many bloody questions, you know that?"

"Why are you angry?"

"I am sorry. 'Tis just that lately I have been feeling unsure of myself. I be confused and angry with myself." Almost shouting, she added, "Yes, I have a strong attraction to Tobias Sampson!"

"And what is that to be angry about, please tell me?"

"I don't know!"

Anne did not know what to say but she was beginning to understand why Mary was so upset. Coming over to where Mary was sitting, Anne took her into her arms, pressing Mary's head against her bosom.

"Mary, I do not feel that by loving this man you love

me any less.''

"How is it possible to love two people at the same time?''

"I don't know how, but 'tis. I want you to be happy. If you love Tobias, tell him so. Discover yourself to him.''

"Why do I feel unfaithful to thee, then?''

"Because you think too much.''

Mary and Tobias walked the deserted beaches of Tobago. They had been on the island a week; the *Maryanne* was nearly repaired and Mary still had not revealed herself to Tobias.

"Wilt swim, Matt?''

Instinctively Mary refused. Tobias took off his shirt and dived into the billowing surf. Moments later, Mary removed her vest and joined him.

When they came out of the water Mary's shirt clung to her full round breasts. Tobias stared at her, wondering if the sight was real. She looked at him and smiled.

"Why, Matt,'' he said, "how hast ye transformed thyself?''

" 'Tis the magic of the sea. Great Neptune has waved his triton over my breast and. . . .''

Tobias smiled "And what of thy other parts?''

"Likewise transformed.''

Mary took off her blouse to let it dry in the sun. The tiny beach cove was deserted. Stretching out on the sand, she felt the warm sun on her naked breasts; the feeling was rare and glorious. Indulging in this glowing sensation, she closed her eyes and waited for Tobias to say something. But he was silent.

Tobias stared down at Mary's beautiful white breasts and thought to himself, I was told the sea held many surprises but I never did expect anything the like of this wonder. This sea nymph is beautiful in every way.

Tobias carefully laid his body on top of Mary's. He never spoke until after he had made love to her, and then he asked softly, "What is your name, sea nymph?''

"Mary.''

"Will you be my sea wife, Mary Read?''

"Aye."

"What do I say next, then? Since we have no preacher and no church, what happens now?"

"We will make vows before one another. God will hear us over the surf. We need no representative. There be the sand here, and the sea, and the trees and the wind. God is all about us."

"All right then. I, Tobias Sampson. . . ."

"Wait. Do you understand, Tobias, that I must continue to live as I have and will not change my pattern of life now that I be wed?"

"Aye, I know that. I do not ask it. You are an uncommon woman, Mary Read; I want simply to share your life with you. Shall I go on?"

"Aye, please."

"I, Tobias Sampson, take thee, Mary Read, to be my wife. I promise I will never do anything to dishonor you, and I shall cherish thee till the day of my death."

"And I, Mary Read, do take you, Tobias Sampson, as my husband and I shall honor you always."

That night Rackam broke out an additional butt of rum. The crew never knew exactly what they were celebrating, but they were grateful for the extra ration. Rackam was anxious to set out to sea again but in the light of these new circumstances he allowed Anne to persuade him to stay on an extra week at Tobago.

By mid-May the pirates stood for the Virgin Isles. They spent a month in that neighborhood without sighting one sail. Rackam then decided to sail for the Caicos Islands.

Jason Presgrove, gunner aboard the *Maryanne*, was a burly, bullish and sullen man. All his life he had used the sea. His seamed, pockmarked face was burnt deep red-brown. He had no friends, no messmate, because no one liked his company or his rough manner. The ship's great guns were his only friends; he cared for the cannons as if they were his children.

Tobias never came to the deck for gun drills. Jason complained to Captain Bonny. Anne told him that Tobias was a pressed man and a carpenter besides, and would not take an active part in any engagement. Presgrove was not satisfied and decided to confront Tobias Sampson.

To have no concern for weaponry be not manly, he thought. The whole ship be talkin' about him and Read anyway. They do lie together every night. Bloody buggerin' fool, he flaunts my authority besides. Why can he not discharge his duty like an honest man?

The next day at breakfast Jason Presgrove stared at Tobias Sampson. For two weeks now Tobias had taken the morning meal without his messmate. Nauseated by the smell of food, Mary had spent the better part of each morning in Anne's cabin.

It was late June; the men, sweltering on the decks by nine o'clock, were out of sorts. Jason took pleasure in calling gunnery practice at high noon.

Tobias left the deck and went below to check on Mary. This morning Anne was in the galley so Presgrove put his mate in charge and went below to confront Sampson. Catching his arm just as Tobias was about to knock on the cabin door, he said, "Where be your messmate?"

There was a touch of acid in his voice. Mary recognized who it was and stood next to the door in order to hear what the men were saying.

"What business be that of yours?" retorted Tobias.

"He be needed on the gundeck—you too, for that matter."

"I am no fighter, man, and therefore need not to learn the use of guns."

"What are you, then, a friggin' sodomite?"

Tobias went for the man's throat. Presgrove brought his arms upward in a powerful thrust and broke Sampson's hold.

"I be hurtin' to kill thee here and now," said Presgrove, "but 'tis against our articles. We must wait till we reach the next harbour."

"Any time, you name it, man," Tobias growled angrily.

"Four of the clock on the afternoon we put in."

"Aye. I'll be there, you can count on that. Get away from here now."

Mary went back to the cot as Tobias knocked on the door.

"Enter."

Tobias came in and knelt beside the cot, taking Mary's hand in his and kissing it. "How be you this afternoon?"

"Better, now that you are here."

"What is the matter, think you? Why are you sick so much lately?"

" 'Tis seasickness, that is all. I have spells o't now and then. It will pass. We'll be in the Caicos in a day or two. Time ashore will help me."

"We come to those islands so soon? I thought perhaps 'twould be a week or more."

"Nay, only two days at the most. Why? You seem troubled."

" 'Tis nothing; I have work I must finish. Will you come up soon?"

"Aye. In an hour or so."

"I love you."

"And I love you. Don't bang your thumb again."

Tobias laughed and left the cabin. He was afraid, but he could not tell Mary what had transpired between himself and Jason Presgrove. His pride would not let him, so he locked the secret within.

Below, Mary thought to herself, Dear God, I must find a way to stop him. Jason be too hard a man for Tobias. I can keep a secret as well as he can.

Mary was ill the morning they dropped anchor but by noon she managed to get up to the deck. Anne and Tobias were on the *Invincible*. Rackam was inspecting his vessel for a suspected leakage in the hold.

Mary sat on one of the cannons. She still had not thought of a plan to stop her husband from dueling. Jason came to the deck and loaded one of the small boats with cutlasses and pistols.

He can't go ashore so soon. I thought four was the ap-

330

pointed hour. Dear God, I wish I felt more myself; perhaps I could think.

Unconsciously Mary was striking the butt end of her pistol against the cannon.

"Hey, mate," shouted Presgrove, "what are ye doin' there?"

Mary had attracted his attention and aroused his anger by abusing the ordnances. Realizing this, she smashed the pistol repeatedly against the cannon. The pistol broke up and fell in pieces to the deck. Presgrove grabbed her by the shirt front and raised her to her feet.

"Hey, Read, what are ye about?"

"Not anything of your business, Presgrove."

"All the ordnances aboard this vessel be my business, Mister."

"Be that so, here is another then. This be what I think of your fuckin' ordnances." Mary broke her other pistol on the cannon.

Presgrove was fuming. "Ye be lookin' for a fight, Mister!"

"Aye, where and when?"

"On that island there, at six."

"Two!"

"Fine, two!"

"Go around the south point, out of sight of these vessels."

"I'll be there!"

Lowering the boat over the side, he jumped into it and rowed for the island of the parrots.

Mary put her hand on her stomach. Oh, dear God, please, I must not be sick any more today.

At one thirty Mary strapped on her sword, lowered a small boat and rowed ashore.

It was a few minutes after two when Tobias, Anne and Jack returned to the pink. Anne had ordered a small lunch to be brought to her cabin for the four of them. Jack, his feet propped on the table in the great cabin, was drinking rum, while Anne was washing herself at the basin. Tobias had gone in search of Mary.

Food was brought in and Jack dived into it as if he had not eaten in a week, swallowing mouthfuls of beef without chewing.

"Can't you wait, Jack?"

"I'm starvin'. Leave me be."

Tobias came in. "I can't find her anywhere. Robin said she rowed off to the island about half an hour ago."

"She's probably gone swimming."

Tobias could not hide his concern; it was in his voice, and sweat was dripping off his handsome face. "Robin said she had her sword and a pistol."

"Perhaps she went hunting," mumbled Jack, his mouth full of food. "Come on, man, sit ye down and eat."

"I think not . . . I think. . . ."

"Tobias, what is it?" asked Anne, sensing danger. "What's the matter with you, man? Tell me at once if you think something is amiss here."

"Oh, God!" he said, realizing that Mary could have overheard his argument with Presgrove.

"Out with it," coaxed Anne. "What is wrong?"

"A few days ago I had a quarrel, just outside this door, with Jason Presgrove."

"God, no!"

"We arranged to meet on the island at four this afternoon, and I fear Mary may have heard us, for she was here in this cabin."

"Jesus God!" exclaimed Anne. "You dolt, you idiot! Why did you not tell me, at least? She has gone earlier to fight him first. I know her. What's more, she is with child."

"Oh God in heaven, no. I never did guess that was the cause of her illness."

"Aye, 'tis true. And now God only knows what will happen to her. She is a fierce fighter when roused, but I fear Mary is no match for Jason Presgrove in her present condition. Come on, arm yourselves! We must hurry. Pray God we be not too late."

"Why? Why would she do it?" questioned Tobias.

"She loves you, you dolt; that's why!" thundered Anne. "Rackam, damn you, leave that food and come on!"

332

Mary was so weakened that her feet seemed ballasted as she plodded through the sand. When she reached the other side of the point, Jason was waiting with his pistol pointed directly at her.

"Hold there, Read, and fire."

Mary stopped and, raising her pistol, took aim. Presgrove fired first and missed. He was in her sights. Mary lowered her pistol, drew her sword and advanced.

The pistol was her ace; if she fired now and missed, she would have to fight to the death with her sword. Mary knew she was not strong enough to hold out against Jason's powerful assault.

Metal clashed. Ringing sounds came forth each time his cutlass caught her sword. He was not skillful but he had the advantage of a more powerful weapon and Mary was tiring quickly. Her reactions were delayed only seconds but, in the business of swordsmanship, a second's hesitation could prove fatal.

Mary cut across a thrust aimed at her belly, deflecting his cutlass, which put a deep slash across the top of her thigh. Wincing in pain and charged with anger, Mary advanced. Jason fell backward over a piece of driftwood. Mary, almost blinded with sweat and pain, had to deal the final blow now before she lost consciousness.

Anne arrived ahead of the rest just at the moment Mary's pistol discharged.

"Mary!"

Turning around, Mary took one step forward on the leg which could no longer support her, and fell to her knees. Anne caught her as she fainted away.

"How bad is it?" shouted Tobias.

"I don't know yet. Please back away from him, give him room to breathe." Anne saw the blood gushing from Mary's thigh. "Ah, here is the wound. Robin, come here. Remove the left boot—gently now."

Robin removed Mary's boot and poured a quantity of blood out onto the white sand.

"Jesus God!" Tobias turned away.

"Jack, take some men back to the sloop for clean cloths,

fresh water and my medicines. Put a tent up here. And hurry!''

Jack went off in the direction of the small boat with three other men. Anne turned around for a moment and saw the dead man. His face was gone.

"Robin, you and another man bury Presgrove. Take him away from here."

" 'Tis my fault, all my fault!" Tobias was on his knees beside Mary.

"There is no time for tears now. Rip away the leg of her breeches—gently, man, God damn it. I hope Jack returns quickly." Anne tore off her shirt and held it against Mary's bleeding thigh. "Tobias, help me carry her into the tent."

Lifting her gently, Tobias carried Mary into the tent and put her on the blanket.

"Fetch me a log to prop her leg, and tell me when Jack returns with medicines. I must remove her clothes, so keep the other men away from here."

Anne cut away Mary's breeches with her knife and tied a strip of her blouse around Mary's thigh just above the gash.

Tobias returned with the log.

"Place it under her knee. 'Twill keep her leg up somewhat."

"Is the cut deep?"

"Aye, deep enough. If she does not bleed to death, . . . I must have a quantity of clean rags, soon. Please go and hurry Jack along."

Mary was groaning in pain. Anne untied and retied the cloth every few moments, brushing away her own tears as she ministered to her friend. When he returned with the medical supplies, Jack was surprised to see Anne's bloodstreaked face.

"Canst handle this yourself, Anne, or do you need help?"

"I can do it. Leave everything here. Dost have any drug to ease her pain?"

"Aye, some opium. I'll lay the vial beside you."

"The babe," asked Tobias, seeing the blood smeared

over Mary's privities. "Is the babe hurt as well?"

"I think not, Tobias. 'Tis only blood from her leg wound."

"Come on, man," said Jack gently, "wait outside with me."

Anne put a few drops of opium on Mary's lips; she would be parched and lick them enough to get some benefit from the drug. Concentrating all her energies on the wound, Anne willed the flow to cease.

Hours later the bleeding stopped. Anne cleaned the wound carefully and applied a dressing. Exhausted, she stretched out beside her friend and slept.

The next morning Anne was up before daybreak. She stepped from the tent.

"How is she?" asked Tobias.

"Still asleep. I have stopped the bleeding. She is very weak, but I think she will live."

"Thank God for that."

"You had to challenge him, didn't you? Why in the name of God did you do it?"

"He called me a sodomite."

"Jesus fuck, so what! Mary is hurt near to death. You would have been killed, that's certain. And for what?"

"I have some pride."

"Pride! False pride, that's what it is."

"'Tis not false. . . ."

"Man's false pride. There is no jot of courage in't. 'Tis her fault, too, to help thee keep this empty pride. She is not the first woman to have done that and very likely will not be the last. But I'll tell thee this, real courage is lying in that tent there!" Anne walked away, cursing to herself. "Lucifer's balls! Men! Sometimes . . ."

After three days of delirium Mary regained consciousness. Anne was at her side as she had been day and night since the moment of the duel.

"You were asleep a long time."

Mary struggled to raise herself.

335

"No, stay still. You must not move. The cut in your thigh is dangerous. You must be very careful not to move your leg."

" 'Tis funny. I remember going away into a blinding white light. There were people talking . . . about me. Then I woke up and saw you here."

"I am glad you came back."

"How long must I lie here?"

"A week, perhaps a month."

"A month! I shall go mad."

"You will be dead unless you do exactly as I say. 'Tis no trifling wound, I tell thee! Would you like more opium?"

"Uh . . . no."

"Tobias wants to see you."

"Is he angry with me?"

"He has no cause to be. He is sad, and cries a lot, that I know."

"I did a foolish thing. You are angry—I can tell that."

" 'Twas a rash deed."

"I didn't want Anne Bonny to think she be the only one to have impulsive actions."

Anne laughed. Then she saw a pained expression come over Mary's handsome face.

"Here, squeeze my hand. Let me help you through it."

"I . . . I don't want to hurt your hand."

"You can't hurt me. I am not delicate. You have always been too protective of me. I am stronger than you in some ways."

"Aye. . . ." The pain stopped Mary from speaking.

Anne took Mary's hand. She could not help feel Mary's agony as her own. Anne closed her eyes and waited for the series of pains to pass; then she called Tobias.

The pirates spent nearly two months in the Caicos Islands. The men fished, explored all the cuts and inlets, and made excursions to Hispaniola to hunt wild hog. Anne spent her time making new trousers for Mary, who could no longer fit into her breeches.

Anne had been right: Mary knew that without Anne she would never have been able to get through that painful time, and her feeling for the woman grew stronger with each passing day. Having learned to give of herself freely to another person, Anne found her love for Mary deepening. A bond of love between the two was sealed, not with the restricting bands of steel, but with the elasticity of freedom—freedom to give of self, freedom to love, freedom to be.

By mid-August Rackam and his crew left the Caicos Islands and cruised up the Bahamas for the last time. Anne had insisted on it. She had troublesome thoughts she needed to resolve in her mind. The often peaceful and always colorful Bahamian water was the balm necessary to soothe her spirit.

Rackam sailed as far north as Harbour Island. On the third of September he attacked a fleet of seven fishing boats and ransacked the vessels, taking fish and tackle as well as the goods and chattels of the fishermen. Afraid to linger in that neighborhood so close to Woodes Rogers, Rackam steered south again, riding down the ocean side of Eleuthera out of sight of New Providence.

Mary and Anne had a desire to visit Nassau. At this moment both would have given all their wealth for anonymity. Sitting on the deck of the *Maryanne* they considered their situation.

"It hurts me to think there is no place for us to go. We are outcasts of society. Many of our own company do not accept me because I am a woman. It is hard at times to be a woman. I sometimes try to think of myself disguised as a man like you and all alone aboard a vessel bound for some unknown port."

"And?"

"The thought frightens me. I cannot be alone as you have been most of your life. I weep even now to think of you and your solitary life. But 'tis not only compassion which makes me weep, but my own fear of loneliness."

"I pray God you may never chance to be alone. Put these fears out of mind, Anne. We have gotten ourselves too deep in heavy thoughts. We must leave off."

"Aye. Look at the sea. Hast ever seen such color in your life? And think of the vastness of the ocean. Such glorious space and fresh breeze."

"Life is good on the sea. We should enjoy every minute while we can."

Rackam landed on the French side of Hispaniola and took away some cattle and two Frenchmen, Peter Cornelian and John Besneck, who were hunting wild boar. The two men were skilled in curing meat in the manner of the buccaneers and Rackam forced them to use their skills on behalf of his crew. They were shipped aboard the *Maryanne* so that they would have the benefit of conversation in their native language. They spoke no English.

On the first of October, three leagues from Hispaniola, Rackam sighted two merchant sloops, fired upon and then boarded them. Both sloops were heavily laden with nets and tackle and well stocked with provisions. Rackam put out the master and crew and took both vessels. Rounding the east end of Hispaniola, he sailed down through the Mona passage into the Caribbean sea to run with the wind to Jamaica.

Jamaica: October 1720

Jamaica. The Arawaks called it a land of forests and streams. Columbus described it as a magnificent scrap of deep green crumpled paper floating in the blue Caribbean. In the last quarter of the seventeenth century, Port Royal, the wickedest and most sinful city in the world, became the stronghold for the British buccaneers. Destruction visited often. In January of 1704 a devastating fire had consumed what buildings the earthquake of June 1692 had left standing in the town.

Sir Nicholas Lawes, Knight, was the Captain-General and General-in-Chief, Chancellor and Vice-Admiral of the island of Jamaica. His main interest, like that of all Jamaicans of the period, was planting. Lawes maintained that planting was the mother of trade and Negroes were the support of planting. Pirates were the chief enemy of trade, and Lawes found that with the promise of pardon the pirates in his area had grown more numerous and insolent.

Rackam and his fleet of three sloops and one pink chanced to encounter a British slaver en route to Jamaica. The entire fleet converged on the vessel, clapped her aboard, and took her without any loss of men.

Before they even boarded the vessel, Mary knew it to be a slaver, and she was prepared to make this day her last. Her life in the Caribbean had come full circle. Every detail of the torturous passage aboard the accursed *St. Job* rushed into her consciousness. Now the captain and all the officers of the *Grace of God* had been killed in the battle.

Letla, now you are avenged at last, Mary whispered to herself. I am free to die in peace. But I am afraid suddenly, because standing here victorious over my enemies I feel I will not die the honorable death of a soldier. I have found my own honor. I, Mary Read, a woman, have done a courageous and honorable deed by saving these people and destroying their persecutors.

Mary stood in silence as Rackam's men brought the prisoners up from the hold. Tobias was on one side of her, Anne on the other. Both sensed her suffering and both were hesitant to take her hand in the presence of this company. Mary stood alone, as she had done most of her life.

Black Robin looked at the frightened faces of the men, women and children who now stood expectantly on the deck.

A few more than three hundred remained of the eight hundred captives who had left the Guinea Coast in this two-hundred-ton vessel. Robin came and stood before Jack Rackam. He spoke no word; his request was clearly outlined on his face.

"Robin, you may take the largest two of our sloops," Jack said.

"And the pink," offered Anne.

Jack raised his voice. He wanted no misunderstanding about what he was going to say next. "Anyone who wishes to go with Robin and these people is free to do so. Anyone who wishes to leave our company may come and stand here beside Robin."

All the blacks on Rackam's crew, plus a few others and the crew of the slaver, stood beside Robin. Tobias looked at Mary. Seeing this, Anne walked over and stood beside Jack. She was apprehensive and waited to hear Mary's response to Tobias' silent request.

"I cannot, Tobias."

"Aye."

"Wilt bring my chests of gold from the pink?"

"Aye."

Fetherston, Corner, Davies, Howell, Harwood, Dobbins, Carty and Earl elected to stay with Rackam. They began to transfer their personal belongings from the pink to the sloop.

"All right, Robin, load the sloops. We will sink this stinkin' vessel after. Fetherston, keep aboard our sloop only what we need in the way of provisions. We will be at Jamaica soon and can get more there. Robin has many people to care for, we but few."

"Aye, sir."

"Where will you go, think you, Robin?" asked Anne.

"To the great Caicos island. There be a large pond at the northeast end with good farm land all around. We will settle there."

"Luck to thee, my friend."

"And to thee, Mistress."

"Robin," said Mary, offering her entire wealth of coin and gems, "take these chests."

"I thank thee, Matt. 'Tis generous of thee."

"I do not need so much; you will, my friend."

"Will the Frenchmen go?" Jack asked Anne.

"Nay. They say they will not ship with niggers."

"The scum! Think they be too good for anybody, eh? They'll do our dirty chores now, I warrant, or I'll feed their rotten hides to the fishes!"

"I think you should kill them, Jack. They are not good men."

"Aye . . . I will," he said hesitantly, "when I have done with them."

Jack Rackam had changed; he had no stomach for pirating any more. Weary of killing, he avoided bloodshed whenever possible. Anne remembered Bellamy's remark the day Black Bart had killed his ship's boy on the street in Nassau. "Killing is a necessary part of piracy." Rackam had lost heart on board the slaver; Anne had seen him waver. She was fearful; the fate of the entire crew was in the hands of this fainthearted man. Moreover, she regretted that once again she was carrying a child of Jack Rackam's in her womb.

Because of the close quarters in the sloop it became necessary to inform the crew of Mary's identity. Fetherston, Corner, Howell and Davies, who had shipped with her for almost a year, were greatly surprised. Since they were all friends, this disclosure made it easier for everyone, especially Tobias and Mary. The Frenchmen presented the only serious problem. Confined to the galley for the most part, they were kept apart from Rackam's company.

Cruising the north coast of Jamaica, about five leagues from Port Maria Bay, Rackam took a schooner. Thomas Spenlow, the master, and the crew offered resistance and were assaulted but no one was killed or hurt. Rackam detained the vessel for forty-eight hours, taking off fifty rolls of tobacco and nine bags of pimiento; then he returned the schooner to Spenlow and bid him go where he would.

The next day, the twentieth of October, Rackam fired upon the sloop *Mary and Sarah,* which was riding at anchor in Dry Harbour Bay. The master, Thomas Dillon, and his crew abandoned the vessel and went ashore.

Rackam had chosen to cruise the north coast of Jamaica at the wrong time. His presence in these waters would prove fatal to him and his company. This lee side of the island, usually peaceful and pleasant, had recently been a scene of turmoil and tragedy. Pirates, cruising the coast in piraguas, had been menacing the planters by stealing slaves and carrying them to Cuba to sell.

Two notorious pirates, Nicholas Brown and Christopher Winter, had committed a vicious act in St. Ann's parish. During a slave raid they had set fire to a house with sixteen people in it. One old Negro man, hearing the tortured screams of the children within the house, had tried to save them but was badly burned for his futile efforts at rescue. The assembly had asked the governor to offer a bounty for the taking of Brown and Winter, but Lawes had informed them that there was no money available in the treasury. He assured them, however, that he was determined to hang any and all pirates captured within his jurisdiction. The citizens in the north were angry and continually watchful.

Ochos Rios lies midway between St. Ann's parish and St. Mary's. Here the pirates stopped on a beach near a point of land covered with palms. While the crew put up leantos and posted watch, Anne and Mary walked the beach. Not far from their camp they came upon a waterfall. Its wide steps cut through dense growth and large trees. Still fully clothed, Mary floated in the milky pool at the bottom of the falls while Anne climbed the rocks alongside.

" 'Tis a river fall," shouted Anne from the top. "I think I will slide down in the water."

"Be careful!" Mary shouted back.

Anne climbed to a plateau and walked across the slippery rocks; then she sat in the rushing water and let it carry her down the falls.

"Oh!" Mary gasped, watching her.

Anne slid to the bottom, then floated head down in the water. Alarmed, Mary hurried over to her and lifted her out of the water.

"Anne, Anne, be you all right? Answer me! Dear God, not drowned, I hope!"

Mary sat holding Anne in her arms. The falling water beat against her back. She put her lips against Anne's and breathed into her mouth. When Mary realized that Anne was kissing her, she exclaimed, "God's Death! You she devil! You had me frightened out of my wits. God damn you anyway!"

Anne was laughing now. "I can't resist. 'Tis so easy to fool you."

"Ooh, damn your blood, Anne Bonny. You anger me past my limits sometimes."

Mary splashed water in Anne's face to avoid striking her, which was what she really wanted to do.

"So you want to play, eh, little mother?"

Anne grabbed Mary around the torso and brought her down on top of her into the shallow water.

"God damn you, woman!" Mary shouted, as she wrestled to free herself from Anne's hold. Freeing one hand, she took a fistful of Anne's hair and pulled hard.

"Aargh!" screamed Anne. "Not fair! Leave it to a woman with child to think of such a low, sneakin' trick as that. Some soldier you are, *ma cherie*!"

"Cruel bitch, to fight with a woman so indisposed. Have ye no shame?"

The women stopped fighting momentarily. Anne looked into Mary's beautiful eyes. They were black now and Anne knew that Mary was really angry.

Anne smiled and said, "You're right; we should not fight. I am sure we can think of something better to do here in this beautiful place on this glorious afternoon."

Anne watched Mary's eyes slowly return to their natural deep-brown color, then she saw tears well up in them.

"Why do you weep? I did not hurt you, did I?"

"Aye, you did."

"Where! *Mon Dieu!* Show me! Your Leg? Where?"

"No, my heart. You bloody well hurt my heart."

" 'Twas only pretense. You are too serious always."

"I do not like your jokes! Promise me you will never do that again."

"I promise, little mother. Now don't weep any more."

Anne took Mary into her arms.

"I thought you were dead. You don't know, you can't know how that moment felt to me."

"I am sorry, truly sorry. Never again, I promise."

Mary closed her eyes and rested against Anne's bosom. Looking down at her friend, Anne suddenly felt an emptiness, a frightened intense longing, she did not completely understand. She kissed Mary's forehead and eyes in an effort to drive out those foreboding thoughts. Angry at her own fears, Anne fought passionately against thoughts of death, desperate to give Mary the ultimate expression of her deep, undying love.

Late that afternoon Dorothy Thomas left the bay at Ocho Rios in her canoe loaded with supplies for her small farm in St. Ann's Parish. She was a large woman in her middle forties, possessed of a hearty determination and fortified in the strength of the Almighty. At dusk she stopped on the east side of the point near the falls to spend the night before continuing on to St. Ann's Harbour and home.

The family burned in their house by the pirates Brown and Winter had been her neighbors. Since that time Dorothy had taken a pistol on these frequent but usually uneventful excursions. Dobbins and Carty, keeping the watch that night, saw her and the next morning reported her presence to Rackam.

Jack, doubtful that the woman would invite them to breakfast, decided to attack and carry away her provisions. Mary was to steer the small boat around the point. She took along the three men to load the stores. Jack, Anne and George Fetherston planned to cross the point on foot and take the woman by surprise. As Mary rounded the point she heard a shot fired. In haste she approached the beach. The men helped her out of the boat as she came to shore.

Furious, Anne was cursing loudly at the heavyset woman, who stood almost triumphant, legs wide apart, hands on hips. There was a red mark across Anne's left eyebrow. Startled, Mary almost called out Anne's name but restrained herself just in time. She shot a desperate glance in Anne's direction and pulled her sword.

"Whoreson bitch! Bloody fen!" shouted Mary. "Dost want further action? Have at me, then, ye hobbyhorse!"

Mary threw a cutlass at the woman's feet. She did not like the smug look on Dorothy's face and wanted a chance to teach her another expression. Jack was instructing the men regarding which of the goods to load into the boat. As far as he was concerned, Anne and Mary would be able to manage one woman. He ordered his men to take only food and things necessary for their survival. They were to leave the locks, nails, hinges and the like.

Dorothy Thomas refused to pick up the cutlass and stared in fascination at the two women.

"Dost ye not 'ave the fear of God afore yer eyes?" she shouted. " 'E'll not forgive these vile sins. Ye be gross, barbaric. Thy crimes be abhorrent to all Christian folk!"

"We but steal a bite of breakfast," replied Anne. "I'd hardly call that abhorrent, old woman."

"Ah, if this be thy only wicked deed, 'twould be so; but I know ye 'ave committed a 'undred vile, gross and wicked deeds that even Lucifer would shake to look on."

"Jesus God, she be a female Nicholas Trott!" groaned Anne in disgust. "Enough of her mouth. Dispatch her, Matt!"

"I cannot till she pick up that cutlass. Pick it up, you gutless bitch!"

"I will not. I stand secure in the Lord!"

"You'll not stand secure in the Lord if I decide to send thee headlong to hell!" shouted Anne.

"What is the trouble here?" asked Jack. "We must be off now."

"Kill this woman, Jack."

"Why? I have no cause."

"She tried to kill me before."

"Why did you not shoot her? Be there something wrong with that pistol in your hand?"

"I was stunned by the wound, else I would have killed her. Jesus fuck! Can't ye do anything any more? This woman will bring witness against us all. Mark my words, Jack!"

"She's right, Jack," said Mary. "Still her mouth before 'tis too late for all of us. 'Tis the captain's duty."

"Do it, Jack!" demanded Anne.

"All right! All right!"

Jack raised his pistol and took aim. Dorothy Thomas stood defiantly before him. Just as his finger closed on the trigger his hand began to shake. He tried to steady it with his left hand but could not. Finally he dropped his gun hand to his side and stared at the white sand at his feet. Then he looked up at Anne and said, "Not a bloody word! Not one fuckin' word. Hear me! Into our boat now. Move your arse," he threatened, drawing his cutlass.

Corner hoisted the sail and Mary took the tiller and steered around the point toward the sloop.

Jack set a westerly course. Dorothy Thomas rowed out beyond the point to take note of his direction; then she made the long trip to Spanish Town to inform the governor of the presence of pirates on Jamaica's north shore.

Negril, Jamaica: 1720

On a bright November afternoon Rackam's sloop rounded the western tip of Jamaica, and he put out his anchor at a beach north of Negril Point. The men repaired lines and tackle and fished. Tobias was busy about some minor repair to the bow of the sloop. Anne and Mary viewed the immediate landscape. They could see that the shallow water was only a short distance from the boat and decided to swim to the shore. Once ashore, they stretched beneath a palm tree and gazed out over the water.

"The Caribbean Sea. Dost ever tire of looking at this water, Mary?"

"Nay. I find I spend more and more of my time of late just staring at the sea."

"See how the colors grow deeper in greens and blues."

" 'Tis black at the horizon though, like death."

"But consider the whole of this scene. Colors stretch from milk white to black, flat and endless. I feel as if I've had been here before."

Mary was fascinated by the blackness of the horizon. Suddenly she felt the child kick in her womb, and she smiled. Here was life. Pulling herself away from the black distance, Mary watched the small milky-white waves lap the shore and she pushed her feet deeper into the sand. Taking Anne's hand, Mary placed it on her stomach.

"Active little rascal, isn't he?" Anne remarked.

"Do you think 'twill be a boy, then?"

"I think so. Your time is soon now, less than two months, I think. Are you afraid?"

"Somewhat."

"Don't worry. I will be with you."

"I know you will."

"Do you like this place? Should we stay here till your baby is born?"

" 'Tis a peaceful place. Yes, 'twould be a fine place to birth a babe."

"I'll speak to Jack. We should not leave now. I feel that the babe may come early."

"Promise me something?"

"Aye, anything."

"Deliver me here on the beach, in the open, where I can look up at the sky and out to the sea."

" 'Tis a promise."

Anne and Mary watched, enthralled, as the sun set on Negril beach. Anne was speechless but Mary finally said, " 'Tis the most beautiful sunset I ever did look upon."

They lingered many hours past the sunset. Anne was tempted to remain ashore all night. The moonlit beach was seductive. But, lest their men worry, they waded back to the sloop.

When they arrived on board they discovered that their presence had not been missed at all. Rackam had invited some sailors aboard to drink with them. Cutlasses and muskets were strewn about the deck. Rackam and most of his crew were by this time almost incoherent and their guests were also fairly well pickled. Even Tobias had tipped one too many glasses of Richard Corner's punch. Only the two Frenchmen were sober and they were not what the women would consider pleasant company. The indisposition of Rackam and his men was indeed unfortunate, for at this ill hour one Captain Bonnavie and one Jonathan Barnet were sailing in company toward Negril Point.

After the war with Spain there were many seafaring people in Jamaica. The governor did not know what to do with them so he sent them out after pirates. Jonathan Barnet was one such experienced seaman. He was a stout, brisk Irishman whose guard sloop was well manned with bold fellows like himself.

At ten that night Captain Bonnavie spotted Rackam's vessel and, being ahead, lay by till Captain Barnet's sloop came up. Bonnavie informed Barnet of Rackam's vessel and he made swiftly for it.

When Barnet's sloop came in sight, Anne harshly issued rapid orders to weigh anchor and stand away. Somehow the men managed to comply. In the moonlight Rackam could now clearly see the guard sloop bending its sails in a case toward them and he issued more orders to hasten their departure. But Barnet, having the advantage of some little breezes off the land, soon came up to Rackam's sloop and hailed him.

"What are you?" shouted Barnet.

"John Rackam from Cuba," answered Jack thickly.

"I bid thee strike to the King of England's colors!" ordered Barnet.

Anne answered, "We'll strike thee no strikes, Mister!"

Mary fired the swivel gun on the guard sloop. Barnet ordered a broadside and a volley of small shot which carried away Rackam's boom.

Jack shouted to his men, "Throw our colors into the sea!"

Barnet and his men boarded Rackam's vessel. After a minor skirmish, Rackam and all his men went below, leaving Anne and Mary to hold the deck against Barnet and his men.

"Cowards! Fuckin' cowards, the lot of you!" shouted Anne, as she wielded her cutlass against the king's men.

During the fighting Mary caught a glimpse of Tobias unconscious on deck. Roused to vengeance by the thought of her husband dead, she fired into the hold, killing one of the visitors and wounding others.

"Rackam, you friggin' coward! Damn your blood, all of you! Come out and fight like men!"

Cursing and swearing vengeance against their enemies,

their fellows and the whole world, the women fought desperately, but they could not hold the deck against so many. Finally they were seized and disarmed. Barnet's men brought Rackam and the rest up from the hold. One of the sailors roused Tobias out of his drunken sleep. Mary, relieved that he was alive, was suddenly angry that he would so besot himself.

"Be you all right?" Tobias asked drunkenly.

"Aye, no thanks to you."

"What has happened here, I. . . ."

"Speak no words, Tobias. 'Tis all over now."

The Frenchmen were protesting their innocence.

"Tell it to the gov'nor, mates. Perhaps he'll understand thee," replied Barnet. "Bloody foreigners!" he mumbled.

Anne was furious. She cursed Rackam in the vilest terms as everyone was taken aboard Barnet's sloop. At Port Royal Barnet delivered his prisoners over to Major Richard James, a militia officer who procured a guard to carry the prisoners to the gaol at Spanish Town.

Anne and Mary were left manacled and confined in a damp, nichelike cell which was not tall enough for either woman to stand upright. It had no window. The gaol was in fact one large open room where most of the men were chained to the wall. There were a few small cells hacked out of the thick walls. Rackam was placed alone in one of them. A grinding wheel for sharpening swords, standing in one corner, was the only object in the room.

St. Jago de la Vega had been first settled by the Spanish in the early 1500's. Now it was the capital of Jamaica and the seat of His Majesty's government on the island. On the morning of November 5th the cathedral bells woke the pirates from their drunken sleep.

At two in the afternoon the prisoners were brought before Governor Lawes. The twenty-three pirates were escorted by the militia guard down the street to the courthouse, where a hostile crowd had gathered. The building was already packed with people and more crowded in. The prisoners

351

stood before the bar and had to suffer the jeers and taunts of the mob until the governor arrived.

There was nothing to distinguish Nicholas Lawes from any other island planter in the room. He wore a loose-cut coat of a coarse light woolen fabric, and a full-bottomed wig. Owing to his great age, he used an ivory-handled cane. Settling his fleshy body into the president's chair, he was ready for what proved to be lengthy proceedings.

His first statement informed the audience that this was not a formal trial but an informal hearing. However, any evidence brought out here would be used against the prisoners later. Mister Gomersall set his motion before his excellency and Lawes approved the expenditure of one hundred pounds to Barnet and his men for the capture of John Rackam, pirate captain.

"A very good piece of work 'tis, to bring in so many," remarked the governor. "But I daresay 'twill cost us a fortune to construct gallows for all of them."

Peter Cornelian began to jabber excitedly in French.

"What? What's this? Calm down, man. What language be that?"

"French, Your Excellency," volunteered one of the counselors.

"Dost any one of you speak it?"

All the counselors shook their heads no. Lawes then ordered the court attendant to go into the town and fetch an interpreter.

"Now, John Rackam, step forward. Be you the captain of the vessel taken by Jonathan Barnet?"

"Aye, sir."

"I am here to tell thee, Mister, that ye are a bloody and notorious villain and will hang for your wicked crimes."

Cheers rose up from the crowd.

For a split second Jack saw Anne clothed in a tarpaulin and sitting in a tree. It was hard for him not to smile.

"Quiet in the court! Quiet, I say! Well, Mister Rackam, what do you have to say?"

"Sir, I. . . ."

"Enough! Be all these men of your crew, sir?"

"Nay!" shouted Thomas Quick.

"Who are you, sir?"

"Name's Thomas Quick, Your Grace. Myself and eight other men here were visitors aboard Rackam's sloop. We be not pirates, sir, but honest turtlers."

"Is this true what he says, Mister Rackam?"

"Aye, sir, 'tis true. Those nine men there came aboard my vessel to drink a bowl of punch the night we were captured. I never did see them afore that time."

"Canst not refuse a dram of rum, Mister Quick, when 'tis offered to ye by bloody pirates?"

"Sir, at first we did run away and hide in the bushes. Then Rackam hailed us, saying he were an honest Englishman. After much persuasion we got into the small boat he sent ashore for us and came aboard his vessel. That be the truth of it, Your Honor, sir. We be no pirates."

Besneck blasted out a flurry of French clearly meant to accuse Quick and the others.

"Shut it, I say! You hold your tongue till we have an interpreter! One more outburst and I'll send thee back to the gaol. Understand me?"

Besneck well understood the hard look in the old man's eyes, and kept silent.

"All right, then. Mister Quick and you eight men stand to one side. You will be dealt with later. Now, you—Rackam's men—state your names to the court."

One by one Rackam's crew addressed the court: Master George Fetherston, Quartermaster Richard Corner, Seaman John Davies, Seaman John Howell, Seaman Thomas Earl, Seaman James Dobbins, Seaman Noah Harwood, Helmsman Matt Read, Seaman Bonn, Tobias Sampson.

"And what is your occupation, sir?"

"Carpenter."

"Mister Rackam, what are the names of the Frenchmen?"

"John Besneck and Peter Cornelian."

"Seaman Bonn, have you no given name?"

353

"None that I know of," said Anne in a deep voice. "My name is Bonn."

"Very well, sir."

Simon Clarke came into court to act as interpreter to Besneck and Cornelian.

"Mister Clarke, find out what those men have been trying to say to me."

"Aye, Gov'nor."

A few moments of intense communication took place between the three men. Lawes lit his pipe and waited. Rackam sniffed the aroma and fell into despair to be denied such a simple pleasure. Now the proceedings were very real to him.

"Gov'nor Lawes, these men say they were pressed, taken by force by John Rackam while they were hunting on the shore of Hispaniola."

"Mister Rackam, is this true?"

"Aye," said Rackam, too despondent to go into any further explanation. "This man, Tobias Sampson, was likewise forced."

"Say true? What do you say, Mister Sampson? Are you a forced man or are you as guilty of piracy as the rest?"

Tobias said nothing.

"Tell me, sir, are you guilty or innocent?"

Tobias remained silent.

Mary could not understand why Tobias refused to answer and save himself. She stared at him in an effort to perceive what was going on in the man's head.

"The rest of you, how do you plead to the charge of piracy?"

All answered, "Not guilty."

"And you, Mister Sampson?"

He said nothing. The governor's face turned beet red, and he raised himself a little out of his chair to address Tobias more directly.

"Dost understand you cannot be condemned lest you say aye or nay to the charge?"

"Yes, sir, I understand that."

"Then how do you plead? Silent still. Well, tortures will open your lips, I assure you. The Frenchmen are hereby released, but ordered to stay in town to serve as witnesses against these men. Clarke, tell them what I have said. Rackam, you and your men here, except for Mister Sampson, will be tried by the court of Admiralty on Wednesday, November 16th. You, Mister Quick, and your crew will be tried at a later date after the fate of these others has been determined. This hearing and meeting of the assembly of His Majesty's Island of Jamaica is hereby adjourned."

"Wait!" Simon Clarke shouted. "These men have something more to say."

"Tell them to save it for the trial. We cannot listen to their jabber all day; 'tis nigh suppertime."

"Sir, they say these two here, Read and Bonn, are women."

A shock of near hysteria erupted in the room. People chattered to their neighbors and climbed over one another to get a better look at the two.

"What?" shouted Lawes.

"Bloody fuckers," muttered Anne under her breath.

"Bleedin' pricks!" murmured Mary.

"Women! Can't be! Not in my court! 'Tis outrageous! 'Tis not to believed. You, Read and Bonn, step closer." Lawes adjusted his spectacles. "What are you, sir?" he demanded, addressing Mary.

"A woman, sir."

"And you, Bonn, what are you?"

"Likewise a woman."

"Incredible! What are your names?"

"Mary Read."

"Anne Bonny."

"Well, now, how can we try you, then?"

"Like the rest."

"They be worse than the rest, Gov'nor," said Clarke. "According to these Frenchmen they are more fierce fighters than any of these men."

"Sir."

"Yes, Mister Quick."

"That one, Read, when we were taken, she cursed and swore at the men to come out and fight, and she shot into the hold, killing one of my men and wounding poor John Eaton here."

"Outrageous!"

"I deny it!" shouted Mary.

"Hold your tongue, woman. Ye should be ashamed. Are ye both spinsters?"

"Spinsters! Jesus God!"

"Watch your tongue, woman," Lawes threatened Anne. "Ye answer my questions with a civil tongue or I'll hang ye this very day. I care not what ye are. Women or no, ye be bloody pirates like the rest, perhaps worse, if these men speak true; 'tis for the court to decide. But we will hear now how your wicked and perverse lives have brought you to this place. Now, are you a spinster, Mistress Read?"

"I have a husband, sir. One of these men here."

Loud whispering came from the audience.

"Quiet, all of you! Continue, Madame."

"I say husband, sir, because we did make a vow each to the other and 'tis as good a marriage in conscience as if it had been done by a minister in a church."

"The Church of England will not sanction it, Mister . . . ah Mistress."

"I honor it. I have never committed adultery or fornication with any man in my life."

"Who is this man?"

"I will not tell you, for I would not have him condemned by his association with me. He is an honest man, sir, and has no inclination to piracy."

"Tell the assembly how it came to be that you are here before us."

Mary told the counselors and the audience the story of her adventures since the time of her birth. With honesty and pride, she presented an unadorned account of her life. She knew that what she said here would be reported to the world. Yet this was her story, unique, bizarre, fascinating, adventurous, but true.

"Mister Rackam," said the governor. "Did you know your helmsman is a woman?"

"Aye, sir."

"Didst ever try to dissuade her from such a wicked life?"

"I once asked her why she pursued such a dangerous manner of existence."

"And what did she say?"

"She said she thought hangin' no hardship; 'twas fear, she said, what kept dastardly rogues honest. If not for such a harsh penalty, those who cheat their neighbors on land would rob at sea and soon the ocean would be crowded with rogues like the land."

Anne muttered to Jack under her breath, "Damn your blood, Jack! Why is your tongue so loose now?"

"I am a dead man. It matters not what I say any more."

"Indeed, Mistress Read," responded the governor. "No care for hanging, eh? Well, that can be proved. And you, Mistress Bonny. Be that your family name or some other?"

"I will not reveal my father's name, now or ever."

"Very well, 'tis honorable for a daughter to protect her father's name. Are thee well born?"

"Hardly, sir."

"Tell us."

Twitters were heard in the audience as Anne began the story of the humorous events surrounding her birth. Surprisingly, she had remembered every detail and her father would have been proud of her manner of delivery. Anne manipulated the emotions of the audience, taking them from laughter to tears and back again. Everyone, including Mary, was enthralled, almost spellbound by her story. Then she synopsized the events from her marriage to James Bonny in Carolina to the present.

"Am I given to understand that you deserted your husband in New Providence?"

"Aye."

" 'Tis an ugly circumstance against you. Have you given

a true and complete account of your life?"

"Aye."

"You left out a few details, I think, Mistress Anne," said a voice in the crowd.

"Who are you, sir? Approach us."

"My name is George Daniels, late of Bath Town, North Carolina."

Young Daniels was living in Jamaica because his family was paying him to stay away from home so that his scandalous actions would no longer embarrass them. Notorious as a womanizer and gambler, Daniels had been caught cheating at cards and was no longer socially acceptable in the Carolinas.

"State your purpose here, Mister Daniels."

"I have evidence against this woman Bonny's character."

"And what about your own, sir? What is your character that you may accuse another? You are a remittance man, are you not?"

"Aye, sir. You look puzzled, Mistress Anne. You don't remember me? Well, 'tis true we have never met," he said acidly, "but perhaps you remember my cousin Philip Daniels?"

"Mister Daniels, come to your point," demanded the governor.

"Your Excellency, this woman beat my cousin nearly to death because he wanted to marry her."

"God's Nails!" expostulated the governor. The audience went wild with protest and rage.

"Harlot!" screamed one woman.

"Brazen wench, filthy baggage!" shouted another.

" 'Tis not all, sir," continued Daniles. "She killed her serving maid with a case knife."

"No! What are ye, woman, a witch, a devil or what?"

The audience was in such an uproar by now that the governor could not silence them. He finally called the militia to clear the room. When all was quiet again he went on.

"You, Mary Read, and you, Anne Bonny, alias Bonn,

358

will be tried before the high court of Admiralty on Monday, November 28th, for your crimes of piracy. Take the prisoners away to the gaol. The assembly is adjourned until Wednesday, November 16th.''

As they were escorted back to the gaol, the streets filled with a jeering mob who in their hearts had already convicted these prisoners of every act of piracy committed against the island of Jamaica since 1716.

For all the prisoners the waiting was long and damp. Imprisonment was especially hard on Mary, whose leg ached continually and whose advanced state of pregnancy would have made comfort impossible even under dryer circumstances.

"St. Jago de la Vega," remarked Anne. "St. John of the Way, and the way is hard. Thank God we are together. I could not bear this confinement alone."

"Not one bloody window," Mary said despairingly. "No light of day visits this place."

"At least Jack has been allowed his pipe. Look at him there; he doth shiver all the day. I could pity him if I weren't so angry."

Mary's eyes were clamped shut.

"What is it, Mary? Are you in pain?"

"Aye, but that I can bear. 'Tis the darkness I cannot bear. I will die without the light and warmth of the sun. I know I will."

"You must not despair; remain strong for the child's sake. Do as I do—think yourself away to some warm, dry, sunny place. 'Tis the only way."

"Where do you go?"

"Watlings. There are a hundred beautiful places I can remember. I fly over the blue-green rainbow of the Caribbean Sea, then I lose myself in a tree, a rock, a blade of grass or a grain of pink coral. Where would you go?"

"Negril, I guess, or the falls at Ocho Rios, or perhaps the mountains of Hispaniola."

Suddenly Mary began to laugh.

"What is funny?"

"Is the story really true?"

"What story?"

"The one you told at the hearing about your birth."

" 'Tis too incredible to have been invented, don't you think?"

"So it's true, then?"

"As far as I know. My father told it me. He said 'twas true. That is all I know."

"Did you really hurt that man's cousin as he said you did?"

"Aye, bloody fucker! That bastard spread vile stories about me in the town. Every man thought me no better than a whore and felt he had the privilege of having his way with me, any time and in any place. 'Tis what the world will think of me now when this news reaches London. There was such a hue and cry against me in the courthouse that I had no opportunity to defend myself. Do you believe me, Mary?"

"Certainly I believe you. I know you well, Anne."

" 'Tis a comfort."

"Did you indeed kill a serving wench in Carolina, too?"

"Aye, but 'tis not something I am proud of."

"Canst tell me the cause?"

"It happened in a moment of passion. I regretted the action the very instant I plunged my knife into her belly."

"You know I have killed scores of people in my lifetime and the very thought makes me shudder even now. I never did get used to killing."

" 'Tis a wonder and a blessing. You are the most beautiful and sensitive creature it has been my good fortune to meet. Will you do something for me?"

"If I can."

"Tell me every detail of your life. There were things at the hearing that you hinted at which I would like to know more about. And 'twill help to pass the time here."

"Where would you like me to start?"

"At the very beginning."

On Wednesday, November 16, 1720, John Rackam and his eight crewmen were tried before a court of Admiralty. Vice Admiral Lawes presided. Members of the council constituted the jury of twelve. On the table lay an ornate silver oar, about thirty-three inches in length, which was the symbol of the admiralty court's jurisdiction over crimes on the high seas.

The King's commission was openly read. This mandate was contingent upon the Act for the more Effectual Suppression of Piracy. The act clearly stated that according to a statute made in the reign of King Henry the Eighth, all persons convicted of piracies should be executed and should suffer the loss of their lands, goods and chattels.

After this lengthy document was read, the oath was issued to all the judges. Then the crier recited the following proclamation three times in a penetrating and irritating voice:

"All manner of persons that can inform this honorable court, now sitting, of any piracies, felonies or robberies committed in or upon the sea, or in any haven, creek or place in or about this island, or elsewhere in the West Indies, where the admiral or admirals of our sovereign lord the king hath, or have any power, authority or jurisdiction, let them come forth, and they shall be heard."

The nine prisoners were set at the bar to hear the charges read against them. Four charges were made concerning Rackam's seizing ships and goods on four separate occasions: the seven fishing boats at Harbour Island, the two merchant sloops off Hispaniola, Spenlow's schooner at Port Maria Bay, and Dillon's sloop at Dry Harbour Bay.

After these charges were made, all nine men pleaded not guilty. The witnesses called against them were Thomas Spenlow, Peter Cornelian and John Besneck. John Spatchears of Port Royal gave an account of their capture at Negril.

Governor Lawes asked each man if he had any defense to make. Each said that he had no witnesses and further stated that he had never committed any acts of piracy. Rackam avowed that their whole design had at all times been against the Spaniards.

"Frivolous and trifling excuses!" shouted Lawes. "Attendant, take these men away from the bar and clear this room!"

The courthouse doors were closed, but the judges deliberated for only a few moments. Then the doors were opened and the prisoners once again brought before the bar.

"This court has unanimously found each and every one of you guilty of the third and fourth articles charged against you. You, John Rackam, George Fetherston, Richard Corner, John Davies, John Howell, Patrick Carty, Thomas Earl, James Dobbins and Noah Harwood, are to go from here to the place from whence you came, and from thence to the place of execution, where you shall severally be hanged by the neck till you are severally dead. And may God in His infinite mercy be merciful to every one of your souls."

The next afternoon Thomas Quick and the other eight visitors to Rackam's sloop on the night of the capture were taken to the militia stockade, the same place Tobias Sampson had been taken after the hearing. They would wait there for two months until the assembly saw fit to hear their case. Rackam and the ten condemned men would be taken away that night, some to Port Royal, some to Kingston, for the act provided that the executions of pirates must take place on or within the ebbing and flowing of the sea.

The provost marshal escorted the men from the gaol, carrying the silver oar before them. Jack was allowed to visit Anne. She considered telling him that she was with child, but dared not with the officer standing by. It would have been small comfort to him anyway.

Sadness filled his large brown eyes; fire filled hers. The couple was silent for a long time. As the officer took Jack's arm to lead him away, he asked, "Have you no word of comfort for me, then?"

Anne replied, "Jack, I am sorry to see you here, but if you had fought like a man you would not need to hang like a dog!"

Rackam looked deep into Anne's eyes and his smile instantly washed away her bitter anger. Reaching through the bars, she took his hand tenderly. "I am sorry, Jack."

"I have loved you, Anne Bonny, like no other woman I have ever known. I will think of you at the last."

In a moment he was gone.

On Friday the 18th day of November, 1720, Captain John Rackam, Master George Fetherston, Quartermaster Richard Corner, John Davies, and John Howell were executed at Gallows Point at the town of Port Royal. The bodies of Rackam, Fetherston and Corner were afterward carried to Plumb Point, Bush Cay and Gun Cay, where they were hung on gibbets in chains as a public example.

On the next day Noah Harwood, James Dobbins, Patrick Carty and Thomas Earl were executed at the town of Kingston. Rackam's calico-clad frame had been stuffed into a small iron cage and hung to rot at Bush Cay in Port Royal Harbour in order to terrify seafarers and discourage them from taking up such evil practices as piracy. From that day Bush Cay became known to mariners as Rackam's Cay.

" 'Tis a hard thing to accept, Anne." said Mary. "All of our company be gone. I am sorry for Jack; he was not himself at the end."

"Aye, rum had defeated him long before the king's justice took his life."

"There were some good things that we did. I cannot believe that we be as wicked and profligate as they say."

"What we consider charity the government names as crimes. Just think on what we did; freed criminals shipped at the crown's expense, as well as slaves worth thousands of pounds. Pray God that the governor learn not of those deeds."

"To think of all the great ships we have plundered, and now they will hang us for stealing fishing tackle."

" 'Tis ironic indeed."

"There be no chance of acquittal for us, 'tis certain now.

We be charged with the same crimes as Rackam and the rest. Nothing can save us.''

"No, but we can do one thing.''

"And what be that?''

"Ask for a stay of execution by pleading our bellies.''

"Are you with child? Why did you not tell me before this?''

"I had it in mind to tell you but there was no good time. Besides, I am just recently certain of it.''

"How many months, think you? They will examine us. Can you be detected?''

"Two, maybe three, months; I am not certain.''

"Then we are both saved.''

"For a time.''

"A short time for me.'' Mary was lost in thought for a moment. Then she said, "I think such a plea be cowardly for me. I have lived as a man all my life and I stand as accountable for piracy as the rest; 'tis cowardly to take the woman's way out.''

"We will not offer a defense or excuse; we ask only for a stay. 'Twould be worse to kill the innocent babes.''

" 'Tis a wonder no one suspects me now.''

"You are tall and thin and do not show much under your loose garments.''

"I feel enormous. It cannot be long, a few weeks at best. Then I'll hang, I know I will. Jack might as well have put the noose around my neck himself by repeating what I said to him about piracy.''

" 'Tis not over yet. Our trial is tomorrow. We must have a little patience. Mary, did you ever imagine that I would have to ask you to be patient?''

"Oh, dear God, how can I be patient when I do not know what has happened to Tobias? We hear nothing in this place. No one will talk to us.''

"He has not hanged with the others. Perhaps there is some hope.''

"But where is he? What are they doing to him? Why did he not say he was forced? He be no pirate, Anne!''

"I know that, but he did fight with us on the slaver. That is piracy."

"God's Nails! That be mercy. Besides, he did it to help me. I was crippled and weak and . . . oh, God, why must the man be so bloody honest? He'll not allow any excuse to himself. Jesus God! This not knowing whether he be dead or alive is torture to me!"

"Mary, please, 'tis not good to excite yourself this way. I'll ask the guard when he brings our supper. Perhaps I can persuade a little information out of him. Calm yourself for now. We cannot help him nor he us."

"Useless! Never before have I felt so useless—never. 'Tis hard to accept defeat."

"We are not defeated yet. Trust to time."

On Monday, November 28, 1720, Anne and Mary were tried before the court of Admiralty. The courtroom was packed with people, who came chiefly out of curiosity. Never before had women been condemned of piracy.

"Bring the prisoners to the bar!" demanded Governor Lawes. "Hearken to the charges against you, Mary Read, and you, Anne Bonny, alias Bonn, late of the island of New Providence, spinsters, for piracies, felonies and robberies committed by you on the high seas, and within the jurisdiction of this court. William Norris, Esquire, register of this mighty court of Admiralty, read the articles against them."

"Article One: That they, the said Mary Read and Anne Bonny, alias Bonn, on the first day of September in the seventh year of the reign of our said lord the king, did feloniously and wickedly consult and agree together with John Rackam . . . to rob, plunder, and take all such persons, as well as subjects of our lord the king. . . ." The register droned on and on until all four charges, the same articles on which Rackam and the others had been convicted, were read.

Anne and Mary pleaded not guilty.

The two Frenchmen were produced as witnesses against

them. Mister Simon Clarke, sworn interpreter, spoke for them. "The witnesses declare that the two women were on board Rackam's sloop at the time that Spenlow's schooner and Dillon's sloop were taken and that they were very active on board and willing to do anything. When they saw, gave chase to, or attacked any vessel, both women wore men's clothes and Anne Bonny handed gunpowder to the men. The witnesses say that the women did not seem to be kept or detained by force, but of their own free will and consent."

Thomas Spenlow was sworn in; he stated that when his schooner was taken, the two women were with Rackam.

Curiously, Thomas Dillon had not testified against Rackam and his men, but he appeared in court this day to give testimony against the women.

"Aye, sir, they were with Rackam the day he carried away me sloop. The woman Anne Bonny had a gun in her hand, sir. And they were both very profligate, cursing and swearing much and ready and willing to do anything on board."

"Thank you, Mister Dillon. Call the next witness!"

"Dorothy Thomas, approach the bar!" shouted the court attendant.

"God's Death!" muttered Anne under her breath. "Worse luck! We are undone now. That old trot has come all this way expressly to put the noose round our necks."

The bitch will cannonade us with her righteousness, thought Mary.

"Well, sir," said Dorothy Thomas, "the day Cap'n Rackam took most of my provisions from my canoe, these women were with him."

"How were they dressed?"

"Well, Your Honor, much the same as they be now. They wore men's jackets, long trousers and handkerchiefs tied about their heads. And sir, each of them had a cutlass and pistol. What's worse, sir, is that they cursed and swore most villianously at the men that they might murder me."

"Why did they want you killed, Mistress Thomas?"

"Why sir, to prevent my coming against them!"

"Well, here you are, eh? Seems that you will have the last word after all."

"Aye, sir!" she said vindictively. "Besides, Your Honor, 'tis a disgrace to womanhood for them to behave in such an unseemly manner."

"Did you know them to be women at the time?"

"Aye, sir, by the largeness of their breasts."

"Uh . . . well, Mistress Thomas, you may stand away. Now then, do you, Mary Read or Anne Bonny, have any witnesses who may be sworn in your behalf? Have you any questions to ask this court or the witnesses produced against you?"

No questions or statements that would do us any good, that's certain, thought Anne.

"Sir, we have no witnesses," said Mary.

"And we have no questions, Your Excellency," replied Anne.

"Remove these prisoners from the bar and put them into safe custody. All the standers-by withdraw from the court."

The president and commissioners deliberated the circumstances of the prisoners' case and unanimously agreed that both women were guilty of piracy in the plundering of Spenlow's schooner and the taking of Dillon's sloop. The prisoners were brought back to the bar.

"This court has unanimously found you both guilty of piracy in the third and fourth articles of the articles exhibited against you. Do either of you have anything to say or offer why the sentence of death should not be passed upon you for your said offenses?"

"No, Your Excellency, I have nothing material to offer," responded Anne.

"Nor I, Your Honor," replied Mary.

"You, Mary Read and Anne Bonny, alias Bonn, are to go from hence here to the place from whence you came, and from thence to the place of execution, where you shall be severally hanged by the neck till you are severally dead. And God in His infinite mercy be merciful to both your souls."

A hushed silence fell over the audience. A handsome young planter standing in the back bent his head in despair. It was Anne who spoke.

"Your Excellency, we are both quick with child and pray that the execution of the sentence may be stayed."

"Both of you?" Lawes asked, looking at Mary.

"Aye, sir, I am also with child," Mary responded.

"Very well then, this court orders that the execution of said sentence be respited. And I hereby order than an inspection be made forthwith. This court is adjourned till Monday the nineteenth day of December next."

The young man hurried from the courtroom and tried to push his way through the crowd. He called out Anne's name, but when she looked around she could not see anyone she recognized. The few guards could not keep the people away from the prisoners. Many of them were pressing up against the women, shouting obscenities and tearing at their clothes. Mary felt as if she were being strangled; turning her ankle on a loose stone, she fell. Anne helped her to her feet and half carried her back to the gaol.

"Are you all right?"

"Aye. So many people! Where did they all come from?"

"Friggin' thrill seekers! You could have been seriously hurt out there."

"I never thought I would be happy to return to this cell. 'Tis almost a relief to be here."

"I did fear for our very lives in the street. My coat is ripped to shreds. 'Tis useless to me now." A sudden cold chill shuddered through Anne's body.

"Be you cold? Here, take my jacket."

"Nay. I am not cold. The thought of so long an imprisonment doth chill my blood."

"Remember when we last sailed from Harbour Island, how we talked? Little did I know then I would be shut away in this tiny cage."

" 'Twill be a long time now."

"Aye, for you. I have only a few weeks at best."

"Oh, Christ, if only we had some friend on the outside. Perhaps escape would be possible."

"Our only friend left is poor Tobias and he may be dead, too, for all we know. Oh, 'tis all hopeless, Anne!"

Days passed. Both women were rudely examined by the garrison doctor and the court was satisfied with the results of his inspection. Sentence was suspended until after each woman had given birth. There was still no word of Tobias. Twice a day the guard brought food. Anne barraged him with questions but he said not one word in response.

One afternoon, a full two hours prior to the evening meal, the large door of the gaol swung open. Anne and Mary, blinded by the afternoon sunlight, did not recognize the man who entered. The guard stayed at the door and pointed to the cell across the room.

A tall figure approached and whispered, "Anne, Anne O'Brannon?"

"Aye. I am Anne O'Brannon," said Anne, as she peered through the bars at the handsome, well-dressed man standing before her. "Ah . . . you have the advantage of me, sir. I cannot for the life of me place your face. Should I know you, sir?"

"I am somewhat changed, taller and fuller in the face. Perhaps you will recognize this." He reached under his coat in back and pulled out a battered tomahawk handle. He handed it through the bars to Anne.

She studied the object for a long time. Her fingers passed over the carved heart, which was impossible to see in the dim light. The impression of the letters had been worn almost smooth but she was able to make out the faint initials which were carved there.

"A, Anne, and B, Baldwin! Baldwin Sommerwood, is it you?"

"Aye, 'tis I."

"Oh, thank God, we were near despair to see a friendly face. Mary, this is Baldwin Sommerwood. His father is a friend of my father's. Baldwin, this is Mary Read."

"Pleased to meet you, Mistress Read," he said, bowing.

" 'Tis a pleasure to meet you, Mister Sommerwood," replied Mary.

369

"Are you a barrister now, Baldwin, as you had planned?"

"Aye."

"How did you get here? When did you come?"

"I was here at your trial . . . I . . . ."

"Oh," said Anne despondently.

"Your hearing did make a great noise. I happened to be in Port Royall on some business when John Rackam was hanged. Many people in the town talked of the two women of Rackam's crew who were to be tried in Spanish town, so I came here. I had no idea you were one of the women until I heard the name."

"Didst recognize me right away?"

"No, not until you spoke. Afterward I tried to reach you but could not fight my way through the crowd. I called your name. Didst hear me?"

"That was you? I looked around but the mob was frightful; I saw no one I recognized. The crowd drew my attention. I feared they might lay hands on us and murder us in the street."

"Aye, the town has gone wild. Thank God you have been granted a stay. 'Tis hoped the town will forget its wrath against you. Are . . . are you truly a pirate, Anne?"

"Aye, but we are not as wicked and bloody as they say. We have done some good, I hope. But the world will never know it."

"I believe you. The court will hear no extenuating circumstances. The law is concerned only with facts. 'Tis a grieveous fault in the system of justice."

"Can you help us?"

"I will do everything in my power. 'Twill not be easy. I had to petition the governor for three days before I was allowed to visit you."

"Mister Sommerwood, have you heard anything about my husband, Tobias Sampson?" asked Mary. "They threatened to torture him because he would not answer aye or nay to the charge of piracy. We do not even know where he has been taken. I have not seen him since the day of the hearing." Mary was on the verge of tears.

"Please, Baldwin, find him!" pleaded Anne.

"Do not worry, Mistress Read, I will learn all I can."

"How can we thank you? You be our only friend."

"I have seen to some of your comforts. The food should improve and they are to bring blankets tonight. Let me know if they comply with my requests. Also the guard promised to let you walk in the courtyard once a day."

"Oh, thank you!"

"I shall solicit for your freedom every day. Believe me, I will not rest till you both be free. Have you any other particular need which I have overlooked?"

"Mary's time is near. We will need some things for her lying in. Could she have a midwife, do you think? We may need help."

"I have a woman servant here with me who will collect what you need. I will ask about the midwife but I fear the governor will refuse any such request."

"Baldwin, if you see Tobias, please convince him to plead innocence. Tell him for me that I find it no disgrace or sign of weakness in him that he should save his life. Tell him I love him and I would have him keep his life."

Baldwin came to visit every day. He brought them clean clothes, candles, books, any little thing he felt might add a measure of comfort to their brutal imprisonment. But he had no good news to relay concerning Tobias. The captain at the stockade had told him Tobias had been tortured but had not uttered aye or nay to the charge of piracy. He had been sentenced to be pressed to death on December 14th. Baldwin withheld that last bit of information from the women.

Uselessly, Baldwin petitioned the governor to release the women. Even his father's word that he would make assurance for their conduct did not soften the governor's resolve.

"They be hardened criminals, Mister Sommerwood," said the governor. "I cannot allow such creatures their freedom. 'Tis against all principles of law."

"Canst give them a better place when comes the time for their lying in? Must you deny them even a midwife?"

"No, they can birth their bastards alone in the gaol. 'Tis no concern of mine."

"But sir, Mistress Anne be a lady of means from the Carolinas. She deserves better treatment."

"That woman is no lady, sir. She is a bloody and villainous pirate, a despicable wench. But if you can produce several good accounts of her character from any of the planters here, we will consider them. I make thee no promises, Mister. There will needs be many and notable accounts to offset the bad witness against her already."

"Aye, sir. And what of Mary Read?"

"She will hang as soon as she has been delivered of her bastard."

"Sir. . . ."

" 'Tis the law, Mister Sommerwood. We must stand firm on the law, sir; you should know that."

"Aye, Your Excellency."

Law or no, Balwin Sommerwood was grieved by this news. Surely the law must sometimes temper justice with a little mercy. Tobias and Mary were condemned to death and he had only a thread of hope for Anne.

Anne was frightened at the prospect of delivering Mary's child alone in the filthy gaol, but she concealed her fear from her friend. Mary did not look well; she was feverish, her eyes lusterless, her skin cold and clammy.

On the morning of December 14th Mary's pains began. She labored all that day.

In another part of the town Tobias had been stripped naked, except for a cloth covering his privities, and taken to a low, dark room in the stockade. There he lay on his back while his arms and legs were stretched with rope and tied to the corners of the room. A great weight of iron and stone was laid upon him. That day he was given only three morsels of barley bread without drink. If he lived, the next day and each day until he died, he would be given as much foul water as he could drink.

Tobias died some time during that first night.

Mary suddenly sat up on the bench.

"What is it?" whispered Anne.

"I don't know. Didn't you call out my name? I heard my name."

"No, I had dropped off to sleep."

A fierce pain gripped Mary. Anne held her hand tightly. When the pain eased and Mary could breathe again she said, "I think the babe will come very soon now."

"Thank God. If you labor much longer you will not have enough strength to give birth."

Anne and Mary struggled together for hours. Finally Anne eased the child out of Mary's womb.

"At last!"

Anne had been denied a sharp instrument; she was obliged to chew through the cord. She washed the baby and put it in Mary's arms.

"Mary, you have a fine boy. You must hold him now while I minister to you."

"A boy?"

"Aye, a beautiful, healthy boy. I wish Tobias could see him."

"I think he does see him."

"Sleep now, you need rest," she said, puzzled by Mary's response.

"Who will care for him when I am gone?"

"Do not worry. Baldwin will come for him. He has promised to raise my child, too. Just think, Mary, they will play together and grow together. Baldwin has promised me that our children will be given every advantage."

"He be a good man. Thank him for me, please."

"You can thank him yourself in the morning."

"If I am asleep, do not wake me. Give him the babe, for it will tear my heart to see him go."

"Aye."

"And one more thing, Anne. Ask Baldwin to find my sword and buy it back at any price. Did you find my belt?"

"You mean this? 'Tis heavy. How on earth could you have carried it all this time? Why would you?"

"It contains Spanish gold. Give it to Baldwin. Tell him to exchange all this money for my father's sword. You will do it, won't you, Anne?"

"Aye, I will."

The intensity in Mary's eyes was alarming as she gazed in wonder at her child. Her fingers felt over every part of his tiny body. She held him close and fell asleep.

Baldwin came in the morning as he had promised. Mary was asleep; Anne gently extricated the child from her arms. The cell was opened and Baldwin took the child and put him into the arms of the young black woman standing behind him. Anne gave the cloth moneybelt to Baldwin and told him Mary's wishes.

"I will find her sword, Anne. Trust me."

"You must. It was her father's."

"Aye."

"Any word of Tobias?"

"Anne, I am sorry, but he is dead."

"When? How did he die?"

"He was pressed to death yesterday and died in the night. He remained silent to the end."

"Last night, you say?"

"Aye. You must forgive me for not telling you, but I saw no need to trouble Mary further."

"I think she knew it. How long does she have now?"

"Not long. Anne, I tried, I even related to the governor what you told me of Mary's distinguished military career, but he will not bend. Mary will hang as soon as she is able to walk to the scaffold."

"Christ Almighty!" Anne gripped the bars and shook them viciously. " 'Tis a sin, you know that. I finally know what sin really is. Sin is to waste a noble, courageous, tender woman. Go now, Baldwin, and leave me to my grief."

"Aye."

The door of the gaol thundered closed and seemed to initiate in Anne a flood of angry sobs. Her hands slid down the grimy bars as she sank to her knees in the muddy earth.

For four days Mary took very little nourishment; she seemed to languish. Her husband was dead; her son had been taken away; soon she would lose her own life. But a deep desire stirred within her and she longed to see the sun once more. On the fifth day her appetite suddenly improved; the guard reported this to the provost marshal, who in turn informed the governor.

Mary walked back and forth in the cell testing her legs.

"Mary, please lie down! I do not want the guard to see thee out of bed; word will get back to the governor soon enough that you are well."

"Anne, do you not think it a grand joke? Why must one be healthy to die? 'Tis ridiculous. 'Tis a contradiction in nature."

"Aye. All the same, I cannot bear to lose you so soon."

At ten that morning, William Norris came into the gaol and approached the cell. Both women knew what he was there to say.

"Mary Read, I am here to inform you that at nine in the morning, tomorrow the 20th day of December, you will be taken from this place to Port Royall to be executed."

"But she is not well!" Anne protested.

" 'Tis no matter. Time enough has passed. If she cannot stand the rope will hold her up awhile. You are to wear woman's clothes."

He shoved a coarse woolen garment through the bars. Anne took it.

"Have you any last request?"

"May I walk outside this afternoon?"

"Aye. I will instruct the guard. Be there anything else?"

"No, nothing."

The marshal left. Mary was silent. Anne tried to quell the sick feeling rising in her throat. A bitter taste in her mouth stopped her from shouting out vile obscenities.

After the marshal had gone, Baldwin Sommerwood was admitted.

"Hast heard?" asked Anne bitterly.

"Aye. I was with the governor earlier and no amount of reason would change his mind."

"Reason!" Anne laughed sardonically.

"Mary, I brought your clothes, freshly laundered, as you requested."

"She must wear this rag for the occasion." Anne angrily shook the dress in his face.

"Thank you," said Mary, taking the garments from him. She sank down wearily on the bench. Anne stood against the wall trying to gain control of herself. Her fury would not help Mary now.

"How be my boy?" asked Mary weakly.

"He is healthy, Mary; do not fear. I shall take good care of him."

"Hast found my sword?"

"Aye. 'Tis safely stowed in my rooms."

"That is well; the sword is all the legacy I have to give my son. You will see that he gets it, won't you?"

"Aye."

Anne buried her face in her hands and turned to the wall, sobbing quietly.

"I would like to see my son once more. I am to walk in the courtyard this afternoon."

"I can stand outside the gate with him. They will not permit me to come inside where the prisoners walk."

" 'Tis well. And will you wear my sword?"

"I will, and proudly too."

"I have one final request to make of you."

"Anything."

"You must promise me that you will not rest till Anne be released from this place. And you must care for her till the end of your days."

"Aye, I promise."

" 'Tis not enough to save her life; you must love her and cherish her always, as I have."

"I will. I promise. I promise on your sword. I . . . I will go and get the child."

Anne helped Mary into her clothes, not the crude dress provided by the provost marshal but her own clothes: the trousers Anne had made for her and a soft white shirt. As

Anne buttoned Mary's Guinea cloth vest she remembered when she had repaired it after Jack, in a jealous rage, had slit the buttons off. Anne touched the scar on Mary's chin tenderly. Mary took her hand.

The two women sat silently side by side on the wooden bench. There was nothing more to say.

At three o'clock the guard opened their cell. Mary, refusing assistance from Anne, limped across the room and out into the courtyard. The guard stopped her about ten feet from the gate where Baldwin was standing. He held the child up so that Mary could see him. Mary stood a long time, smiling at her baby.

A fine boy, she thought. You be a good boy for your mother. List what she has to say to thee. My father's sword be yours now. See that you bring no dishonor to't. Care for Anne as I would; love her as I do. Give her no cause to grieve as I have. She has had enough grief in her life. You hear me, boy?

The baby seemed to smile at her.

The sunlight flashed off the hilt of her sword hanging at Baldwin's side and triggered a moment in her past long ago when she had first taken the sword in her hand.

Mary, gazing up at the sun, seemed to spiral up into the air. Whirling in a cyclone of sunlight, she shouted, "M. R., M. R. Mary Read, a soldier! Seaman Mary Read! What? Soldiers do not fight in velvet. There! I be free! Mary Read, pirate of the Caribbean Sea, is free! I am free!"

After Mary had collapsed in the dirt, the guard helped Anne carry her back to their cell. He brought in pails of water as Anne had requested.

Anne sponged Mary's burning face with cool water, but the fever raged on. That night Mary waged a mighty battle against death. 'Twas a battle greater that Malplaquet and all her sea battles put together.

"Charge!" she shouted out in her delirium. "Spit in the cannon's mouth! Our only enemy is fear. Max . . . Max, where are you? Didst lose you in the bloody fray?! Take that, you dastardly rogue! Whoreson knave!"

377

Anne tried to restrain Mary's swinging arm, but it was too powerful for her.

"I'll have thee yet, villain! Ah . . . ah . . . take that . . . and that. . . ."

Exhausted, Mary fell back into Anne's arms and she gripped her hand.

The fever has consumed her, thought Anne. But she has had her wish after all. Mary Read will die in battle.

"Anne?"

"Aye, Mary, I am here."

Mary's body seemed to relax and her face brightened, but she still held a vicelike grip on Anne's hand.

"I can see it! I am almost there!"

"What? Where?"

"Negril."

Anne freed her mind in order to help Mary reach that place of perfect peace.

"Do not be afraid, my friend, I am there with you. I can see it too: the swaying palms, the white, white sand, crystal sunlight glancing off the water."

"Aye . . . aye, the water. . . ."

"Yes, 'tis creamy white, and azure, and green and. . . ."

A smile suddenly appeared on Mary's face; she closed her eyes and loosened her grip on Anne's hand. Anne knew she was alone now, for Mary was gone, drifting peacefully in the blue water toward the black horizon.

Historical Afterword

In his correspondence of November and December of 1720, Nicholas Lawes, erstwhile governor of Jamaica, neglected to mention to the Colonial Office that of the pirates recently captured, tried and condemned, two were women. It was fortunate that Robert Baldwin, printer, published *The Tryals of Captain John Rackam and Other Pirates,* which in 1721 was submitted to the British Public Records, branding Anne Bonny and Mary Read as notorious criminals.

In 1724 Daniel DeFoe, under the pseudonym of Captain Charles Johnson, wrote *A General History of the Pyrates . . . with the Remarkable Actions and Adventures of the Two Female Pyrates, Mary Read and Anne Bonny,* a work which propelled the women into the history books. The source of DeFoe's information about the early lives of Bonny and Read is unknown, since there is nothing of the background of either woman in Baldwin's trial transcript. The only startling bit of information was the fact that both women stated they were "quick with child and prayed that execution of the sentence might be stayed."

It is possible, therefore, that Governor Lawes conducted a hearing, of which there is no written record, wherein the women told the stories of their lives. And it is entirely possible that some of the people present at that hearing in Jamaica made their way to England and were interviewed by DeFoe. It is unlikely that DeFoe's journalistic integrity would permit him to fabricate a story as outrageous as that of "Mistress Mary and the Three Spoons."

Throughout the novel the historical facts have been preserved, with a single exception: Bartholomew Roberts did not begin his piratical career until 1720, but all the other despicable and not so despicable rogues mentioned in the novel were active during the Great Age of Piracy.